FOR ALL
THEIR LIVES

BY FERN MICHAELS
(Published by The Random House Publishing Group)

All She Can Be
Captive Innocence
Cinders to Satin
Desperate Measures
For All Their Lives
Free Spirit
Seasons of Her Life
Serendipity
Tender Warrior
To Have and to Hold
To Taste the Wine
Valentina
Vixen In Velvet

THE CAPTIVE SERIES
Captive Passions
Captive Embraces
Captive Splendors
Captive Secrets

THE TEXAS SERIES
Texas Rich
Texas Heat
Texas Fury
Texas Sunrise

THE SINS SERIES
Sins of Omission
Sins of the Flesh

FOR ALL THEIR LIVES

A Novel

FERN MICHAELS

BALLANTINE BOOKS TRADE PAPERBACKS
NEW YORK

2010 Ballantine Books Trade Paperback Edition

Copyright © 1991 by Fern Michaels

Published in the United States by Ballantine Books, an imprint of The Random House Publishing Group, a division of Random House, Inc., New York.

BALLANTINE and colophon are registered trademarks of Random House, Inc.

ISBN 978-0-345-52384-6

Printed in the United States of America

www.ballantinebooks.com

4 6 8 9 7 5 3

As a mother, a sister, an aunt, a writer, and as a human being, I want to thank all those fine, dedicated, wonderful nurses who took care of our sons so willingly and selflessly in Vietnam.

—F.M.

PART
ONE

PART
ONE

Chapter 1

HE WATCHED HER . . . with clinical interest.

And he wondered why he felt so removed.

The object of Mac Carlin's intense scrutiny was Alice, the woman he'd been married to for eight years. He felt like a sneak, a Peeping Tom, watching her.

Mac's index finger automatically rose upward to adjust his aviator glasses, which were slipping down his nose.

How was it possible, he wondered, for this woman to spend eight solid hours sleeping between lace-bordered satin sheets, and then wake up with every blond hair still in place? There was color on her high cheekbones and a smudged line under her lower lashes. And not one, but two diamonds winked in each ear. Her lips were a glossy deep pink that matched the polish on her exceptionally long nails. He wasn't sure, but he thought the nails were artificial. He wasn't sure about the glossy pink lips either. It had been awhile since he'd kissed his wife or even looked at her up close.

The peach-satin creation that swirled about her was one he'd never seen before. He knew that it must have cost as much as two good suits from an expensive tailor.

Once he'd thought her delectable as a bonbon. He'd wanted her, but the only way he could have her was to marry her. Which he did, the day he graduated from West Point. Crossed swords and all.

To his mind, Alice now more closely resembled a shellacked mannequin, and her personality, if she'd ever had one, was brittle and artificial.

When he'd first met Alice Summers at a pool party ten years

3

ago, during his third year at the Academy, she looked like the girl next door. She'd been a flirt, a tease and a virgin. She told him in no uncertain terms that she was a "good girl" and didn't "put out" for anyone. He'd done everything but howl at the moon in his desire to have her, but she wouldn't even let him put his hand near her breast, much less *inside* her dress. He couldn't really remember now, but he thought that back then he'd respected her for holding out.

Marriage to Alice had been, and still was, the biggest disappointment of his life. Alice's idea of sex was: I give you something and you give me something back. What he had to give were material offerings: a new fur jacket, a gem, a trip, a sports car, trinkets, elegant handbags, lizard shoes, anything so long as it was expensive. With every promise of a new treat, Alice performed. Once a week. If he held out in the gift department, once every two weeks. If the check from his trust fund was slow in arriving, every three weeks.

It took him a full year before he got it through his head that he was buying his wife's sexual favors, and another year before he realized Alice had married him for his money. He couldn't recollect anything about the third and fourth years, but he did remember the fifth year because he'd asked for a divorce. Of course she'd said no, after she'd had a good laugh. "Do whatever you want, darling," she'd said, "but please, be discreet." He'd never touched her again, until a few months ago when he'd gotten stinking drunk and literally dragged her into *his* bedroom. He hadn't raped her. You couldn't rape someone who was dead from the neck down. In fact, he remembered her exact words: "Just do it and get it over with."

The next day he'd volunteered for Vietnam. He managed to pull the same strings his father had pulled to get him stationed at the Pentagon. His father, Supreme Court Justice Marcus Carlin, had more strings to yank than a hot air balloon. It had worked for him just the way it worked for his father. Captain Malcolm Carlin was to depart the United States of America in two days. He felt like cheering. Maybe he would, after he told Alice.

Mac leaned against the wall. Alice hadn't yet noticed him.

Maybe, he thought, she hadn't put the startling green contact lenses in her eyes yet. Cat eyes. All she needed was a tail.

For the thousandth time he wondered what it would take to make Alice give him a divorce. He'd already offered her the house in Palm Springs, the chalet in Aspen, this monstrous house in McLean, Virginia. He'd even offered her his prize stallion, Jeopardy. She'd laughed and said, "It's not enough." He'd raged, demanding to know what *was* enough. "Put a price on it, Alice."

"Some day, Mac, when your father goes to that big court-room in the sky," she'd said, "you will be an incredibly wealthy man. When that happens we'll discuss it, and not a moment before." She'd stunned him with that. He'd called her a ghoul and she'd laughed again, a weird, tinkling sound that gave him goose bumps.

What bothered Mac even more was his father's blindness with regard to Alice. The old man thought she was right up there with sliced bread. On those occasions when the old man needed a hostess, Alice willingly played the part, which gave her a perfect entrée into Washington society.

Mac had no illusions about his father, none at all. Marcus Carlin was a lecher, if a discreet one—a good ol' boy, salivating, geriatric, ass-pincher.

The old man was as fit and trim as a frisky pup. He still worked out, jogged three miles every morning, had the wicked-est backhand at the country club and could belt down a half bottle of Old Grand-Dad and never blink an eye. He was also the youngest Supreme Court judge on the bench.

Mac sighed. Time to get on with his day. He glanced at his watch. Just enough time for a quick cup of coffee and another minute to tell Alice he was leaving. He wondered now for the first time what his wife was doing up at the ungodly hour of seven-thirty. He allowed his eyebrows to shoot upward in sur-prise.

"To what do I owe this *early* morning breakfast?"

"It's *too* early for humor, Mac," Alice murmured.

Once again Mac wondered how she managed to talk without moving her facial muscles.

Mac poured his coffee into a fragile little cup, which looked like it belonged to a child's tea set. He shrugged.

Alice looked down at the piece of dry toast on the gold-rimmed plate. Would it stay down if she nibbled on it? She rather doubted it. Panic coursed through her. She knew what was wrong, and she didn't need a pelvic exam or a urine test to confirm it. She was pregnant. The whole idea was so repulsive, so abhorrent, she almost gagged. A baby wasn't in her plans—not now, not later, not ever.

Last night in the privacy of her bathroom she'd wadded two towels into a ball and slipped them under her nightgown to see what she would look like with a protruding stomach. Her father-in-law would be delighted. Mac would be delirious. But she had gagged.

She needed to give her condition a *lot* of thought. It was only nine months out of her life. She'd demand a trip to the south of France, where she'd live out those months so that none of her friends would see her stomach grow fat.

"Dieting again?" Mac said, stalling for time.

Mac was such a disappointment to her. She'd expected wonderful things from him, and he hadn't come through. He was still a captain working at the Pentagon. Nothing prestigious about that. He *did* look dashing in his dress uniform, but otherwise he didn't stir her in any way.

"You should think about dieting yourself, Mac," she said. "You look like you've put on a few pounds." It was a lie, she thought sourly, he was as fit as his father.

"Alice, I have to talk to you about something, and no, it cannot wait. I'm leaving for Vietnam in two days. I volunteered. We'll have time away from one another, and when I get back, if I still feel the same way I do now, I'll file for a divorce. I want that clear and out in the open. If you still refuse, I'll simply walk out."

Alice raised her green eyes guilelessly and smiled. "I'm pregnant, Mac. So it's hardly the time to think about divorce. Or for you to be going off and leaving me. Well, say something."

He did, but it wasn't what he intended to say. "Did you tell my father?" A baby. The thought was mind-boggling.

Alice's brain raced. *What did that mean?* Did he suspect? "What a perfectly silly thing to say. Of course I didn't tell him. You're the first one I've told."

"I'm having lunch with Dad. I'll tell him. He'll look out for you while I'm gone." Jesus Christ! Of all the things in the world she could have sprung on him, this was the worst.

Mac found himself staring at his wife. She was beautiful, cold, and brittle. He now realized, of course, that he'd never loved her.

Alice's long nails tapped on the dining room table. "How long will you be away?" she asked in a disinterested voice.

He didn't want to tell Alice he would be in Vietnam a year, so he shrugged.

"Be sure there's enough money in the account to take care of things. I don't want to have to beg your father for handouts. I think I'll go to France and have the baby there. I'm sure you have no objections. Of course, I'll need enough money to rent a villa. And I mean carte blanche, Mac," she said warily.

"I wouldn't have it any other way," Mac said sarcastically. He saluted her smartly before striding out of the dining room.

Alice wrinkled her forehead. She hadn't counted on Mac's being gone for the birth of the baby. The manicured nails tapped on the shiny surface of the dining room table. When Plan A doesn't work, switch to Plan B. Or C or D.

While her mind raced, rejecting, sifting, collating, Alice's eyes raked the dining room she'd inherited from Mac's father. After their marriage the judge had turned over the Carlin homestead to Mac and moved into a house in the Georgetown section of Washington.

She remembered that day so well. She'd walked through the house, awed at the magnificence of it, but she couldn't imagine Mac, as a little boy, scampering about the huge rooms. He certainly wouldn't have been allowed to bounce a ball on the old, polished wood floors, or to slide down the banister of the splendid staircase. She'd only given the Carlin ancestry, which graced the walls, a cursory glance. They were history and had nothing to do with her.

She had never changed anything in the huge colonial mansion, because to do so would have angered Marcus Carlin, and if there was one thing she vowed never to do, it was to upset her father-in-law. In the beginning the heavy, antique furniture depressed her, but once she made it her business to learn its value, her attitude changed. Now she had it all catalogued, right down to the last silver spoon.

She'd also had her jewelry catalogued and appraised, which comprised all the fine pieces she had weasled out of Mac and her father on her birthdays and Christmas. She had the neck for diamond chokers, and just the right earlobes for the three-carat clusters that once belonged to Mac's grandmother. Her wrists were slender and graceful enough for the several diamond bracelets she constantly wore. She had a total of seven valuable rings, so valuable that Marcus Carlin insisted she keep them in a safety vault, but it annoyed her that she and Mac had to pay the outrageous insurance premiums on them. Once she'd had to cancel a trip to the Virgin Islands because premiums were due. The following day she'd taken her entire jewelry box to Marcus Carlin and with tears in her eyes told him that she and Mac couldn't afford to keep them. The judge had immediately written a check. Mac and his father had serious words over *that* incident. She and Mac had had serious words too.

Alice looked down the length of the cherrywood table, which was set with two magnificent arrangements of fresh tulips and greenery. It would seat sixteen comfortably. She fancied she had an eye for beauty, but none impressed her as much as her own. She presented a lovely picture sitting there at the head of the table in her elegant dressing gown, and she knew it. The fine crystal, bone china, and sterling silver inspired her eyes to sparkle. The Irish linen cloth and napkins felt like satin in her hands. Her eyes turned to the sideboard, where an elegant silver service stood. All this now belonged to her, the mistress of Carlin House.

And she was fucking pregnant.

The birth alone would be worth a palatial estate in Hawaii. Or perhaps a chalet in Switzerland. She did love to ski. Then again, she loved the sun.

The Carlin money was so old, it was moldy. It had been made

in tobacco and cotton, which was another way of saying the sweat, blood, and tears of slaves. There was so much of it, it boggled her mind. And she wanted it. All of it. If *she* couldn't have it all, then her child would get it. Either way, it would be hers.

On her way up the majestic stairway that led to the wide, central foyer, with its decorative balcony, Alice vaguely wondered, and not for the first time, about her feelings toward Mac. He'd certainly given her everything she'd ever asked for, even the family home. He'd grumbled about accepting it, of course, but in the end he'd given in, because he thought it would make her happy. And then he'd taken her around the world, again, to make her happy.

Alice removed her dressing gown and hung it carefully on a scented hanger. She wanted her own maid, someone to pick up after her, but so far that little treasure had eluded her. A cook, a housekeeper, and a gardener were all she had. Now, though, with the baby coming, she was almost certain she could cajole a personal maid out of her father-in-law. She would also have to give some thought to a nurse and a nanny.

An ugly look crossed Alice's face as she ran her hands over her flat stomach. Soon it would bulge like a watermelon, and she'd have to wear those damn tent dresses. Maybe she could have Dior whip up something that wouldn't shriek pregnancy.

Today was one of her nothing days, a day when she could sit and read, drink a mint julep, watch television, or go shopping. She hadn't been shopping in two days. By now Garfinkle's would have new merchandise. A day for herself. Or she could read a book on pregnancy, the one the doctor had given to her last week. As if she wanted to read about a uterus, ovaries, and the birth canal. Just the words were enough to make her heave.

She could have stopped by her father-in-law's office and invited him to lunch to tell him *the news*, but Mac had already planned lunch with him. Better to let the judge come to her. Much better.

Poor Mac. Poor, poor Mac. Where had it all gone? She pulled on a sheer nylon, careful to keep the seam straight. She wasn't certain if she had ever loved Mac. She rather thought she had, in the beginning. But maybe it had only been his dashing cadet uniform, his potential, his background, and all that wonderful, old, crackly, green money. Mac and his family were everything her family wasn't. Her father was a landscaper, her mother a nurse. They'd lived in a square little house that was manicured and pruned, so much so that it screamed at you when you walked up the flagstone walkway to the little front porch with its two wicker chairs. She'd never wanted for anything. She'd had everything the other youngsters had, possibly a little more, as her mother worked. She'd had her own car at seventeen, a spiffy Pontiac with real leather seats. She'd even been popular in school, a cheerleader, and she had sung in the school choir because her voice was high and sweet. By the time she left for Syracuse University, she knew she never wanted to return to Rockville, Maryland. Instead she wanted to find a rich husband and get married as soon as she finished college.

The secret to anything, she thought as she twirled in front of the smoky mirror, was planning. For her anyway.

She had a plan now. It was committed to memory. Later, at some point, she would decide it was time to put it into effect.

Poor Mac. Poor, poor Mac.

Alice climbed behind the wheel of her Mercedes sports coupe for an exhilarating day of shopping at Garfinkle's.

IT WASN'T UNTIL Mac parked in the lot nearest the Pentagon's Seventh Corridor entrance that he started to wonder if Alice would deliver a girl or a boy. A baby! Son of a bitch!

It wasn't that he didn't like babies. In fact, he loved kids. As an only child, he'd often been lonely growing up and had always wished for a house full of siblings. He knew he'd make a good father if given the chance. He debated a full minute about the strings he'd pulled to get transferred out. He could pull them again and have his orders changed. *If* he wanted to. But he'd made a commitment and he would stick to it. Alice would survive as long as she had a housekeeper, a butler, a chauffeur, a cook, and round-the-clock nurses.

Mac Carlin turned more than one head when he strode down the corridor to the office he shared. He was tall, well over six feet, and he carried himself like a commanding general. The Academy did that to a man. Chest out, chin in. People called him handsome. He saw himself as clean-cut and all-American. He had the kind of bright blue eyes that women loved, and sinfully long eyelashes that swept upward and matched his unruly dark hair, which he threatened to brush-cut every time it fell over his eyes. He also had a sense of humor. He could laugh at himself and was fond of playing practical jokes on the secretary, Stella, who took it all with good grace.

Stella thought of him as a son and brought him cookies and brownies from home. She was Polish, and once in a while told him a silly Polish joke. She also told him, over and over, that if he wasn't happily married, she could fix him up with one of her hundred cousins. Captain Carlin always laughed, but he never said he was happily married.

Stella wiped her eyes. She was going to miss him. How handsome he looked, she thought, as he strode past her desk and winked at her, something he did every morning. She pretended to swoon, as *she* did every morning. It was a standing joke between them.

The buzzer on her desk sounded. "Stella, will you get Phil Benedict on the phone for me and call my father to confirm our lunch date? By the way, you look beautiful today. That husband of yours must be treating you right." He chuckled.

Stella beamed. "Yes, sir, I'll take care of it right away. Stash always treats me right, Captain."

"That's because he knows a good woman when he sees one," Mac joked. He was going to miss Stella and her sweet, homely face. He was going to miss a lot of things.

He thought about the baby while he waited for his old roommate to come on the line. He'd miss the birth, the first bottle, and everything that came afterward. Would Alice send him pictures? Out of sight, out of mind. He'd have to discuss that with his father.

Mac's fingers drummed on the desk. The ease with which Alice had announced her pregnancy puzzled him. She'd made it clear early on that she didn't want his children, even though she'd said otherwise when they were dating. Once she'd made the rash statement that she couldn't wait to cook a meal for him. He was still waiting. Alice couldn't boil water, much less cook a meal. Sometimes he wondered how she got herself together in the mornings. This whole thing was confusing, to say the least. The Alice he knew would have demanded he find a doctor to perform an abortion. She would have ranted and raved and blamed him. The Alice he knew would have thrown a fit at her circumstances, and more so when she found out he was leaving for Vietnam, but even that hadn't bothered her.

"You son of a bitch, I just heard!" Phil Benedict hissed into the phone. "I want to go too!"

"Sure you do and sure you want to leave those twins and that cute little wife. Don't shit me, Benny."

"Sounded good, though, didn't it?" Phil laughed. "Personally, I think you're nuts. Let the marines go. They come by that kind of stupidity naturally."

"I need to put some distance between me and here, that's all. The thing at home, it's not getting any better. My old man is leaning on me real heavy. I hate staff duty. This is nowhere to be, Phil, and we both know it. By the way, Alice told me she was pregnant this morning. *Before* I delivered *my* news."

"But . . . You told me . . ."

"Yeah . . . Yeah, but I never told Alice," Mac said tightly. "Since I exercised my conjugal rights one night when I had too much to drink, she thinks I'm responsible . . . or she'd like me to believe I am."

Phil Benedict whistled. "Hey, why don't you pull some of those awesome strings your father pulled the first time around?"

"I thought about it and decided against it. This is something I feel I have to do, Phil. I don't want to deal with Alice and *her* pregnancy now."

The faceless voice on the other end of the phone was silent for a moment. "I understand, Mac. Is there anything I can do, anything you want me to take care of while you're gone?"

"Write to me. I have a feeling I won't be getting many letters. Alice said she's going to rent a villa in the south of France and have her baby there."

Phil whistled again. "Hey, you know what I always say, it's probably meant to be. Listen, I can meet you for a drink after work if you want. We should at least shake hands and all that crap. You can tell your wife you had a flat tire."

"The hell I will. I'll say I stopped for a drink with the best friend a guy ever had. Sadie's, right? Five minutes past five okay with you?"

"I'll be there."

Mac looked at his cleared desk. There really was no need for him to be here. He had his orders, and his time was his own. Something had prompted him to come in today, possibly the luncheon with his father. Marcus Carlin was the kind of person you had to make an appointment to see. Marcus Carlin didn't believe in time off.

From childhood on Mac had always had to play the part of a little soldier for his father. He'd done it to please him, and when he pleased his father, his mother smiled. In his formative years he'd never said more than "yes, sir" and "no, sir" to his father. A regimented life, according to the judge, built character. So first there was boarding school, then prep school, and then the U.S. Military Academy and his commission in the army. "Ten years," his father had said, "ten years and you're out and headed for a bright future in politics." Well, his goddamn ten years were almost up, and he didn't want to go into politics, and Vietnam was his one and only chance to show independence from his father. Maybe, if he was lucky, he wouldn't come back, and he'd *never* have to go into politics. Or he could take off and disappear when he mustered out after his tour of duty in Nam. The coward's way out, he thought miserably, although in his gut, he knew he was a coward only when it came to confronting his father. Otherwise, nothing cowed or frightened him.

Where Vietnam was concerned, the old man would surely expect him to come home with every medal the army had to offer. Once, that is, he got over the shock of Mac's decision.

Mac's stomach rumbled ominously. A grimace of pain stretched across his face. Once the judge heard about Alice's pregnancy, he would have a press release scheduled by three o'clock. It would be full of saccharine and bullshit.

Mac pounded his clenched fist down on the shiny desktop. A pencil skittered to the edge, teetered, and dropped to the floor. Dust particles swept upward. They reminded him of the sawdust in a carnival. He'd run away with a local fireman's carnival when he was twelve. The carny people had hidden him for two months. That two months had been the happiest time of his life. He'd loved eating with the Fat Lady and all the roustabouts. His only concern was his mother, who was in failing health. He'd called her once from a pay phone to tell her he was safe, but he hadn't told her where he was. The worst part was being found by state troopers and taken home. His father hadn't done anything normal like taking a belt to his behind. Instead, he'd banished him to his room without a radio. The only reading material he was allowed to have was *Webster's Collegiate Dictionary* and a book consisting of maps of the entire world. His punishment was to learn the spelling and the meaning of every single word in that dictionary. Every night for a year his father quizzed him. Weekends were spent drawing maps and penciling in remote places, half of which he couldn't pronounce at twelve years of age. To this day he could close his eyes and pinpoint any place on the world map. It was his personal nightmare.

Still, he didn't start to hate his father that year. The hatred started two years later, when he found out that his father was having an affair with a diplomat's wife. He thought he was being a good son when he returned home from the city and told his mother about seeing his father with a strange woman. If he lived to be a hundred, he would never forget the awful look on her face. Two weeks later Elsa Carlin packed her bags and returned to her home in Charleston, leaving him behind. The old man had handled it by pensioning her off like a servant. His mother had taken the money too; she'd marched out of the house like a soldier, her head high, her eyes brimming with tears. How cold her face was. He had thought then that the hatred in her eyes had been for him. Even now he wasn't sure that it wasn't. What he did know now was that he was responsible for breaking up their family.

They'd never divorced, and his mother had died five years after she left. A coronary. The old man had given out some kind of piss-assed statement about his wife having had a breakdown and, good husband that he was, he had insisted she return to her family, where the atmosphere was conducive to a complete recovery. In the meantime, he and his son would manage to get along on their own. From that day, his father had totally ruled his life.

Now it was time for a change. When he got back from Vietnam, he would be mustered out and take his place in the civilian world. Then he could do whatever he wanted. He could get his divorce, provide for Alice and the baby.

His bottom line was his personal happiness. He wanted to be loved by someone, and he wanted to love that person in return. He wanted to watch sunsets, to walk in the rain, to discuss his old age, to raise a family born out of love with a partner he loved.

Maybe it would happen. Maybe it wouldn't. Right now he had a luncheon to attend with his father, and then a year to serve in Vietnam.

MARCUS CARLIN WAS every bit as imposing in his Saville Row suit as he was in his black judicial robes. His peers described him as formidable. Friends called him distinguished. Women said he was magnificently handsome and they plotted and schemed to be seen with him. The President of the United States considered him capable and austere. Media reporters treated him with deference, while they mumbled and muttered among themselves that yes, he made good copy, but not good enough to lose your job over. Most of them had come close to the unemployment line when they'd taken his political dossier to their chiefs just as he was about to announce his entrance into politics. Publishers and television network presidents immediately descended on his home and suggested to him, as friends, that he should withdraw from the race. In his study, over Havana cigars and Jim Beam whiskey, he agreed to do exactly that.

With his political ambitions in ashes at his feet, Marcus

Carlin got drunk and slept on the Persian carpet that night. When he awoke with a colossal hangover the following morning, he decided all the media were his enemy. But if he'd had to pay their price this once, he wouldn't pay it a second time.

Now his son Mac would do what he, Marcus, hadn't been able to do, the elder Carlin thought. There were no skeletons in his son's closets. The boy had promised him ten years in the army. He had one to go, and then his hat would go into the ring for the governorship of the state of Virginia. With Alice at his side, the beautiful, dutiful wife, they would make a perfect couple. The idol-loving public would go wild over them, he was sure. He'd *make* sure, by orchestrating their private lives and feeding tidbits to the hungry press. Once he whet the public's appetite, he would have the election in the bag.

Marcus rarely smiled, but he smiled now. Mac would be a figurehead, and he would be the power behind his son. It would be *almost* as good as being governor himself.

Judge Carlin stepped from his chauffeur-driven stretch limousine, and within seconds was ushered to his favorite table at the rear of the room. Almost immediately a drink was set in front of him. He nodded when a copy of the *Washington Star* appeared on the table. Carlin allowed himself one quick glance around the room. There was nobody of importance there. Not that it mattered. He rarely spoke to anyone, and he never invited anyone to join him at his table if he was lunching or dining alone.

He did like being seen with his son, however. Although they didn't look much alike, Marcus felt he looked as youthful as Mac, and he wanted people to notice that. As far as he was concerned, the only sign that he was older than Mac was his hair, which was gray, while his son's was dark chestnut, almost black. The judge was fit and trim, weighing exactly 180, which was also his son's weight. He had blue eyes, like Mac's, but his own were calculating and shrewd, where Mac's were trusting and open. They both had the same straight nose and the same cleft in what one reporter called a Grecian jaw. Fully clothed, Marcus Carlin could easily pass for a dashing forty-eight, thanks to a skilled plastic surgeon in Switzerland. When associates commented on his youthful appearance, he gave the credit entirely to a line of vitamins he said he took religiously. But he also worked out regularly, played tennis and squash, and jogged three miles every morning. However, he never wore shorts or short-sleeved shirts. Marcus didn't want any observers to see what he detested about himself—loose, flabby skin. For that, he hated his son's rippling, muscular thighs and hard biceps.

The judge sensed rather than saw his son approaching. Sensed because he noticed the slight rustle of moving chairs, was aware of craning necks and a soft murmur of voices, especially from the women. Mac was almost as distinguished in his captain's uniform as the judge was in his English-tailored suit.

"Dad, good to see you," he said, slipping into his chair.

Marcus wondered with annoyance how his son could be so unaware of the stir he was creating. He himself was always attuned to the effect of his own entrances.

Mac reached for his glass of wine, which appeared as if by magic. His father was lighting a cigarette, and Mac wanted one too. He waited a moment to see if his father would offer him one from the crocodile leather case, but he didn't. His father never offered anything.

"How's everything over at the Pentagon?" the judge asked in a bored voice.

Mac watched the perfect smoke ring rise and then waft toward him. He brushed at it impatiently. He didn't like the Jockey Club, because it was one of his father's favorite restaurants. He also didn't like his father's narrowed eyes or grim jaw. Mac's heart fluttered. Had the old man somehow gotten wind of what was going on? It was unlikely, he decided, since he'd learned to *play the game* almost as well as his old man.

Mac leaned back in his cane chair, a picture of nonchalance. He took his own cigarettes from a pocket, a crumpled pack of Chesterfields, and lit up. It amused him when his smoke ring circled the judge's head. Rather like a halo. He thought he could see little tufts of hair resembling horns on the sides of his father's head. He found himself grinning. "Things are about the same as they were yesterday and the day before that. I don't sit in on policy-making decisions."

"By your choice," the judge snapped.

"Yes, by my choice," Mac said quietly.

He wasn't going to miss his father at all. How could you miss someone you were never allowed to know, to get close to? He could feel his eyes start to spark when a bowl of French onion soup was set before him. He detested onion soup. He waved it away, his jaw tightening. He wasn't going to touch the cobbler's salad either. He could almost picture the grilled salmon steak that would be forthcoming shortly. His father's favorite meal; his guests too, like it or lump it. He'd seen people force down food, stifle their gagging impulses, just to impress his father. He'd done it himself, and all he'd gotten for it was acute indigestion. But not today. Not ever again.

Mac lit a second Chesterfield, then drained his wineglass and signaled for another. His father's eyebrows shot up. One drink at lunch was his father's motto, two for dinner. All things in moderation. Mac gulped at the dry wine.

Judge Carlin dabbed at his lips. He worked his tongue around the inside of his mouth.

He's worried there might be specks of spinach on his teeth, Mac thought.

"Just spit it out, Malcolm, and let's see what we can do with it," the judge said, patting his lips a second time.

Mac crossed his legs and fixed his stare on his father, across the table. "I volunteered for Vietnam. I leave the day after tomorrow. My orders are carved in granite, if that's your next question." He signaled for a third glass of wine.

"You did what!" the judge hissed.

Mac smiled. He wondered how his father did it: his jaw had barely moved, his lips hadn't parted, but the angry horror was there for anyone to see. "You pledged me ten years, Malcolm. An honorable man doesn't go back on his word."

"I'm not going back on my word. One year in Vietnam will finish up my time in the service. I'm giving you exactly what I promised. When I get back, if I get back, we'll discuss the second part of my career," Mac said tightly.

The salmon steak arrived just as Mac knew it would. He waved it away. Today there were two sprigs of parsley on the plate.

The judge leaned across the table, a ghoulish look on his face. The other diners were supposed to think he was smiling. It was such a neat trick, Mac thought, being able to talk and not move your lips or jaw. "This is about the most stupid thing you've ever done. I've pulled strings, I've called in favors, and I've gone out of my way to get you a comfortable job in the Pentagon. Now you toss it all aside."

"I'm not needed here, and I hate staff duty," Mac replied. "I want to contribute."

"Do you have any idea of what's going on over *there*?" the judge demanded. He didn't wait for a response, he never did. "You don't have to go. Let someone else go."

"Father, I am the someone else. I'm not going to change my mind," Mac said firmly.

"You didn't answer my question. Do you know what's going on over there? Well, do you?"

"I'm in the army, for Christ's sake, of course I know what's going on over there. I hope to make a difference. At least I'm going to try."

The judge laid his fork down across his plate next to his knife. Now he's going to tell me all the things on his mind, Mac thought, all the things that are important right now, more important than me. He sat back and fired up another cigarette.

"I have a lot going on, Mac. I don't want to have to worry about you, and contrary to what you believe, I will worry. They're yellow-eyed weasels, and they don't fight the way you've been taught. There are no rules over there. You've learned jungle warfare from a book. The real thing is nothing like what you've been taught.

"LBJ told me himself he had a meeting with Premier Nguyen Cao Ky on the seventh. Ky said his government would never deal with the Viet Cong. They talked about economic and social reforms to win the war against the communists. We both know that's bull. This war will be won or lost by force of arms. That's why I prefer you stay stateside. I don't want to stand by your casket the way I stood by Chester Nimitz's. Do you hear me, Malcolm?"

"I don't want your blessing," Mac said firmly. "I just want your support. I need you to tell me you understand why I'm going over there."

Judge Carlin picked up his fork and poked at his salmon. It was the most Mac would get. There would be no words, no pat on the back. He would finish his lunch. Mac found himself grinning.

"What's gotten into you, son?" the judge asked.

Son. Mac couldn't remember the old man ever calling him son. It was always Malcolm or Mac around his friends. It was too late for words like son. It was too late for a lot of things. He steeled himself to maintain the outward show of respect that was demanded of him.

"Jesus, Dad, I'm supposed to be a goddamn combat leader. They couldn't wait to change my orders. They need me over there. I'm going. Do you want to say good-bye here or stop by the house? You will keep an eye on Alice for me, won't you? Maybe this will take the edge off things. Alice is pregnant. She told me this morning. I'm not changing my mind. She wants to go to France and have the baby there," Mac said cooly.

The elder Carlin snapped his lips shut. He hated having his judgment questioned. He never backed down. Never. And now, on top of everything else, a brat! *That* wasn't in his plan. He didn't like children, never had liked them. He tolerated Mac because it was expected. It was wholesome. It was the way things were done. But he didn't have to like it.

"You could have asked me first."

Mac laughed, a loud guffaw that made the other diners stare at the two good-looking men dining alone. "When? As I was unzipping my pants, or when Alice couldn't find her diaphragm? I guess there was a minute there when I could have called you." His laugh sounded bitter. For once, he noticed, the old man actually looked embarrassed.

"That's not what I meant, and you damn well know it," the judge seethed. It was a shock and he hadn't been prepared for it. Then again, a baby, a toddler, would look good when he announced his son was going into politics. Mac was better looking than Jack Kennedy. Alice had the same kind of savoir faire as Jackie Kennedy. Maybe a stint in Vietnam would add to the political flavor of things. Providing Mac came home a hero. He gave voice to the thought.

Mac winced. He'd known the old man would think of it. "Well, hell yes, Father, I wouldn't have it any other way," he said mockingly. "You will keep tabs on Alice, won't you?" He waited for his father to nod, then said, "Then you won't mind if I skip dessert. My sweet tooth runs toward apple pie, not rice pudding. And I don't like chicory in my coffee."

"Your mother must be rolling over and over in her grave," the judge muttered.

Mac could feel the beginnings of a heat flush on his neck. He wasn't going to get suckered into *that* game. The old man always pulled out his mother as a last resort.

Mac stood, every eye in the room on him. "I guess this is good-bye, *sir*," he said quietly.

There was little the judge could do but extend his own hand. Mac crushed it. "Good-bye, Malcolm. Make me proud of you."

"You bet, *sir*. Yes, *sir*. Right, *sir*. Whatever you say, *sir*." Mac fired off a snappy, mocking salute to his father before he strode from the restaurant.

And that was the end of that.

Outside in the brisk air, Mac inhaled deeply. He'd wanted the old man to slap him on the back. He'd wanted some encouraging words. Wanted, but never expected.

He started to walk; it was the only thing he could think of to do to get rid of the knots in his neck, the tension in his gut. Maybe a long walk in the brisk air would heal his heart.

He wandered aimlessly, up one street and down another, until he didn't know where he was. Not that he cared at that moment. He walked until he was almost numb with the cold, then he hailed the first cab he saw. Forty minutes later he climbed into his own car and headed for his and Benny's favorite bar. Their favorite because Bill's Bar and Grill was the only place that served them when they'd been underage.

As he was locking his car, Mac surveyed Pennsylvania Avenue. Not much traffic. The bar would probably be empty. He could sit in the back and nurse his misery until Benny arrived. He stared at the garish neon sign that burned twenty-four hours a day. It looked like a sleazy, ramshackle tavern from the outside, but it was clean inside, warm, and full of camaraderie. The clientele, for the most part, wore three-piece business suits and Brooks Brothers shoes. There were no fistfights here, and the place didn't smell like stale beer and cigarette smoke. It was, in his opinion, a class operation. Sadie Switzer ran the place. There was no Bill. She had named it, she said, after her only true love, who had left her high and dry when he found out she was pregnant. Sadie was fond of saying she kept the exterior shabby on purpose in case old Bill ever decided to come back and ask for a part of the profits.

There was a picture of Bill on one of the walls; it doubled as a dart board. Sadie gave free draughts to anyone who hit Bill's nose dead center. During Mac's senior year in prep school he'd practiced throwing darts every evening, but he'd used a picture of his father for a target. He'd gotten a vicious kind of pleasure out of plucking out the old man's eyes and shredding his nose. Jesus, he'd used up a whole week's allowance having pictures of his father blown up just so he could mutilate them. The day Sadie got tired of serving him free draughts, she asked him how he got so good at throwing darts. He told her. She'd hugged him, tears in her eyes. It was the best hug he'd ever had, sweet and motherly.

Warm, lemon-scented air wafted toward Mac when he opened the door. He blinked several times till his eyes adjusted to the dim interior.

In a way, coming to Sadie's was like coming home. He felt comfortable both here, in the bar itself, and upstairs in her four-room apartment. When he was younger, Sadie had never let him drive even after just one beer. Serving him when he was underage was one thing, but letting him drive under the influence of alcohol was something else.

If there was such a thing as a beautiful bar, then Bill's Bar and Grill was beautiful. The bar was solid mahogany with a shiny brass rail, which Sadie polished herself. There were always bowls of pickled eggs as well as nuts and pretzels on the bar. The stools were made of matched, polished mahogany that smelled lemony and clean. The cushions were real leather and *swoosh*ed when you sat down. He'd always liked the sound. He also liked the oak floor, which was washed and waxed every night, even on Christmas Eve. The tables and chairs were also made of oak and were bright with polish. Green and white checkered cloths covered the tables. Sadie insisted that this was because Bill was Irish and his favorite color was green. Once in a while, especially on St. Patrick's Day, she placed green candles on the tables and served green beer. It took him almost two years before he figured out that Sadie still loved Bill and would take him back in a heartbeat if he should ever walk through her front door.

Mac sat down at the bar and ordered a bottle of Bud. His eyes scanned Sadie's memorabilia wall. Snapshots of patrons and their families covered it, but by invitation only. One did not, ever, sneak a picture onto the wall. To do so meant instant banishment. When Sadie decided you were worthy enough, she would casually mention that it was time for a picture. Mac had waited almost a year before she asked the bartender to snap a picture of him and her standing together outside the bar with the neon sign behind them. There were all kinds of pictures of Sadie on the wall, usually taken during one of the bashes she was famous for, but there were no pictures of Sadie posing with anyone but Mac. He'd puffed out like a peacock that day, and still did when he thought about it.

As he sipped his beer, Mac decided that someday he would do something really nice for Sadie in return.

Her scent arrived before she did. Mac sniffed appreciatively when she walked into the bar from the kitchen.

"Mac, honey, no one told me you were here." She smiled, walking around the bar. "Is anything wrong?"

The concern and worry on her face made him force more lightness into his voice than he felt. Sadie already knew he was going to Nam, she'd been the first person he'd told. "No, not at all. I'm meeting Benny here, and I wanted to say good-bye.

I just had lunch with my father." He swigged from the bottle and shrugged at the same time.

Sadie Switzer was a tall woman, five-eleven, and she carried her height regally. She wore the best clothes, always had her hair expertly coiffed, and her makeup was so professional that it looked as if she wasn't wearing any. Her hair was naturally white, and she refused to color it. "An old broad like me, come on," she'd say. "I'm sixty-five. If I change myself, Bill won't know me when he finally decides to look me up." She was pretty, with eyes as green as grass and a straight little nose that she twitched when she was annoyed. But it was her smile, all crinkly and warm, that attracted people to her. In turn, she knew everything there was to know about her customers and their families, their pets, their in-laws, and she dispensed advice like a professional psychiatrist.

She sat down on the bar stool next to Mac. "Ginger ale," she said to the bartender.

"You're lookin' good, Sadie." Mac chuckled.

"I should, it took me three hours this morning to get myself together. God, I didn't think I was ever going to get old. Then one day I woke up, and there I was, an old broad. I think it was the same day I realized Bill was never going to come back here for me."

He had it, the nice thing he could do for Sadie. Find Bill.

"Where did he go, Sadie?"

"He *said* he was going to San Francisco, but that was a lie. He just didn't want me to find him. He didn't want a kid, that's what it was all about. For sure he wasn't father material, but at the time, I wasn't exactly mother material either. I would have learned, Mac. Honest to God, I would have learned. I wanted that baby more than anything in the world, because it was part of Bill. When I miscarried, I wanted to die. I kept myself going all those years by convincing myself Bill would eventually start to think that he had a son or daughter and want to see his flesh and blood, but it never happened. I didn't care after that, and I let myself go—physically and mentally. Then you walked in here, angry and belligerent, with a chip on your shoulder. It would have been my son's birthday, if he had lived. Me and you, we hit it right off. I didn't even give a damn if I got arrested for serving you, you being underage and all. Kid, when you invited me to West Point for your graduation, there wasn't a prouder person in the world. You screwed up by getting married, but we aren't going to talk about that. Swear to me you're going to write to me at least once a month."

"I swear—every two weeks. I wrote you when I was at the Academy, didn't I?"

"That was different, you were lonely. You're going to a hellhole. I can read, Mac. It's all jungle over there. Once a month will be fine. But in the meantime, I would like to know why you're doing this."

Mac signaled the bartender for a second beer. "I have to get out from under. I need some time, some space. The old man took it rather well, all things considered. He ordered me to come back a hero."

"It figures." Sadie snorted. She would never forgive the judge for the way he treated his son. Neither would she ever forget the humiliating way he'd looked at her at Mac's graduation. She didn't like Alice either, and she had tried to steer Mac in other directions, but he'd been stubborn. If she'd had her way, she would have taken him to a high quality cathouse and turned him loose, but she didn't have any say. It was a real pity; now Mac was shackled to someone he didn't love with no way out.

"And your wife?" she asked gently.

"Ah, my wife. Well, Sadie, this morning my wife told me she's pregnant." He hated the pitying look in Sadie's eyes. He took a long, hard pull at the beer bottle, almost draining it. "Say something, Sadie."

She shrugged her shoulders.

Sadie was wearing a raspberry-colored silk blouse with a cream-colored skirt and beige pumps. A slender strand of pearls adorned the front of the blouse, Bill's one and only gift to her.

She felt tears prick her eyes. She loved this boy—this *young man*, she corrected the thought. She felt his pain, had always felt it, and somehow she always knew when he was going through a bad time. She'd called his home for a while, but Alice usually managed to forget to give Mac her messages. When she couldn't reach him at the house, she called the Pentagon. It was her mothering instinct, she said, which she'd never gotten the chance to nourish until Mac came along.

"A baby is a wonderful thing for two people, Mac. Perhaps it will cement your marriage." She didn't believe it for a minute.

"I'm going no matter what, Sadie," Mac said glumly. "I have to do this—for me. If I don't, what the hell kind of father am I going to make? Let's not talk about this, okay? It's my last night to howl. Me and Benny. The TFB kids. Remember? You christened us."

"The Trust Fund Boys. Yes, I remember," Sadie said softly. "I think that's the only time in my life I made a bad judgment call. I apologized to both of you."

"Yes, you did, and we took it real well, Benny and me." Mac's voice was beginning to slur. He was on his fourth beer. "Benny's okay. My best friend. He's happy, did I tell you that?"

"Uh-huh. How about some coffee, Mac, and a sandwich? Let's go upstairs before you start giving my place a bad name." She almost laughed then at the way Mac snapped to attention. He removed his uniform blouse, loosened his tie, and rolled up his sleeves. He stood back and pitched his visored service cap toward the bar. It landed neatly on two bottles of Bombay gin. This time Sadie did laugh as she linked her arm with his.

In Sadie's apartment, Mac leaned back in the comfortable chair and did his best to concentrate on her favorite show, *Dark Shadows*. It was four o'clock, so he still had an hour to kill until Benny arrived. Sadie was right. He needed to sober up before his best pal in the whole world arrived.

Sadie set down a plate of thick sandwiches full of every cold cut known to man. "I put lots of mustard and mayo on, just the way you like it." Three pickled eggs and two sour pickles, along with some potato chips, completed Mac's meal.

"Alice never makes me anything. The cook does it," Mac mumbled as he chewed obediently. "Thanks for bringing me up here. The last thing I wanted to do was embarrass you. I shouldn't have had all that beer on an empty stomach."

"It wasn't me I was worried about, it was you, Mac."

"I know, Sadie," Mac muttered as he gulped the last of the coffee. He was more clear-headed now and he felt less woozy. "Did I tell you I'm going down to Charleston tomorrow on an early flight? I want to see my uncle Harry before I leave. I didn't tell my father I was going. Shit, I didn't tell Alice either. I should call her now and tell her I won't be home for dinner."

"Now, that's a thought." Sadie grinned.

Mac laughed. "I said I *should*, I didn't say I would. Alice . . . Alice doesn't care."

From long experience, she knew it was time to steer the conversation in another direction. "You haven't been to your mother's home for a long time, have you?"

"The last time I went was when I was in high school. It was pure rebellion. My father forbid me to go, so I sneaked out at night and hitchhiked. I was kind of proud of that. My uncle Harry thought it was cool. He hates my old man, but then, my old man hates him too."

"What about you, Mac, how do you feel about your mother's side of the family?" Sadie asked carefully. This was a touchy subject with Mac. A look of pain crossed his face and she felt sorry she'd asked. "Listen, kiddo, that's none of my business, and I'm sorry I asked. Shoot, the program's over. Did Jonathan declare his love for Josette?"

"If he did, I didn't see it. You have to stop watching this crap, Sadie."

"I watch Huntley and Brinkley, what more do you want?"

"What I feel about my mother's family isn't the issue, it's what they feel about me. I guess you could say I'm persona non grata where they're concerned, but my father is at the bottom of it somehow. My uncle Harry is a strange man. I've always had this feeling he wanted to like me, did like me, but something held him back from showing it. Maybe he'll welcome me and maybe he won't. Maybe he'll tell me why my mother turned her back on me and left me with my father. I think it's time I knew. If he won't tell me, then I'll have to live with it."

Sadie's eyes sparked. "Mothers don't leave their children unless there's a reason that's so . . . God, it would have to be something monumental to make me leave a child. Mothers just don't do that, Mac. Look, I know you saw your father with a chippie and you told your mother. That's not it. There's more to it. She probably knew all along your father fooled around. If that was the case, then for sure she would have grabbed you and taken you with her. Maybe you should leave it alone."

Mac snorted. "That's what I've been doing all along. Now it's the right time. I might not get another chance. My old man is certainly never going to tell me what went on, so what other choice do I have?"

She shrugged her shoulders, bunching the slender strand of pearls between her breasts. "Listen," she said brightly, "how about a slice of cheesecake? I made it myself."

"I'm stuffed. Thanks anyway. Look, Sadie, don't feel you have to babysit me. Go downstairs if you want. The early birds will be out in full force. Send Benny up when he gets here."

Sadie smiled, and Mac thought her one of the prettiest women he'd ever seen. She was even prettier than he remembered his mother being. "If Bill calls, bang on the floor."

"You got it."

THE ROOM WHERE he waited was a *Bill* room, Mac had decided long ago. A shrine, for want of a better word. It wasn't that it was an uncomfortable room in any way. It was more like an expectant room, a room waiting for one of its occupants to return. Somehow Sadie had managed to pull everything together in the narrow space so that it was comfortable and cozy. In the winter there was always a fire going in the fireplace and the scent of popped corn in the air. Bill, Sadie said, loved to pop corn, and they used to fight over what Bill called the "fluffies," those first kernels that popped high and white and were crunchy and delicious. In the summer, huge clay pots of flowers decorated the hearth and called attention to the rogue's gallery over the mantel: pictures of Bill fishing, pictures of Bill on the first day of hunting season, Bill in his best suit on Easter, Bill sleeping in a folding chair at the beach, Bill in a wraparound apron, flipping pancakes. All the frames were identical, which made him think Sadie had bought frames by the dozen. Over the mantel was a huge oil painting of Sadie, painted when she was twenty-five. Whoever the artist was, he'd captured her perfectly, Mac thought. Sadie had the warmest, softest, kindest eyes he'd ever seen. The smile on the portrait was just as warm, soft, and kind.

The carpet was thick, almost ankle deep, a pure wheat color which was picked up in the drapes covering the long, narrow windows. Threads of bright orange and deep hunter-green shot through the drapes and were again picked up in the sofa cushions, which seemed to be crafted from the same color dye as the carpet. Two chairs, one a recliner, the other a rocker, were side by side at the far end of the room. At the foot of the recliner was an ottoman covered in brilliant orange. This chair, *Bill's chair*, was like new, still unused. Sadie's headrest, on the other hand, was punched in and the seat cushion dented from hours of use. The small piecrust table separating the chairs supported a lamp, an ashtray holding a pipe, and Bill's glasses. Next to Bill's chair was a magazine rack filled with copies of *Field and Stream*, Bill's favorite magazine. The magazine rack, a twin of Bill's next to Sadie's chair, was filled with copies of *Redbook*, *McCall's*, and *Ladies' Home Journal*. All of the magazines were still glossy, never read. It was no fun to read alone, Sadie said, because there was no one to discuss the articles or stories with. It was all part of Sadie's dream. Underneath the triple windows a pool table with balls racked and cue sticks at the ready waited for Bill. The balls were always clean and shiny, with never a speck of dust. To the left of the pool table was an entertainment center. A stereo system, television, and record rack. Bill liked Big Band music. Sadie had every record ever made. To the right of the entertainment center was a floor-to-ceiling bookshelf filled with all of Bill's favorites. All classics, all bound in beautiful leather. On the lower shelf were Sadie's books, novels of suspense and mayhem. Her favorite author in the world was Erle Stanley Gardner. They looked new too, but that was because Sadie never bent the spines of her books. She'd cock the book at a weird angle, lean toward the light and read. She never turned down the corners of the pages either. Bill had a thing about book pages, she'd said. He wouldn't even read the paper if someone touched it before he did.

Early on, Mac and Benny had decided that Bill was a royal pain in the ass.

Mac's eyes drifted to the coffee table in front of the sofa with the soft pillows; it was extra long, custom made. A bowl of fruit, the latest issues of *Field and Stream* and *Redbook*, along with a dish of Spanish nuts, waited.

Rage rushed through Mac. He wanted to smash the room, to rip and gouge everything in his sight. He'd had the feeling before, and it always left as quickly as it surfaced. All of this was by Sadie's choice. If she wanted to live in a fantasy world, who was he to say she should or shouldn't? Downstairs she was as normal as everyone else. Probably more so. The tension in his shoulders eased.

It was a room, and that's all it was.

It was dark outside, Mac realized. He switched on the lamp and closed the draperies, loving the way the room took on an even cozier atmosphere when the fireplace at the far end was lit.

"Mac, you here?" Benny called from the foyer.

"In here," Mac responded.

"Sadie said to put these in water. She said there's a vase in the bottom of the sink. Good to see you, Mac," Benny said, slapping his friend on the back. "I called you a couple of times over the past month, but Alice said you guys were busy. So I said shit on you and waited for you to call me."

"I appreciate your concern," Mac said with friendly sarcasm. "Let's get those flowers into a vase, and then I want to talk to you. There's something I want you to do for me while I'm away. Are you hungry?"

"No, I'm not hungry. I eat a big lunch because Carol is such a lousy cook. We don't have a cook the way some people do. What do you want to talk about? We can do two things at once." Benny grinned.

For some reason, Phil Benedict would do anything Mac wanted, and that included letting him call him Benny. He'd deck anyone else. He was tall, pencil thin, with big ears and reddish hair the color of ripe wheat. Light brown freckles danced across his cheeks and nose. His eyes were soft, warm, mellow; Mac called them cow eyes. Benny always retaliated by saying they were good enough to get him the prettiest girl in New York City. He had a dashing, sporty grin which lit up his whole face. Benny was a good friend, a caring friend.

"I want you to find Bill Trinity for Sadie."

"You want *what*!"

"You heard me. I'm going to give you a check, and you hire a private dick and tell him to find Bill. Snitch one of those pictures off the mantel. With what we both know, maybe we can give the guy enough to come up with something. I don't care what it costs. Don't tell the dick that though. Make him earn his money. Whatever it takes, do it. The only thing is, if it turns out he's dead, don't tell her. If they find him, I want you to go to him, wherever he is, and talk to him before you bring him back, providing he doesn't have a wife. Then I want you to beat the living crap out of him for running out on Sadie."

Benny's freckles bunched up. "Are you sure we should be sticking our noses into Sadie's business?" he asked worriedly. "I'll do it, I'll do it," he added hastily. "Have you given any thought to him not wanting to come back? Jesus, Mac, it's been a hell of a long time. I can't force him."

"When you tell him the way it is here, he'll come. Sadie said he loved her, and women know these things."

"It's probably going to take forever."

"So what? You aren't going anywhere but back and forth to the Pentagon."

"What the hell is that supposed to mean?" Benny asked with an edge to his voice.

"It means I'm getting edgy. I guess I didn't tell you I'm going down to Charleston tomorrow. I kind of want to see my uncle Harry again."

"Is this the same Uncle Harry who never wanted to see you or talk to you after your mother died?" The edge in his voice was rougher now, almost jagged.

"That's the one. I'm gonna ask him some questions."

He looked nasty, Benny thought, which meant he would be like a terrier with a rat between his teeth. He also wondered why his friend had waited so long to visit his mother's old home. He knew for a fact Mac had only been there twice in his life, and he'd been too young to remember one of those times.

"If it's something you gotta do, then you gotta do it," Benny said, pouring himself a cup of coffee. He carried it to the Formica table and sat down. Mac joined him.

"Look, I don't want to get into all that family jazz. I wanted us to have a friendly visit so I wouldn't feel so damn bad about leaving you behind. I figured we'd reminisce about the good old days, belt a few beers, and then shake hands. I screwed up. Sorry about that, Benny."

"This coffee is fine; my stomach's been out of whack for a week or so. I think I have an ulcer. Beer would kill me right now. Besides, how in the hell could we reminisce downstairs in the bar with all that racket going on?"

They talked for a long time, Benny doing most of the talking. Mac plucked an orange from the luscious bowl of fruit on the table. Benny watched as his friend ran his thumbnail up one groove and down the other, his thoughts everywhere but on the subject at hand. Finally, their conversation slowed and disappeared into a depressing silence.

"Goddamnit, this is turning into a wake," Mac said sourly after a few moments. "This might be a good time to clap one another on the back and head home. Me to Alice, and you to your happy little family. Jesus, I envy you, Benny, but at the same time I'm happy for you. Can you understand that?"

"Sure. Look, Mac, why don't you go home and make some sort of peace with Alice?

"Did I ever tell you the only time Alice and I had good sex was the night before her beauty parlor appointment? On Thursday nights she didn't worry about her hair getting mussed up. That's a hell of a thing, isn't it, Benny?"

"Yeah, it is, Mac," Benny said, straightening his tie. He felt like crying for his friend. "Listen, let's go downstairs, hug Sadie, and shoot two darts at your old man's snoot. Winner buys drinks for the entire bar."

"Dead center on his nose. You never even came close. It's a sucker bet, but I'm game," Mac said tightly.

Sadie watched the two favorite men in her life walk over to

the dart board. She immediately reached under the bar for a picture of Judge Carlin, blown up three times its original size. She personally thumbtacked it over the bull's-eye and moved back. Tears glistened in her eyes when Mac squared his shoulders before pulling on his cap. This was something new, she thought. Mac never attacked his father when he was dressed in what she referred to as full regalia. Benny either.

The room grew quiet. A dart game required everyone's full attention.

"You first, Benny," Mac said, stepping back.

Benny felt the urge to cry again. Mac had been right, he'd never even come close to hitting the judge's nose. Usually he got him high on the cheekbone or low on the chin. He squinted, crossed his fingers on his left hand as he said a silent little prayer. He threw.

Sadie's eyebrows shot upward. "Dead center, Mac. You can see the hole real clear."

Mac waited for the round of applause to quiet down. He adjusted his cap at a rakish angle before he stretched his neck muscles. He didn't wind up, didn't stare at the picture the way he usually did. He threw.

Sadie expelled the long breath she was holding. "You hit the same hole, Mac. Now it looks like there's a pimple on his nose." No one laughed. They weren't supposed to.

"Two rounds of drinks for the house, Sadie. Benny's buying one and so am I." He ripped the picture off the dart board and handed it to Sadie, along with two twenty-dollar bills. Benny forked over the same amount.

"I'll . . . guess I'll see you around, Sadie," Mac said in a choked voice.

Sadie bit down on her lower lip. "I'll be here, Mac. Write, okay?"

"You bet. Allow extra time for the mail, you know . . ."

"I will. I'll write once a week and send you packages. Come here, you big lug."

The bar grew suddenly noisy, the juke box blared "The Witch Doctor" as Mac folded Sadie in his arms. "Thanks for everything," he whispered. Sadie struggled from his arms and

ran upstairs. To cover the emotion of the moment, Mac playfully punched Benny on the shoulder before he shot off a salute
that was so professional, Benny blinked. His own was sloppy in
comparison.

"See you, Benny."

"Yeah."

When Benny left Bill's Bar and Grill, there was no sign of
Mac or his car. He cleared his throat three times before he could
take a normal breath. "Fuck you, Judge Carlin," he muttered
through clenched teeth.

MAC GARAGED THE car. It was a clear February night and
extremely cold. Overhead, the sky was black and sparkling. So
many stars. He wished, the way he always had when he was a
boy, for peace within himself. He always wished for the same
thing when he saw the first spring robin. He'd never told anyone, not even Benny.

He entered the house through the kitchen door, but he didn't
stay long in the kitchen. Once it had been his favorite room in
the house. It was the place where his mother took him to give
him sugar cookies and milk. Sometimes in that room, she told
him stories about giants and kings and queens. Now it was
for him a tidy, sterile area where food was prepared by a
woman whose name changed monthly.

Alice was sitting on the sofa with her legs curled under her.
She looked pretty, Mac thought, but she evoked no emotion in
him. She wore a mint-green peignoir with lace ruffles. She had
one in every color imaginable. He craned his neck to see if she
had on matching mules with feathery tendrils. She did. Benny's
wife, Carol, didn't own things like that. She wore a pink flannel
robe with a belt and slipper socks. He knew because he'd seen
her once when one of the twins was sick. He'd stopped by to
give Benny a ride to work so she could keep the car that day.
The house had smelled like perked coffee and fried bacon.

"Alice," he said curtly.

"Mac," Alice said without taking her eyes from the television
screen. *The Man From U.N.C.L.E.* was her favorite show.

"I need to talk to you, Alice. Now. I have to be up early. I'm going to Charleston, and from there on to the West Coast. I want to discuss a few things. Are you listening to me, Alice?"

"I can hear every word you're saying, Mac. What do you want to talk about?"

Mac walked over to the television set and turned it off. He stood with his back to the screen and faced his wife. "I want to know how it is you got pregnant when you used a diaphragm?" He asked though he knew that diaphragm or not, the baby couldn't be his; he wanted to know how she would explain it.

"What an insidious thing to say. You wait here and don't you dare move. I'll be right back." She was off the sofa, her peignoir flying behind her, the heels of her mules clicking on the polished floor. She was back a second later with a plastic pouch in her hand. Her face was triumphant. She led her husband over to the table lamp, from which she removed the shade, and held the round piece of rubber against the light. A minute hole appeared as a bright little spot in the latex. "I knew you would say just what you said, that's why I didn't throw this away. It's not *my* fault!"

"Isn't it going to bother you being alone in a strange country? If you stayed here, at least my father could look after you. All your friends are here."

"Friends? I don't want them to see me looking like a blimp. I want to hide, don't you understand?"

"No, I don't understand." He remembered Benny's wife and the way she had trundled along, waddling like a duck, up until the day she delivered. She constantly made jokes about her appearance, and she had let him put his hand on her stomach when the baby kicked. He'd been awestruck, as awestruck as Benny. Benny had worn a sappy expression for the whole nine months. He'd loved the way his wife looked. But then Benny and Carol were in love.

"It's not important for you to understand. As long as I do, that's all that's important. Anyway, why are you going to Charleston? What did your father say?"

"I want to see my uncle Harry, and my father didn't seem too interested in becoming a grandfather. I asked him to keep an eye on you. As for money, I took care of everything."

"I want *enough*, Mac. Make sure you understand that."

"I understand, and I said I provided for you. Now, I want to talk about us."

"Not again, Mac," Alice said wearily.

"Yes, again. Because I'm not happy, and I don't see how you can be happy. I don't love you, Alice. I want you to think about this marriage. I meant what I said this morning. When I get back, we're going to discuss a divorce seriously."

Alice felt a flutter of panic. He sounded different than he had this morning. She believed he meant what he said. Where would that leave her? Out in the cold with a kid, that's where.

"I never understood what it was you wanted from me, Mac," she whined. "Tell me now. If I'm supposed to think about this while you're away, I have to know what it is you *think* I did wrong."

"I wanted you to be a wife," Mac said coolly. "Do you know that in our entire marriage, you never even made me a cup of coffee?"

Alice's laugh was shrill. "Listen, Mac, you were the one who hired the cook. You said you didn't want me to do anything but be here for you. That's exactly what you said. And that's what I did. I got used to this way of life to please *you*, and now you tell me you're going to take it away from me when you get back? No you're not. I'll fight you. I've made a life for myself, and I'm going to keep it, and that's all I have to say about it," Alice snapped. "Is there anything else?"

"Only this." Mac seethed. "If the baby is a girl, I want it named after my mother. If it's a boy, I want it named after me, not my father."

"Fine, I agree. Is there anything else?" Alice asked coldly.

"Good-bye, Alice."

"Good-bye, Mac."

Mac fumed all the way up the steps. The television set was already back on.

ALICE REACHED FOR the little notebook she had stuffed under the cushion when she heard Mac's car in the driveway. Her skin positively itched and the tips of her fingers tingled. Her heart took on an extra beat at what she'd done between the hours of five and seven. She forced herself to close her eyes, take a deep breath, and count to ten. Her eyes snapped open on the count of ten. If anything, she was even more excited. She tried again; this time her eyes circled the room, trying to focus on something that would relax her.

This was *her* room. She'd decorated it herself in all the colors she loved, brilliant, flamboyant fabrics, eye-watering carpet, and glass and chrome furniture. The pictures were a mishmash of color and brush strokes by unknown artists in outrageous gilt frames from a bygone era. Because she didn't like the idea of a wood-burning fireplace, she'd cajoled and whined until the elder Carlin permitted her to change it to gas. Now the flame was constant and her stark white walls didn't have sooty smudge marks all over them.

She took another deep breath. She had work to do. She had decided it was time to look into numbers that equaled assets. If he went through with his threat of a divorce—and she didn't believe for one minute that he would—then she'd need records of everything to give to her attorney.

As far as she knew, Mac hadn't put her name on anything, so there were no joint assets. There was no *ours*, only *his*. But, Mac had said he was going to leave her power of attorney. All she had to do was weep and wail, and the judge would come across with what she wanted.

A delicious feeling filled her when she opened the little notebook. She'd had to write small to get everything down on the square little pages. Bank account numbers, balances, property deeds, exact locations, the cusip numbers on the stocks, the bond balances, the dates on the trust fund. She'd been startled when she saw the bank record, and was stunned to find out Mac was the recipient of two trust funds: one from his mother and one from an aunt. She'd actually had to close her eyes and put her head between her knees when she saw the amount of money the funds generated. And four full pages of assets. My God, she hadn't known there was that much money in the world.

Damn, where was the power of attorney? She hadn't seen it in the desk. She brightened momentarily when she remembered

Mac had had lunch with his father. He'd probably given it to him. Mac was thorough. If he said he was going to do something, then he would do it.

The Princess phone was in her hand in a flash. Should she call the judge to confirm it? She would wait until tomorrow, she decided. She didn't want the judge to think she was money-grubbing.

She stuffed the notebook under the sofa cushion. Tomorrow she would retrieve it and lock it away in the bottom drawer of her jewel box along with some of the heirloom jewelry the judge allowed her to keep in the house.

She was nervous now. Had she put everything back into the manila folder just the way she'd found it? Guilt made her uncurl her legs and rush to Mac's study. The huge brown envelope was gone. She ran to the hall to see if it was on the table in the foyer. It wasn't. Where in the hell was it? she wondered irritably. It must be in Mac's room. She crept up the steps, careful to make no noise. She opened the door a crack, then waited until her eyes became accustomed to the moonlight. Mac's bags were packed and standing by the door, as they had been earlier that day. There was no folder, no envelope on the wide triple dresser.

Alice watched her husband for a long moment. She felt a second rush of guilt. How vulnerable Mac looked in sleep. She had a sudden urge to run over to the bed and kiss his cheek, but squelched it.

She hated thinking about Mac; it made her feel disloyal. After all, he *had* been good to her. Why wasn't she happy? Why couldn't she be like Benny's wife? Was she as self-centered and selfish as Mac said? Why couldn't she give back a little? Mac wasn't all that bad; in fact he was kind of nice as far as husbands went. If he were only more aggressive, more motivated, she might feel differently.

She wished she loved Mac. She *liked* him. But then, she didn't know anyone who was *in love* with their husband.

When the phone rang at eleven o'clock, Alice was so startled, she almost fell off the sofa. She picked it up on the second ring.

"Hello," she said in a froggy voice.

"Congratulations, my dear," Marcus Carlin said.

"Thank you, Marcus," she replied. "Is that why you're calling so late? Mac is asleep." She should ask him now about the power of attorney, she thought.

"I've been thinking all afternoon, Alice, and I've decided the south of France is not the place for you to be all alone. No, I want you to stay right here. I can't imagine what Mac was thinking to allow you to go traipsing off to France. The boy is just too indulgent where you're concerned."

"But, Judge—"

"There will be no buts. I would be derelict in my duty to allow you to go. I know what's best for you. It's settled—you'll stay right here. We don't want to take any chances with the new Carlin heir, now do we?"

Alice's eyes narrowed. She wanted to tell the old coot to go fuck himself. She really meant to say it aloud, but what came out of her mouth was, "As usual, you're probably right."

"I knew you'd see it my way. I know Mac will be relieved. What do you think about him going to Vietnam, Alice? He'll come back a national hero." He didn't wait for her response, said, "Tomorrow will be trying for you. I'll come by in the evening and have dinner with you. Seven-thirty. Have the cook prepare a leg of lamb. Give her the night off. We'll have some sherry, I'll read some Robert Browning, and you'll forget about Mac for a little while."

Alice swallowed past the lump in her throat. She knew what *that* meant.

"I'll see you tomorrow then. Good night, Marcus."

Alice crunched the pillow at her side into a ball. Bitter tears rolled down her cheeks. "Nobody gets it all," she muttered.

IT WAS STILL dark outside when Mac walked down the steps and carried his bags out through the kitchen. He looked longingly at the coffeepot. There was no time. If he was lucky, Benny might have two cups ready when he stopped by to pick him up.

His guilt vanished when he pulled to the curb outside Benny's split-level house in Alexandria. He grinned, seeing his friend

walk out the door with two cups of coffee in his hands. Behind
Benny, Carol waved at him. Jesus, some guys had all the luck.

In the car, Mac gulped at the coffee. "You don't know how
badly I need this."

"Yeah, I do. Listen, you son of a bitch, you better come back
all in one piece."

"Hey, the old man gave me orders to come back a hero. Let's
not fuck this up, Benny. We went through it all last night."

"Yeah, but what about that old man of yours? What if he
comes down on me about . . ." He patted the thick brown folder
on the seat.

It was the power of attorney, and Phil Benedict was the name
on it. Phil, Mac had decided, would take care of his fortune
until he returned. It was his slap in the face or kick in the gut
to his father and wife, his final act of defiance.

"There's a sealed letter in there with my father's name on it.
All you do is hand it over if he so much as says a word. Don't
take any crap from Alice either. That's another way of saying
turn a deaf ear to all her demands. She gets a check the first of
the month. If she decides to go to France, then you simply pay
the bills."

"You sure you want me to keep your car?"

"Hell, yes, let Carol drive it so she won't have to drive you
in in the morning. Everything's in the glove compartment, including a letter that says I'm giving you permission to use the
car. The insurance has been paid for the year. No problems
there at all. You'll be doing me a favor by driving it."

Mac pulled to the curb in front of the airport. "You're probably the best thing that ever happened to me, Benny. I don't
think there's another person in the whole world I trust the way
I trust you. Sadie, maybe, but that's different. I'll see you."

"Yeah," Benny said, clapping him on the back.

When Benny pulled away from the curb, he felt as if he had
left part of his life behind. "He's got it together now, this is the
first step. Be happy for him, Benedict," he muttered as he
moved with the early morning traffic flow.

* * *

IT WAS EXACTLY eleven o'clock when Mac drove his rental car through the gates and down the long poplar-sided driveway to the white-pillared plantation house his mother had grown up in. He stopped the Ford and rolled down the window. It was unseasonably warm. A black-winged fly and a mosquito buzzed through the open window. His mother told him once there were wetlands behind the house that bred all kinds of things. Snakes, she'd said, a devilish light in her eyes, and rats bigger than tomcats. He remembered shivering at the thought. She hadn't liked living here in the big house with the huge white columns, but she hadn't told him why. The only thing he knew for certain was she'd loved her brother Harry and the cook, a Negress named Maddy. He'd met each of them only twice, but he remembered them as if he'd just met them yesterday. Maddy was dead now, and Harry was in his eighties.

In the morning sunlight and at this distance, the house looked magnificent, but he knew that it would be full of dry rot. He sat hunched over the wheel trying to see everything all at once. The low brick wall that was so perfect for laying on and staring at the stars was still there, listing slightly, but intact. To his right was another low brick wall, with an iron gate that led to the azalea garden. Film companies still came to shoot footage there, and in April brides paid handsomely to be married in the formal garden. His mother and father had been married there. He'd seen the pictures.

Every year, no matter what, his mother said, a fresh coat of paint was slapped on the mansion. Usually around the first of February, before the weather got too warm and sticky. Obviously, Mac thought, the painting had been done already, for the mansion was blinding to the eye.

The veranda was wide and full of lush green ferns. Maddy used to bring them out each morning and take them in in the afternoon. The ferns were old and never died off, his mother said. He wondered if the swing was the same one his mother sat on when she was young. How sad that he didn't know this side of his family. He'd been forbidden to come here, and he couldn't help but wonder why in his rebellious years he'd only tried once. He knew this house and grounds as well as he knew his own house in McLean. He remembered every single thing his mother had ever told him, and he'd studied the pictures in the family album.

Mac got out of the car. He knew if he walked to the left he would come to the wash house and the stable that had been converted to a six-car garage. If he walked to the right, he would see the smokehouse and caretaker's cottage. Around the side of the house, in front of the kitchen door, would be an apron of cobblestones. He wondered if the wash lines were still strung between the angel oaks. The old slave quarters were down a little hill from the back of the house. They'd been maintained and refurbished because the plantation was a historical building.

Mac was heading toward his left when he stopped in his tracks at the sound of a shotgun blast. "That's far enough," a voice roared. "This would be a good time to announce yourself, young man."

"Captain Malcolm Carlin, sir," Mac shouted. "I'm Elsa's son. Is that you, Uncle Harry?"

"I'm Harry. Come closer so I can have a look at you." Mac obliged but stopped ten feet away. "Why are you here, young man?"

"I came to see you. I'm leaving for Vietnam tomorrow. I . . . wanted to say . . . hello and good-bye."

"How old are you?" Harry demanded.

"Thirty-one, sir."

"You're too late, boy. The time to come here was when you became a man. You're ten years too late. Now, get back in that car and head out to wherever it is you're going. You're more Carlin than Ashwood. An Ashwood would have been here the minute he came of age."

There was nothing for Mac to say to that. He watched the shotgun come up level to his chest. The old man had the spookiest eyes he'd ever seen. At that moment, Mac swore his uncle could see into his soul. The shotgun crept up another inch or so.

"I'm sorry I didn't find a way to do it. I did try once. I don't know, maybe I didn't want to hear you tell me what I've come now to hear."

"What would that be?" the old man asked brusquely. His hand on the shotgun was steady. His left hand hitched up his pants.

"I want to know why my mother left me behind and didn't keep in touch with me. My father said she wasn't capable of caring for me because she had a mental disorder. Did she ever talk about me? She never even sent me a Christmas card," Mac said in a stricken voice.

"You hold on to your britches, laddie. Your mother did nothing but talk about you. There were many presents, many cards and letters written every day. I know because I mailed them myself. But it's up to your father to tell you why he did the things he did. I don't want anything to do with him or you. If you had real Ashwood blood in you, you would have come to your mother."

"For God's sake, Uncle Harry, I was only a kid. I thought my mother didn't want me. She just up and left. If she sent letters and presents, I never received them. I thought she blamed me."

"You don't fix blame on the one thing in the world you love," Harry said tightly.

"That's why I didn't understand the trust fund. I knew I had one, but I didn't know the extent of it until I turned twenty-one. I didn't understand about the fund from Aunt Rita either."

"Your mother fixed that too. You're a rich man, Mr. Carlin, thanks to Ashwood ingenuity." Harry lowered the shotgun. Suddenly he looked tired and ill. He waved his free arm about. "This will eventually go to you, the whole hundred acres. The whole ball of wax, as the young people say. Elsa made me promise. Easy promise to make, since there were no other heirs. Come back and see me when you finish up with the war. If I'm still alive, we'll talk then. Good-bye, Mr. Carlin."

Mac stood with his mouth hanging open. The meeting was over. He got back into the rental car and took a last, long look at his mother's old home before he backed out of the long driveway. He felt as if he'd been slammed in the chest with a full round of buckshot.

He drove aimlessly, his eyes looking for landmarks that would lead him to the graveyard—his last stop.

It was well past noon when Mac drove through the monstrous gates of the Calvary Cemetery. He drove carefully along the narrow brick road lined with magnificent angel oaks dripping Spanish moss. If cemeteries could be called beautiful, this one was gorgeous, Mac thought crazily. His eyes zeroed in on the caretaker's cottage, which seemed an exact replica of a Hansel-and-Gretel fairy-tale house.

The door opened with a loud *swoosh*, and a man dressed in a white three-piece suit emerged. The fedora he wore was made of white felt with a scarlet and green band around the crown. Mac thought it early in the year to be wearing white, but he really didn't know. Alice was the one with the fashion sense. He climbed out of the car and met the man halfway down the brick walk.

"Malcolm Carlin," Mac said, extending his hand. "Can you tell me where the Ashwood plot is?" He felt embarrassed. It was a hell of a thing that he had to ask a total stranger where his mother's grave was. And he had no one to blame but himself. He could have come here any number of times if he'd *really* wanted to.

"Hilary Carter," the caretaker drawled. A cigar found its way to his mouth. Mac fired up a cigarette. They blew smoke in one another's faces. He was a stranger, and the South didn't take kindly to strangers. The suspicion and annoyance on Carter's face angered Mac.

The caretaker hooked his thumbs into his vest pockets as he rocked back on his heels to get a better look at Mac. "I see Ashwood in you. That can only mean you're Elsa's son. You were just a sprout when we lowered her. I remember you."

"I'm in a bit of a hurry, so if you'd just—"

The caretaker lifted a manicured hand, complete with clear nail polish, and pointed to his left. "Walk down around the curve and to the right of that angel oak, where the moss is dripping to the ground. It's a prime plot, the best in all of Calvary. There's three plots left: one for Harry, and I suppose one for you and one for your wife or child. It's spelled out on the deed. Paid in full, if that's of interest to you."

"Thank you, Mr. Carter," Mac said, stamping on his cigarette. He knew without having to look over his shoulder that Carter bent down and picked up the butt. This place was so tidy, it made his skin crawl.

When he came to the Ashwood plot, he wasn't prepared for the rush of emotion that roared through him. His eyes filled and his shoulders shook. He squatted down, his eyes level with the chiseled words. ELSA ASHWOOD. BELOVED DAUGHTER. WIFE. LOVING DEVOTED MOTHER. Mac bit down so hard on his lower lip that he tasted his own blood.

"He told me you didn't want me. He said you left me behind because I would get in your way. For a long time I believed him, and when I stopped believing, I was too ashamed to come here. Benny's mother said parents love unconditionally. She and Sadie are the ones who convinced me that you must have had a reason for what you did. It's all mixed up in my mind, Mama. First I had to forgive you, and then . . . I needed to know you forgave me. I tried to call you those first years. I even wrote you a letter, but it came back, addressee unknown. I guess I had the wrong address on it. Father whipped me good for that. I just want you to know I *wanted* to come; I just didn't have the guts to do it. It's not important anymore for you to forgive me. I'm sorry if I hurt you. Listen, you have to know something," Mac said in a strangled voice. "I hate that bastard. I mean I *really* hate him.

"So far, Mama, there hasn't been a whole hell of a lot in my life for you to be proud of. This is my turning point. I've coasted because it was easy. I didn't want to make the effort. It was all this hatred I'm still carrying around, and I don't know how to unload it. Uncle Harry said I was ten years too late. He was wrong, I'm eighteen years too late. I should have run after you that day and hung onto your skirt and made you take me with you. That's what I should have done, what I wanted to do. I'll be back, Mama, you can count on it."

Mac shook down the creases in his pants. He wished he had a handkerchief. He put his knuckles to his eyes the way he'd done when he was a kid. Carlins didn't cry, his father always said. *Bullshit!* He turned and would have toppled his uncle Harry if Harry hadn't stiff-armed him. What the hell was his uncle doing here? He shouldered his way past his uncle, his eyes on Hilary Carter, who must have been watching all the time.

"Boy?"

Mac stopped and turned. "I have a name, Uncle Harry. If you want to call me, then call me by my name," he snapped. He didn't need this crap, this intrusion into . . . his what? His grief, his misery, his shame.

"Malcolm." There was a soft chuckle in the old man's voice. Mac reacted to the sound. His mother used to chuckle the same way. He thought it one of the happiest sounds of his childhood. It was a warm, cozy sound, which seemed to wrap itself around the small boy he was.

"Did you follow me here to say good-bye or are you just curious by nature?" Mac asked, an edge to his voice. It was the voice he reserved for his father.

"Both. I brought something for you. It's in the car."

"The old family crest?" Mac asked bitterly.

The chuckle was back in Harry's voice. "Better than that. Follow me out to the main road and pull over. Hilary's the local gossip, and I see no reason to give him something to talk about." He slapped Mac on the back as they strode past the caretaker.

"Y'all have a good day now, y'hear?" Carter called after them.

On the shoulder of the road, Mac got out of his car. His uncle was lifting a box from the trunk of his own car. It was cardboard and tied with string. It wasn't heavy, Mac noticed. His eyes were full of questions.

"This was your mother's. When we packed up her things, this was kept separate in case . . . you ever decided to come for a visit. Elsa said we weren't to seek you out. She said if you ever came here under your own steam, I was to make the decision to give or not to give."

"What is it?" Something of his mother's. He felt light-headed.

"Books," Harry said succinctly.

"Books," Mac said stupidly. He'd expected something . . . meaningful. But he knew he shouldn't be surprised. His mother loved reading. She'd read to him almost every night of his life until she left.

"When the war gets bad . . ." Harry let the words hang in the air.

Mac was already opening his flight bag. It took him five full minutes to arrange, shove, and squash his belongings to make room for the oversized shoe box. He snapped the bag closed. It made a loud sound. Now he had to turn and face his uncle and thank him. He wondered what had made him decide to come all the way out here. He voiced the question and prepared himself for a tongue-in-cheek answer.

"Didn't want you going off to that place you're going to without something of your mama's. She'd never forgive me. I'll be joining her one of these days, and she did love to ask questions. It's a wise man who has answers." He allowed himself a small smile. Mac grinned. "The other reason is you came here to visit her. If you hadn't come here, I wouldn't have given you the box. Now that makes sense, doesn't it?" he demanded fretfully.

"Yes, sir, it does."

"You look like your grandpa Ashwood. Spitting image, I'd say." The thought seemed to puzzle him. "See Elsa in you too. You come from good stock, bo—Malcolm."

"Half of me is Ashwood, Uncle Harry," Mac said gently.

"The best half," the old man cackled, and slapped his thigh in delight.

Mac stretched out his hand and the old man crushed it a second time. Mac winced, exerting as much pressure as he could. He thought he saw approval in the watery old eyes.

"I'll be back."

"I believe you will, Malcolm. You give those . . . what do they call those people where you're going?"

"Vietnamese." Mac grinned. "You aren't going to tell me to come back a hero and all that jazz, are you, Uncle Harry?"

"Hell's bells, no. You're an Ashwood. You'll distinguish

yourself. Ashwoods always distinguish themselves." The laughter bubbling in Mac's throat died when he realized the old man was serious.

"Yes, sir, I'll do my best."

"I don't like this place, did I tell you that?"

"I kind of figured, Uncle Harry."

"Well, sometimes I like it and sometimes I don't. Right now, I don't like it. It's always here, waiting for me." He pursed his mouth into a round O of disapproval before he got into his car, jerked it into gear, and drove off without a backward glance.

Mac wore a smile all the way to the airport. He turned in the rental car, checked his bags, and headed for the nearest restaurant. He had a three-hour wait for his flight to California, where he would board a military flight to Vietnam.

It was time for Mac Carlin to soar, *time for the dream to come alive*.

Chapter 2

CASEY ADAMS SMILED as she hugged each of her guests. "Thank you for coming. I'll miss you. Yes, yes, I'll write even if it's just a postcard. If I find a rich American who wants to marry me, of course you'll be invited to the wedding. Adieu, my friends. Don't forget me, for I'll not forget you."

When the bright blue door of the apartment closed for the last time, Casey fell into her friend's outstretched arms. "It was wonderful of you to give me this party, Nicole. I'll treasure the memory of it. Everyone had such a good time though, it's hard to believe we fit thirty people into this tiny apartment." Her voice broke and then strengthened when she stared down into Nicole's misty eyes. "We'll be friends forever, Nicole. The United States seems far away, but I can come back sometimes, and you can come to visit me. Promise, Nicole."

"Of course I promise, but I don't know about me coming to visit you in California. The airfare alone must be outrageous. I'll marry a rich Frenchman and then I'll come. With my seven children. Will you have room for all of us?" Nicole teased.

"Of course. I'm going to miss you, Nicole. Danele too."

"For a little while you will. But you're going to have a new life. I'm so happy for you, Casey. I cannot comprehend how, after all this time, all those years we spent in the orphanage . . . I just . . . you had a father. You really did have an American father. I hate him for never claiming you," the tiny French girl cried passionately. "You should hate him too. He claims you in death. How is that fair?" she demanded hotly. "Well?"

Casey shrugged. She was a spitfire, this tiny creature she called best friend. Ninety pounds of pure energy with great

49

luminous eyes that blazed with love or anger, depending on her mood. She was dressed now in an outrageously clingy dress that was hiked above her knees to reveal matchstick-thin legs that ended in spike-heeled shoes, which made her all of five feet tall. She was brushing now at what Casey referred to as her "nineteen hairs," her pixie bob.

"And a grandmother. You had a grandmother. Oh, Casey, you are going to be so happy. I'm jealous." Nicole pouted. "Come, come, there is one bottle of wine left that I saved for you and me. We're going to curl up on the floor with pillows and have our last talk. Oh, Casey, what am I going to do without you?"

"You will go on making women beautiful. Without you, what would your customers do? And, it isn't every beautician who has Madame Chanel for a customer. Besides, Jacques is going to ask you to marry him. I saw it in his eyes tonight when he looked at you. Will you say yes?"

Nicole became coy. She shrugged. "Maybe yes, maybe no. He's poor. I need to be rich to have seven children. How many will you have, Casey?"

"At least nine. That makes sixteen between us." Casey giggled. "Won't our reunions be wonderful?"

Nicole felt her throat constrict. She wondered if Casey knew how beautiful she was. When they were little in the orphanage and sharing side-by-side cots, they talked into the night, sharing dreams and fears. In those days, she had always thought of Casey's eyes as the color of bluebells that grew in the garden. Now she called them electrifying. Both girls wore braids back then. Casey's were the color of corn silk. Now that hair was gold, thick and beautiful, with a natural curl Nicole would kill for.

She had only seen Casey truly angry once, and that time those electric-blue eyes had turned purple with passionate anger. They'd giggled over that a lot. Passionate purple eyes were something to giggle about when one lived in the drab St. Gabriel's orphanage, where laughter was seriously frowned upon by Sister Ann Elizabeth.

"I really hated Sister Ann Elizabeth as much as you hated her," Nicole blurted.

Casey laughed. "Now, where did that come from? We were talking about the children we're going to have."

"I know. And my children are going to be happy. There won't be any Sister Ann Elizabeth in their lives," Nicole said vehemently. *"No Catholic school for my children."*

"Mine either," Casey said just as vehemently.

"Yet you went back to St. Gabriel's two days ago, didn't you? Danele said she saw you."

"I . . . I went for selfish reasons. I wanted to see that nun's face when I told her about my . . . inheritance, about having a real father and a grandmother. I thought I hated her. I wanted to hate her. I lost count of the times she took a switch to me."

"Three times on my behalf," Nicole said softly.

"It was worth it." Casey smiled. "Incorrigible misfits, she called us. She said we had delusions, and when one is an orphan one can't afford delusions because they get in the way of life. Remember?"

"Casey, there's nothing about St. Gabriel's I'll ever forget. I'll never forgive her for the way she treated us. Never! But you damn well forgave her, didn't you?" Nicole accused. "After we swore in blood we never would."

"It doesn't matter anymore, Nicole. We got through it. Look at us now. I'm a fine nurse. You have your own shop, this marvelous little apartment, and a man who loves you. You have guts, and you gambled on a dream. Don't tell me you didn't follow through just so you could rub Sister's nose in your success."

"So what?" Nicole blustered.

"She made us tough. She made survivors out of us. She told me that. She said we had no idea what the real world was like. She had tears in her eyes when she was telling me how every night she prayed for the two of us. She really believed that the switchings we got, the detentions, the rosaries she made us say, the raps on the knuckles, were for our own good."

"She's a fanatic, Casey, and she lied to you. Nuns aren't supposed to lie. She lied to you, said there was no note on your basket when they left you at the orphanage. If it wasn't for Maryann copying down the note from your file in Mother Superior's office, Sister Ann Elizabeth would have beaten you down to nothing. Little kids don't have to have guts or be tough. They need dreams and something to hold on to. She took that away from you! You had a father and a grandmother."

"They didn't want me. She knew that. Do you think that back then I could have come to terms with that? No, Nicole. It was better I dreamed and took the switchings and the rosaries."

"I still don't understand how you can forget the hell she put us through."

"She was sweeping the leaves off the walk when I saw her. She looks old and tired. Very tired. She still smells like Noxema and she still has the little white flecks around her nails. She's just older. I told her I was sorry."

"You're crazy! Why would you tell that old tyrant such a thing?"

"So it was a little lie. I think she needed to hear it. She's never going to forget me, that's for sure." Casey laughed. "I always wanted to be unforgettable."

"I'll never forget you," Nicole cried.

"That's enough for me," Casey said, hugging her friend.

"Me too."

"If I don't leave now, Nicole, both of us are going to be blubbering in our wine. I want to remember you with a smile and to know I skipped out to leave you to clean up this mess."

"Au revoir, chérie," Nicole said, wrapping Casey in her arms.

"Au revoir, Nicole." A moment later Casey was out the door, tears streaming down her cheeks.

Casey walked slowly, her hands jammed into her pockets for warmth. She was spending this last night in the student quarters because she'd turned over her apartment to a young intern who'd taken possession of her quarters at noon. She smiled when she realized she was homeless, though not for long.

Tomorrow, today actually, was all planned. She would say her own personal good-bye to Paris. Then, at four o'clock, she would take a taxi to the airport and fly to California with one stopover in New York City.

She had a house now, a home, and a small bank account in U.S. currency. Six thousand American dollars. Her inheritance. She'd read the letter from the American law firm of Quigley, Quigley, and Archmore a dozen times before she fully comprehended it. It had taken her a full hour to digest the information the attorney had given her over the phone when she'd finally made the decision to call. She'd called again when she made the decision to travel to California. Nolan Quigley said he would see that the utilities were turned on and he would leave the key in the mailbox. He'd told her to stop by his office at her convenience to sign the necessary papers. He also told her he would tell her what little he could about her father, though Jack Adams had only been a client for a year.

Casey shivered in the cold night air. She really did have a father, one who thought enough of her to leave her his house and his money. She knew her name was a real name, not one made up by the nuns, the way Nicole's name was. The lawyer had told her in a kindly voice that her mother was a streetwalker and her name was Rene Beauchamp. She'd cringed a little at the news, but having a real mother with a real name was the only thing of importance.

It was all behind her now. Tomorrow she would start a new life. No regrets.

The dimly lit hospital lobby had seemed like home for many years. She'd worked double shifts more times than she could remember. She always worked the holidays so the married nurses could be with their families. She stayed on extra hours to be with critical patients, on her own time with no pay. She lived for her work. It was her life.

She'd been stunned two nights ago when she went off duty to find the nurses and doctors assembled in the day room shouting, "Surprise! Surprise!" It had been a wonderful going-away party. More wonderful because her colleagues had meant it when they said she was a good nurse and she would be sorely missed. They'd given her a beautiful gold watch and the biggest bouquet of flowers she'd ever seen. She'd wept then. At the end of the party the Chief of Surgery took her aside and said, "There will always be a job for you here if you want to come back. You are one of the finest, most dedicated nurses I've ever worked with." Then he'd handed her such a glowing letter of recommendation that she'd cried all over again.

The lobby was deliciously warm and very quiet. Casey walked through the corridor that led to the student nurses' wing. Midway she changed course and turned left to the stairway that led to the third-floor surgical wing.

She walked on tiptoe down the polished hospital corridor until she came to her daytime station. Seated behind the desk was the night charge nurse. She was reading a novel. When she looked up, she smiled at Casey.

"So, you can't leave us after all. You just happened to be on this floor and just thought you'd stop by and see how Mrs. Laroux is doing. How am I doing so far?" Casey smiled. "She's restless, but that's to be expected. She asked for you several times, though she's going to be just fine and we both know it."

"She's scared. She's seventy years old. I'm only twenty-six, and I'd be scared and frightened out of my wits to have my hip socket replaced."

"Well, you can peek in, but if you wake her up, you're on this floor for the rest of the night and I go home. Agreed?"

Casey laughed softly as she made her way down the hall, her high heels in her hands. When she came to Room 306, she quietly inched the door open.

Claire Laroux was a feisty, wizened woman who always said she was seventy years old and followed that with, "I always lie about my age." She looked to Casey like a baby bird in her nest of pillows. Little tufts of hair stood on end, testament that she constantly raked her gnarled fingers through the thin strands. She was awake, as Casey knew she would be. In one hand she held a rosary, and in the other was one of her sexy, steamy paperback books. She was addicted to them. She was fond of saying that all she'd ever wanted in life was to be ravished and plundered. She'd wave her rosary and cackle, "See, I pray for it every day, but does He listen? No, so I have to pretend."

"You're supposed to be asleep," Casey admonished quietly.

"I knew you'd stop in. I stayed awake to say good-bye."

"We said good-bye this afternoon," Casey said softly.

"That was just good-bye, this is the real good-bye, when no one else is around. I said a rosary for you before so that you would have a safe trip to the United States."

"Are you in pain?" Casey said with concern. "Be truthful."

"Of course I'm in pain. The pain never leaves me. I wanted to make you feel good, so that's why I said I waited up for you. I haven't been reading, I've been praying. I don't want to die, Miss Adams. I'm afraid to die. That old biddy out there doesn't understand. She's sixty-eight, you know."

"She's lying to you." Casey grinned. "She's sixty-nine. You aren't going to die and you know it. People don't die from hip operations. You've been here for six weeks, Mrs. Laroux, and have you ever once heard me lie to you? This is what I'm going to do. I'm going out to ask Nurse if she can't give you something for the pain a little ahead of schedule. Then I'm going to give you the Casey Adams special back rub. I'll fluff your pillows just the way you like them. Then I'm going to read to you from this . . . this piece of trash you are so fond of. You have to promise to go to sleep though. Is it a deal?"

"Do I have a choice?" the old lady muttered.

"I can leave."

"All right."

Casey was back a moment later with a sugar pill in her hand. "This," she said, holding out the pill so the old lady could see it, "is the strongest medicine we have. It's going to work very quickly, so it will behoove us to move right along here."

Fifteen minutes later the patient was propped up in her nest of pillows, a contented smile on her face. "Chapter Four. I'll pray while you read," the old lady said, blessing herself.

Casey opened the book and started to read. " 'He ripped her blouse, exposing a creamy white breast. Julian's eyes glazed. Megan's eyes filled with tears. "Oh, Julian, I've waited so long for this. Do it! Do it! I can't bear it a moment longer! Make wild, passionate love to me right here on the kitchen floor. Do it, Julian!" ' "

Casey risked a glance at her patient. Sound asleep. She closed the novel and laid it on the night table. She tiptoed around the bed to turn off the overhead light. "Good-bye, Mrs. Laroux," she whispered.

At the desk she stopped one last time. "Her bedsores aren't getting any better. Take care of her. Good-bye, Michelle. Oh, by the way, I left off where Julian is going to do it with Megan right on the kitchen floor. I'd read that instead of the one you're reading."

"Are you kidding? This is one of hers. Have a safe trip, Casey, and all the luck in the world."

Casey blew her a kiss as she headed for the stairs.

CASEY ADAMS LOVED Paris.

And she was leaving.

Tears rolled down her cheeks.

She loved this café by the Closerie des Lilas. She longed for spring and wished she hadn't made the decision to leave during this drab month of February. She wanted to see the monstrous horse chestnut trees in bloom, not these naked, angry-looking trees. She worried now that she was making a mistake. The crazy urge to run and throw her arms around the ancient chestnut trees was so strong, she gripped the edge of the wrought-iron table.

It was cold here in the café, but she didn't want to get up, to move indoors. She wasn't in the mood to hear the hushed whispers of young lovers. The French were so passionate in everything they did, be it soul-searching stares, hand-touching, or wine-drinking. Perhaps she was angry that she was only half French and half American. Over the years, she'd told herself the American side of her accounted for her caution and intensity. Most of the young people she knew subscribed to the philosophy that they should live, love, and be happy, while she believed in work, work, and more work. Danele, her outspoken friend, often said, "Fix yourself up, Casey, smile, and men will drop at your feet." As if she wanted men to drop at her feet.

It wasn't that she didn't date; she did. Young interns constantly asked her out, but they were boring dates: full of shop talk and life and death. They all wanted sex—casual or intense—they didn't care. What they weren't prepared for was any kind of commitment, and none of the young men she knew were husband material.

When the fourth cup of coffee was set in front of her, Casey realized she didn't want it. She just wanted to sit here and never move. She was tired because of all the walking she'd done earlier. Her last good-bye to Paris. Some day she would come back, but not for a very long time. Earlier she'd gone by the little apartment house in Ile St. Louis one last time, a stone's throw from the gardens of Notre Dame which were dormant now, but she'd walked through them anyway, crying with every step she took. She'd sat on a bench overlooking the Seine for hours, thinking of the bench as a kind of scaffolding giving her different views, views she'd taken for granted all her life. She'd looked downstream and set her watch by the clock of the Institut Français. If she'd stayed longer, waited for the sun to set, she would have seen the way the light filled the towers of the Louvre and the muddy green water of the river. She'd burned into her memory the sight of the Pont Neuf crossing the prow of the Ile de la Cité. From her position on the bench she couldn't see the Ile St. Louis, which to her was the world's most perfect village.

She'd spent an hour in the Grand Galerie of the Louvre. The Louvre always left her breathless, and today was no exception. She'd wept and then cried again when she trekked under the chestnut trees in Luxembourg Gardens. She'd walked, one last time, the promenade of the Champs Elysées, her eyes misty with tears. She'd shed so many tears today, her eyes ached with strain.

She'd made her way then to Sacre Coeur at Montmartre to see Paris at her feet, and once again she'd promised herself to return.

Casey glanced at her watch. She'd been sitting here in the café for a very long time. She signaled the waiter for her check, stood up and buttoned her coat. Even though it was cold, she decided to walk back to the hospital for her luggage.

She was short, more French in that way than American with soft blond hair the color of fresh-churned butter. Nicole said she was wispy and angelic. When she smiled, which wasn't often, the smile always reached her eyes. She believed her high cheekbones came from her mother, and she dusted them lightly with rouge every morning. Her hands were soft and capable-looking. She kept her nails cut short and applied a coat of light polish after she buffed them. Casey's hands were one of the first things people noticed about her, after they got over the shock of her buttery-colored hair which she wore pinned on top of her head so her nurse's cap would stay secure.

A furious gust of wind swooped through the sidewalk café. It had turned colder too, Casey thought as she buttoned her camel-colored coat close to her throat. The waiters were carrying the tables and chairs inside. She sucked in her breath when another gust of wind, this one stronger, fussed about her knees, whipping the hem of her short coat away from her wool skirt.

Casey took one last, long look at the café where she'd spent so much time over the years. When she was satisfied she would remember it, she shoved her hands into the pockets of her coat and strode off.

The airline ticket in her pocket felt comforting. Her cold fingers traced lines across the smooth paper. She could hardly wait to see California.

CASEY SET FOOT on American soil for the second time in twenty-four hours.

She walked around the airport to get the feel of the way Americans did things. They walked in a hurry, she noticed, just the way they did in New York, and they were wearing incredibly short skirts.

Everyone had tanned skin and poufed-out hairdos. It took her all of five minutes to realize people were staring at her the way she was staring at them. Her pink sweater set looked childish, as did the garbardine skirt that fell below her knees. The models were wearing short skirts in Paris, but the locals never bent to the fast-moving trends until they were certain a hemline was going to be around for a while. She wondered what kind of underwear the women and young girls wore and if they dared to bend over. She looked schoolmarmish by comparison.

Her natural curly hair, which she had cut two days before, was short and feathered about her face. Even if she wanted to change to the pageboy curl or the teased-up cotton candy 'do, she didn't have enough hair. She found herself blinking at the eyeliner on the women. At first she thought all the women were movie stars, until she saw several elderly ladies with blue eyelids and dark lines around their eyes. Raccoons. Casey felt a bubble of laughter begin to build in her throat. Touring the airport, she marveled at the gift stores, coffee shops, bookstores, and lounges, and at the hordes of people bustling about. She loved it all, itched to buy something, but she was unsure of the currency and wouldn't know if she was being overcharged or if an item was too expensive.

Coming toward her was a gaggle of military personnel, both men and women. Casey stepped aside as the laughing group swept past her. She liked uniforms, possibly because she'd worn them all her life. These young men and women were so pressed and shined, they positively glowed. The women's skirts were knee length, Casey noticed, their pumps the same as hers, their hair short, their caps at jaunty angles. She wondered where they were going.

She was outside now. Why in the world had she thought California was going to be warm and sunny? It wasn't. It was dismal with rain falling steadily and a low, swirling fog. She read a novel once where the author claimed the air in California was perfumed, and women didn't have to buy exotic French fragrances. To her the air smelled moldy and earthy. She longed for sun and warm air. She snuggled deeper into her coat, glad that she hadn't dressed for a southern climate.

"Taxi, miss?"

"*Oui.* Yes, I wish a taxi," she said, mindful that she had to speak English. "I want to go to 3345 Lombard Street, Russian Hill," Casey said, settling herself in the backseat, her bags secure in the trunk.

The taxi driver started talking the moment he moved from the curb. Casey listened intently, certain she was about to receive a firsthand education on life in America. She changed her mind a moment later when the driver started to curse the antiwar protestors in the middle of the road. "That singer, what's her name, Joan Baez, tried with a bunch of others to block the doors of the Selective Service Center in Oakland. That's not too far from here either. It's not American to do that," he snorted, giving the wheel a vicious tug. He laughed, a bitter sound. "They arrested her and charged her with disturbing the peace. Can you beat that!" Casey shrugged. "You know what else?" the cabbie said angrily. "Just last month a Catholic priest and a few other idiots poured blood over Selective Service files in Baltimore. Then they parked themselves and waited for the FBI to arrive and arrest them. Can you beat that?" Casey shrugged again. She wasn't into politics, French or American.

"Are you a native Californian?" Casey asked, hoping to change the subject.

"Nope. I hail from Philadelphia, Pennsylvania. You sound like a Frenchie. Are you a Frenchie?"

"My father was American. My mother was French. I have dual citizenship. Is my accent very noticeable?" she asked anxiously. Damn, she wanted to blend in so desperately, and she'd worked so hard on her English. Now this babbling cab driver was telling her he was astute enough to know immediately that she was French.

It was the cab driver's turn to shrug. "I pick up all kinds of people. I've been driving a hack for twenty-five years. After a while your ear can tell a foreigner. No offense."

"No offense." Casey smiled.

"Is this your first visit to California?"

"Yes. I'm going to live here now. Is the weather always so terrible?"

"At this time of the year it is. You'll have to get used to it. I did when I first moved here. I thought the sun was going to shine all day long. If you want sunshine, you'll have to go to Los Angeles. I have a cousin who lives there. If I knew there were no protestors there, I'd go in a heartbeat. It's not right for famous people to let their names be used for such things. Because then ordinary people start to believe it's okay. Either you're American or you're not, that's the way I look at it. I don't like to see our boys getting killed any more than the next person. You can't believe what the papers tell you either. Only Washington knows what's going on, and they don't share it with us little people."

"I guess that means you're for the United States' involvement in Vietnam," Casey said, craning her neck to squint through the fog. She wished he'd talk about someone famous like the Beach Boys. "Do the Beach Boys live here?"

"I mind my own business and don't get involved, and I think they are from here. Are they the boys who sing 'Barbara Ann'? I hear it on the radio all day long."

"Yes, yes, that's the latest song they sing. It sounds wonderful in French."

The cabbie snorted as he steered the cab around a stalled car. "I like Perry Como and Bing Crosby."

Casey smiled.

The driver, his window rolled down, was switching his gaze from the windshield to the side window. Gray fog rolled inside the open car window in slinky tendrils which reminded Casey of snakes. "The fog is really bad today. Lombard Street is not my favorite street at any time of the day, and in the rain and fog it's worse."

"Why is that?" Casey asked nervously.

"Lombard is the crookedest street in San Francisco. Tomorrow in the daylight you'll see for yourself. It's every cabbie's nightmare."

Casey believed him as she slid from one side of the cab to the other. Visibility, she knew, was about zero. She blessed herself as she settled against the right side of the cab. She was jostled almost immediately to the left side. Her handbag slipped to the floor. Before she knew it, she was on the floor too, groping for a handhold.

"This is it!" the driver said in a relieved tone. Casey's tone was just as relieved when she thanked him.

She wished she could see what the house looked like. First impressions were so important. But like the driver said, tomorrow was another day.

It was so dark, Casey stumbled twice going up the brick

walkway to the house. The driver, carrying her cases behind her, offered up a muttered curse as he too stumbled.

"I'm sorry there are no lights on. Just leave the bags on the stoop. I have to find the key and the light switch. Thank you very much. Be careful driving back."

"Thank you," the driver called back. She must have given him too much money.

Casey fumbled in the mailbox for the key Nolan Quigley said he would leave for her. The moment her fingers touched the key, she let her breath out in a long sigh. Her hands searched her pockets for a match. With trembling fingers she tried to hold the wavering little light steady while she fit the key into the lock. It turned easily. She sucked in her breath. Another second and she would be inside. She turned the knob quickly. If she'd been less cold, if her teeth weren't chattering, she would have delayed the moment. Warmth won out.

She was inside, her bags in the foyer. To the left and down low she saw a small night-light. Mr. Quigley must have left it on for her. She noticed it was also warm in the house. Heat. How wonderful it was.

Casey walked around, the low beam of light guiding her way as she flipped on switches. It was a lovely little house. She walked back to the kitchen. Quaint. Cheerful. Colorful. Even comfortable. But definitely a man's kitchen. The round oak table and four chairs looked strong and sturdy enough to weather a hurricane. The word comfortable popped to mind a second time. The windows were curtainless; there was no rug on the floor by the sink, no plants on the windowsill. There was a cookie jar, though, in the shape of an oversized mushroom. She lifted the lid. It was almost full of date-filled cookies.

She hadn't asked the attorney when the man who had claimed to be her father had died. Now she wished she had. She bit into one of the cookies. They were fresh.

The stove was clean. The refrigerator was clean and bare, save for a carton of milk and a can of Maxwell House coffee. She looked in the cabinets. Soup, lots of soup. Canned vegetables, lots of corn. Lots of spaghetti and macaroni. Lots of dry cereal too. A man's pantry, and one who didn't cook much, she decided.

The dining room was square, as was the living room. Probably twelve by fifteen. The furniture was plain. The dining room set looked as if it had never been used. A layer of dust covered everything. She liked the living room, with its two comfortable rockers covered in a dark, coarse, plaid material. The sofa was hunter-green. Again, a man's sofa, long, deep, and comfortable. Copies of *Time, Newsweek,* and *Business Week* were stacked neatly on the round coffee table next to a huge crystal ashtray. A lighter and a fresh pack of cigarettes sat next to it.

She loved the fireplace. She stooped down to peer inside. A fire was laid. She withdrew a long match from a brass container on the hearth. The wood sparked instantly.

There were no bookshelves or pictures to give a clue about her father. No extra furniture. The corners were bare. Women always stuck things in corners to round out a room. Tears brimmed in Casey's eyes. There should be something on the mantel, but there wasn't. She felt cheated. Tears dripped down her cheeks.

She retraced her steps to the kitchen, where she measured out coffee and water into the percolator. She would have coffee by the fire. She wondered if she had the right to go through the rolltop desk against the living room wall.

The moment she heard the comforting plop of the percolator, she resumed her tour of the house, turning on more light switches in the hall and bathrooms.

There were two bedrooms and two bathrooms. Brown towels hung in the master bathroom. Brown rugs lay on the floor. The shower curtain was brown and white. Casey found it depressing. In her father's bedroom was a large bed—king-size, she supposed—with a brown plaid spread. The bed was neatly made, with slippers at the side. Again, the windows were curtainless, with venetian blinds pulled to the sill. The second bedroom startled her when she turned on the light switch. She blinked and wiped at her tears with the back of her hand. She looked down and for a minute likened the carpet to a spring meadow. Little bits of green fuzz were on the surface. New carpet. A wicker chair with green and yellow cushions sat alone in a corner. Two wicker chests stood side by side against the wall. The bed, the kind she always dreamed of having, a four-poster with an eyelet canopy, took up most of the room. The bedspread was green with a huge spray of yellow tulips in the center. Pillow shams of the same color had smaller sprays of tulips in their centers. Here there were drapes on the windows to match the meadow-green carpet. The blinds were drawn. Her eyes swiveled to the four walls. On each one, in a simple white frame, were pictures of French flower stalls. Casey felt her throat tighten. Her hand went to her mouth to stifle a cry of pain. Had this room been intended for her someday? Was that possible?

She opened the mirrored closets. Empty of clothing. A dozen padded satin hangers hung on the rod. Two brass hooks were on each side of the closet, for hanging purses or scarves. There was a shoe rack on the floor. She counted the prongs. Six pairs of shoes. She had four pairs, counting her nursing shoes.

The bathroom was as pretty as the bedroom—all green and white tile. New, thick yellow carpets were on the floor. Equally thick yellow towels were on the racks. A yellow plastic soap dish and a yellow plastic glass sat on the vanity. She picked up the glass and saw the price tag still on the bottom—sixty-nine cents. The soap dish was seventy-nine cents. The toilet paper was yellow too, the first piece still attached to the roll and not hanging down. A dusty, off-white ruffled curtain hung over the window. A small, green porcelain frog perched on the window-sill. Casey bit down on her lower lip. Tears burned her eyes again as she tried to blink them away. She did her best to clear her throat. When she didn't succeed, she threw herself on the green and yellow spread and howled her grief for a man she'd never known.

Casey cried all the tears she'd never been allowed to shed because Sister Ann Elizabeth said big girls didn't cry. Tears brought swift punishment. Tears brought ridicule. Tears brought misery.

When she was tired of beating the pillows, tired of sobbing, tired of cursing Sister Ann Elizabeth, Casey swung her legs over the side of the bed. She hated to do it, but she unrolled the yellow toilet paper and blew her nose lustily. She loved the powerful sound of water rushing into the bowl. California must have a wonderful sewer system. She felt pleased with the thought as she made her way to the kitchen for coffee.

Back in the living room, she settled herself on the floor in front of the fire, with the cushions from the couch at her back. She got up a minute later and turned on the television set. She had no idea what she was watching. Three silly men hopping around, punching each other in the nose. She closed her eyes, the volume turned low. She was asleep within minutes.

WITH THE OBLIGATORY appointment with the legal firm representing her father behind her, as well as numerous visits to the supermarket, and having gotten what she thought of as her American legs planted firmly on the ground, Casey settled into the fourth day of her new life in California.

It was dusk now. She'd argued with herself about going to the cemetery to see her father and grandmother's final resting place. Part of her didn't want to see the cold marble with their names chiseled into the stone. The other part of her said she needed to see the place, needed to know there was a place to go to say thank you, to find a kind of secondhand comfort if that was possible.

She hadn't cried. She'd tried to conjure up a picture in her mind of what her father and grandmother looked like, but she'd been unsuccessful. The best she could do was to frame a mental picture of Mrs. Laroux. Her father remained faceless. Probably because of Nolan Quigley's words. She flinched even now when she remembered them. "He didn't want to be bothered with a child. He didn't want to remember the harlot who created you. Whores were supposed to take care of themselves. He believed you were your mother's responsibility. He said you would be fed and clothed and have a roof over your head, and that was more than a lot of people had. Your father was a very cold man. He told me the only reason he was leaving his house and what little else he had to you was so the state wouldn't claim it." Then Quigley said the words that burned into her soul. "He didn't love you, didn't love your mother either. He said he never loved anyone. It pains me to tell you this, but it's better you know the truth. I'm very sorry, Miss Adams."

What that all meant, Casey thought miserably, was she shouldn't make up stories about the family she never knew and delude herself. She would take the house, the six thousand dollars, and be damned glad she didn't have any other problems like bills and liens she would be responsible for.

Casey slid the single pork chop and baked potato onto her plate. Maybe she should have said a prayer at the cemetery. She'd wanted to, but she hadn't. She looked at the food on her plate as she said grace. Then she mumbled a short prayer for her unknown grandmother and father.

Her dinner over, the dishes washed, Casey carried her coffee into the small living room and lit a fire. She wondered what she would do when the last of the wood was gone from the back porch. Where was she to get more? Whom did one call? The problem went on her list of things to do. The list was getting longer, but she would handle it all.

The pad was on her lap, the coffee cup in one hand, a pencil in the other, her eyes and ears turned to the six o'clock news. The moment Walter Cronkite signed off, she turned the volume down on the set to concentrate on the note pad in her lap. The words hospital and then job were written on the first line. Transportation was on the second line, and on the third, driving lessons. Taking taxis until she learned how to get about with mass transportation was going to seriously eat into her budget. She blinked. The list seemed endless. Utilities and taxes had to be looked into. Car insurance too, if she was going to learn how to drive her father's Dodge. Right now, though, she had to make a list of hospitals, along with their addresses and phone numbers, and make appointments to see their nursing administrators. She would deal with the other problems on her list on a daily basis. Things would work out, fall into place, she was sure of it. She sighed mightily as she stared into the blazing fire that was raging up the chimney. Why in the world had she built such a monstrous fire?

Casey slid down onto the floor and stretched out on her belly.

It was so toasty, so warm. In France, central heat in her small flat was something she only dreamed about. She'd always been cold, always worn a sweater, even to bed. Mrs. Laroux would love America with its wonderful central heat.

She thought about Nicole and Danele then, and wondered what they were doing and if they missed her. So far she'd been too busy to think much about her old friends. "I hope I make friends here," she muttered sleepily.

Casey woke a long time later, shivering. She threw two huge logs on the fire and watched as sparks shot up the chimney. She curled up and, hugging her knees, watched the dancing flames. Her little four-hour snooze had left her wide awake—so wide awake she decided to write to Nicole and Danele before going back to her lists.

From time to time she dozed off, awoke, and then dozed again. When her new gift watch said the time was six-thirty, she showered, made breakfast, and called for a taxi. At seven-thirty the taxi arrived. With list in hand, she climbed into the cab. "San Francisco General Hospital," she said.

Thirty-five minutes later she exited the hospital so stunned at what she'd heard that she felt light-headed. The director had been kind but direct. "You need to be state certified," she had said. "The nursing exam will be held July ninth at ten o'clock. I'm terribly sorry." Her glowing letter of recommendation had meant nothing to the director. She would have to get a tutor. Even with a tutor, there was no way she could be ready to take State Boards in only five months. She felt like crying when she climbed into a waiting cab and ordered the driver to take her to the Medical Center at the University of California. There she was told exactly the same thing. The director, a kindly white-haired woman, offered to find her a tutor.

Casey spent the remainder of the day going from clinic to clinic. Then, in a last desperate measure, she asked the taxi driver to take her to a medical employment agency. The answer was the same everywhere. She needed an American nursing diploma, and the only way she could get a diploma was to take the State Boards in July.

She did cry then, hiccuping and sniffling into her handkerchief. The taxi driver, who'd decided to stay with her after her third stop, cleared his throat and voiced an opinion because he hated to see women cry. "Listen, miss, it isn't the end of the world. Why don't you go to work for a doctor in his office? There are thousands of doctors in the telephone book. And if that doesn't work out, I know where you can get a job like," he snapped his fingers, "that."

Casey blew her nose. "Where's *that*?"

"The military. They're always looking for nurses."

"Do you mean join the army?"

"Yeah, you wear a uniform. You'd probably be an officer."

"Are there military hospitals here in California?" Casey asked tearfully.

"They're all over. The really big ones are in Washington, D.C. If you went to work there, you'd be nursing all the top brass with their ulcers and hemorrhoids. Of course, if you want to *really* make a difference, you can sign up to go to Vietnam. Our boys could use you over there, and they won't care if you're French, English, or Mongolian. Whatever you decide, I wish you luck, miss," the driver concluded, pulling to the curb in front of her house.

"Thank you very much," Casey said as she paid him. She added what she thought was a generous tip. He smiled gratefully.

"Tomorrow is another day. If you want to make the rounds again, call and ask for me. My name is Jake Connors. I go on duty at seven-thirty."

"I'll do that," Casey said, and thanked him again.

In the warm, lighted kitchen, Casey found a can of chicken noodle soup in the cabinet. While it heated up, she made fresh coffee and toast. It wasn't much of a dinner, she thought, but she wasn't very hungry.

Before she ate, she carried in wood from the back porch. The pile was dwindling. There were twelve logs, at best, with a few that were little more than kindling. God, what am I going to do? she asked herself. She wasn't certain if her concern was for the wood pile or the fact that she couldn't find a job. "The hell with it," she muttered.

With her dinner on a tray, Casey sat in front of the fire. The soup was too salty, the toast cold. She set it aside and sipped at the coffee as she smoked one cigarette after another. She sat through the news and a game show before she got up to wash the dishes. She took a shower, washed her hair, filed her nails, replenished the fire, finished the coffee, and then got out her tattered list along with the phone book.

The cab driver was right, tomorrow was another day. She'd go to one of the medical registries that hired nurses to work in offices. Maybe she could get a job working in a dentist's office. If tomorrow wasn't more promising than today, she would give serious thought to the cab driver's suggestion about joining the military. He said there was a real need for nurses in Vietnam. Or she could hire a tutor and study like mad and try for the State Boards. She had an ear for the English language, but she didn't have an eye for the words. She knew her limits, knew she couldn't possibly make it by July, which meant she'd have to study all the way through the year and try for the Boards in early February.

Go home. Go back to Paris, an inner voice chided. You're needed there. They'll welcome you. Mrs. Laroux will be delighted. Go.

But did she really want to go back to her old life? If she did that, she'd be admitting failure. There were still so many things to do here. She wanted to find out more about her father and grandmother. She wanted to see California sunshine. She wanted to smell the famous orange blossoms, tour a movie studio, and perhaps actually *see* a real film star. Of course, she'd have to go to Hollywood to do that. She owned a car, and once she learned how to drive, she could visit the whole state if she wanted to. "I can get a job as a shop girl," she muttered, "and study for the Boards at night." And waste a whole year of your life? the niggling inner voice replied.

She was angry now, up and stomping about the small living room, her hands clenched into tight fists. It wasn't fair. She'd come here filled with hopes and dreams, and now they were in ashes at her feet. The urge to throw something was so strong that she bit down hard on her lower lip and tasted her own blood. She wiped it with the back of her hand. "Damn!" she exploded.

A nurse's aide. She could do that. But would a hospital hire her in that capacity? She hoped so. And, of course, she would see if she qualified as an office nurse. At least she'd be working in her profession instead of selling hosiery and gloves to house-wives.

Her bad moments over, Casey sat down cross-legged in front of the fire and reached for her pad and pencil. She worked steadily for over three hours writing down names, telephone numbers, and addresses. In her father's desk she found a map of the area and a bus schedule. She mapped out her route, frowning over some of the names she had difficulty pronouncing. She felt better now that she had a plan, so much so that she brewed a second pot of coffee. She showered while it perked.

Casey watched a late night show while she worked on a budget. Eventually she dozed and then drifted into a sound, dreamless sleep, and didn't awaken till six-thirty the following morning.

Dirty-gray drizzle greeted her when she left the house to step into a waiting cab, which would take her to the medical center. After that she would test her homemade map and bus schedule.

WHEN SHE ENTERED a steamy coffee shop at three-thirty, she was drenched. In her life she'd never felt this battered and bruised by her peers. She wasn't wanted. She wasn't needed. She'd put up with rudeness, and she had to bite her tongue so she wouldn't snap back a sassy retort. There was no place for her here, it was that simple. State Boards be damned.

Casey ordered a tuna sandwich that tasted like glue. She pushed the plate away and concentrated on the coffee in front of her. She was startled a moment later when a crisp voice asked, "Would you mind sharing this table? All the others seem to be taken."

Flustered, Casey looked around and for the first time noticed how full the shop was. She was taking up a table with four chairs. She felt embarrassed when she nodded, a flush creeping into her cheeks.

"I hate to ask, but I'm starving. If I'm intruding . . ."

"Not at all. I didn't realize . . . I've been sitting here . . . I'm just about to leave," Casey said self-consciously. She raised her eyes then. His smile was so real, so warm, she could only respond in kind. Nicole would call him a heartthrob. She waited a moment to see if her own heart would thump the way Nicole said it would when she met a handsome man. When nothing happened, she almost laughed.

"Mac Carlin, newly arrived in San Francisco."

"Casey Adams, also newly arrived. And soon to depart."

"Me too. My orders got snafued. I have two weeks to either cool my heels or kick them up." He grinned. She had to be the prettiest girl he'd ever seen. He loved her accent. He'd never seen such riveting blue eyes before. They were taking stock of him. He wondered how he was measuring up.

Casey wondered if he was flirting with her. Nicole would have known instantly. "What does that mean, snafued?" she asked.

"SNAFU stands for situation normal, all fouled up. That's the way the army does things sometimes. I'll have the number four," he said to the waitress, "and a cup of coffee." He looked back at her. "Where are you soon to depart for?"

What a wonderful smile she had. He likened it to his mother's smile when he was little. It was the kind of smile that wrapped itself around you. The smile reached her eyes, as he knew it would. He felt like clapping his hands. He didn't of course. That would have been childish.

"France. Paris."

"Ah, Paris in the spring. Is it as beautiful as they say it is?"

"It's very beautiful. I think Paris has a soul. I have lived there all my life." He was easy to talk to. Surely this couldn't be classified as flirting, not this easy, natural conversation.

"Then you must be on vacation. What do you think of California?"

Casey made a face. "All it does is rain. I don't care for the fog. I think it's . . . impersonal. No one speaks to anyone, everyone is so . . . busy. Actually, I'm not on vacation. I came here to find a job. It appears my services are not needed, so I decided this morning that I will return home."

After the waitress set down his order, he said, "I agree with your assessment of this city one hundred percent. What is it that you do?" he asked, biting down on his sandwich. A look of panic rushed across his face when he chewed what was in his mouth.

Casey laughed, a sound of pure delight. "If your number four is tuna, I could have given you mine."

"It tastes like Elmer's glue and wood shavings."

Casey laughed again. "I believe that's a good assessment. The coffee is fine."

"Which just goes to prove my theory. A coffee shop should serve coffee. They do that well. As soon as they start messing with food, it goes wrong. I should have ordered cornflakes. Would you like some? Cornflakes with a banana?" Casey nodded.

Mac flagged the waitress. Casey continued to smile while the tired waitress simpered and apologized for the tuna sandwiches.

"What is it you do that you can't find a job?"

"I'm a nurse."

"And you can't find a job?" Mac asked incredulously. "Wait, wait, wait, I didn't mean that the way it sounded. But hospitals always need nurses, don't they?" He felt stunned at how indignant he felt in this young woman's behalf.

"My credentials are French. They tell me I have to take the American Nursing Boards, which are given in July and February. I cannot . . . I speak English well, but I would need a tutor, and there is no way I can be prepared by July. I don't want to stay until next February and not work at my profession. I have a dual citizenship, but that makes no difference," Casey said mournfully.

"I never heard of such a ridiculous thing," Mac said huffily. "You should show them all and join the army. They need nurses."

Casey's eyebrows shot upward. "How do you know this?" she demanded.

How did he know this? "I don't, not for sure, but it stands

to reason. I saw in the *Washington Star* that nurses are in short supply everywhere."

"You mean Vietnam!"

"Please don't tell me that you're one of those antiwar protestors."

"I won't tell you that. Were you in Vietnam?"

"No, but that's where I'm headed as soon as my new orders come down."

"Did you volunteer or are they sending you against your wishes?"

"No. I volunteered," he replied, as the waitress set down their bowls of cereal. "It's a year's tour, but I've already decided I'll volunteer for a second year. It's the right thing for me to do. I guess it was like that for you when you made the decision to come here from France. I mean, the right thing for you."

"At the time."

"You might like working at Walter Reed Hospital. The Washington-Virginia area is quite nice." *And I might get to see you again sometime.*

Under the cover of her eyelashes Casey observed him. He looked tall and strong. Possibly he had been an athlete at one time. She liked the strong look of his hands. A wave of heat surged through her when she wondered what it would feel like to be touched by those hands.

She knew he was staring at her. He had said something to her. Lord, what was it? "Yes, the cornflakes are quite nice," she stammered.

He laughed deeply. "The banana is a little green, don't you think?"

"Yes, and hard. Bitter too."

He laughed again, revealing perfectly aligned white teeth. American orthodontia, she decided. She felt self-conscious when she remembered her slightly crooked eye tooth, the one Nicole called "endearing."

Sadie would approve of this girl, Mac thought. So would Benny. His brow began to knit when he thought of his lacquered, polished, coiffed wife. He pushed her from his thoughts.

She looks nervous, Mac thought. He felt a moment of panic when he realized she was groping in her bag for money to pay her check. She was going to get up and leave, and he'd never see her again. The thought brought an immediate ache to his chest.

Mac reached for the check. "I'm the one who ordered the cornflakes, so I should be the one to pay. Please, I insist," he said at the doubtful look on her face. "Besides," he grinned, "it's the American way."

She was slipping into her coat. In a few minutes she'd be gone. The ache intensified. "Listen, would you like to join me for a drink someplace? A decent place. Perhaps one with a piano bar. We could have dinner too." He held up both hands, palms toward her. "Look, it will be two people enjoying each other's company. Then on the stroke of midnight, or before, if you wish, you can ride off in your pumpkin. I don't know anyone else here. What do you say?"

If Nicole and Danele were here, they'd subtly kick her under the table and blatantly hiss in her ear, "Go, go, go. *Mon Dieu*, do we need to draw you a picture?"

"That sounds very nice. My evening is free," Casey said breathlessly. There was such a buzzing in her ears, she felt light-headed, and she thought her shins hurt. She laughed then for no reason.

Mac joined her, not knowing why. He wondered vaguely if what he was about to do came under the heading of unfaithfulness. No, he decided, dinner and conversation were social pastimes. Anyway, at this point, he didn't give a roaring fuck what heading they came under.

Heads turned, Casey noticed, when Mac walked to the register to pay the check. She watched as one girl rolled her eyes and pretended to swoon, while another whistled soundlessly. She felt like whistling herself. American girls called it a wolf whistle, but somehow she'd thought it was the men who were supposed to whistle at girls, not the other way around.

Outside the fog swirled about them. It was late in the afternoon. "Would you like to walk for a while?" Mac asked. "It's not quite so dismal when you're with someone. When we get tired, we'll take a cab to a French restaurant I've heard about called La Folie. What do you say?" He waited anxiously, hardly daring to breathe for fear she'd say no.

"Oh, I'd like that very much. Do you like French food?"

He didn't, but he was going to learn to love it in short order. Still, for some reason he didn't want to lie to this girl. "It's a little rich for my taste, but everyone knows it's the company and the wine that make for a delightful dinner."

"I think you're right." Impulsively, Casey linked her arm with Mac's. "Wouldn't you love to catch it?"

"The fog?" He thought it was the most wonderful thing he'd ever heard. He found himself chuckling. "Shall we try?"

"Absolutely." Casey laughed as she let loose of his arm and started to chase a tendril of fog. They were children, laughing and giggling as they ran down the street, their arms outstretched. Mac had never done anything so outrageous or silly, especially in uniform. He hadn't laughed like this in years. He suspected Casey Adams hadn't either.

"I give up," Casey said a long while later.

"Thank God. Ten minutes ago I realized we weren't going to make a fortune catching and bottling this stuff. I hate to admit this, but I'm winded. Let's hail a cab."

Casey giggled. "I agree."

Warm and gentle. A sense of humor. Her arm was in his again, her breathing as labored as his own, but there was a smile on her lips. He *liked* this girl with the delightful French accent. Damn, he felt like he was nineteen again.

"I'd like to hear all about France and what it's like to live there." He wasn't just saying the words. He really did want to know.

"Where do you come from, Mac?" Casey asked quietly.

"McLean, Virginia. It's not far from Washington, D.C."

"I will tell you all about France if you tell me about Washington, D.C."

"It's a deal. Hey, here's a taxi." Mac flagged the Checker cab. "Polk Street, La Folie," he said to the driver.

"You're familiar with the city then?" Casey asked curiously.

"Not really. I used to come to California on vacations," Mac said shortly. "San Francisco is not one of my favorite places. I prefer Los Angeles."

"I see," Casey said, because she felt she had to make a comment.

Mac laughed. "No, you don't. My mother used to say 'I see' all the time. What it meant was she didn't understand and she was going to be polite until I explained. My father likes California. He has friends here, and we used to come here every year when the school term was over in the spring. Going on a vacation with one's father isn't exactly the best way to have fun, especially when father and son don't get on all that well." He forced a light tone to his voice. He wasn't about to allow his father to infringe on this evening.

It was dark when the cab pulled to the curb in front of the pretty storefront café. "I have to warn you," Mac said, holding the door for her, "service here is supposed to be lackadaisical at best. Well meaning, of course. But I've heard it's a fun place. The sort of restaurant my father would hate."

There was no warmth in his eyes when he spoke of his father, Casey noticed.

"Sazerac cocktails and fresh oysters," Mac ordered. "Shall I try out my French on you? It isn't half as good as your English." He leaned across the table and blurted, "You have the most incredible blue eyes. Is that the *real* color of your hair or does . . . is it artificial? It looks like soft butter. It's important for me to know, but I can't explain why." A boyish grin stretched across his face. Casey's heart thumped.

"My hair color is real. My friends always teased me in school. I tried to be so French, and they all said I looked American. Right now, I don't know what I am. Thank you for the compliment," Casey said lightly. *She was actually flirting.*

"It's your turn," Mac teased.

Casey blushed.

"I've embarrassed you, I'm sorry. That wasn't my intention at all." He liked her elegant Gallic shrug. Sadie would call him a clod for what he'd just said and tell him that, no matter what, you never embarrass a lady.

They talked of the weather while they ate their oysters and sipped their drinks. When they exhausted a discussion on the bay's smell, the fog, the cold, and the rainy winter months, Mac asked where she lived in France.

"In a very small flat. I sublet it to a young intern. From my yard I could sneak into the gardens of Notre Dame. I used to pretend I was a grand lady out for a stroll when I went there. The priests were very indulgent with me. I love flowers, you see. They allowed me many liberties."

They talked and nibbled, whispered and smiled, laughed and touched hands across the table. Casey told herself it was a pleasant interlude that would end when she walked through the doors to catch a cab.

A guilty expression crossed her features when she looked around the room a long time later to find they were the only patrons in the café. "I think they want to close," she whispered.

"I think so too. It is late. I can't tell you how much I appreciate you . . . it was one of the nicest evenings in my life. Tell me something, though, how is it you have an American name?"

Casey smiled. "It's really a French name. It's spelled Casée. If you were writing it, you would put the little mark over the first e. To be stubborn, I adopted the American spelling."

"I see." Mac chuckled. They were both laughing when they swept through the café doors. She could have eaten for a week with the tip Mac left on the table. She said so.

"We took up that table all night. They could have turned it over three times. I had to make it up to our waiter." Casey thought it a wonderful gesture.

A taxi pulled to the curb. "Lombard Street, you said." Casey nodded. Mac relayed the information to the driver. "Will you have dinner with me tomorrow?" he asked impulsively.

"Yes," Casey answered just as impulsively.

"Give me your phone number."

"Oh! I don't know what it is. It must be in the telephone book under Jack Adams."

Mac stood back from the curb. "I'll call you tomorrow."

"Thank you for a wonderful evening."

"My pleasure. I'll see you tomorrow." He snapped off an airy salute in the general direction of the cab, and watched it disappear into the swirling fog.

Casey swept into the house, her steps light, her eyes sparkling.

A fire would be nice, she decided. While she laid the twigs and crunched up papers, she pushed all thoughts of Captain Mac Carlin as far back into her mind as she could. She waited a moment while the pyramid of sparks raced up the chimney before she added two solid birch logs. Satisfied with the steady blaze, she trotted off to her bedroom to put on her robe and slippers. She carried her pillow and the comforter bordered with yellow tulips and sprigs of green fern out to the living room. She settled herself in front of the fire. She thought about Mac's promise to phone her, and reached out of her cocoon for the telephone book on the shelf under the end table. Her eyebrows shot upward when she discovered all the columns of Adamses. Like a child, she ran her index finger down the page to search out her father's name and phone number. Once she saw it and committed it to memory, Mac would be more real. She could almost picture him dialing the number and then waiting for her to say hello. Ohhh, she could hardly wait for the call. However would she pass the time until that wonderful moment happened? She was on the fifth column on the second page when she realized there was no J. Adams, no Jack or John Adams listed on Lombard Street. Panic seized her. Once a number had been printed on the little paper circle, but it was nothing more than a blur now. Completely illegible. Where was the number? *Mon Dieu*, where was the number? Her throat tightened. She swayed sickeningly. Her finger found the O on the dial. "Operator, I need to know the number of this phone I'm calling you from. Could you give it to me please?"

"One moment. The address and name, miss?"

Casey gave her the address and spelled her father's name slowly. "Possibly the number is listed under Jack or John or maybe just the initial J."

The silence on the phone while the operator looked up the number thundered in Casey's ears. "I'm sorry but that number is unlisted."

"What does that mean?" Casey croaked. "I'm new here in California. This is my father's number, and he . . . what does it mean?"

"It means the number can't be given out. To anyone," the operator said irritably.

"But it's my number now. I'm the one who will be paying the bill. I should have the number. Please, this is very important to me."

"I'm sorry, miss. Contact the business office tomorrow. The hours are nine to five." Casey stared at the pinging phone clutched in her hand. This couldn't be happening to her. It wasn't fair.

Casey slumped down on the floor again. Lord, she was stupid. What was she going to do with the phone number when she got it from the telephone company? Stupid! Stupid! She didn't know where Mac was staying, so how was she to give him the phone number? She pummeled the padded comforter, tears streaming down her cheeks.

Two weeks. Mac had two weeks in San Francisco, time enough for them to get to know one another. Time enough to explore the area. Time to laugh and perhaps cry when it was time for him to leave.

If she'd been more experienced, more worldly, she would have made sure the handsome captain had her address. If she'd been more sophisticated, she would have gotten the name of his hotel. Sister Ann Elizabeth would say this was nonsense, and that's why fate intervened to create an impossible situation. Casey didn't believe it for a minute.

She fought the urge to stamp her feet and scream. Nicole and Danele would tell her to leave no stone unturned. "Go, go, go," they'd say. "Where?" she wailed. "I don't know enough about this city. I don't even remember the name of the coffee shop where I met him."

The logs shifted, teetered on the iron grate before they settled between the wide prongs. What was Mac Carlin doing right now, this minute? She wished she knew. She longed for a dog or a cat to snuggle with. She'd always wanted a pet. Someday she was going to surround herself with cats and dogs. Once she'd had a goldfish she kept in a cracked cup. It had died in a day's time. She'd cried for a whole day when Sister Ann Elizabeth flushed it down the toilet and then threw the cup in the trash. She'd wanted to bury the fish in the gardens at Notre Dame. She wondered if Mac Carlin had had a pet as a child. Once she'd caught a flicker of sadness in his eyes, but it disappeared almost immediately.

What had they eaten? *Soupe de poissons, crudités, pâté, potage de légumes,* and *glacé panachée.* She found herself giggling when Mac gave the order in his strangled French. She'd laughed aloud when she saw the garnish on the soup. Mac said it looked like a giant ladybug. It had been one of the most enjoyable evenings of her life. Damn! She wanted to see him again. How delighted she'd been when he asked to see her tomorrow. Now it was like everything else in her life that didn't work out.

"What I need is a fairy godmother," Casey muttered. She flopped over on her stomach, propping her chin in her hands. "A fairy godmother who knows San Francisco, and knows about men."

Where *was* he staying? Had he said anything, given a clue she hadn't picked up on? She yanked at the telephone in her lap. Hotels. She would call them all until she found him. Sleep was the farthest thing from her mind as she flipped through the telephone book to the section that listed hotels. She blinked at the long list. It would take a full night and day to call all of them. Her jaw set tightly. Either she would call them or she would have to forget about Mac Carlin. She dialed and dialed. At one in the morning she was perturbed, at two she was annoyed, at three she started to get angry, at four she threw down her pencil in disgust to head for the kitchen to make coffee. She'd called over a hundred hotels in the San Francisco area and had that many still to call, if not more. She sipped coffee while she continued to dial one number after another. By seven her eyes were red and full of grit from the smoky fire. At eight o'clock she threw her pencil into the dying flames. She was so stupid. Mac said when he visited San Francisco with his father it was to visit friends. He wasn't staying at a hotel at all but with friends. She felt like a fool when she replaced the telephone on the end table. *"Bête, bête, bête,"* she chastised herself on the way to the shower.

Casey rubbed at the steamy mirror with a yellow hand towel. She looked awful, felt awful, her eyes red and puffy. She wanted to scream at her reflection, to keen, to wail her lament. Instead she cried silent tears of frustration. She toweled her hair as she wept, with the same yellow towel she'd used to wipe the mirror. Satisfied with her damp curls, she made her way to the bed, where she crawled between the cold sheets. She'd never considered sleeping in the nude before, she thought as she drifted into sleep. When she awoke from her nap, she was going to do something else she'd never considered: she was going to join the army.

THE FIRST THING Mac Carlin did when he finished his breakfast was to write Sadie's address on the box his Uncle Harry had given to him. He had checked into a civilian hotel in order to have more services than would be available at an army BOQ. And now he called the hotel desk for a bellhop to mail the package. He hadn't looked at the books. It wasn't time for him to touch his mother's things, even though they were meant for him. Maybe it would never be time. He scribbled off a note to Sadie and slipped it into one of the hotel's envelopes. When the bellhop appeared, he handed him a ten-dollar bill and asked to have the letter attached to the box. "Keep the change," he said generously.

The second thing he did was pull out the hotel telephone directory to look up the Jack Adams number. He ran his finger with his blunt-cut nail down the long list of Adamses. There had to be at least five hundred, but not one that lived on Lombard Street. He felt his heart twitch. It was Lombard Street, he'd repeated it to the taxi driver. The information operator told him in her nasally voice that the number was unpublished. His heart gave a second twitch.

Mac knew what he was feeling was wrong, but he didn't care. He also knew what he was about to do was just as wrong. He didn't care about that either. Yesterday he'd met a delightful young woman, a woman who made his blood sing. He'd chased tendrils of fog with her, laughed with her, eaten with her, and held her hand for the briefest second in time. It was fate. Kismet. Preordained. It was *something*, and he wanted to experience it again. Jesus Christ, he was a "star man" of West Point, top honors, a captain in the United States Army. He was trained to do the impossible. A little thing like an unlisted phone number and lack of address would not, *could not* deter him. What he had to do, he told himself, was change the situation around and think of Casey Adams as the enemy. Search her out—that's what he had to do.

Mac Carlin was a man with a purpose when he strode through the wide double doors of his hotel in search of a taxi. He was oblivious to the admiring glances of the female hotel guests and envious stares of the potbellied men toting their briefcases. "I want to go to Lombard Street," he said briskly. "I don't have an address. Just drive."

The morning was quiet, Mac noted, perfectly windless, and that surprised him for some reason. It was cold, though, and damp. He hated dampness and the smell dampness brought. He thought of one of his father's rental houses on the Chesapeake which always smelled like someone's wet galoshes. The air smelled the same way today. He wondered if it was some kind of omen.

He needed to find her. He wasn't sure why. He wanted to see her again. He'd made a date with her. He'd promised to call. What the hell was she going to think? It bothered him that she might think he was some kind of pickup artist. It had been so natural, their meeting. He'd loved every single minute of it.

Moments later, when the taxi driver turned right off Geary Street onto Divisadero, the heavens opened in a downpour. "I have to pull over, son. I can't see to drive. I can tell you this is going to last for a while," the driver said authoritatively. "We get rain like this at least once a week at this time of year."

Mac grunted as he smacked his closed fist into his open palm. "Damn it to hell."

"If you don't mind me asking, son, if you don't have an address, how do you know which house you want? This isn't a good street to be a looky-look, if you know what I mean. It's so crooked, you can kill yourself if you don't drive at the right speed."

"Are there a lot of houses?" Mac asked, a note of desperation in his voice.

"A right fair amount. It's not a good street to stop and start on, if you get my point. Can't hold up traffic. Be a lot easier if you know what you're looking for."

"A girl," Mac blurted.

"Okay, that's different," the cabbie said, grinning.

"I put her in a cab last night, but I didn't have the address. I just told the driver to take her to Lombard Street. She's visiting here from France, and her father has an unlisted phone number. I want to see her again, and I have only two weeks, possibly less if my new orders come through. Any suggestions?" So much for his West Point education, he thought wryly.

The cab driver removed his cap and scratched his grizzled head. "What about the cab driver who brought her here? You could call them if you know the name of the company. The dispatchers keep logs of all drivers' trips. If you have the time, the driver who picked her up should be able to get the address. Or you can try the post office. They *might* tell you. The electric company or the water company might help. I don't know how free they are with their information, but it's worth a try."

"Thanks," Mac said, grateful for a course of action.

"If you strike out at the post office, you could think about waylaying the mailman. Of course, you'll have to sit somewhere along the way if you don't know what time he delivers on Lombard."

He hadn't thought of that either. He thanked the cabbie a second time.

"I think we can take a stab at driving through this now. I got new wipers last week. They seem to be working pretty good. What's the plan, sir? Do I just drive up and down or what?"

Or what. "Yeah, I guess that's all we can do. Do you know where the post office is or the utility companies? I'll make it worth your while," Mac said. "I don't know the name of the cab company. The cab was cruising."

The drive up and down Lombard Street was an exercise in futility, Mac decided an hour later. He was wasting his time and he knew it. He wasted his time at the post office too. They also refused to tell him the name of the mail carrier for Lombard Street and the time the mail was delivered. He fared no better at the utility companies.

It was two-thirty when the cab driver dropped Mac off at his hotel. He smiled and tipped his hat when Mac handed him a fifty-dollar bill. He promised to call Mac at the hotel if he found out anything on his own, as he thought he might ask around, among his friends, just in case.

In his room Mac ordered a ham and cheese on rye and a bottle of beer. While he waited for it, he put through a call to Sadie. His spirits lifted the moment he heard her voice. He explained about the box of books and then proceeded to dump his immediate problem in her lap. "Do you have any ideas, Sadie?"

"When you come into this country from another country, don't you have to give the address where you're staying?"

"Yes, you do. She has a dual citizenship. Still, there should be a record. I'll give it a try."

"Mac, honey, don't get your hopes up, okay? I've never been able to find Bill. You need more to go on. Didn't she say anything that would give you a clue? What about France? Did she mention any names you could call over there? I know that sounds rather extreme, but if you're determined to leave no stone unturned, it's worth a try."

"She mentioned a friend but only by her first name. She said she worked in a hospital, but she didn't say the name of it. She can't get a job here because her nursing credentials are from France. It's hopeless, isn't it, Sadie?"

"It sounds that way, honey. Listen, why don't you go back to the place where you met her or where you had dinner. Go back and forth. She might realize by now that you have no way to get in touch with her, and she might be doing the same thing. Does she know where you're staying?"

"I didn't tell her. I have to see her again, Sadie, I just do. I know I shouldn't . . . it's just that she was special . . . I never felt the way I felt with her. Jesus Christ, you should have seen us. We were trying to catch fog. She made me happy, Sadie, she made me laugh. I know it's wrong, but I can't help myself. Alice ... Alice is ... when I get back we're getting a divorce. It's been over for a long time. That doesn't make this right, but it makes me feel better to say it out loud. I'll write, Sadie. Take care of yourself."

"Good luck, Mac. I hope you find her."

"I do too. Bye, Sadie."

"Good-bye, Mac."

The airport and Customs took up another two hours of Mac's day with no results. He spent three more hours going back and forth between the diner and the French restaurant on Polk Street, with no better results. At seven o'clock he left the restaurant and headed back to his hotel.

IT WAS TWO-THIRTY in the afternoon when Casey called for a taxi. In her purse she carried all her credentials along with her passport. "Take me to the nearest army recruiter," she ordered firmly.

Twenty minutes later Casey leaped from the cab before she could change her mind. She thrust bills at the driver, not knowing if she was giving too much or not. Her teeth were clenched so tightly, she thought her jaw would crack.

She sucked in her breath, squared her shoulders, and moved through the door of the recruiting office with the same force she used to shoulder her way through the doors of the operating room. She didn't lose a second when she marched straight to the sergeant on duty and said in a clipped voice, "I'm a nurse and I want to join the army. I would very much like to work at Walter Reed in Washington. Is this possible?"

The sergeant blinked. "Uh-huh, you bet. You'll be offered a commission. As to Walter Reed, well, they're staffed right now," he lied. "Sit down and let's talk a bit. You seem like you're in a hurry."

"Yes, yes I am. Where are your other hospitals here in the United States?" she asked, hating the desperate sound of her own voice.

"There's nothing available stateside. Those posts are the first to fill. What is your speciality?"

"The last three years I worked in the operating theater. In Paris. My certificate is French. Does it make a difference?" she asked anxiously.

"What's your feeling about working out of the country?" the sergeant asked, ignoring her question.

"I just came from 'out of the country,'" Casey said quietly. "Why?"

The sergeant chewed on his lower lip. "Our boys sure could use a good nurse in Vietnam." He shuffled through a loose-leaf binder. "Well, it says right here in paragraph 1–6 of AR 601–139—this is about commissioning in the Army Nurse Corps—that 'waiver of professional requirements will not be considered.' But let me work on that. They require an examination, and with your experience, you'll pass with flying colors. You'll go in as a second lieutenant. Now, that's not too shabby. I'll tell you what," he said, "you go out and get a cup of coffee, walk around a bit, let me make some phone calls, and I'll see what I can do. Leave all your papers here, they're safe with me. Come back in, say, an hour and a half." At the doubtful look on her face, the sergeant pressed his advantage. "Our boys sure could use someone like you. It's the patriotic thing to do."

"Vietnam? Well . . . I don't . . . it's not that I'm unpatriotic, it's just that I . . . I was thinking of returning to France . . . I can work there . . . I never . . . it's so far away. I really wanted to work at . . . Walter Reed. I'm not sure about joining the army if I can't . . . all right, I'll think about it," Casey said, making her way to the door.

Outside in the brisk air, she did think about it as she walked up one street and down another. Mac Carlin was going to be in Vietnam soon. Why shouldn't she go too? There was nothing holding her here. Going back home meant failure. She would be an officer, the sergeant said. Mac Carlin was an officer. Not too shabby, the sergeant said. It would definitely be a new start. "I'll do it!" she muttered, spinning around on the sidewalk to head back to the recruiting station.

Inside the building the recruiter looked up from his paperwork and smiled.

"How big is Vietnam?" Casey demanded.

The sergeant shuffled his papers. "Here's a map. Judge for
yourself."

"It looks very large," Casey said quietly. The sergeant
shrugged.

Casey's second question surprised the sergeant even more.
"How many American soldiers are in Vietnam?"

"Around three hundred thousand at last count. Why do you
ask?" the sergeant asked curiously.

Instead of answering him, Casey asked another question.
"How difficult will it be to locate a captain in the army?" She
flushed a bright pink to the sergeant's amusement.

"As long as you know where the captain's stationed, it won't
be a problem. Your own personnel sergeant can help you."

Casey debated a full five seconds, shifting her balance from
one foot to the other. "I wish to . . . accept the commission,"
she said firmly.

"Atta girl!" the sergeant said enthusiastically.

The sergeant started his paperwork. He prided himself on his
fast and accurate judgment of character. This girl, this young
woman, cared about people; he could see it in her eyes when he
mentioned "our boys." He'd had only one bad moment of
guilty conscience. There were six openings at Walter Reed, but
this girl would be wasted there. He knew it as sure as he knew
it was going to rain again later that evening.

A FEW DAYS later Casey Adams, and two student nurses, were
sworn into the United States Army.

Casey mourned the loss of Mac Carlin as she packed her bags
that evening. She unbuttoned her stiffly starched caps and laid
them on top of her uniforms. She looked around doubtfully.
What should she do now with her winter clothing? She made
piles on the bed: packing her girdles, stockings, and underwear
in the bottom of the bag. Assorted blouses and skirts followed,
then three dresses she wondered if she would ever get to wear.

Shoes and sandals came next. She still had room in her bag when she was finished.

Casey called a taxi to take her to the nearest drugstore, where she filled a shopping bag with aspirin, shampoo, soap, talcum powder, toothpaste, two new toothbrushes, deodorant, and anything else she could think of that she might need. When she paid for her purchases, her brow creased with worry. What was she going to do about her money? She'd meant to open a bank account, but for some reason, she hadn't gotten around to it. *Mon Dieu*, this was all so sudden and so out of character for her. The bank check in her purse, wrinkled now and creased, had to be deposited somewhere. Not here though, an inner voice cautioned. Then where? she fretted. Nicole. Send it to Nicole with a letter of instruction. She trusted Nicole.

Jack Adams's desk was full of writing paper, envelopes, and stamps. Casey scribbled off a note to Nicole explaining her situation. She added a long postscript telling her about Mac Carlin. Uncertain about postage, Casey licked five stamps and scrawled AIR MAIL across the envelope.

For the second time that evening, Casey put on her coat and walked down the street to the corner where she'd seen a mailbox. She heaved a sigh of relief when the lid snapped shut with a loud clang.

An hour later her winter clothing was packed in a box from the garage. She carried it to the attic, along with her second suitcase. The writing materials were back in her father's desk drawer. Her clothes for the morning were laid out on the chair in her room. Earlier she'd called the attorney at his home to explain her situation, and she asked him to take care of closing up the house and to pay the bills with the money in her father's small bank account.

The long evening loomed ahead of her. She built a fire, then watched television for a while. Her nerves twanged with anxiety.

Evening television programming turned out to be so silly and ridiculous that she soon turned down the sound and reached for the telephone directory. On a whim, she flipped to the list of hotels and started to call the ones she hadn't reached the several days before. It was twenty minutes to twelve when the switchboard operator at the Hotel Savoy announced she would put Casey's call through to Captain Carlin's room. Casey's grip was so tight on the receiver that her knuckles turned white, and her heart was beating so fast, she thought it would leap out of her chest. *He was there. She'd found him. Mon Dieu.* She listened to the ring, knowing there would be no answer. "Captain Carlin isn't picking up. Would you care to leave a message?"

Would she? Did she want to? Could she even speak? She worked her tongue around her dry mouth. "Yes, yes I would. Tell . . . say . . . Casey Adams called."

"Would you care to leave your phone number?" the operator asked.

Would she care? Of course she cared. She wanted to demand the operator take her number, but she didn't know what it was. She looked down at the square black phone. Her shoulders slumped. "No . . . yes, I would, but you see, I don't know what the number is here. It's not on the phone, and I believe it's unpublished."

"What would you like me to say then?" the operator queried.

"Just that I called, operator. Thank you."

Casey curled into the corner of the sofa. She was trembling from head to foot. She'd found him, for all the good it was doing her. *Mon Dieu*, now what? What would Nicole and Danele do? Go to the Hotel Savoy! Of course, that's what they would do. That's what she should do too. He's not there, her inner voice argued. You could wait in the lobby. And be conspicuous? Proper young ladies do not chase men or go to their hotels. Could she even get a taxi at this hour of the night?

Casey raced to the bathroom, washed her face, brushed her hair, and added fresh lipstick. "What do I have to lose?" she asked her reflection. "Nothing, not a thing." She was smiling when she called for her taxi, and she held her breath while she waited for the dispatcher's confirmation. "Fifteen minutes," he said briskly.

"Thank you. Thank you very much."

Unable to wait inside a moment longer, Casey let herself out and stood in the drizzle. She barely noticed the misty rain.

She'd persevered, and now she was going to prevail. Nicole and Danele would be so proud of her.

The taxi pulled to the curb right on schedule. "The Savoy Hotel," Casey said sliding onto the seat. She yanked the door closed with a loud slam. "I'm in a hurry, sir."

"I can see that," the driver said tartly.

The ride was short, ten minutes at the most. Casey was stunned when she realized Mac was so close, and yet, until an hour ago, she hadn't been able to find him. Ten minutes away. Her heart fluttered in her chest. Just ten minutes, and now all she had was less than five hours until she had to report to the United States Army. Less than five hours. She felt weak suddenly, and her stomach, queasy. Only ten minutes away. She'd spent *hours* calling every hotel in the area. This was all a bad dream, she told herself.

The hotel suited Mac Carlin. It wasn't fancy or ostentatious. It looked comfortable, the prime requisite for weary travelers. The oak-paneled lobby was restful somehow, the touches of brass just right. It was clean, Casey noticed, another requisite for travelers away from home.

In less than three minutes Casey was seated in a deep leather chair after being told that Captain Carlin hadn't returned. She would wait. How long she didn't know. Probably until the desk clerk started to look at her suspiciously, which happened at twenty minutes of three.

Casey did her best to stare down the desk clerk the way Nicole would have done. "I'd like to leave a message for Captain Carlin, but I'll need paper and a pen," she said stiffly. She carried both to a small alcove. Thinking in French and writing in English proved to be a chore. She wasn't sure it was all proper, and at this point she didn't really care.

Dear Mac,

I feel very foolish writing this note to you, but I want you to know I enjoyed dinner with you the other night and the time we spent together. I looked forward to spending the time with you. I still don't know my father's telephone number, and it doesn't matter now. I'll be leaving at five in the morning, a little over two and a half hours from the time I write this. I called all the hotels in the telephone book to locate you. You were out, they said, so I came here to wait for you. It is almost three in the morning and I must leave now.

I have never done anything like this before. I now have a pleasant memory to carry with me. Thank you again for a lovely evening.

Casey debated a moment before she signed the note. She added her father's address and her name.

"Would you please call a cab," Casey said as she handed over the note.

"Certainly," the desk clerk said coolly.

"Thank you," Casey said just as coolly. Her head high, her shoulders back, Casey walked through the oak-paneled lobby to wait for the cab outside. It was raining harder now, splashing on her shoes. She didn't care about that either. Where was he? She'd made a fool of herself by coming here. She wanted to run back inside and snatch back her note and rip it to shreds, but she didn't have the nerve. He probably thinks I'm a street-walker, she thought as she stared over her shoulder. The desk clerk was still watching her from behind the desk.

"Take me to 3345 Lombard Street," Casey said to the driver. She pulled the door shut, careful not to slam it the way she had earlier. She wanted to cry, to throw a tantrum. She was a fool. Men who stayed out all night were up to no good. Mac Carlin probably hadn't given her a second thought, while she'd been obsessed with him. She tried to shrink into her wet coat. She'd never felt so humiliated and embarrassed in her life. She wished she could run and hide and erase her meeting with him.

Biting down on her lip, Casey walked through her father's house, making sure the lights were off, her room tidy and the kitchen neat. Her eyes smarted. "It looks like I was never here," she thought miserably.

It was exactly five o'clock when Casey noticed the flash of headlights on the living room wall. She was out the door, suitcase in hand, a moment later.

At eight minutes past six Casey boarded the bus on the first leg of her journey to Southeast Asia. She would attend an officer orientation course at Fort Sam Houston in Texas. Her final destination: Vietnam.

MAC CARLIN CHARGED through the door of the Hotel Savoy at fifteen minutes to five. His stride was purposeful, military. He was tired and irritable, and the irritability showed on his face when the desk clerk caught up with him at the elevator. "Sir, you have two messages."

Christ, the old man found out about the snafu, Mac thought. "I'll get them in the morning," he barked, stepping into the waiting elevator.

"Sir, the young lady looked . . . upset. She waited for over two hours," the desk clerk said. Mac stopped the door from closing. "What did you say? *Exactly?*"

"I said the young lady looked upset. She waited for over two hours. She left a message. You have two messages."

"Well, where are they?" Mac thundered.

"In . . . in your box, sir. I'll get them."

"Son of a bitch!" Mac snarled. "Call me a cab!" he roared.

"Yes, sir, right away, sir," the desk clerk said, never taking his eyes off the angry captain. He just *knew* the captain was going to put his fist through something, and he didn't want it to be his face. He'd seen angry guests before, but nothing like this.

Palms out in front of him, Mac pushed through the doors. He stormed up and down under the skimpy canopy. She'd been waiting here for him while he was sitting in an all-night movie watching French films dubbed in English. "Son of a bitch!" While she was waiting he'd been watching *Babette s'ev va-t-en Guerre* with Brigitte Bardot, a stupid movie in which the sex kitten played a British agent helping the French resistance. He'd seen five movies, all of them French, all of them terrible, but he felt closer to Casey thinking she might have seen them too.

"What time is it?" he demanded of the cab driver as he slid into the backseat.

"Five minutes to five," the driver said tiredly.

"I'll give you a hundred bucks if you get me to 3345 Lombard Street by five o'clock. Two hundred, whatever the hell you want. Just get me there. If you get a speeding ticket, I'll pay it. Move!"

"Yes, *sir!*" Tires squealed. Mac was thrown off balance as the cab shot forward. He held onto the strap over his head as the cabbie did his best to earn the promised bonus. His tires squealed a second time at four minutes past five when he pulled to the curb. Mac was out the door before the cab came to a full stop. He ran up the walk knowing he was too late. He banged on the door and shouted Casey's name until he was hoarse. When there was no response his fist shot out. Pain ricocheted up his arm into his neck. He banged again with his good hand, shouting and cursing. Lights sprang to life across the street and next door. Jesus, he was creating a ruckus. All he needed was a pair of pissed-off cops or the military police.

"Get out of here," he said to the cab driver. "I missed her by four fucking minutes. Four goddamn, lousy minutes."

"Look, son, do you want to tell me what this is all about?" the driver asked kindly. Mac told him.

"We passed a cab on the way up. Maybe it was her. The only place I can think of that someone would go at this time of morning is the airport. Not too much traffic at this hour. If that was her, we might be able to catch up. We usually go off duty at five. Not many calls between five and six when the new shift comes on. The cabbie might have stayed on since the airport is a good fare."

"Let's try it," Mac said, his face full of disgust. "Listen, can't you call in and ask where she's going?"

The box on his dashboard squawked. "Not our cab, son. Sorry. Do you still want to try the airport?"

"Why the hell not?"

The only way Mac could describe the ride to the airport was hair-raising at best. His search of the terminal was futile.

As he walked back to the waiting taxi, he knew one thing for certain: He was capable of killing. With a weapon or with his bare hands.

* * *

TWO WEEKS LATER, when his new orders arrived almost a week behind schedule, Mac headed for Travis Air Force Base to begin the first leg of his journey to Southeast Asia. His final destination: Vietnam.

PART
TWO

PART
TWO

Chapter 3

THE PLANE WASN'T just dirty, it was filthy. It smelled of mildew, dry urine, and something else Casey couldn't define. She was soaking from her own perspiration, her uniform so wet she could wring out the hem. Her girdle was just as wet, chafing her each time she moved. She'd never been more miserable in her life. She knew her own sweat was adding to the obnoxious odor in the plane, so she tried breathing through her mouth the way the others were doing. It didn't help.

It was a day of mishaps. This was the third plane she'd boarded so far, and she had yet to make it to a runway. The first plane was a cargo plane with engine trouble; the second developed a fuel leak; and this one, Casey was certain, was put together with spit and glue. She'd been aboard for the past three hours along with four other nurses and seven enlisted men returning from R & R. Up front were three doctors and two officers playing gin rummy and drinking warm beer. When they took time out to lower their bottles, they cursed the army and Southeast Asia, their voices carrying to the back of the plane.

Earlier in the day her small group had been cheerful, chatty, talking about Officer's Training School, the enlisted men's R & R, and, of course, home. For the most part they were a happy group, until they boarded this last plane, and then fatigue had finally set in. But Casey couldn't sleep. She felt cranky and grumpy and wanted to tell the VIP's up front to shut up. She wanted to get off the damn plane and walk around and take off her girdle. She wanted a cold soda pop and something to eat. What she didn't want was another cigarette, because the air was already so foul she could hardly breathe.

Wake Island, the last stop before Vietnam. They were waiting for another VIP, and he was three hours late. Whoever the son of a bitch was, Casey hoped he broke both his legs when he came aboard.

A sudden shout went up from the men behind Casey when a stewardess came aboard the MAC plane contracted out to the Flying Tigers. She was a pretty girl and she was young, and just as damp and sweaty-looking as everyone else. Casey watched as one of the officers reached out to pat her rear end. She swiveled, swatted at his hand, and dressed him down loud enough for the whole plane to hear. Casey felt like cheering. Catcalls and disgruntled boos from the men behind her set her teeth on edge. God, she was tired.

"Listen up, everyone. We'll be taking off in thirty minutes. We're waiting for the men from Travis to get here. We're going to need every one of these seats, so clear off your gear to make room. I'm sorry about the delay, but the plane from Travis was late. Hang on, guys," she said directly to Casey and the others seated behind her. "They're loading on some cold soft drinks and I'll serve them as soon as we get airborne."

"Is it always this hot?" Casey muttered.

"This is nothing, wait till you get to Vietnam," the stewardess muttered in return. "We have some magazines on board, would any of you like one?" She had no takers. Casey slumped down on the seat and covered her face with her hanky. She had to sleep or she was going to die sitting in this plane. She tried every trick she knew to relax enough to sleep. She was dozing off when a stampeding band of boisterous young men, not more than nineteen, came aboard. Casey felt rather than saw a body take the seat next to hers. He was young, blond, and smelled soap-and-water clean. When she removed the hanky from her face for a better look, she got a whiff of his hair tonic. Casey sighed deeply as she settled back in her seat, and she said a little prayer asking her God to protect the young soldier. A moment later she was sound asleep.

CAPTAIN MAC CARLIN climbed the steps of the plane, his face grim. The good old army credo, hurry up and wait. Bull*shit*!

Mac's eyes raked the brass in front of the plane. He could tell at a glance he was outranked by three majors and one full colonel, and ripped off a salute before he stowed his gear. He hadn't had any sleep for almost forty-eight hours, needed a shower and a shave, was no longer creased and pressed. His only consolation was that none of the others looked any better than he did. He felt like bellowing, "Let's get this show on the road!" but merely slid into his seat and buckled up. He was asleep the moment he closed his eyes. Fifteen minutes later the plane was airborne.

THE FLYING TIGER set down at Tan Son Nhut Airport in Saigon at three-thirty A.M. The flight attendant had both doors open: the rear door for the enlisted men and nurses, the front for the brass and doctors. Mac was the last to leave the forward section of the aircraft.

"Jesus," was all he could say when the heat and humidity smacked him in the face. He smelled rotting vegetation. He took a minute to orient himself as he tried to breathe through his mouth.

He was aware of a line of school buses, military buses, and young lieutenants with clipboards. He gagged from the putrid air as he watched the gaggle of enlisted men head toward the row of buses, and wondered how they knew which one to take.

A second lieutenant had started toward him and was rattling off Mac's name when he saw her. He didn't stop to think; he didn't stop to consider. His heart leaped to his mouth, and he shouted, "Casey!" He dropped his gear, his heart thundering in his chest. It couldn't be, he thought. He was making a fool of himself. God simply didn't make coincidences like this. He didn't care, he had to see for himself.

The young woman, whoever she was, was turning. In a heart-beat he'd know if it was really her. Who else in the whole world had that buttery-yellow hair? He pushed his visored cap far back on his head, needing every bit of help to see her face in the white light glaring off the tarmac.

Her smile was like a sunburst. "Mac!" she cried joyously. "It *is* you!"

They both started to talk at once. "I called all the hotels ... I went to this all-night French movie house ... I waited until I couldn't wait any longer ... I saw all these French movies so I would have something to talk to you about ... I'm sorry about the phone number ... I tried everything I could think of ... There were no openings at Walter Reed ... I missed you by five minutes ..."

The drivers of the buses revved their engines.

"Captain, on board now! This is the army, *sir*!"

Mac turned to the voice calling him. He held up his hand. He couldn't lose her again.

"Where are they sending you?" There was desperation in his voice. He didn't care if they court-martialed him.

"I don't know. The major has my orders. Where are you going?"

"Long Binh. Contact the USO here in Saigon and let them know where you are. I'll find you." He wanted to kiss her, to take her in his arms. "I'll find you," he said again before he turned to run for the bus waiting for him.

"I'm sorry," Casey muttered to the woman at the steps to her bus.

"Sorry isn't going to do it, Lieutenant. You're in the army and you obey orders. You have no personal life now. You've held up this bus for ten minutes. You disobeyed a direct order when I told you to get aboard."

Casey bristled. The woman wore the rank of a major. Right now, right this minute, she didn't care if she was a general. "I'm a nurse, Major, not a soldier. I said I'm sorry." Her back stiff, she climbed on board the bus and immediately craned her neck out the open window. In the eerie yellowish light she thought she could see Mac leaning out. She waved wildly. She heard him shout, "Don't forget the USO!" As if she would forget.

"I won't!" she screamed.

"That will be enough of *that*! You will conduct yourself like the officer you are," the major said coldly.

Casey had learned a lot in the brief time she spent at OTS. She had also picked up a lot of American slang, like "fuck you" for anger or frustration, and her favorite utterance was, "oh shit." Now, she mumbled both phrases under her breath, to her seatmate's amusement. The one thing she hated was taking orders. She wondered if this hefty-looking woman with the steely eyes could do anything to her. When in doubt, she thought, retreat.

Casey forced a sickly smile to her lips. "I'm sorry, Major, but that was my fiancé, and we were separated in San Francisco. He didn't know I was coming here," she lied. Tears rolled down her cheeks, right on cue. She instantly had the sympathy of everyone on the bus, but they were all military enough not to verbalize it.

The officer's voice was as crusty as her attitude as she introduced herself as Major Patricia Ellison. "Welcome to Vietnam, girls. As I call your name raise your hand."

After the major went down the list, and several women asked questions which were rushed aside, they heard the sound of gunfire. "Is that thudding . . . artillery fire?" one of the giddy young girls asked fretfully.

"Yes. It's H and I fire, harassment and interdiction. Our guns. You'll get used to it."

She's wrong, Casey thought, I'll never get used to it. Neither would the giddy young girl. She already looked too white-lipped and frightened. If she was nineteen, she was old.

Casey knew she was the oldest, the one with the most nursing experience. The six young women riding with her were fresh out of nursing school.

She hadn't made friends with any of them on the way over. They were too young, too silly, too self-absorbed to take seriously.

The bus pulled to a stop and the GI's in the back trooped down the aisle and walked into the night.

The major steadied herself by clutching a seat as the bus lurched off. "You'll be spending the next few hours at one of Saigon's BOQ's—bachelor officer quarters," she said. "In the morning, after breakfast, there will be a thirty-minute orientation and you'll be given your assignments. Then you'll be taken back to the airport to board your individual flights to your duty stations."

Casey was the last one off the bus. She followed the others and was reminded of a row of ducks trailing after their mother. She noticed the young girls weren't the only ones wearily shuffling their feet. The major looked as tired as any of them.

So this was Saigon. Casey stared at the stark-looking administration building and then at the departing bus. She felt the urge to spit, to try and get the awful stench out of her nose and mouth. In her life she'd never smelled anything so foul. Cow manure, sulfur, rotting vegetation, and something else—death. Rotting flesh.

She accepted a cup of strong, black coffee. She wanted a shower, would have killed for one, along with a clean change of clothes. She wondered if she had time to go to the bathroom and apply some Mum deodorant. Having gotten a whiff of the other girls, she knew she smelled just as bad. Clean underwear and some sweet-smelling talcum powder would be such a luxury, and she wanted to take off the rubber girdle; it was killing her.

Casey took her seat among the other girls and sipped the bitter coffee. At least the room was air-conditioned. It looked like any other administration building, with curtainless windows and hard plastic furniture. The fluorescent lighting was so bright that the glare off the stark white walls hurt her eyes. She concentrated on the gray floor. A captain stood in front of them, her arms full of clipboards and manila folders. The young girls riddled the officer with questions. Casey listened with half an ear, her thoughts on Mac. She'd found him. He'd looked so happy to see her, had risked a reprimand from his superiors to run after her. He'd been on the same plane, and she hadn't known it. He must have come aboard in the Philippines when they put down to refuel. Or had he gotten on at Wake Island? Not that it mattered now. For that one instant, he looked as if he wanted to take her in his arms and kiss her.

She squirmed, the girdle cutting into her waist. How handsome he looked, even with his growth of beard. She'd smelled his sweat, been *that* close to him. Or had she actually touched him? She couldn't remember. He'd said he would find her. She believed him implicitly.

"Why is it so hot here?" someone whined.

The captain, who was powdered, creased, and polished, allowed herself a small smile. "You're in-country now. It's ninety degrees Fahrenheit, with ninety percent humidity. I'd be lying to you if I told you you'll get used to it. You won't."

"Are the hospitals air-conditioned?" the same person asked.

The captain allowed a second small smile. She shook her head. The young nurse groaned.

The following ninety minutes were spent listening to brief descriptions of the various evac hospitals where each of them was to be assigned. Casey was going to the 85th, in some place called Qui Nhon.

She felt terribly old when one of the young nurses started to cry. "I get heat rashes, you know, something that looks like measles. I have to stay dry and powdered or I itch."

Casey almost laughed. The captain did laugh. The girl cried again.

They were huddled together like sets of frightened Bobbsey twins. If the captain didn't step in and reassure the young nurses, there was going to be a revolt, Casey thought. Evidently the captain was thinking the same thing.

"Now listen up, girls, you're here to do a job. You're in the army, and you're here to take care of our young men, and that's exactly what you're going to do. Now, pull yourselves together.

"Adams, you'll be leaving first. You have exactly fifty minutes to wash up, grab some breakfast, and board the bus for the airport, where you'll take a C-130. That's a transport plane." She pointed down the hall to where the rest rooms were. Casey sprinted off, her travel bag flapping against her legs. Thank God, she finally had a chance to take off her girdle.

Inside the lavatory she hiked up her skirt and peeled the rubbery girdle down over her legs. She tossed it into the trash can next to the sink. For as long as she lived, she would never, ever wear a girdle again. She rummaged in her bag for panties and almost groaned when she realized they were rayon tricot. They would be just as clingy. She doused herself with Lily of the Valley talcum powder.

The water running from the faucet was light brown and

warm. It smelled foul. She wondered what would happen if she brushed her teeth or stuck her head under the water. She'd been told never to drink it. She settled for brushing her hair, which was a mass of tight, damp ringlets plastered against her head.

The captain seemed a nice sort, Casey thought, as she rolled on garters for her stockings, perhaps nice enough to take a message to the Saigon USO. She'd have to lie again and say Mac was her fiancé. She hoped that would make the message more important, less likely to get lost in the shuffle.

Casey headed for the makeshift buffet in the room next to the one in which they'd spent the last two hours. The girls were munching on sweet, sticky buns and drinking orange juice. For some reason, Casey thought there would be eggs or pancakes. Now she realized how stupid the thought was. She went down the line, ignoring the buns and doughnuts. She settled for a glass of orange juice and a cigarette she really didn't want. She carried them over to the table where the captain was going through a pile of papers. If they hadn't been about the same age, Casey didn't know if she would have had the nerve to make her request. The captain looked up and smiled warmly. Casey explained the situation.

"I'll be glad to do it. I go off duty at seven. I'll drop it off on the way to my hooch. By the way, my name is Sue Collins."

"Casey Adams." She took a seat and nodded in the direction of the whispering nurses. "Seems a nervous group."

Sue shrugged. "I wish they wouldn't send us the young ones. Very few of them can handle it. They're fresh out of school, and most of them have never seen operating room duty. The ones with experience prefer to work at home. On the other hand, we have some nurses here who are on their third tour. It's hard to leave, and quite a few come back because they're so desperately needed by the young kids who come in all shot to hell. Wait till you meet some of those crazy medevac pilots."

"Medevac?"

"They fly out the wounded in helicopters patched together with spit and mud. They call themselves dust-off pilots."

"You have great affection for them, by the look in your eyes."

"I should—I've been dating one for about a year. His name is Rick. Of course, I only get to see him about once a month, and then he gets antsy to get back to the kids out in the bush."

"Does he fly into Qui Nhon? I can give him a message if he does. You could write it out. You pass on mine and I'll pass on yours."

"Deal." Sue laughed as she scribbled off a huge I LOVE YOU on a piece of tablet paper. Casey slipped it into her flight bag. "Rick's regular schedule is Da Nang to Chu Lai and sometimes Quang Ngai. He hits Qui Nhon at least once a week. But what about your guy?"

"He's kind of special. He didn't know I was coming here. At first I wanted to go to Walter Reed to work, but they were full up, the recruiter said, so I volunteered for Vietnam. We met on the tarmac. He was on the same plane, and I didn't even know it."

"Good luck to you both." Sue looked at her watch. "It's time for you to leave. Great talking to you. Good luck, and remember what I said about Pleiku, about it being cooler up there in the highlands. Give Rick a hug for me if you see him."

"Will do," Casey said holding out her hand. "Thanks."

"You bet. Now the hard part starts, convincing those babes they're going to love it over here. See you around."

Casey made her way through the huge double doors, her cases heavy in her hands. She felt herself assaulted almost immediately by the foul, humid air. If all of Vietnam smelled like this, she was going to get very tired breathing through her mouth, she thought as she shoved her cases aboard the bus.

Exhausted, she slumped down in a worn, cracked leather seat whose stuffing lay in huge patches on the floor, half of which was rotted away. What was left was so rusty that Casey was afraid to put her feet down for fear she and the seat would fall through to the tarmac.

The bus stopped twice, but no one got on. Each time, the driver cursed, ground the gears, spit on the steering wheel, and cursed again, at which point the bus squealed to life.

The plane, even at this early hour, was full of GI's. They whistled appreciatively when she climbed aboard. She smiled and nodded as they helped her aboard. She'd never seen so many willing hands.

"We've been waiting for you, blondie." One of the soldiers grinned, freckles dancing across the bridge of his nose. "Guess you're the VIP."

"Me? I'm a nurse!"

"Then you're it. We've been waiting for almost an hour. It's not that any of us are in a hurry to get where we're going, but it's goddamn hot in here, as you can see."

"I'm terribly sorry. The bus broke down twice. The driver had to . . . to spit on it and make all kinds of noises before it would work again."

"Oooh, la-la, you're French. She's French, guys!" The freckle-faced young soldier laughed.

"You're supposed to be sitting up front since you're a VIP," a second GI said tightly.

"That's almost funny." Casey smiled. "I would like very much to stay back here, if you don't mind." It was obvious to Casey that some *did* mind. She probably reminded them of their sweethearts back home. She realized no offense was meant.

"First time in Nam?" someone asked. Casey nodded.

"Where you headed?" another asked.

"Qui Nhon. Do you know it?" Several of the GI's nodded.

"You going to the 85th Evac or the 67th?"

"The 85th."

"Hang on, we're lifting off," someone said.

"But . . . the plane is still open," Casey squawked as the ground gave way beneath the plane.

"This ain't Orly Airport in France, honey, this is Vietnam," a voice said sarcastically.

Casey squeezed her eyes shut. *Mon Dieu*, what had she gotten herself into? Buses that have no floors, planes that have no doors, air that smells like death. And Mac. The moment she opened her eyes, a few of the GI's clapped their hands. "Welcome to Southeast Asia, Lieutenant. Now, guys, let's give her the real skinny on this godforsaken piece of shit called Vietnam."

Casey listened as they told her horror stories of their time in-country. After a while she swallowed hard and her eyes filled with tears. She looked around at the group of faces. They were so young, most of them in their late teens. Youthful bodies and eyes as old as God's.

"Do you ever write home?" she blurted.

Home. It was the magic word. Even the sarcastic young man who had snarled at her smiled. Home. She learned about Edison, New Jersey; Hastings, Pennsylvania; Raleigh, North Carolina; Salisbury, Maryland; and a host of other states she'd studied in her American geography class a long time ago. She heard about moms and dads, sisters and brothers. She envisioned gowns worn to senior proms by girls with names like Carol, Patty, Debbie, and Connie. She found herself asking all the right questions and making all the right comments. When the talk switched to their various pets, she found herself choking up. She listened to the good-natured arguing about cats versus dogs until one youngster said he had a dog and a cat who were best friends. They were quiet after that, their thoughts far away.

Home.

Casey felt fear clutch at her heart. How many of these young men would survive to return home?

Ten minutes later the soldiers began to stir. Casey roused herself, straining to look out the open end of the plane. They were flying low. She was aware again of the awful stench of the country. She started to breathe through her mouth the way the soldiers were doing.

The freckle-faced youth grabbed for his gear. "This is Cam Ranh Bay, we get off here. The other guys," he said, pointing to six GI's who were dozing, "are going on to Quang Ngai, north of where you're going. Good luck, Lieutenant."

"Good luck to all of you," Casey said with a tremulous smile. "And remember, I don't want to see any of you in my hospital." She wagged a playful finger in the freckle-faced soldier's face.

"Yes, ma'am."

She watched them straggle off the tarmac carrying M-16's. She'd recognized the guns from one of her basic training classes. A major had shown the class how to load the weapon, but no one had been permitted to touch it. She wondered if Mac would be carrying one.

Casey closed her eyes and daydreamed about meeting Mac somewhere, anywhere, in the lush jungles. Maybe even Saigon. Her mind weaved exotic fantasies, so exotic she felt her neck and ears grow warm. She was feeling something she'd never felt or experienced before, and she *liked* what she was feeling. How long would it be before she saw the handsome captain again? Months, weeks, days . . . hours? The worst scenario would be months. But whatever it turned out to be, she would have to live with it. She was in the army now, and it controlled her life. Damn.

Casey picked at the loose stuffing on the seat, shredding it between her fingers, while fantasies about Mac Carlin consumed her thoughts. Then she felt the plane begin its descent into Qui Nhon.

The moment Casey stepped off the plane, the heat slapped at her, circled her, cut off her breathing, and then wrapped itself around her like a thousand steaming blankets. She gasped, reeling. A hand reached out and then another.

"Welcome to Vietnam," someone said.

If one more person said those words, she was going to jam them up their sweaty butts. She nodded curtly.

"I need a bath," she said to the chief nurse, who identified herself as Major Maureen Hagen.

"Don't we all! The bath will have to come later. I hate to do this to you, but we need you in the O.R. Follow me and scrub up," she ordered.

"Wait," Casey said, digging in her heels. "I've had hardly any food or sleep in four days. I'm in no condition to work in an operating room."

"That's a very nice story, Lieutenant. Now, let me tell you mine. We're short-handed, and the operating room is full of young boys who might die. So move your ass and move it now."

Casey almost ran to keep up with her, and when they reached

the O.R., Casey gasped in horror at what she saw. This wasn't, it couldn't be a hospital. It was too primitive.

"Scrub! You'll assist Dr. Farrell. He's at the third table from the rear. If I see one tear in your eye, Lieutenant, you will work double shifts. What that means over here is you will be working twenty-four hours a day instead of twelve or fourteen." She pointed a finger, with a chewed-off nail, to a corner. "Gowns, masks, caps. Booties are in the bin."

"Yes, ma'am," Casey said. *She looks just as tired as I feel,* Casey thought. *This* was not what she expected. She'd stupidly expected a gleaming, sterile hospital with adequate facilities. This place, she thought grimly, was more like a butcher shop. Stretchers were constantly moving in and out. "Next!" bellowed a corpsman, sending a chill through her body. An assembly line. *Mon Dieu!*

Casey squared her shoulders. "I'm ready, Major." The major's eyes were kind, Casey noticed, and knew intuitively that the major had shed tears.

"I'm glad you're here, Lieutenant. Now a word of advice. We have at least ten hours of surgery to get through. It'll be easier on you if you don't look at their faces."

Casey tied her mask in place. "Yes, Major. I'm ready."

She decided a moment later, when she walked over to Luke Farrell's operating table, that she wasn't ready at all. She did as the major instructed and avoided looking at the patient's face. Instead, she looked at the boy's feet, and saw to her horror that his left foot was hanging by a tendon.

Casey's head buzzed and she knew she was as close to fainting as she'd ever been in her life. She was aware of the intense heat, and of the smell of blood—blood on the floor, blood on the walls, blood staining the surgical garb, spurting blood. Blood everywhere. From somewhere to her left she could hear a conversation about last year's Army-Navy football game, and someone else was complaining about needing a root canal. Suddenly all sound ceased. She swayed, her knees started to buckle. She knew she would have blacked out and fallen into the pool of blood on the floor if the doctor hadn't given her a direct order.

"I need to cut it *now*, Lieutenant! Scissors!"

Her voice returned, somewhere between a squeak and a yelp. "Yes, sir." She reached for the surgical scissors. If she lived to be a hundred, a thousand, she would never forget the sound of the boy's foot hitting the galvanized bucket at her feet. Then she looked at the patient's face. "I don't think he's ever shaved," she said in a strangled voice.

"I think you're right," the voice behind the mask agreed. "I'm Luke Farrell, glad to have you, Lieutenant . . ."

"Casey Adams, sir."

"Your papers said you're an experienced O.R. nurse."

"Yes, sir." Casey's eyes followed the doctor's hands, anticipating which instrument he would need next. She slapped it into his hand with cool efficiency. "Please don't say welcome to Vietnam," she said tightly.

"Clamp! I wouldn't welcome my worst enemy to this hellhole. Suture!"

"Where'ya from, Casey?" Luke Farrell asked as he tied off a bleeder. "Is that a French accent?" There was amusement in his voice. Casey wondered where it came from, considering their circumstances.

They talked as they worked, neither of them looking at the patient's face. It was an hour before Luke said, "Close, Lieutenant, I need to hit the latrine and grab a quick smoke. We're permitted ten-minute breaks. If I hustle, I might be able to sleep for six minutes."

"Close!" Casey said in stupefied amazement.

"Yeah, you know, sew him up and prep the next guy."

"Well, I . . . listen, Doctor, I never . . . I only . . ."

"Worked in a civilized hospital under the best conditions. You only assisted in gall-bladders, tonsilectomies, appendectomies, etcetera, etcetera. Honey, over here you're going to be doing everything. You've eaten into my ten minutes, so I'd get cracking if I were you. I get real cranky when my nurses don't follow orders."

"Yes, sir," Casey bleated.

Stripped of his mask, the doctor looked so weary Casey wanted to tell him to go to sleep, that she would operate for him. He had beautiful eyes, warm and caring, but frustration burned in them. She wondered how many men had died on his table today.

He rubbed his beard stubble and stretched his neck muscles. "I always tell my nurses to pretend the guy on the table is her brother. I pretend he's my father and give him my best shot."

"Yes, sir," Casey said, preparing to close the gaping belly wound on the young man. "Anything else, sir?"

"Nope. Unless you'd like to go over to the Officers' Club after this shift and grab a beer with me. We can tell each other how tired we are before we fall asleep on the bar."

Casey nodded.

"By the way, I'm the chief surgeon here."

Casey nodded again.

"I also like neat stitches, or as neat as you can make them in up to ten minutes. Pretend you're doing embroidery for your mother. It all comes down to home and memories," he said, so wearily that Casey wanted to reach out and pat his shoulder.

The next eight hours were a nightmare for Casey. She didn't know where she found the strength to stay on her feet. Each time a new patient was littered to the operating table, she wanted to cry. Luke, she noticed, had tears in his eyes several times. "Wipe," was all he said toward the end, when he lost two patients, one after the other.

On the wall by the door was a chart checked off by a corpsman. An O with a line through it meant a patient was alive. An X meant a patient was alive with a fifty-fifty chance of making it. A minus sign meant the patient had died. A plus sign meant the soldier was to be airlifted to Thailand. The moment Casey spied the chart, she hated it. There were too damn many minus signs. She shifted her mental gears then, determined to do her best as long as she could function and stand on her feet.

When it was finally over, she sagged against the wall. She was certain she couldn't move to take even one step. Her feet were swollen to twice their size, her ankles were chafed raw, and her neck was so stiff she couldn't move it to either side. Her ears buzzed from the surgical saw used to amputate limbs.

"I feel like my eyeballs have been boiled in formaldehyde," she muttered to Luke Farrell.

"That's about as apt a description as I've heard. Come on, I promised to buy you a drink. Whatever you do, don't take off your shoes, or you won't get them back on."

"I already figured that out for myself," Casey said tartly as she trotted after him.

THREE CHUGS INTO the long-necked bottle, Luke Farrell said, "You did good in there." Casey felt as if she'd just been given the Distinguished Service Cross. She tried to square her shoulders, tried to smile to show her appreciation. She swigged from the beer bottle. Nothing in the world ever tasted so good, and she hated beer.

He was tall, lanky really, and he definitely wasn't handsome Casey decided as she eyed Luke Farrell over the rim of the beer bottle. Freckles, a shade lighter than his rusty red hair, marched across his cheekbones. She'd bet a nickel he hated his freckles. His ears, she decided, were a smidgin too large for his long, narrow face and in no way detracted from his warm, dark eyes. His hands were strong; beautiful, capable hands with clipped nails. Perfect surgeon's hands. If she were to describe him to Nicole, she would say Luke Farrell was ordinary with beautiful hands and eyes.

She liked him. Liked him a lot.

"Eat a couple of those hard-boiled eggs. The protein will pep you up a little. Two more," he said to the bartender.

They were on their third beer when the club came alive. Nurses and officers in clean fatigues walked in, ordered beer and pretzels and carried them to spindly tables made from bamboo. Conversation hummed as Ping-Pong paddles clicked plastic balls back and forth. It looked civilized, Casey thought blearily. The eggs were giving her gas. Her stomach rumbled alarmingly. She felt sick and said so.

"Time for you to hit the sheets," Luke muttered out of the corner of his mouth. "I'll carry on here." He ordered another beer for himself.

"Aren't you going to sleep too?"

"Sleep? I can't sleep. I never sleep. What I do is drink myself into a stupor. When I actually *sleep*, I dream about all those kids who got away from me, so I don't sleep. You want to hear something real fucking silly?' Casey nodded, knowing she wasn't going to like what she was about to hear. "I'm an abdominal surgeon. That was my speciality back in the States. I couldn't hack the hours and the mess, so I went into dermatology. It's a nine-to-five job, dermatology. Man, I was a real whiz on acne and heat rashes. People don't die from acne. None of my patients ever died. Now they all die. I write letters, you know. That's the hard part, writing the letters. I don't have to do it, but I'm the last person to see the . . . patient. Sometimes they say something. Parents have a right to know their son's last words."

"I could help you," Casey said quietly.

Something shimmered in Luke's eyes. "Yeah," he said softly. "We can do it at night when we can't sleep. Yeah, yeah."

There were more people in the club now, although the Ping-Pong table was quiet. Conversation was muted, almost hushed. Casey heard the number seven mentioned as she walked toward the door, every step pure agony. Seven young men had died today, and she didn't even know their names. That meant Luke Farrell was going to write seven letters.

Luke Farrell stared after Casey and wondered if she would be different from the rest. All his other nurses had taken off like scalded cats as soon as they could put in for transfers. But with this one, there was one second, one moment, when their eyes met and he thought he saw his destiny in her eyes. Christ, he should be a writer. How corny could a guy get? He guzzled from the beer bottle, draining it, then held up a hand to signal a refill.

Luke tilted his chair back against the wall. What in the goddamn hell was he doing here? It was a question he asked himself every day, and every day he gave himself the same answer. He was here because of Jimmy Oliver, Jimmy Oliver's mother, an old Mustang, and his own shame.

Jimmy Oliver mowed his mother's lawn. Jimmy Oliver raked his mother's leaves in October, and in the winter Jimmy Oliver shoveled his mother's snow. Jimmy Oliver delivered the *Pittsburgh Press* to his mother, never just throwing it in the driveway, but climbing off his bicycle to walk to the front porch, where he folded it neatly before stuffing it in the mailbox. Jimmy Oliver bought his old Mustang with the money he saved from all that lawn mowing, leaf raking, snow shoveling, and paper delivering.

The day Jimmy Oliver turned eighteen he'd put the Mustang up on blocks, kissed his girlfriend Katy, hugged his mother, shook his father's hand, and left for basic training in the army. He ended up in Vietnam. Luke knew this because Mrs. Oliver felt it her duty to tell him about Jimmy's last good-bye.

The last time he saw Jimmy Oliver was the day his casket was lowered into a grave in the Squirrel Hill Cemetery.

Harriet Oliver, Jimmy's mother, had looked at Luke with tear-filled eyes and said, "There was no doctor for him. He bled to death. Jimmy's buddy wrote and told us." Harriet had lunged at him, and Jim Senior had to physically pull her away while Katy cried great gulping sobs.

"You're a doctor," Harriet shrieked, "you treat pimples. *Pimples.* My son . . . my only son died . . . and you treat pimples. It's not fair."

Two days later the Ford Mustang was in his mother's driveway covered with a tarp. As far as he knew, it was still there.

Luke hadn't done anything stupid right then, like closing up shop and hustling his butt over here. He'd waited *three whole days* before he notified all his patients he was closing his office and referred them to various colleagues who thrived financially on skin problems. Then he'd driven over to his mother's, removed the tarp from the Mustang and vacuumed the interior. He spent all day washing, waxing, and compounding the car. When he was done, he put the tarp back on and cried. The rest was history.

Luke raised his hand again. Maureen Hagen, the chief nurse, slapped a bottle of warm beer into his hand. She moved away, saying nothing.

The warm beer rushed down his throat. He was here because of all the Jimmy Olivers . . . for all the Harriet Olivers.

Damn, this Casey Adams had nice eyes . . . good hands. He wondered what it would feel like to touch her yellow curls. He could feel his hands start to itch. He lit a cigarette, then removed his boonie hat, shook it out then settled it on his rusty hair. His night was over. He counted the beer bottles before he let his chair thump back on all four legs. Maybe he could sleep tonight. Maybe he would see Casey Adams's face instead of Jimmy Oliver's before he sank into oblivion.

Maybe.

THE MOMENT CASEY was outside in the humid air, the eggs and beer spewed from her mouth. Gasping and retching, she staggered down the path to her quarters. Off in the distance she could hear a sort of coughing sound she'd never heard before: mortars. And of course the crackling noises had to be rifle fire.

Inside her room Casey looked over her army cot with its inch-and-a-half mattress, her footlocker, dresser, and regular locker with distaste. She peeled back the blanket and sat down. The sheets were wet. So was the blanket and pillow. She didn't care. She tugged at her shoes, each tug pure torture. Her feet seemed to swell even more, right before her eyes. The relief of freeing them was exquisite.

"Welcome to Vietnam," she murmured before she settled into a sleep so deep she didn't wake until she felt someone shake her to wakefulness.

"Lieutenant, I am Lily Gia. Major Hagen has assigned me to you for the day. It's almost time for breakfast. I'll show you where the shower is, and I've brought some shoes that are a couple of sizes bigger than yours. We're expecting a big push in a few hours, and you're going to be on your feet again. I will ready a footbath for you when you get out of the shower. It will help a little. They have pancakes at the mess hall. You won't die from the coffee." She smiled warmly.

The Vietnamese girl was so pretty, Casey thought, with her silky black hair and flawless complexion. She had the most beautiful smile she'd ever seen. Tiny little pearls gleamed at her ears, as pearly white as her perfect teeth. Model pretty, except she was tiny, elfin really, with long, slender hands, perfect for playing the piano or doing surgery. "Are you a nurse?" she said around the stench from her mouth.

"Yes, but I wish to be a doctor. Can you stand, Lieutenant?" she asked, her fine straight black brows feathering upward in concern.

"I can do whatever I have to do," Casey said through clenched teeth.

Lily was stronger than she looked. She couldn't weigh more than one hundred and five pounds, yet here she was, holding Casey upright the moment her knees buckled.

Somehow Casey managed to get to the shower. Lily handed her a wicker basket that she upended and sat on. She lathered, scrubbed, and rinsed. She repeated the process four times before she felt clean enough to get out of the shower. She used three-quarters of the can of talcum powder she'd brought with her. Her clothes stuck to her body the moment she put them on. With Lily's aid she hobbled back to her quarters for the footbath she promised. It was waiting along with a plate of pancakes and a small pot of coffee.

"I made the decision to bring your breakfast here. I hope it was the proper thing to do," Lily said shyly.

"Who cares if it's proper or not? For me, it's the right thing. You speak excellent English, Lily," Casey said, dipping her swollen feet into the white enamel pan. "Oooh, this is wonderful. What's in it?"

"Many things. Local herbs mostly. One hour and the swelling will lessen. Tonight you will soak again, and by tomorrow you will be able to wear your own shoes. It is wonderful, is it not?" Lily asked impishly. "To answer your question, I learned English in New York City."

"I don't think I ever felt anything this good. Do I detect French somewhere in your background?" Casey asked curiously as she attacked her stack of rubbery pancakes.

"I'm half French. My father was Vietnamese, my mother French. I have relatives on my mother's side of the family who live in the United States. They sponsored me, and I studied there for a very long time. I would have stayed on, but I felt my people needed me. Later, God willing, I will return to your country. Do I detect a French accent in your speech, as well, Lieutenant?" she quipped.

"Please call me Casey. Yes, I'm half French and half American. I think, Lily, that you and I will be good friends."

"It is my wish also," Lily said shyly. "I visited many places while I was in the United States. Your country is wonderful. There are so many places to go. I made wonderful friends. I saw the honeymoon place where much water rushes down. It was a memorable sight. Of course I had no one to honeymoon with." She giggled. "I also went to California one summer and saw orange blossoms and a film studio. One does not need to wear perfume. The air is scented. I loved it. I had many boyfriends," she said with her hands on her hips to make her point. "Do you have a boyfriend?"

Casey laughed. "I don't know. Maybe, sort of, but I'm not sure." She told Lily about Mac Carlin. "I couldn't believe my ears when he called my name. Now, all I have to do is find him or pray he will find me."

"How exciting that you found your love here in my country. My love is from your country. I feel, too, we are destined to become good friends. I feel it here," she said, thumping her chest with her fist. "Tell me, do you like my country?"

"It stinks," Casey said bluntly. "What *is* that smell?"

Lily laughed. "It is the earth. One gets used to it. I truly missed the smell when I went to the United States. When there is no napalm in the air it isn't too bad. You will adjust to it. How do your feet feel now?"

"Much better," Casey sighed happily. "When do we go back on duty? I don't even know what time it is, I forgot to adjust my watch."

"You'll hear the choppers long before they get here. You will have time to dress and report to the O.R. Major Hagen says you are to rest until that time arrives. Is there anything else I can do for you?"

"Just talk to me. Tell me about Dr. Farrell. He's an excellent surgeon."

"The very best, that's why he's the Chief of Surgery. He talks strange sometimes and says . . . funny things. I think it's to hide his feelings. He doesn't want anyone to know the way he feels. I have seen him walking in the middle of the night. He thinks too much of all those young men who have passed on. He cannot free himself of his countrymen. I understand this. One evening when it was quite late and he . . . he wasn't himself, he said his shoulders were heavy with guilt because he wasn't a good enough surgeon. He believes this, but it is not true. He is by far the best surgeon we have."

"Tell me about Major Hagen," Casey said, wiggling her swollen toes in the water.

"She is, how do you say, tough—but fair. She never asks anything of us that she will not do herself. There are only two other nurses besides myself, and now you. It is not enough. We work twelve-hour shifts when there is incoming wounded. You will do your share of ward duty. I must warn you, your heart will never be the same."

"I've never seen anything like yesterday," Casey confided. "At first I didn't think I would make it. I did, though. I really did. Then, listen to this, I ate three hard-boiled eggs and drank three bottles of beer and puked my guts out. Why are these sheets so damp?" she demanded.

Lily chuckled. "It is the humidity. We have local women to do the laundry," Lily explained. "Every day the sheets are laundered, but they always feel damp. You will get used to it."

"It's so much to deal with all at once. I don't know what I expected, but I do know this isn't it. Is Saigon like this?"

"Heavens no. Saigon is a beautiful city. My parents live there. Both of them are doctors, educated in Thailand. I have three sisters and three brothers. I am the youngest. What about your family?"

Casey told her about her life in Paris, the grandmother and father she never knew. She spoke of Nicole and Danele and Sister Ann Elizabeth.

"I will take you to Saigon to meet my family if Major Hagen gives her permission. It won't be for a while. We can catch a ride with one of the chopper pilots. You will like Saigon. It is *very* civilized. We can try to locate your lover and go to parties while we wait for him to come to you. It is a wonderful idea, is it not?"

Casey flushed. "He's not my lover."

"He will be." Lily giggled. "It is meant to be, I feel it here," she said, thumping her chest again. "I will bring more coffee." She gathered up the tray with Casey's dishes. When she turned back, her dark eyes were confiding and full of mischief.

"Yes?"

"I . . . I have a lover in Saigon." The words gushed out of her mouth as though held in too long. "He is an American, a doctor. My . . . my parents do not approve. He's much older than I am, almost as old as my brother. He's married," she blurted, lowering her eyes.

Casey dried her feet, wondering what it was she was supposed to say. "Has he made any promises to you?"

Casey felt inept when Lily winced.

"The same promises all the GI's make to Vietnamese girls. They want to marry us, they say, when the war is over. We cook for them, wash their clothes, and go to bed with them. They give us babies and leave to return to their homes, and they do not come back. But Eric isn't . . . Eric is different." Her voice, Casey thought, was too defensive. She knew the girl doubted her lover.

"I'm sure he's all the things you say he is," Casey said kindly.

"I . . . I had to tell someone," Lily said shyly. "You will keep my secret?" At Casey's nod, Lily left with the tray held high over her head.

Casey slid her feet into soft felt slippers, hitched up her fatigues, and ventured outside. She wanted to see, in broad daylight, what her new home was like. On her trip to the shower, she had not glanced right or left. She did both now, drawing in her breath at the lush, dark greenery surrounding the compound. She saw the concertina wire rolled in what looked like hoops along the eight-foot-high fence. To keep her in or keep the VC out? Both, she decided. She hated the sight. The smell, the humidity, was so overpowering, she felt dizzy. She started to breathe through her mouth again. Would she ever get used to this country?

"A bit awesome, eh?" Someone behind her chuckled. Casey whirled.

Luke was still wet from his shower. His rusty curls were slicked back from his head, but he was freshly shaved, and his robe flapped around his bare ankles. He linked his arm through hers.

"Yes," she said. "Where are the flowers? I thought there would be flowers."

"Jesus, I don't know. I never thought much about it, but you're right. I think we should find out right away, before the next push comes in. Heavy casualities are predicted for today. Predicted," he said, "is the same thing as confirmed. It beats the shit out of me how these brass monkeys know almost to the goddamn minute when wounded are due to arrive. They stick pins in some asshole map, and the next thing you know we have two hundred kids coming through here. Those flowers now," he said, slapping at his head, "are going to bother me. Flowers are important. Don't know how that got past me."

The row of Quonset huts came into Casey's line of vision. They were barren-looking, hot and ugly. She wanted to say something about how ugly they were, but she realized Luke already knew. Instead she said, "Do you know a doctor, an American one, in Saigon, named Eric?"

"Jesus, are you going to tell me you already got a thing going with one of our doctors? You just got in-country yesterday. Or are you going to tell me you're asking for Lily?" He didn't wait for her answer. "Want some advice, Casey? Mind your own business and let Lily handle her own affairs."

"I guess that means the Eric in question is married and is stringing Lily along," Casey said. Her face flushed with the reprimand. "When his tour is up he'll go back to the wife and children. She'll probably be pregnant, and he'll never think about her or the child again." Casey searched her mind for an apt description of the situation. "It stinks!" she said succinctly.

Luke laughed. "You know, it sounds worse when you say it with a French accent. Married men have dalliances with young women all the time, here, in the United States, in France. It's what it is, nothing more. And," Luke wagged a finger under her nose, "Lily has been educated in the United States and lived there for a good number of years. She looks young, but she's thirty years old, so that hardly makes her a young girl who doesn't know the score. Take my advice and stay out of it. She won't thank you later on."

Casey watched the doctor when he stopped in his tracks, his ears and eyes cocked toward the horizon. "Here it comes."

He meant Chinooks full of wounded, but she couldn't hear a thing, couldn't see a cloud on the horizon. She was aware of movement as corpsmen with their insignia on their arms rushed outside the Quonset huts. She saw Lily Gia and the chief nurse head for the hospital. She walked as fast as she could, back to her quarters, where she pulled on the shoes Lily had left earlier. When she was outside again, she still couldn't see anything or hear the rotor blades of the incoming choppers.

Five minutes later she was masked, scrubbed, gloved, and gowned and standing alongside Luke Farrell. He was discussing the flower shortage with two other doctors. One of them promised to have some flown in.

"I just want to know who the fuck is going to plant them," Luke grumbled.

"I'll do it if no one else will," Casey said from behind her mask.

"Do you have a color preference?" the doctor closest to Luke's table asked sourly.

"Red. Purple. Yellow," Casey shot back.

"They'll be here by 0800 two days from now."

When the wounded came in, there was no time to think, no time to do anything but concentrate on the surgeon's hands.

She was looking down at Luke's patient. He had a lacerated liver and was going to lose his spleen. He had multiple shrapnel wounds all over his body. He'd lose one of his legs, maybe the other. His stomach steamed upward. "Wipe!" Luke ordered. "Clancy!" he roared. "This guy has a head wound. When I finish, take over!"

Jack Clancy was the neurosurgeon.

"I think we can stabilize this guy," Luke said from behind his mask. "What do you think, Nurse?"

Casey slapped a clamp into Luke's waiting palm. "I say you're right," she replied softly.

They talked then of inane things, about where she was going to plant the flowers and how many would arrive. When they exhausted the subject of flowers, they talked about hot dogs and hamburgers and ice-cold beer. Picnics, Luke said, were his favorite pastime, ants and all.

They were on their fifth patient; the talk moved on to hula hoops and stuffed animals and two-wheeled bicycles. When a deep belly wound arrived, Lily spelled Casey for her ten-minute break.

Outside in the stifling air, Casey lit a cigarette as she let her eyes travel the length and width of the compound. Now was as good a time as any to decide where the flowers would go. Planting flowers was normal. Planting something beautiful in a place so ugly was civilized. She did a mental count of how many plants she would need. Maybe she should just make a big circle and plant everything in the center instead of trying to decorate the mean-looking Quonset huts. She knew in her gut that the plants and the garden would become an obsession. She felt like crying, but of course she wouldn't. That would mean she was weak, and this awful country wasn't for the weak of heart. She said a prayer then, asking for strength and stamina to do what she came here to do. "Don't let me fail," she pleaded silently.

The day wore on. When the shift crawled toward the fourteen-hour mark, Casey felt as if she would drop in her tracks. All she wanted was to lie down on the wet sheets and sleep forever. She no longer cared about her feet. They were as numb as her brain. When she left the O.R. at the end of fifteen hours, she refused to look at the chart by the door. When she peeled off her hospital clothes, she saw dried blood on her arms. She wondered whose blood it was.

Casey headed straight for the shower. She stood under the spray, fully clothed. She rubbed at her fatigues, trying to squeeze the water toward her swollen ankles. In a daze she walked back to her room and fell on her cot.

Six hours later she heard the Chinooks directly overhead. She bolted upright, knowing she had five minutes at best to get to the O.R.

She pulled the hospital gown on over the same clothes she'd showered and slept in the night before. Until she pulled on her booties, she hadn't realized she was barefoot.

"I had a dream last night," Luke volunteered.

"I thought you said you never sleep," Casey said in an accusing voice.

"Actually, it was a daydream, okay?" Luke looked down at his first patient. "Jesus Christ!"

Casey glanced at the faceless boy, faceless because there was virtually no face left. She reeled and felt one of the corpsmen's backs push against her own. She recovered immediately.

"Who's doing triage!" Luke barked. "I can't help this kid. I don't fix faces. Ah, shit! Corpsman! On the double, move him out! Next!"

Five hours later Luke said, "As I was saying, I had this dr—this daydream. I was sleigh riding with this kid Jimmy Oliver. I didn't have a sled, so I was using an old rubber tire. Man, did that baby go. I was at the top of this huge hill, back in Pennsylvania, and when we got to the bottom, we sailed right into the South China Sea, tire and all. Is that a dream or what? There we were freezing our butts off, and then at the bottom we slid into ninety-degree water. Neat, eh? Close this guy, Adams. Looks like it's going to be an early shift today. Ten and a half hours. Can't beat that. I'll buy dinner at the club. *After* I fight you for the shower. Remember now, neat stitches."

"Yes, sir."

She was tired, but not as tired as she had been the day before. She was also starving. She was clean, her hair washed, and she added lipstick and a dab of powder to her already damp nose. She rubbed it off when she saw the way it clumped on her skin. Au naturel was the way to go. It had to be. There was no choice. She smiled at her reflection. She was adjusting. Even her feet felt better.

The others were already seated when Casey entered the Officers' Club. Maureen Hagen was seated next to Lily Gia, and next to her were Luke and two other doctors, whom she was finally seeing for the first time without their surgical masks. She wondered whose guest Lily was, or if that protocol wasn't a requirement at the club.

Off duty they were a wholesome group. The talk was about home and friends and favorite foods.

"What I really miss is the change of seasons," Maureen said wistfully.

"Hell, we can fix that right up," a doctor named Sam said brightly. "We're getting some flowers. I put the order in last night. Personally. Flowers will make it summer. Can you deal with summer for a while? We can work on the other seasons as we go along. Anyway, you're about due for R and R, aren't you?" Maureen nodded. "Save it for winter and go to Japan. It gets cold there in winter. That's my contribution for the day, ladies and gentlemen."

"And we do thank you," Luke muttered.

They drank beer and ate stale, soggy pretzels. Their dinner, when it arrived, was something that looked like pepper steak and rice. Luke said it wasn't pepper steak at all. No one, it seemed, knew exactly what it was, because it had no taste. Lily giggled.

The talk was easy, friendly. Casey felt as if she truly belonged somewhere for the first time in her life. Then Luke made a toast. She raised stunned eyes to the group when he said, "To the best O.R. nurse I ever worked with! Think I'll marry her someday!"

"Here! Here!" Brian Breen shouted, raising his glass. Casey flushed. Lily hugged her and Maureen winked slyly in her direction. God, she really belonged. It was a wonderful feeling. Of course, she knew Luke didn't mean it. He was just saying whatever came into his head. Luke Farrell was a loner. The Luke Farrells of the world didn't have time for things like marriage. But she did feel flattered.

They all went on about home for a while, but when the conversation came to Casey, she said, "I just got here. It's too soon for me to think about home. The truth is, I don't have a home to go back to." She told them all about arriving in San Francisco. They listened intently. When she wound down, Brian said, "That's shitful! I come from Waco, Texas, and they're always looking for transplants. Think about it." By the end of the evening she had offers from six other states.

When the clock on the wall said it was 10:45, Maureen decided to call it a night. So did Lily. Brian was asleep on the table and Sam was dancing by himself in the middle of the floor. Tomas had left earlier with a young nurse named Patty something-or-other. Casey looked at Luke, and Luke looked at her. "I know what you're going to ask me. You want me to tell you all about Vietnam, right?"

"How did you know?" Casey asked in awe.

"I can see it in your eyes. You wanted to ask before, but we were all caught up in the home thing, so you put it off. Right?"

"Are you a seer or something?"

"Or something. It took me five days before I started to ask about it. I'll pass on what I was told, howzat?"

"Only if you feel like talking about it," Casey said quietly.

Luke tilted his chair back against the wall. He spoke in a low, even monotone. He's reciting a geography lesson the way I used to do in class, Casey thought. She listened, which was more than she did when the other students were reciting their lessons.

"We're on the Indochinese peninsula, bordered on the north by China, west by Laos and Cambodia, east and south by the Gulf of Thailand, the Gulf of Tonkin, and the South China Sea. North and south, I'd say, stretches it to about a thousand miles, east and west about three hundred thirty miles. In the north it's thick, mountainous jungle. The VC love it there. The climate is monsoonal with lots of floods. Here in the south it's flat, marshy, and muddy. Rice grows well in both the north and south. You're gonna get sick of rice. I'm to the point where I'd rather chew on grass than eat rice."   •

"I'm pretty much a potato person myself." Casey smiled.

"Forget it. No potatoes here. Lots of pepper though. Sweet potatoes, does that count?"

"Ohhh, I love sweet potatoes with lots of butter, pepper, and brown sugar. I could eat them every day."

"Jesus, don't tell that to anyone or you will be," Luke groused. "And you'll get a good case of Ho Chi Minh's revenge." Casey flushed.

"How do you know all this?" Casey asked suspiciously, unsure if Luke was putting her on or not.

"Got it straight from a mama-san who helps out in the orphanage in Da Nang. Since it's her country, she should know, don't you agree?"

"I suppose so. Do many of the Vietnamese speak English?"

"The educated ones do, and French, of course. The nuns in the orphanage speak Vietnamese fluently. They translate for us. Onward and upward . . . the biggest cities in the south are, of course, Saigon, which is very modern, and Da Nang. I've been to them when I can get out of here, which isn't often."

"Is it true that there are a lot of Roman Catholics here?"

"It's true. Taoism and Buddhism too, though everyone is so hell-bent on killing everyone else, it's hard to conceive the religion thing at all. What are you?" Luke asked curiously.

"Roman Catholic, and you?"

"I'm not anything right now. Someday I will be though," Luke said curtly.

"I see," Casey said.

"No you don't see at all. Jesus, I hate it when people patronize me. You don't understand how I cannot have a religion and maybe never have one. Since you think it, why don't you say it?" he snarled.

Casey bristled. It bothered her when this man who played second fiddle to God in the operating room could be so blasé about something so important. She minced no words when she said so.

Luke blinked. "It never pays to argue about religion or politics. I was baptized a Lutheran, does that help?"

"Yes." Casey smiled. "It helps a lot. Listen, thank you for the history lesson. You forgot something though." She grinned.

"And what might that be?"

"You forgot to tell me about the money. Well, don't worry. I already know. It's the dong."

"Dong, schlong, what the hell." When he saw her blush, he knew she knew what the second word meant. "Sorry, that was uncalled for."

"Accepted. I wasn't raised entirely in a convent," she said, though actually, she had only learned the word in the past few days. She'd overheard some enlisted men using it. "Guess I'll see you tomorrow."

"And the day after and the day after that," Luke said morosely.

"Are you going to stay here?" Casey asked curiously as she prepared to leave.

"Yeah, I want to write a letter to a med school buddy of mine in Thailand. I've been trying to coerce him into coming here and helping out, but so far he's resisted my efforts. He's probably the best goddamn plastic surgeon in the world. If Singin Vinh were here today, he could have fixed that kid's face, the one we lost. If I'd been able to save him, Singin could have . . . ah, shit, what difference does it make now?"

He was writing the letter in his head, Casey saw. She ceased to exist for him, and that was all right. Whoever you are, Singin Vinh, she thought, I hope you reconsider and come here to help your friend. She walked out into the hot, sultry night.

"Good night, Casey," Lily called from across the compound.

"Good night, Lily. Sleep tight, don't let the bedbugs bite." She could hear Lily's soft laughter follow her.

Inside her stifling room, Casey lay down on the bed, staring at the ceiling. Maybe she should write some letters herself. She could pen off a note to Mac and give it to one of the chopper pilots to deliver to the Red Cross unit in Vinh Long. It would probably go through three or four pilots before it reached Vinh Long, but if there was a way to get something through, be it supplies, wounded, or messages, the chopper pilots were the ones to trust. A letter to Nicole to ask for cotton underwear would go with the regular mail. She closed her eyes, merely to rest them and think about what she wanted to write to Mac, when she drifted off to sleep and didn't wake until the middle of the following morning.

"No wounded today," Lily said in the mess tent.

"Really! That's wonderful. What will we do all day?"

"Scrub down the operating room, help on the medical floor, write letters for some of the men, read to others. Paperwork," she said, making a face.

"Paperwork!" Casey said, aghast.

"Uh-huh. Loads of it."

It was noon before the chief nurse called a halt to the morning's work schedule. The hospital was clean, the mounds of linen counted and neatly stacked, rounds were over, letters written for the wounded, along with small talk about things back home. It was all under control for the moment, Casey thought as she walked outside into the brilliant sunshine. The sky was a radiant blue, the clouds white and fluffy.

"It's all so quiet," she murmured to Lily. "I don't hear any mortar fire or sniper fire. It's weird. What does it mean?"

"It means both sides are taking a temporary break, I guess. Enjoy the quiet. It won't last long. There's a pond not far from here if you want to go and enjoy the quiet for a while. It's a wonderful little place where you can sit on a blanket and read. I would imagine there are places like it where you come from. All we have to do is tell someone we're going, so they can guard us. It's one of the rules. Until now, we've been so busy I don't think anyone has explained to you that you cannot leave the compound without an escort. It will be nice to have some company today, if you feel like coming with me."

"I'd love it. I have some letters to write. What's for lunch?"

Lily made a face. "Macaroni and cheese and Spam."

"I *guess* I can eat that." Casey grinned.

Lunch was a cacophony of chatter, laughter, the clatter of silverware and plates and shuffling feet, as well as some good-natured jostling which resulted in squeals and giggles from the Vietnamese women who were permitted to eat in the mess hall. Casey enjoyed the easy camaraderie.

She ate two bites of the macaroni and cheese and three of the Spam before she pushed her plate away to concentrate on her coffee, which was black as mud and just as thick.

"Mmm, Army coffee," Luke Farrell said, holding his cup aloft. "It doesn't get any better than this," he added dramatically.

"*Mon Dieu*, I hope not." Casey laughed. When she felt her eyeballs were back to normal, she lit a cigarette. "This is something else I'll get used to, right?" Nobody bothered to answer her.

Luke leaned across the table. "Casey, if you were serious about helping me with the letters, I'd like to start after rounds this evening." Sam looked at Lily. She nodded.

"Did any of you fix the shower?" Major Hagen asked. "Look, I want it done today. I will not have those chopper pilots circling overhead to look at my girls naked in the showers. You gave me your word!"

"It's not our job," the doctors complained in unison. The major rose to her feet to tower over them. "We'll do it, we'll do it," they grumbled good-naturedly. "When the sun goes down. Is that okay?"

"In writing, Doctor," the major said, whipping a small pad and pencil out of her breast pocket. "And don't think for one minute that I don't know you cruds have been standing on the dispensary roof looking down into the shower. You're all damn lucky I haven't turned you in."

"To who?" Luke grumbled. "Anyway, why would you want to do a damn thing like that, Maureen? You should be flattered that the three of you are so desirable. It's a goddamn compliment."

"My ass, Captain! You're all perverts." It was said good-naturedly, but there was a ring in the major's voice that told the men enough was enough. By dusk there would be some kind of roof over the shower enclosure, even if it was patched-together cardboard.

To her nurses Major Hagen said, "Free time till four o'clock. And don't, for God's sake, get sunburned. Casey, wear your boonie hat, but take your helmet with you. Remember, flak vests."

"Yes, ma'am," Casey said.

HER ROUTINE WAS established. As the days wore on, Casey adapted easily to the rules and the routine. She was needed. She'd come here to do a job, and she was doing it to the best of her ability. She was helping save lives. She was making a difference. It no longer mattered that she worked fourteen-hour shifts, slept little and ate less. The blood and the chart by the door were now a part of her life.

April Fool's Day was her one-month anniversary in Vietnam. When she checked off the date on her calendar, she winced. A whole month and there had been no word from Mac. He's never going to find me, she thought sourly.

Several things happened on Fool's Day, as Lily referred to it. A C-130 landed with four nurses aboard. Casey no sooner finished clapping her hands with delight than Maureen Hagen handed her a manila envelope and told her she had ten minutes to pack her gear and board the C-130 with Lily and Luke.

"You're going to Pleiku. A new MASH unit is coming incountry. You'll be working out of tents, supporting the Fourth Division. The Air Force is already there. It's my understanding there will be six nurses in all, six or seven doctors, and a few med techs. This is paradise compared to where you're going. Good luck!"

Numb with shock, Casey threw her things in her duffel and ran to the plane. She wanted to say good-bye, but there was no time. No time to leave word for Mac in case he managed to get word to her here. Would anyone know enough, care enough, to say she was in Pleiku? She gave sound to her thought as the plane lifted off.

"One of the chopper pilots will bring your messages. Anything to do with home or," Luke grinned lasciviously, "love is a priority. It might take a month and it might take two, but if there's a message, you'll get it."

"It's going to be cooler in the mountains," Lily said quietly, to change the subject.

"Lookee here," Luke chortled as he held aloft a copy of the *New York Times*. "It's only eight days old. My old man sends me one issue a week so I know what's going on back home." He held up two other issues that were older. "It doesn't matter what the dates are. It's like fresh news to us, so sit back, ladies, and I'll read to you," he drawled. "Let's do it this way. I'll read the headlines, and if you want the story, I'll read the whole thing, okay?" The girls nodded agreement.

"Okay, here goes. Now remember, feel free to interject at any point." Lily tittered. Casey smiled. "Hedda died! That's Hedda Hopper, known for her hats. She's a . . . was a feisty old broad who was a gossip columnist. If she wrote about something, you could believe it. Titillation at its best. Anyway, she's dead at the age of seventy-five. Sophie Tucker died too. She was seventy-nine. Her theme song was 'One of These Days.' Oh, shit, Buster Keaton died. I loved Buster Keaton. Jeez, he was seventy. I hate this, I goddamn hate this," Luke snarled. "These people died last month, and I'm just reading about it now. It's not right, and it sure as hell isn't fair either. Ah, shit!" There was silence for a moment or two before Luke continued. "Nehru's daughter, Indira, is now the Premier of India. He up and died too. I thought only GI's died over here," he said nastily.

"Hey, girls, did anyone tell you the United States troops launched their biggest offensive of the war? They hit a stronghold twenty miles northwest of Saigon. Where the hell is the Iron Triangle?" he asked Lily.

"In the jungle. It's an American term." She wrinkled her nose at Luke.

"Eight thousand army soldiers were involved? There's nothing about the number of . . . of wounded or dead. Guess they don't print that back home. I can't get over this, there's nothing good in this damn paper. Nothing. Look, here's an article on Chester Nimitz." He raised his eyes over the paper. "He was the commander of the United States Pacific Fleet in World War Two. Guess you girls weren't born then, huh? Anyway, he's dead too."

"What's the good news?" both Casey and Lily heckled.

Luke grimaced. "Guess you didn't hear me. There isn't any. There aren't any funnies in the *Times* either." He read on, his voice a monotone.

"You want more?" he asked, lowering the paper to better observe his captive audience, who by now were sound asleep.

He snorted. "Can't say that I blame you, it's all bullshit." He rattled the paper before he turned to the financial section to compute his net worth. He snorted again, not liking the numbers swimming around in his head. He folded the papers neatly before stuffing them into his bag. Later, on one of his sleepless nights, he would read them from cover to cover, line by line, word by word.

He wished he was home, back in his sterile office with nothing more on his mind than what he was going to do for the weekend: play golf, tennis, or take off fishing. He hated this country, hated this goddamn plane, hated the smell, hated seeing kids die who should be back home playing sandlot ball and chasing girls in flowered skirts.

Luke's face scrunched itself into a grimace so he wouldn't cry. Every time he lost a kid he thought of Jimmy Oliver and Katy in her flowered skirt. His sister Betsy wore a flowered skirt the night before he left, when she went out on a date with Teddy Wyler. Teddy was nineteen. The kid had looked so dreamy-eyed when he told Betsy the skirt looked like a flower garden. His mother was wearing something soft and flowery that night too. He thought then about the flowers Casey and Lily had planted around the compound. If he was a poet or a writer, he would have said there was a riot of color, a profusion of rainbows, something corny like that. In the beginning he'd thought the guys would pick the flowers or laugh and make jokes, but none of them had. He'd seen a lot of them staring down at the different rainbows. He'd seen a misty eye or two. But what really amazed him was the lack of weeds. He'd almost wet his pants the morning he'd seen the company commander stop to pull a weed before leaving the compound. Shit, he didn't even know the names of the flowers Casey planted. Didn't know the names of the flowers on Betsy's or Katy's skirts either.

He thought then about Mary Baker, his office nurse. His sister told him Mary was sweet on him. And why the hell shouldn't she be? He'd cleared up her goddamn acne and hadn't charged her a cent. She'd promised to write him, but so far he'd only gotten one letter, a newsy, chatty page or so about what was going on in Squirrel Hill, Pennsylvania. He'd given a lot of thought to answering the letter, but so far he hadn't. He didn't know what to say in a letter. He couldn't talk about all the kids who died under his hand or the kids he'd saved. He couldn't talk about the arms and legs he'd amputated. How could he tell her there were days he literally swam in blood?

He wondered if Casey had a flowered dress. Mary was pretty, with soft brown eyes and a delightful smile. She liked to kid with him, to kibitz and read him the comics between patients. She was young though, twenty-three, and he was thirty-three. He was too old for Mary Baker, he'd told his mother when she asked him for the thousandth time when he was going to get married and give her grandchildren. Too old. Now he was ancient. Casey was twenty-six. Just the right age.

Luke let his mind roam then because he didn't want to think about how old he was and he didn't want to think about flowered dresses either. Poison ivy. If he could come up with something to take the itch out of ivy poisoning, or sumac, or poison oak, he could make a fortune. One thing about the Vietnamese, they had an herb for everything. He dreamed then about seeing his discovery in *JAMA*. He'd be on the six o'clock news. Casey Adams would be at his side in a flowered dress saying, "I knew he could do it. When it comes to poison ivy, Luke Farrell is your man." His stocks and bonds would soar, his bank account would swell. He could pay off his medical loans and still have enough left to join the Squirrel Hill Country Club and put a down payment on a house. He'd move into larger offices, set up a small company in Saigon to import the herbs that were going to make him a force to be reckoned with in the medical field.

Luke woke with a start, his mental being back in Squirrel Hill, giving his interview on the six o'clock news. "Poison ivy!" he said happily.

"What is that . . . poison ivy?" Lily asked, certain it was some dread disease she'd never heard of.

"What do you mean, you never heard of poison ivy? I need you to know so I can take an herb back home for a cure. Oh, shit, you mean I'm not going to be rich and famous and be written up in *JAMA*?"

"Guess not." Casey giggled as she got her gear together.

"Oh, well, it was a hell of a dream. Best one I've had in months. Best one since coming here, actually. What about pit acne and heat rash? What do you use?" he demanded irritably of Casey.

"Calamine lotion," Casey quipped.

"Smartass," Luke snapped.

"It is a compliment, is it not?" Lily asked in a serious voice, her dark eyes sparkling.

"You bet. By the way, Casey, do you have a flowered dress?" Casey nodded. "Good, I'd hate for my dream to be a total waste.

"Welcome to Pleiku."

Chapter 4

He had seen her. It wasn't a dream.

"Jesus Christ, is it always this hot?" Mac demanded of no one in particular as he took his seat on the bus and swabbed his face with the sleeve of his shirt.

A pressed and creased first sergeant eyed him and said, "Just what the hell was that all about, Captain?"

"My sister," Mac said evenly. "She's a nurse." The lie rolled off his tongue so easily, Mac almost laughed. The surprise on the NCO's face held disbelief.

"To answer your question," he said, "yes, it's always this hot. Actually, relatively speaking, right now it's cool.

"Sit back and enjoy the ride," he barked to the whole bus, taking his seat. "Oh, by the way, welcome to Vietnam."

Mac grinned when he heard a fresh-faced lieutenant mutter, "Up yours, Sergeant."

Christ, she was here. He'd seen her, actually touched her arm. He'd been *that* close to her. Now he knew what people meant when they said time stopped for the barest second. Time and his heart. He'd never seen a smile like hers. It had lit up the airfield. Jesus, the chances of finding anyone the way he'd just found Casey, and under these circumstances, had to be about one in a zillion. He felt giddy, light-headed, not like himself at all. Calm and collected, that was his nature.

The bus ground to a halt in front of the BOQ. The Sergeant stood at the front of the bus, his clipboard in hand.

"Straight through the main door. Briefing room is down the hall to the left. Latrine to the right. Twenty minutes before you can get some shut-eye. Move it, what are you, old ladies with blisters on your feet?"

Ninety minutes later Mac was under the shower singing at the top of his lungs, to the amusement of the other officers. They joined in. The sound wafting through the louvered door sounded, the colonel thought, like a bunch of high-strung cats on a fence.

With a towel wrapped around his middle, and a razor in his hand, Mac looked around at the men and asked, "Do any of you know how I can get a message to my sister? She's a nurse. I said I'd leave word at the USO."

"That sister on the runway?" a baby-faced lieutenant asked, smirking. "Listen, man, don't shit me. If she's your sister, then I'm your brother. Level with me and I'll take your message. I'm catching a ride up to the Continental for a breakfast meeting."

Mac looked at the fast-talking lieutenant and grinned. "Long-lost love and all that. Give me five minutes and I'll scribble off a message. How far is Long Binh from Saigon?"

"Twenty miles or so. Hurry it up, okay? I'm meeting one of my lost loves for breakfast, and she doesn't know what it is to wait around. She'll go off with the first grunt who's willing to buy her steak and sweet potatoes."

A ripe discussion followed, so ripe Mac could feel his ears burn. The lieutenant, Phil Pender, was on his second tour and seemed to know the ropes.

Pender shuffled his feet when he saw Mac pull out a clean uniform shirt with his insignia of rank. "I guess that means you want the info as soon as possible," he muttered.

"It would help, but it isn't an order. I'll be leaving here in about an hour, two at the most. Mac Carlin," he said, holding out his hand. The lieutenant took it and squeezed. Mac's eyes watered, but he didn't relax his grip. He was glad he'd written his message before the bone-crunching handshake. He gave a lazy salute, then attacked his three-day stubble of beard.

Dressed, shaved, cigarette in one hand, coffee in the other, Mac passed up breakfast and walked outside. He wanted to see Saigon in the bright light of day.

He drew deeply on his cigarette. It was hard to believe a war was going on. Saigon, from what he could see, looked like any other city back in the States. He saw Western clothes on the men, though the women mostly wore loose black trousers and long-sleeved shirts. He also saw many women, most of them older, in *ao dai*, their native gowns.

He was aware, too, of the many smells of the city. A green, decayed smell, cheap gasoline, and of course cooking foods, including the powerful fish sauce called *nvoc mam*. And sewage. He hated it. He realized now he'd been breathing through his mouth since he'd come outdoors.

Mac lit a second cigarette from the stub of the one he'd been smoking. There was sound now, from the corner where a peddler was setting up shop and hawking his wares. He was joined by a second man and then a third. From out of nowhere children appeared, neatly dressed in uniforms. School. The thought was so alien, he stopped in his tracks. Just miles away people were killing one another, and still children went to school while their mothers and fathers sold vegetables, fruits, and anything else they could lay their hands on. Dried fish hanging from a smoky rack nearby made Mac gag. No matter what, life went on. He headed back to the building he'd just come out of and wondered what it was. A public building of some kind, that much he could tell. He hurried back inside to take advantage of the air-conditioning. He was drenched in his own perspiration when he sat down with the other officers.

"Gentlemen, welcome to Vietnam. I'm Colonel Arlen Morley and I'll be conducting this briefing. Get comfortable. If you want more coffee, I'll wait till you get it." Mac joined the mad scramble to the coffee machine on the paper-covered table. "Smoke if you like." Another three minutes were used up while the men fired their cigarettes. The room grew quiet.

"We're all going to Long Binh. I assume you already know that, but I like to keep things clear from the git-go so there's no confusion later on." Mac smoked and sipped, one ear tuned to the colonel, the other tuned backward in time, listening to Casey's thrilling voice.

"Now listen up, men. I'm going to give you some statistics. Last year, in the first three months, seventy-one of our guys were killed. We lost another nine hundred and twenty during the last three months. The powers that be do not like this. Right now we're into the third month of a new year, and so far we're down twelve hundred men, that's four hundred men a month, if you're counting, most lost to land mines, booby traps, and ambushes. We don't have fronts here and we don't have any kind of strategic objectives except one—to interdict the Ho Chi Minh trail. The Ho Chi Minh trail is crucial to the Cong's supply operation. It runs for hundreds of miles, through the mountains of Laos. Without its use, the enemy cannot fight because he can't get arms and ammunition. General Westmoreland wants us to strangle the supply line along that damn trail."

An aide to the colonel drew the shutters on the windows. As if by magic a map appeared on the stark, white wall. "This is an aerial photograph of the trail. In practical terms, it's a six-thousand-mile network that's at least thirty miles wide." The pointer in Morley's hand jabbed at the map. "Trails, river crossings, dirt roads and paths, most of it covered by triple-canopy jungle." The pointer stabbed again, first at Cambodia and then South Vietnam.

"Defectors have spun a story for us that reads like a fairy tale." Mac listened with one ear to Morely's droning voice speak of transfer points, ox carts, bicycles, and human hands. "Our best sources of information tell us there are seventy-five thousand working along the entire network. You will be a part of a huge effort coordinated with the other branches of the military. Every day we'll have hundreds of aircraft in the skies, including B-52's to hammer the trail with high-altitude bombing."

"What are the odds of our succeeding?" Mac asked quietly.

The colonel bristled at the question. "Some supplies will get through, no matter what we do. This is a jungle with thousands of places to hide. There are more roads, trails, and paths than you can even begin to imagine. But we hope to cripple them. Does that answer your question, Captain?"

"Yes, sir," Mac said coolly.

"If there are no other questions," the colonel barked, "you are dismissed."

Mac looked around at the other officers getting to their feet. Aside from Morley, he was highest in rank. The other nine men were lieutenants, three of them fresh from the Academy. Before it was over, they'd be calling him Pappy. The thought pleased him. He wondered if any of them knew or if it showed exactly how green he was when it came to combat. Bivouacking and fighting mock wars on maps were a hell of a lot different than the real thing. He had a gut feeling book warfare wasn't going to cut it out here.

The bus ride to Saigon's Tan Son Nhut Airport was made in virtual silence. The UH class helicopter, better known as a Huey, was gassed and ready. Its rotor blades were chopping at the thick, humid air when Lieutenant Pender raced to board. He snapped off a salute in the general direction of Arlen Morley and then handed him two pure Havana cigars.

"Damn, I knew it," Mac muttered. There was one in every crowd.

Once the chopper was airborne, Pender grinned at Mac. With a thumb and middle finger he shot what looked like a spitball, which fell into Mac's lap. The lieutenant's broad wink let Mac know it wasn't an ordinary spitball. He grinned broadly as Mac read the message on the crumpled-up piece of paper. NURSES SENT TO QUI NHON. 85TH EVAC HOSPITAL. YOU OWE ME!

Mac nodded, sat back and closed his eyes. His thoughts weren't on the Ho Chi Minh trail or the tunnel rats he'd heard about, but on Casey. He had the name of a place. He knew where she was.

Phil Pender nudged the lieutenant next to him. "I just made the captain's day. We're gonna be like this," he said, crossing his fingers. "Count on it."

"Yeah, yeah, yeah. How'd you get out of that briefing is what I want to know," Paul Dawson demanded.

"Shit, I heard that crap so many times, I could recite Morley's words verbatim. He wanted cigars, I got him cigars. You're new here, but young man, you better learn how to play the game where Morley is concerned. See this pocket?" he said, pointing to his right breast blouse pocket. "Morley is in here.

See this one?" he said, pointing to his left pocket. "The captain is in this one."

"You ROTC guys are all alike," Dawson grumbled. "The rest of us go by the book, and look at you. Where the fuck did you take your R and R?"

Pender's round face split into a wide grin. "Tokyo, Japan, and then Hong Kong. The colonel wanted some raw silk from Macao to send home to his wife. And a few other little . . . lacy things."

"Next thing you'll tell me, you're a procurement officer."

"What do you have in mind?" Pender demanded.

"Stuff it, Pender. I'm not interested in anything you're peddling."

Pender sniffed like an outraged virgin. "Your loss, Dawson."

"You know, Pender, I heard about you back at Travis. They say you're a maggot. You're a legend in your own time."

"I'm going to take that as a compliment, Dawson. Look, each of us does what he has to do to get on."

Pender settled back and closed his eyes. He felt like crying. He'd give his eyeteeth to be one of the guys, but it would never happen. Maybe it was his own fault. Early on he'd set himself apart simply because he knew how to wheel and deal. He knew in his gut he'd make a crackerjack used car salesman, and that's exactly what he was going to do when he went back home after this stinking war. The other thing he'd learned early on was how to suck up to the brass and make himself indispensable. When you were indispensable, you didn't go out on night patrols or stand guard duty. You sat in the Officers' Club and played cards and drank gin. You made sure your C.O.'s laundry was done on time and his boots polished.

Hell, he had his own hooch, his own girl, and he knew how to provide nice clean girls for the brass. And he knew how to keep his mouth shut.

Mac's eyes snapped open the same time Phil Pender's did. They were descending.

"We're home," Pender chortled.

"Can it, Lieutenant," Colonel Morley snapped.

When they had disembarked the Huey, Morley gave them yet

another lesson about Vietnam. "I'm only going to say this once, men. Long Binh has the only organized detachment of WAC's in Vietnam. The compound to your left belongs to them. Them. Not you. Never you. The high fences and the concertina wire at the top is not to keep out VC but to keep American military personnel out of that compound. There are security guards, as well. So the message is clear: keep out."

Mac looked at the two-story barracks with their bunkers in front. He couldn't help but notice the smirk on Phil Pender's face. He knew without a doubt that the baby-faced lieutenant had managed to get more than one man past the fences and guards.

Morley was speaking again. "The rest of the day is your own. Tomorrow's orientation will be in the mess hall. Lieutenant Pender will show you around. By the way," the colonel added airily, "the temperature today is ninety-five degrees. We post it daily in front of the mess tent."

"The grunts have a daily pool, Captain," Pender said out of the corner of his mouth. "I can put you in for a sawbuck every day if you like."

"What do you get out of it, Pender?"

"Two bits on a buck. Helps to defray expenses, if you know what I mean."

Mac wasn't about to ask him what expenses he had in the jungle.

"Your home away from home, Captain," Pender said, pointing to the third tent in a row of five. "If you need anything, just ring. I'm on the other side. Showers at three o'clock."

Mac waved away a swarm of gnats bent on attacking him. The first thing he saw when he entered his new quarters was the insect repellent. He'd douse himself good once he took a shower. If that didn't work, he'd chew the tips off a book of matches and let his body absorb the sulfur.

It wasn't the Ritz, he thought tiredly. Hell, it wasn't even a flea bag. But he could make it more comfortable for himself. He made up the one empty cot with damp sheets and blanket. He hung his dress uniform on a length of cord stretching from one end of the tent to the other. The rest of his clothing went into his footlocker. He'd used up three and a half minutes unpacking. The small, framed picture he set on top of his footlocker, along with his shaving gear, was of Sadie, Benny, and himself. "When I write to you guys, I don't think I'm going to be able to tell you what this is *really* like," he muttered.

Jesus, he'd thought it was going to be a little more civilized. He'd expected a certain amount of heat and humidity, but nothing like this. He hadn't expected the stink either. *That* was bothering him, but he noticed he was no longer breathing through his mouth. Phil Pender was almost a relief. He'd expected a Phil Pender. He was sure he could whip Pender into shape in a heartbeat. Finding Casey was going to be something else. Hope, the poet said, springs eternal.

Stripped to his underwear, Mac sat down on his cot. He gave in to fear then, his shoulders trembling, his hands sweating. Had he done the right thing by volunteering to come here? The reality of his circumstances had mule-kicked him. He was competent, he was capable. He'd graduated in the top percentile of his class. He'd done his best at playing desk jockey in the Pentagon. He could think on his own and act on his own decisions. But was he good company-commander material? Could he cut it? Would he be able to gain the respect of his men, or would he be just another Pentagon pussy to them? He shuddered. It would be his job to ensure the safety of his men. He *had* to cut it. When he walked away from the army, he wanted to walk with his head high and his shoulders back. Not for his old man, not for the brass, but for himself.

The fear gripping him now was normal. It was a wise man who understood fear. One of his instructors at the Academy had told him that. But how to deal with it? Gut it out, Mac supposed. Another instructor had told him that in war a good soldier had buddies, and buddies looked after one another. A good soldier did not make friends, because friends had a way of dying on you and that was something a good soldier didn't have time to deal with. No friends. Only buddies. He could handle that. He hoped.

"Towels, Captain," Pender said through the flap opening in the tent. "And they're almost dry." He handed over a stack of khaki towels. "There's no one in the shower now, if you want to use it. I'll be in the club. If you come over, I can introduce you to some of the men."

"Thanks, Pender. Which way is the club?"

"To the left. We have a piano with six missing keys. You'll hear the music. Just follow your ears. Is there anything else I can help you with?"

"Yeah, Pender, tell me about Colonel Morley. Off the record."

Pender eyeballed the captain, weighed the possible consequences, and decided to put his money on him. "Well, sir, it's like this. He hasn't endeared himself to the men, and that's as it should be. He's not running in a popularity contest. He's been known to change his mind . . . changing his orders three or four times before he makes a final decision. It seems the men . . . ah, what the men say is he's . . . what he is is . . . Jesus, Captain, are you gonna make me say it out loud?"

Mac pretended to be puzzled. "Are you saying our full bird is indecisive, doesn't put his ass on the line, and makes sure his own is always covered? Shit, those attributes fit half the United States Army, Pender. Is there something else?"

"He's lost a few good men, sir, because he was . . . uncertain . . . He turned tail and ran is what he did," Pender said indignantly. "I don't know this for a fact, sir, it's scuttlebutt."

Mac digested the information. "Thanks, Pender." When Pender had gone, Mac flopped back on the cot. He wondered again if he'd made a mistake in coming to Southeast Asia. "Shit," he muttered.

He thought about Casey then and his mood changed immediately: it darkened. He had a vision of the two of them sending messages and never making contact until they met stateside after their tours were over.

"Bull*shit*!" he said, getting up, stomping his way to the makeshift shower. He sang lustily, even angrily, as the tepid water sluiced over him. When he stepped out, he didn't feel any cooler.

He envisioned a map of Southeast Asia in his mind. Some way, somehow, he was going to Qui Nhon. If he had to, he wasn't above pulling some strings, providing he could find the strings to pull.

He had a few bad moments when he thought about his file. Inside was a special notation about his ability to pinpoint any given place on a map, but he was not a topographer. The army had tested him, retested him, and tested him some more. He'd even thought about cheating, but he couldn't bring himself to do it. It was all in his file, and if Morley found it, he would capitalize on it. The same way any good officer would.

Not only the stink of the country, but his own smell hit him full force when he walked through the military compound. Jesus, he was dripping wet again. Why in the hell had he even bothered to shower in the stinking water? He was going to have to give some thought to getting some better deodorant. If there was one thing he hated, it was his own body smell. Long ago, when he was a small boy and permitted to play in his mother's room, he remembered her mixing different powders before she sifted them into a fancy crystal bowl. Baking soda, cornstarch, and something else. She'd said her old mammy in South Carolina had taught her how to make it so she'd smell sweet all the time. The humidity in South Carolina had to be almost as bad as it was here. The powder went on his list of things to do. He looked down at the fine hairs on his arms to see at least a hundred gnats stuck in the fine furring. "Shit!" He rubbed at his arms with the damp towel. He choked as he sprayed and rubbed in the insect repellent. Goddamn, now he was sticky. Which was worse, the problem or the remedy?

He wondered how Casey was adjusting to this place. Women, he thought, wouldn't be as tolerant. He closed his eyes trying to imagine the nimbus of gold curls over her head. That night in the damp and fog, her hair had curled all about her face. The face of an angel. Catching fog. He still thought it the silliest, the most endearing thing that ever happened to him. He wished he could reach out and touch her hand. Even here in this awful place they would have things to talk about.

His wife crept into his thoughts along with a vision of his father. In a place like this, Alice would turn tail and run. And she would squawk all the way back to the States. A frown descended over his face when he tried to picture what Alice's sticky, poufy hair would look like in Vietnam's humidity. Then he laughed.

He wiped at his face again before he pulled on his fatigues. Time to meet his fellow officers and bend his elbow a little. Maybe there would be some men who'd been to Qui Nhon, or at least know a little about the area. Something he could store in his mind on his road map to finding Casey. And he *would* find her. This one wasn't going to get away from him. Casey Adams was his dream.

Tomorrow was orientation and after that, training missions. And after *that* he would be on his own. The old do or die thing. That place all men dread where they separate the men from the boys.

IT WAS AN hour before midnight when Mac made his way back to his tent. He was three sheets to the wind on bad whiskey and sad stories. He'd contributed, blended in. His last conscious thought was that he was going to have a hell of a hangover for his orientation and his first training mission.

The God of Dreams invaded his sleep and took him down the Ho Chi Minh trail a step at a time. At every bend in the trail there were golden-haired nurses with huge red crosses on the bibs of their nursing aprons. Like vampires they were sucking the blood from the Viet Cong, then spewing it out on the trail until he was ankle deep in Vietnamese blood. High in the trees, hidden from all eyes, voices like his father's fell in the thick air. "This is totally unacceptable." It was a cadence set to fife music.

MAC WAS THE last to leap to the ground from the Huey. He staggered slightly as he followed his NCO, who suddenly stopped in mid-stride. Mac danced to the side. "You did okay out there, Captain," the sergeant said out of the corner of his mouth.

Suddenly his tiredness was gone. He *had* done all right, but hearing the sergeant say it aloud made all the difference. "The beer's on me, Sergeant."

"You got it, Captain," the sergeant said, sprinting to Colonel Morley's offices.

Thirty days in the bush. Thirty fucking days without a shower or shave. Thirty solid days of itching and sweating. And, he'd dropped fifteen pounds. But none of the above was important. What was important was he'd cut it out there.

He was ready now for his own command.

Mac's step lightened and he started to whistle. Twenty-four hours to do nothing but sleep, eat, and shower. Hot damn.

Mac dumped his field pack and headed for the showers carrying nothing but a towel and his shaving gear. Christ, he smelled.

His boots came off first. He looked at his feet in awe. It was a miracle his socks came off without taking half his skin. He had blisters, corns, and calluses. Maybe he'd just go barefoot the rest of the day. He tossed his socks in the trash can. He saw Pender do the same thing.

The awe was back on his face as he watched Pender attack his beard with a delicate-looking pair of manicure scissors. He'd been wondering about the best way to remove it. "You do it in degrees, Captain," Pender said. When he was finished he handed the scissors to Mac.

Four showers, three naps, three shaves, and two meals later, Mac felt like himself.

It was time to go to the club and get shit-faced drunk, something he promised to do the moment he returned to Long Binh. Tomorrow would take care of itself. His heart took on an extra beat when he thought of tomorrow. So, maybe he wouldn't get shit-faced drunk. He'd belt a few with the men, do a little nibbling, belt a few more, and hit the sack.

Mac flopped back on his cot. Tomorrow he would be leading his senior NCO and his men, three-quarters of whom were "cherries," men new to the bush, just the way he and Pender had been new thirty days ago.

"Enough of this," Mac muttered. Tonight the drinks were on him. He stuffed money into his blouse pocket.

MAC LOOKED UP from the piano stool he was sitting on when Pender entered the club. "I don't suppose there's anyone around here who knows how to play 'Alexander's Rag Time Band,' is there?"

"I can find out, Captain, if you think it's important," Pender said in a high, squeaky voice that sounded like it came from someone else. Mac's eyebrows shot upward.

"No, it's not important. Is something wrong, Lieutenant?"

"No. Yeah. Well . . . Tomorrow is for real. This other . . . I'm scared, Captain," he blurted in his normal-sounding voice.

"Guess what, Pender? So am I. If you weren't scared I'd worry about you. Maybe scared is the wrong word here for both of us. Let's just say we're anxious. Sounds a hell of a lot better, doesn't it?" Mac said lightly.

"No, sir, I'm scared. Piss-ass scared," Pender bleated, his eyes rolling back in his head.

"Listen, Pender," Mac said quietly, "every man in this army is scared and if he tells you he isn't then he's a damn fool liar. We've been out in the bush for four weeks and in those four weeks I've seen what you can do. The only difference tomorrow is that you answer to me. What it comes down to, Pender, is, do you trust me? On second thought, Lieutenant, see if you can find someone who can play this relic," Mac said, waving him off. Doing what he did best might take the edge off his fear. At least he hoped so.

Mac plunked at the piano keys. When he'd first arrived there were six missing keys, now a month later there were seven. Did someone steal them? He thought the question crucial and wished there was someone who could give him an answer.

Eventually someone came in and sat down at the piano. He *said* he was playing "Alexander's Rag Time Band." Mac clapped his hands so loud and long they started to hurt. "And on that note, gentlemen," Mac said, draining his sixth beer, "I think I'll turn in."

One by one the men straggled out of the club in the captain's wake, but not before they took a vote as to the captain's capabilities. To a man they said yeah, the captain could cut it.

Pender was the last to leave. "Yeah, but can I cut it?" he muttered. He wanted to cry. Needed to cry. Why the fuck shouldn't he cry? Because, he answered himself, soldiers don't

cry. "Fuck that," he mumbled, tears rolling down his cheeks as
he made his way to what he called home. He didn't give a good
fucking shit who saw him. He'd bop the first man in the snoot
who even looked at him crossways or said one word. His
mother always told him if he cried when something upset him
he'd feel better. Back then it worked. He crossed his fingers.

Pender slept with his fingers crossed and tears on his cheeks.

IT WAS 3:30 in the morning when Mac bolted from his sleep.
"Jesus, Christ!" he muttered as he tried to remember the dream
that woke him. He flopped back down on the wet cot. His own
sweat dripped from every pore of his body. His head pounded
and his stomach roiled. He would not throw up. By God, he
just wouldn't. He tightened his stomach muscles and forced the
bile back to the pit of his stomach.

Mac gritted his teeth and dropped to the floor to do his
morning calisthentics. He was victorious when he completed his
last jumping jack. He took an additional four minutes to dress
and lace his boots. His map case was ready, along with his field
gear. Jesus, he could hardly wait to write Benny and tell him he
was taking a platoon out on the Ho Chi Minh trail.

Something skittered around in the depths of his stomach:
fear. A desk jockey turned company commander, on the trail,
responsible for lives, was not something to take lightly, and
he wasn't taking it lightly. He was piss-assed scared; just like
Pender, but that was good, he thought, as he mopped at the
perspiration dripping down his face. Fear was healthy. Fear
could save lives, his men's and his own.

Mac walked out to the still-dark compound. He ground to a
halt immediately when he ran into a swarm of gnats and flies.
They were in his eyebrows, his ears. His first thought was he
was being attacked by a squadron of leeches. He knew if he
breathed through his nose, he would ingest them. "Son of a
bitch," he swore.

"Close your eyes, Captain," Phil Pender ordered. A moment
later Mac felt the sting of insect repellent. "Now breathe," the
lieutenant ordered.

"Thanks, Pender. How's it going?"

"I'm okay, Captain."

"You're sure?" Mac said.

"Yes sir," Pender said smartly.

"This is it," Mac said quietly.

"Yep," Pender said just as quietly.

"We're all going to be just fine, Pender. That's a promise."

"I'm gonna hold you to that, Captain," Pender grinned.

"And I'm gonna make your mama proud of you. Get aboard, Lieutenant," Mac said, motioning to the waiting Huey.

Mac was the last to board. He didn't look back.

Arlen Morley watched Carlin's men as they boarded the Huey.

So far, Carlin was above par. His men liked him, his NCO gave him a glowing recommendation. Carlin cared about his men, you could see it in his eyes. His NCO said he'd worked well with the ranger and airborne-qualified volunteers who conducted long-range raids on enemy depots and other sites along the Ho Chi Minh trail. Carlin's leadership qualities are above the norm, Sergeant Laker had said.

Arlen's eyes narrowed. In his opinion West Point turned out tin soldiers and every real soldier knew it. It didn't matter that at one time he would have given his back molars to be accepted, but his congressman didn't have enough clout to have him appointed. He'd been turned down, shamed in front of his family. It was guys like Carlin, who had fathers with pull, who got into the Academy. Never guys like him. He'd showed them though, he'd climbed up the ladder. He'd keep climbing too. On all the Carlins' backs, to the top.

Morley watched as Mac Carlin boarded the Huey. He expected him to look back, but he didn't. He felt disappointed for some reason. The guy was out to prove something, not to him, not to the army, but to himself. He'd probably damn well succeed. That was okay too. If Carlin looked good, he looked even better.

Never one to fool himself, Morley decided the U.S. Army, Vietnam Provisional Reconnaissance Detachment that he commanded was damn lucky to have Carlin.

Morley yawned elaborately. Now if he could just find a foolproof way to give every single shit detail to the captain, he could stay right where he was, snug as a bug. From now to the end of this fucking war, Carlin would be on the trail. He was personally going to see to it. If any new orders, new paperwork, or strings pulled crossed his desk, well, hell, this was the jungle. Shit like that got lost all the time. Carlin was in the bush and that was the end of it.

TWO HOURS INTO the bush left Mac feeling he was in his own worst nightmare. He called a halt. He itched and he smelled. He worried he would drown in his own sweat. He popped a salt tablet and ordered his men to do the same. He motioned to his squad leaders to form a perimeter. "Listen up, men . . . " Overhead a sleek squadron of Phantoms thundered in the hot, blue sky.

"It's got to be a hundred degrees," someone mumbled. Mac grimaced. The temperature felt more like 140, though it probably wasn't more than 95 degrees. "I assume you've all put your Halazone tablets in your canteens," he said.

The men nodded.

"That's good. We don't have time to wait around while you crap in the bushes. Tie those strings tight, soldier," Mac said to a corporal. "You want leeches crawling up your leg? Don't piss me off. I might be new to this command, but I'm no fool. Next break we're going to check our M-16's. I kick ass real good, and take names later—bear that in mind. The first man's rifle that malfunctions because he didn't clean it will wish he had. Any questions? Okay, move out."

This time Mac sprayed his face himself with the insect repellent, for all the good it did. The minute he started to sweat, he wiped it off. He grinned when he heard one of the men say just loud enough for him to hear, "I thought you said this guy was an Academy turd and didn't know his ass from his elbow." They were looking a little more confident, Mac thought. Christ, he had no idea the men thought so little of West Point. Like everything else, he thought philosophically, you have to prove yourself. He felt himself tingle with anticipation, a feeling of

exhilaration he'd never experienced before. He'd made contact
with his men.

Twenty minutes later two of the men at his side started to
gag. Mac wrinkled his nose and found himself retching. This
was a new smell, one he hadn't experienced before. He knew
without a doubt that he was smelling his first corpse. One of
them, a corporal from Maine, pointed to the right, his binocu-
lars at his eyes. He held up three fingers, meaning there were
three corpses, Viet Cong. They kept on walking.

It was midday when Mac called a halt. They were within
fifteen klicks of their objective, a man-made bridge, and what
they thought was one of the truck depots. The heat was hotter
than an oven. He knew the blisters on his feet had blisters of
their own. If he took off his jungle boots, he'd never get them
back on. He'd never wanted a cigarette so bad in his life.

"The men want to know if they can smoke, sir?" Pender said,
coming up behind Mac.

Mac's face registered disgust. "No!"

Mac hacked himself a space large enough to spread out his
maps and gear. He closed his eyes for a full five minutes the
moment he finished scanning the maps in front of him. When
he was satisfied he would remember every detail, he mentally
positioned his squads and tried to calculate the outcome. He
was momentarily sidetracked when he tried to identify the
sound that was popping his eardrums. The sounds of war. Real
war. M-60's.

A noise resembling a rusty foghorn burst from the sky. Mac
raised his eyebrows as he sought to identify the sound. An
AC-47, a Spooky, or Puff the Magic Dragon. It carried mini-
guns and a whole planeload of ammo and it was capable of
covering an entire football field in eight to ten seconds. The
sparks and tracers he was seeing were tracers from the mini-
guns.

"It's a Spooky, sir. Ivan Mojesky, sir, demolitions," he said
lazily.

"I kind of like Puff the Magic Dragon. The kid in me I
guess," Mac said, just as lazily. "You any good, Mojesky?"

Mojesky thought about the question for a minute. "They

don't come any better than me, Captain. When I set a charge, even if it's with spit and chewing gum, it goes off."

"I'll remember that, Mojesky."

"Captain, has anyone warned you about the bamboo vipers?"

"No, Sergeant, no one has, but I'd appreciate your enlightening me," Mac said uneasily.

"Snakes, sir. They call them 'two steps.' You get bit, you take two steps and you're dead."

"Jesus Christ!"

"Yeah, he's the only one who can help," the sergeant drawled. "It's not my place to question you, sir, but are you sure you want the men humping through this jungle after dark? Personally, I like to do my work in the daylight. Darkness, as the men can tell you, is just as much our enemy as the Viet Cong. I got the eyes of a cat. My mama made me eat my carrots." He chuckled. "I been on this trail seven times in the past eighteen months. Daytime, nighttime, makes no difference. What does make a difference is the odds are a little more favorable for our side in the daylight. The Cong favors night."

"Okay, Sergeant, thanks for the tip."

The sergeant was probably right, he thought. Wasn't it better to see your enemy, to know what you were up against? Morley hadn't ordered him to lead his men under cover of darkness. It had been a suggestion. One he decided he was probably going to ignore. He'd give the darkness one shot, tonight, and make his final decision tomorrow.

"Move out!" Mac said.

They hiked, they struggled, they humped mile after mile with no break, until sundown, that gray time when a soldier could spook himself every time a leaf moved, every time a twig crackled. Overhead the birds were silent. "An omen of some kind," Pender muttered to his men.

The moment the perimeter was set up, Mac hunkered down; the men did likewise. "This is not the dinner hour, men. We're within ten, maybe fifteen klicks of the village we know is a storage depot for the Viet Cong. Now listen up . . ."

When he was on his feet again, ready to move out, he looked

closely at Pender and wondered if the fear he saw in the lieutenant's eyes was reflected in his own. He thought of the seventeen and a half miles of corridors in the Pentagon that he'd more or less walked every day for the past ten years without once becoming winded. He clenched his teeth. This wasn't the Pentagon. This was goddamn fucking Southeast Asia. "And this, Mac Carlin, is your life," he muttered under his breath. He offered up a prayer then that he wouldn't fail, that he wouldn't let his men down. He asked for the strength to be brave; not fearless, just brave.

It was completely dark now. The temperature dropped a little, possibly five degrees. He was still sweating, the perspiration dropping past his lashes into his eyes. The salty sweat made his eyes burn, but he couldn't wipe at his face with his sleeve for fear of getting gnats and other minute insects into them. He tortured himself for a few seconds while he thought of standing under a cool shower in his gray-tiled bathroom back home. He could see the thick, thirsty, gray-on-gray towel hanging on the towel bar. He was working on a dive into his sparkling clean pool when he became aware that something was different in his surroundings. His point man bore out his awareness a minute later.

"It's too quiet, Captain. There's a nest of them at the end of the village. They're smoking and drinking. Dope, sir. They're smoking dope."

"How many?" Mac asked with a catch in his throat.

"I saw nine. There could be more. Too dark to see how many, if any, are in the trees. If this really is a depot, then they're all over."

Mac closed his eyes to visualize the map he'd looked at earlier. The village was carved into the side of a mountain, with one or two huts out in the open, where it was thought the villagers conducted their daily routines.

"That funny noise you hear is fish splashing around in the river, sir." Mac gaped at the point man. "Sure enough, sir, that's what it is. I seen it with my own eyes when I humped my way back."

"It's not on the goddamn map, Corporal," Mac snarled.

"Sir, we been smelling it all day, we just didn't know what it was. This is the junction where they either truck out their supplies or take them down on sampans. This could be a double kill, sir. I seen three bicycles with heavy wire baskets on the back. The women fill the baskets with frags and ride them to the next drop-off spot. Kids ride the bikes too, sir."

"Jesus Christ!"

"Just your ordinary Viet Cong village, sir," the corporal muttered as he made his way back to his squad.

"Mojesky!" Mac hissed.

"Yes, sir."

"We've come across a river we didn't know was here. It's not on the map," Mac said. "I want you to take two men and string claymore mines all along the water's edge."

"The coordinates, sir?"

Mac gave them to him. A moment later he was part of the blackness surrounding the perimeter. A goddamn river. Shit! How in the hell could a recon plane miss a river?

FIFTEEN MINUTES LATER, when Mac was satisfied that each move was synchronized, he and his men moved out. "By the manual, Carlin, this is goddamn by the manual," he muttered to himself. But he told himself as he moved on that the manual meant diddly-squat. There were no rules as long as the other side didn't have the same book.

He called a halt at the edge of what could pass for a clearing. It appeared to be about thirty-five meters across and as round as a grapefruit. A path was cut through the center, veering off to the left into the dense jungle, and it seemed to reappear on the other side. A trick of light, Mac thought uneasily. He looked closer, saw another path, and then another, all criss-crossing like the latticework on a cherry pie. He knew rice paddies lay beyond each, stretching all the way up the mountains. Which path to take? He dropped to one knee and studied the packed-down path. He hoped to find some telltale sign, but there wasn't one. It was a crap shoot, and he knew it. He closed his eyes, visualized the map and pointed.

He didn't have to tell the men to be quiet. Still, their boots crunched on the knee-high saw grass. A brass band would have had the same effect, he thought sourly. Then they settled in, three to four feet from each other, and hunkered down to wait, their eyes never leaving the maze of paths.

Sweat poured into Mac's eyes and down his face. He was dripping wet; even his socks were soaking inside his boots. He knew he had leeches on his legs, but he'd have to wait till later to burn the suckers off. He thought about the pool in his backyard and imagined he could smell the chlorine.

An hour crawled by, and then two. Thirty more minutes passed before Mac raised his hand to signal there was no activity on the trail. It was time to move out and attack the nine-man post at the edge of the village. He looked around cautiously. The fine hairs on the back of his neck prickled in alarm. Each shrub, each tree, looked like the enemy.

It was blacker than a witch's lair as they humped their way through the saw grass. Suddenly, the point man stopped in his tracks and signaled for everyone to drop down. Mac raised his head to see the shadowy figure of a squat man, then a second, not more than fifty feet away. They were crouching, like crabs, as they moved, their heads turning right and left in perfect synchronization. He could feel his heart start to pound. This wasn't a page in the manual or a training exercise; this was so real he was about to wet his pants. He felt hard movement in his chest and knew his heart was taking on extra beats. He swallowed past the lump in his throat. He waited. He saw a third silhouette and then a fourth. Did that make the command post minus four men, or were these men from somewhere else? Then again, the point had said earlier there might be more than nine. There was no way he could know for sure. Five minutes crawled by, then three more, before five more crouching figures snaked their way on their bellies from the undergrowth. The first four were crouching, the second batch humping. Why? Jesus Christ, he knew why. He could smell it all the way to where he was hunkered down. Some fool was splashing insect repellent. If he could smell it, so could the Cong. Son of a bitch! He'd thought he and Pender were the only ones new to the jungle. *That* was in the goddamn book!

"You're on, Sergeant," Mac said to his senior NCO, a man named Stevens.

At the sergeant's signal, bodies moved to the right and to the left. For the briefest second Mac wanted to turn tail and run, to hide in the dense shrubbery. The sound of an explosion ripping through the air convinced him hiding was not his answer. He was up and running, his M-16 belching fire as his sergeant ripped the jungle to shreds.

It took fifteen seconds for Mac to hop, crawl, and run to cover where he'd seen the last batch hump their way through the clearing. He opened fire and heard a squeal of rage. Wild animal or Cong? He didn't wait to find out as he fired off another blast. Another squeal and then a shriek. Hot damn! His elation was short-lived when a grenade went off nearby, showering him with dirt. He threw one of his own. No Yankee pitcher could have done it better. Bodies tumbled in the brush.

"It's a kill! Three! Medic, over here!" Mac's eyebrows shot up to his hairline. One of his men was wounded. A call for a medic meant the man was still alive. No one was fucking going to die under his command. *No one!*

They fought like the soldiers they were. And when it was over and Mac called a halt to the shooting, they set up their perimeter. "How many?" he asked hoarsely.

"Nine wounded. No one bought it, sir."

"Get on the radio, give our coordinates, and get a medevac chopper in here for these men. *Now* you can smoke!" he declared.

"How'd we do, Captain?" the sergeant asked.

"You did great, Stevens. We'll know shortly, when the patrol gets back. I think we got them all."

There was disgust written all over the sergeant's face. "You *never* get them all, Captain. I might not get the chance to say this later, sir, but I'll soldier with you any time."

Mac felt his chest puff out. He *had* done all right. There was just that one bad moment, and he was going to live with it. He'd done what he was supposed to do. He'd goddamned performed like a real soldier. He buried his cigarette before he issued his next order.

"Let's find that depot we came for. Mojesky!"

"Here, Captain," he said, grinning from ear to ear. "Listen, they're popping, sir. Every single one. I strung eight and fired up all three sampans. No business conducted here for a while, sir!"

"They'll be back in business by tomorrow night," Stevens said out of the corner of his mouth. "Bastards!"

"Not if we get that depot," Mac said. "Let's go find it."

THEY FOUND THE depot a little before dawn, and then it was by accident. A youngster, no more than six or seven, was rolling a string of rocks tied with a vine in front of his cave. At first he refused to look at the American soldiers. At one point he'd been called inside. Before he obeyed the stern voice, he'd pointed to one of the thatched huts. It took a good ten minutes before Mac realized it wasn't the hut the boy had been pointing to but the cave beyond it. A quick glance, even a lingering one, wouldn't have picked up the covered entrance to the cave.

Mac was first to enter, Mojesky second. Mojesky whistled, Mac gawked. Along one wall on makeshift shelves were sacks and sacks of rice along with boxes of beer and wilted vegetables. Cartons of Lucky Strike and Chesterfield cigarettes were dumped haphazardly on top of the wilted vegetables. It was floor to ceiling rice and beer. The second wall held identical rough shelves. Boxes of grenades, some American and some Russian, filled two shelves. The third and fourth shelves held thousands of rounds of AK-47 ammunition. Piles of AK-47's still in their oiled boxes stretched to the ceiling. On the third wall were additional boxes of M-16's and five M-60's. The two walls flanking the entrance of the cave held enough C-4 plastic explosive to blow up the state of California.

"In here, Captain," one of his men called. "We got ourselves a makeshift clinic with guess what, good ol' U.S. of A. penicillin, Johnson and Johnson bandages, and lookee here, a whole bale of happy weed. And, oh, this is . . . why, it's medical instruments."

The voice was short of hysterical, Mac thought. He ordered the man out when he opened a wooden box filled with GI dog tags, wristwatches, rings, and pictures of smiling young girls, happy-faced youngsters, and wide-eyed parents. All American.

He felt meaner at that moment than he'd ever felt in his life. He hated totally, completely, when he bent down to pick up the box, to heft it to his shoulders. It didn't feel heavy at all.

"Mojesky, blow this motherfucking place off the map. Give the residents five minutes to clear out, then set the charges."

"Yes, *sir!*" Mojesky said smartly. The captain was *all right*.

"Pender!" Mac roared. "You see this box. You're in charge. If you lose even one picture, your ass is going in a sling. Divvy it up among the men to carry."

"You got it, sir," Pender said, snapping to attention.

"Freeze, get these civilians out of here and don't let them buggy-lug anything. We don't have time for packing luggage. They go as they are. Double-time, mister!"

"O'Brien, what's the body count?"

"Nineteen confirmed. They come back for their dead, sir, what do you want me to do?"

"Nothing, O'Brien, the sun will french-fry them or the explosion will toast them. It's an either/or."

It was six-thirty, dawn, Mac saw by the hands of his watch, and already the temperature was climbing. He looked upward to see the mountains, and a gray, purplish haze obscured his view. In another fifteen minutes the blazing-hot sun would burn off the haze.

Out of nowhere he heard the *pop-pop* rotor blades of a helicopter. The pilot was zooming in at full tilt toward the greenish plume of smoke that signaled his landing zone. Directly behind the first chopper was a second, its rotors singing. He walked over to his wounded, saluted smartly, and said something to each of the men. When the last man was secure in the choppers, Mac approached the pilot. "Do you fly anywhere near Qui Nhon?"

"Just about every day."

"Do me a favor and deliver this to one of the nurses. Casey Adams."

"Are you by any chance a guy named Mac Carlin?"

"I was when I woke up yesterday, why?"

"Have I got something for you. You guys pen pals or what?" he said, handing over a filthy, tattered slip of paper. He was grinning. "Sorry, Mac, I have to get airborne. But call anytime!"

Mojesky, Mac saw, was standing outside the cave, giving him a thumbs-up sign.

"Saddle up and move out!" Mac roared as he slipped Casey's note inside his breast pocket.

It was day two on the Ho Chi Minh trail.

Chapter 5

THE FAMILIAR NIGHT sounds Casey had grown accustomed to over her sixty-day stint in Pleiku were gone. It was so quiet she thought she could hear the blood running through her veins. There was an ominous feeling to the quietness. Something was going to happen, something terrible, she could feel it, sense it in every breath she took.

God, she was tired. Sixteen straight hours of surgery today, eighteen yesterday, and fourteen the day before, and a puny, tepid shower wasn't going to help ease the tiredness. She thought about the package that had just arrived from Nicole. Cotton underwear, French talcum powder, and possibly a few other goodies would be in it. She'd been too tired to open it. Shampoo, wonderful fragrant shampoo, would be a godsend. She hadn't asked for shampoo though.

Inside her tent she flopped down on her cot. How many more days of this could she take? Twice she'd put in for a transfer to Da Nang, but so far she hadn't heard a thing. Guilt settled over her shoulders, cloaking her in misery. Why did she have to feel guilty? She'd done her share, more than her share, and she hadn't had a day off since she arrived. Maureen Hagen, newly assigned to Pleiku, had looked at her as if she'd sprouted a second head when she said she needed time off, time to do nothing but what she wanted to do. Time to see if she could arrange a meeting with Mac.

She smiled in the darkness. Thoughts of Mac were what kept her going, the notes they sent to each other by way of chopper pilots. Rick had promised to fly her down to Da Nang if she could get the time off. "You'll love China Beach," he'd said. He must have said the same thing to Mac, because Mac was trying for China Beach too. Miracles did happen, she thought wearily. God, if she could only be that lucky.

Casey was crying when Lily Gia poked her head under the flap of the tent and held up two bottles of pop. "They were cold when I got them." She grinned. "Casey, you're crying. What's wrong?"

"Nothing, everything. I have to get away from here, or I'll go out of my mind. I thought I was tough, that I could handle anything in the O.R., but this . . ." She wiped at her eyes with the hem of her tee-shirt. "I'm not a crybaby," she said hoarsely.

"I know that, Casey. We all feel the same way. But you get numb to it, you hitch up your socks and keep going. There's no other answer. If there was, I would have found it by now. Anyway, I have good news. At least I think it's good news. I heard Major Hagen talking to some of the doctors, and she was discussing you. I think—and mind you, this is just my opinion—it was about giving you some leave for a few days." The Asian girl's eyes were alight with happiness for her friend.

"Really, Lily, do you think so?" Casey asked hopefully.

"I really think so. You deserve it, Casey. I even heard Luke say you needed time off. It's all up to Major Hagen. If you go, I get to go next. All I dream about is leave. Hey, when are you going to open your package?" she said, swigging from the pop bottle.

"Right now." Casey grinned, gulping at the lukewarm orange pop. She ripped at the string and the tattered paper. Her eyes sparkled when she looked at Lily. "Half is yours. We share whatever is in here. Agreed?"

Lily clapped her hands before she dropped to the floor. She sat cross-legged, her eyes glued to the lid of the box Casey was about to remove. "Oooh, hurry up!" she dithered.

"Aaah, cotton panties," Casey said, holding up a bundle of briefs. "Fourteen pairs, and the day is on each one. A set for you and one for me. We're the same size, isn't that great? Talcum powder. Four. Two for you and two for me. God, it smells heavenly. Chocolates!" she squealed. "We can gorge! Toffee! Macaroons! We've died, Lily, and are in heaven. Look here, a tin of coffee. Real French coffee! We're dead. Lie down, Lily, but not until you fill your mouth with this wondrous, this fattening, this exquisite chocolate. And oh, my God, look, licorice too!" Casey said, digging into the bottom of the box. Suddenly she crossed her arms over her chest. Her eyes rolled back in her head when Lily lifted a tissue-wrapped bundle from the very bottom.

"I know what it is, I know what it is," Casey cried excitedly.

"Tell me before I unwrap it," Lily cried, just as excited as her friend.

"It's a dress, an outfit of some kind. I told Nicole about Mac in my letter. She would do this—send me a dress, I mean. She always nagged me about the way I dressed. She said I was too conservative, too old-maidish. This is going to be spectacular, I just know it. Quick, open it before I have a fit of some kind."

The dress was so simple in line, it was elegant. At a glance she could tell it wasn't a mini, but close to it. The hemline would touch her knees. "Chanel!" she gasped. "Oh, look, here's a note."

Chérie, this is for you to knock that captain off his feet. Later I will send you the bill. The color is called Mediterranean-blue. I imagine by now you are a glorious bronze color, which means this color will be set off to perfection with your tan and the color of your hair. I am so jealous of your nineteen-inch waist. There is not another dress like this in the world. Madam Chanel made it up especially for you, my friend. I explained about the captain and what you are doing over there. The scarf and the small purse are Madam's gift to you. Isn't it wild, Casey! I want a full report when the handsome officer sees you. Danele sends her love.

Much love and affection,
Nicole

"The way things are going, I'll be old and gray and sitting in a rocking chair before I get to wear this dress," Casey said. "This isn't a China Beach dress though. It's a Saigon dress, and that's where I'm going if the major gives me leave. What do you think of that?"

"I think it's a wonderful idea. Will you take a letter to my parents and one for—Eric. I know he's married. It doesn't change my feelings. I must believe the promises he made to me. I love him, Casey," she said softly.

Casey's expression didn't change. She had to believe Lily knew what she was doing. "Of course. Oh, Lily, I can feel a regular shower pelting my skin already. Just the thought of air-conditioning leaves me giddy. I can't wait to dine in a restaurant and eat regular food that actually tastes like it's supposed to taste. Napkins, glassware . . . silverware . . . sleeping on a bed that isn't soaking wet. Luxury beyond belief. I'll get to read a newspaper, maybe even a book, go to a movie."

"If you're going to do all that, when will you have time to see Mac?" Lily asked anxiously.

Casey giggled. "Somehow, I'll fit him in. He's probably as hungry for civilization as I am. We'll do all these things together."

"Will he sleep in that same dry bed?" Lily grinned.

Casey shrugged. "Nothing is impossible. I suppose you'll want a full report."

"Absolutely, right down to the wrinkles in the sheets. When are you going to try that dress on?"

"Not till I get to Saigon. God, Lily, it will smell just like this place. I want to be clean and powdered. It's a size six, so it will fit. If anything, it might be a little loose across the bosom. I'll bet *you* could wear it. It would look beautiful on you. I can't get over how close we are in actual build. When I get back, it will be your turn to wear it. You'll look like a princess. I'll write Nicole and thank her from my air-conditioned room. Maybe she'll send us another one."

Lily picked up on the word *us* immediately and hugged Casey. "You are a wonderful friend, Casey. Without you, I would have gone back to my family and given up all hope of being a doctor. If there's a way for me to go back to the States when you leave, I want to go with you. I want us to be friends all our lives."

"I feel the same way toward you," Casey said.

"Right now we have to think about how we're going to preserve this beautiful creation, otherwise it will be full of mildew in three days' time. Come along, my American friend, we are going scavenging. Someplace in this compound we will find rice paper and a plastic bag." Lily giggled. "First though, we must eat these sweets. Ah, I never thought my sweet tooth would be fed again." This last was said as she stuffed three half-melted chocolates into her mouth. As she chewed she unwrapped pieces of toffee. When her sweet tooth was stated, she sighed and pulled Casey to her feet. "Follow me and be quiet. We could get shot for stealing."

"No!"

"Oh, yes, your American officers frown on pilfering. So," she drawled, "I will point out the places where we will find what we need, and you will steal it. Agreed?"

"To preserve this dress I'll do whatever is needed," Casey said happily. "If they shoot me, Lily, wear the dress in good health."

"Okay. Now follow me."

Three hours later, when the moon was high, the conspirators were back in Casey's tent, their arms full of cellophane, wax paper from cereal boxes, and rolls of surgical tape. They spread their precious loot out on Casey's cot, trying to smooth the crinkly paper.

"The worst thing that will happen is your dress will smell like cornflakes," Lily said, doubling over with laughter.

Ninety minutes later they had an airtight bag held together with surgical tape. The designer dress was folded between the wax paper of twenty-three cornflake boxes before it was placed lovingly by two pairs of hands inside the makeshift bag. They used the last of the surgical tape as a seal.

"Have you given any thought to what will happen in the morning when the cooks find all those cornflakes in their mixing bowls?" Casey asked fretfully.

"A lot of thought," Lily muttered. "The cereal will be damp in another hour, so that's what's for breakfast. Lunch too. Dinner also. I personally love cornflakes."

"I adore cornflakes," Casey said, bobbing her head. She'd agree to eat cornflakes for the rest of her life to preserve the dress, in the hopes of wearing it when she finally met Mac.

"It was a fun evening, wasn't it, Casey?" Lily asked as she munched on the macaroons.

"It sure was, and we didn't even get shot."

ON MAY 10, 1966, United States planes blanketed a Viet Cong base with napalm, on Mac Carlin's orders. It was an order that enabled Mac and his men to destroy the base and wipe out a series of smaller trails, temporarily crippling the enemy. The order earned him a Bronze Star with a V device for valor. He also managed to get a three-day pass to China Beach.

The word went out on the Bamboo Pipeline: Captain Mac Carlin respectfully requests the honor of Casey Adams's presence in China Beach at a mutually agreed-upon date. The return message via the Bamboo Pipeline was: Saigon has air-conditioning and dry sheets. Confirm time and date.

ON TUESDAY, JUNE 7, 1966, the day Ronald Reagan won the Republican nomination for governor of California, Mac Carlin boarded a Chinook with stops at Phuoc Binh, Dong Xoai, and Bien Hoa. At Bien Hoa he caught a dust-off for Saigon.

Casey wasn't as fortunate. When she boarded the chopper at Pleiku, she was told she might make it to Saigon on time, but not to count on it. She changed choppers four times: in Qui Nhon, Tuy Hoa, and Nha Trang, where she waited nine hours for a pilot who would take her to Cam Ranh Bay, and then waited eight more hours for a chopper to Saigon. When she walked off the field at Tan Son Nhut Airport, she had less than seven hours to spend in Saigon before heading back to Pleiku. She wanted to cry with frustration, both at her circumstances and at the way she was dressed—in the required jungle fatigues and jungle boots. Her hair, which had grown almost three inches, was pinned on top of her head in messy disarray. The little makeup she'd started out with had long since washed away with her perspiration.

She held her breath as she walked through the double doors

of the elegant Tu Do Street Princess Hotel in downtown Saigon. The cool air blasted her. The small suitcase she carried, with the blue dress inside, was a child's case. It was bright red with a colorful picture of Mickey Mouse on the front and brought smiles to the faces in the lobby. She felt silly, but exhilarated, a megawatt smile on her face.

She saw him then. He was getting to his feet, but he was moving slowly, as though afraid. His eyelashes were still incredibly long. He was as tanned as she was. And then she saw his smile, saw the warmth in his eyes. "You made it," he said hoarsely.

"I would have walked," Casey said simply.

"Me too." Mac grinned.

"Have you been waiting long?"

"All of my life," he said.

"Me too."

"I only have eight hours left," Mac said.

"I have seven."

He was dressed in clean jungle fatigues. She couldn't wear the blue dress after all, it was too fancy. Her heart thumped. "I can be ready in fifteen minutes," she said breathlessly.

"I can carry your bag to the room," Mac said in a strange voice he barely recognized as his own. "I'll come back down here to wait for you," he added hastily. "You look just the way I remember."

"You do too. I told everyone about your long eyelashes. I didn't think we'd ever . . . what I mean is, I hoped, but . . . the pilots, they're just super. If it wasn't for them, I wouldn't be here."

"Thank God for the Bamboo Pipeline," Mac said at the door to her room. He handed her the Mickey Mouse bag he'd been carrying. He shuffled his feet. "The shower is great. Don't take too long, Casey."

"I won't. Wait for me." She smiled.

"You bet. Fifteen minutes."

He walked on air. He felt the same way. She was the same. Everything was the same as it had been in San Francisco, but now they were half a world away from California. He shivered with a delicious feeling of triumph. *They* were the same. Casey thought so too. He could see it in her face.

God, she was beautiful, just the way he remembered. Her hair, bleached almost white from the sun, was like a nimbus around her head. He liked it piled up with all the wispy curls about her face. In the lobby again, he literally danced his way to the elevator so he could touch her the moment she stepped out.

What would they do, where would they go? He'd have to ask her what she wanted to do. If it was left up to him, he'd take her to the fanciest restaurant in town and stare at her for seven straight hours. He'd hold her hand, smile, and they'd talk the way they had the last time. "You lucky bastard," he said to himself.

The moment Casey stepped into the lobby, Mac swept her up in the air. "I had to do that." He grinned. Casey laughed, a delightful trilling sound. "What shall we do?" he asked.

"I have this list . . ."

"I do too," Mac said, waving a crumpled piece of paper under her nose. "Let's get the shopping out of the way. Then I want to be alone with you, just the two of us, so I'd suggest the zoo and botanical gardens. It's a weekday and there won't be many people there. And, it's safe. Of course, first we have to eat. The time will go by so fast we—"

"I know, so let's not waste time. I also have to drop a letter off at my roommate's parents' house. It's only two streets away from the hotel, so we can walk. Hurry, Mac, let's get all the chores out of the way." She couldn't believe she was being so bold. She linked her arm with his.

"You look lovely," Mac said. "That's a pretty dress."

She told him about the dress Nicole had sent and how she'd planned to wear it, until she saw his fatigues.

"You should have worn it. Blue's my favorite color. Sorry I screwed up."

"Next time, when we have more time."

On the walk to Lily's house, Mac said, "The chopper pilots told me about you nurses and how hard it is on you. They say

all you nurses should get medals. How do you do it? I see death,
but not the way you do. I don't understand how you can—"

"We make a difference. In the beginning it was . . . a nightmare. After a while you sort of get numb. You do what you're
trained to do. You do the best you can. For a while we were
working with outdated penicillin. There are days when I think
it's all a bad dream and I'll wake up in my own bed. But it's
real, so real I constantly find myself questioning my own ability, my training. How do you handle what you're doing?"

"For a while I didn't think I would be able to cut it. Sitting
behind a desk in the Pentagon did nothing to prepare me. Like
you, I've been doing my best. I've lost some men. I've learned
to hate. I don't know if that's good or bad. The hate has kept
me alive."

"It's a pretty house," Casey said, pulling on the bell outside
the walled garden. "We have houses like this in the south of
France. We call them villas. I think it looks a little like the
mission houses in California."

Mac peered into the darkness. "Yes, it does," he agreed.
"Are you sure this is the place?"

Casey nodded.

"Do they speak English?"

"A little. Lily said I should hand them the letter and smile.
This must be her mother. Oh, Mac, isn't she pretty? That's an
ao dai she's wearing. She's so tiny. It all looks so normal."

Tears momentarily blurred Casey's eyes when she said,
"From Lily." The porcelain doll that was Lily's mother repeated her daughter's name in Vietnamese and smiled. Casey
smiled too, and handed over the letter. The Vietnamese woman
bowed low. Casey bowed, so did Mac. Casey leaned closer to
the grilled fence. She touched her fingertips to her lips, said
"From Lily" again, then placed them gently on the little
woman's cheek. She touched her lips a second time. "For papa-
san."

"Please wait one moment," the little Vietnamese said softly.
Moments later she was back at the ornate fence offering a small
package to Casey.

Tears shimmered in Casey's eyes when she unwrapped a

delicate, gold filigreed bracelet. "Thank you. I'll tell Lily you are well."

After more bows of farewell, Mac said, "Okay, we have five hours and fifteen minutes left. What shall we do?"

"Why don't we go back to the hotel dining room, where it's cool."

"That's about the best idea I've heard today," Mac said. "We can kill two birds with one stone. We can eat, and I can look at you. I've thought about you every day. Even when my head was full of . . . other things, you managed to sneak in. I can't believe we only have a few hours."

"They'll go by so quickly," Casey said sadly. "Our visit will be over just as it's getting started."

HE WAS HOLDING her hand across a linen-draped table. "I've made it my business to find every Bird Dog pilot and every chopper pilot in Vietnam. I've sent word out on the Bamboo Pipeline that you and I are engaged. They'll carry our messages back and forth. It's done all the time. I think we'll be seeing more of each other. Forget this Saigon bit for now. Besides, it's too difficult to arrange transportation. We'll meet in other places so we don't waste time. That is, if you're willing to give up dry beds and air-conditioning."

Casey laughed. "I'm not going to sleep in that dry bed. And anyway, I'm getting used to the heat and the humidity, something I never thought would happen."

He realized he was holding his breath, waiting for her reply. What she'd said wasn't what he was hoping to hear. Then, a moment later, she said, "Engaged!" and he let his breath out in a soft swoosh. Her face turned pink. She lowered her blue eyes, but he could see a small smile start to form at the corners of her mouth.

"Does it upset you? It was the only thing I could think of. Everyone seems willing to promote a romance over here. I can rescind the order," he said, biting down on his lower lip.

"No, no, it's fine. It's rather amusing. I agree." She chuckled warmly.

"Good. Here," he said, withdrawing a small package from

his jacket pocket. "I picked this up from a vendor. It's a sort of engagement ring and cost seven ninety-five American." He was laughing, and so was she when he slipped the gaudy, tacky ring on her finger.

"Will it make my finger turn green?"

"Your finger will probably fall off." Mac threw back his head and laughed deeply.

Casey thought the sound was the most wonderful she'd ever heard. She was aware of the other diners watching with amused smiles. Everyone, she thought, loved lovers.

"Tell me everything about yourself—from the day you were born," Mac said huskily.

She told him. Everything. "Your turn." She smiled.

Mac felt something squeeze his heart. Of course she would want to know everything about him. He knew in his gut she wouldn't understand about Alice. Casey would want to believe him, but in the end she'd get up, smile down at him, and say good-bye. In later years, when he thought about her, he'd remember that she walked out on him in a hotel in Saigon. As soon as possible he was going to write to a lawyer he knew in New York City and tell him . . . tell him to file for a divorce. He wasn't going to cheat the girl sitting across from him. He wasn't going to tell any deliberate lies either. He just wouldn't mention Alice until the paperwork was in order. Bullshit, letters took too long. Later, before it was time to return to the airbase, he would excuse himself and see if he could get a call through to the States. The decision made, he felt better. He started to talk. For the first time in his life he was telling *everything* about his life to someone, everything that was in his heart.

Casey said softly, "Marriage for me is forever and ever. I want to have a wonderful life, because I didn't have a wonderful childhood. When and if I get married, I want my children to be loved by me and their father. I want us both to sit by their beds when they're sick. I want both of us to take them on picnics. I want a close, loving family. I don't care if we're poor, as long as we have love. A pet too. A big, shaggy dog who will love and protect the little ones and be protective of us as well. A little house, a charming house I can decorate with a fence around the yard and all kinds of flowers. The impossible dream. Someday," she said wistfully.

It would never work with this man, she thought. He came from a wealthy family with oodles and oodles of money. His servants would live in the kind of house she described. Servants felt the way she did, not rich, powerful people. She was suddenly embarrassed. She raised her eyes defiantly, daring him to make fun of her. The look she saw in his eyes stunned her.

"Jesus, that's all I ever wanted myself," he said. "Two dogs though. I want a swing on the front porch, and a back porch where you can eat on a real picnic table, food you can eat with your fingers. I never gave a crap about that shiny glassware and six rows of forks. Paper napkins are just as good as linen. I want to eat breakfast in the kitchen, with those dogs begging for bits of bacon. I want to live on a budget, to plan a vacation for months. I want the whole ball of wax."

"Then why don't you have all that?" Casey asked, her eyes intent.

"Because I hate going up against my father. I hate to see the disappointment in his eyes when he looks at me. You see, I don't like my father. Maybe I hate him, and that makes me feel guilty. I came over here to get myself together, so when I go back I can do what I please, when I please." His voice turned urgent when he asked, "Do you like to walk in the rain? I mean really walk, without an umbrella, or don't you like to get your hair mussed?"

"I love walking in a spring rain. My hair is curly, so it doesn't matter to me. I don't even own an umbrella. Do you like to walk in the leaves in autumn and smell those same leaves burning?"

"Autumn is my favorite time of year. When I was a kid, I always wanted to steal a pumpkin and carve it out myself. I think I wanted to be Tom Sawyer and Huckleberry Finn rolled into one. The cook always bought the pumpkin and the gardener carved it. I wasn't allowed to light the candle either, and it stayed in the kitchen window, so no one got to see it. I never even got to go trick-or-treating. Hell, I missed half my life, now that I think about it. Listen, we're getting morbid here, let's talk about something else. Us."

Casey smiled. She didn't mean to give voice to the thought in her mind when she said, "I thought most men were married at your age." The absolute, totally blank look on Mac's face confused her. He was being so open, so confiding. She blinked. Perhaps he had been involved with someone at one time and it hadn't worked out. "I'm sorry, I shouldn't have said that."

"No problem," he said tightly. She looked like a daffodil in her yellow dress. He thought of fresh-churned butter; not that he'd ever seen fresh-churned butter, but he had read the term and fixed a picture in his mind of a mound of pure yellow, like fresh gold. She was slim, willowy, with tanned legs and arms. She also had goose bumps on her arms from the air-conditioning. She must be freezing, he thought, as he realized he too was cold. Maybe, like himself, she hadn't wanted to disturb their confiding moments.

"Listen, honey, it's freezing in here. Let's go outside, where we have to fight the heat to get our breath." He peeled off some bills and handed them to the head waiter, who bowed, smiled, and bowed again.

"I'm going to buy a blanket," Mac said when they were on the street, "and we're going to the zoo, where we can sit and look at each other. If I can find some peanuts, I'll buy them too. Are you game, Casey?"

"This heat feels delicious. Yes, I am game. Another hour in that restaurant and I would have gotten frostbite."

"We have three hours," Mac said, when they got to the zoo. He spread the blanket under a leafy tree. "I haven't even kissed you. In my dreams I've kissed you a thousand times. In my daydreams I've kissed you two thousand times. I think you're supposed to say something before I make a fool of myself."

Casey looked around. "I don't see anything here that can stop you. I'm certainly willing. If you hadn't brought the matter up, I meant to."

"Ahh, a forward wench. Come here," he said huskily.

She was standing in his arms, staring deeply into his eyes.

What she saw there allowed her to close her own eyes and give in to the moment she'd hungered for all these months.

Their lips met and whispered sweetly against each other. Her lips parted to feel his tongue in the warm recesses of her mouth. She felt dizzy, faint, never wanting what she was feeling to stop. She clung to him, pressing herself against the length of him, her arms locking fiercely around his broad shoulders. They swayed, seared together, in the hot, humid air, neither willing to be the first to move. She heard him murmur her name, felt him run his fingers through her hair. She tried to move closer, to melt into him until she thought she couldn't bear it a moment longer. She moved then, stepping away from him, her eyes dreamy and glistening.

When she stumbled, Mac held her in his strong grip, gently lowering her to the shell-pink blanket on the ground. His eyes, Casey saw, were warm and soft and full of . . . love, or was it lust?

She almost fainted a moment later when Mac reached for both her hands. "I think I'm falling in love with you," he whispered hoarsely.

Casey licked at her dry lips. She felt the same way, but her inexperience with love only allowed her to nod. She didn't trust herself to speak. She wanted to, tried to. Tears gathered in her eyes. She fell against him, crying into his shoulder. She nuzzled, feeling more contented and safe than she'd ever felt in her life. He was cradling her, murmuring soft words she couldn't understand, and it didn't matter. Finally, hiccuping, she said, "I have never felt this way before. I don't want to leave. I don't want to go back. I want to stay here with you." She was blubbering, acting like a sixteen-year-old. She said so, to her own dismay.

Mac held her away from him for the barest second before he brought her close to him. "Would it surprise you to know I feel exactly the same way? We have the rest of our lives. This is just a moment, a slice of time we have to get through until we can leave this place and move into that little house with a front and back porch. What do you think we should call the dogs?"

Casey bolted from his arms. "But that . . . that means . . ."

"What that means is you'll have to marry me, because I have

no intention of living in sin behind a picket fence. My God, what would those dogs think?"

"Who cares what they think? You hardly know me," she croaked.

"I know everything I need to know. I found you. That's all that's important to me. Besides," he said lightly, "we're engaged."

Casey wiggled her finger. "I thought it was a joke," she whispered.

"Back there it was. I had to make a joke out of it so you wouldn't see how devastated I was if you'd handed it back to me. I guess you can say I'm a coward."

"We haven't slept together," Casey blurted.

Mac grinned. "A small matter that can be rectified in a moment. Next time."

"Are we sure there will be a next time?" She snuggled against him, content with all she was hearing. God, wait till she told Lily.

"Damn right there will be a next time, and a time after that. As often as I can I'll see you."

She sighed happily. "Promise me one thing, Mac."

"I'll promise anything, just tell me what it is you want."

"Just promise me honesty. If you can do that, then we can have a wonderful life together."

At that moment Mac would have promised to gift wrap the moon and sprinkle the package with stars. He promised. He believed implicitly that he wasn't lying. He held her closer, burying his chin in her sweet-smelling hair.

He wanted to take her back to the hotel and make love to her, but the hands on his watch signaled danger. He told her so.

"Next time," she whispered. "I guess I should tell you now that I'm a virgin."

Mac pretended mock alarm. "No!"

Crushed by his response, she said, "Does it make a difference?"

"Not to me, it doesn't. But if you weren't, it wouldn't make a difference either. Before, when I told you I thought I was falling in love with you . . . that wasn't quite true. I fell in love with you in San Francisco. When it comes to women, I'm afraid I don't know too much about the way they react to certain things. I guess you could say I was feeling my way, hoping you felt the same. Do you?" he asked boyishly.

"Oh, yes," Casey sighed happily.

"Will you wear the blue dress next time?"

She nodded, burrowing into the crook of his arm.

"Then it's settled," Mac said exuberantly. "We're in love. It's official!"

Casey laughed. "I've never been in love before. It's wonderful!"

"I haven't either!" It was true, he'd never been in love the way he was in love with this beautiful girl. Now, finally, at long last, he had someone to call his own. Someone who loved him, who wanted the same things from life that he wanted. There was no way in hell he was going to even *think* about his wife now.

They snuggled on the blanket, their cheeks brushing. They talked in soft whispers about the future and the remainder of their tours in Southeast Asia.

When it was time to leave, Mac couldn't find the words. He held his wrist out so she could see the luminous hands. Her shoulders slumped, as did his. They were like two beaten, tired warriors when they left the zoo, the soft pink blanket under Mac's arm.

"Do you mind if we stop at the hotel before we head out to Tan Son Nhut?" he said. "I want to see if I can get a call through to the States."

"Not at all. I have to get my bag anyway."

FIFTEEN MINUTES LATER Mac saw Casey get off the elevator in the hotel lobby. He spoke hurriedly into the receiver. "Listen, miss, I'm calling from Vietnam, interrupt Stewart. What do you mean, you can't interrupt him? I'm his client too," he said angrily. He listened a moment. "Okay, then take down this message and repeat it back to me verbatim." He was listening to the tail end of his message when Casey approached him. She winked at him. In his life no girl had ever winked at him. He felt himself grow light-headed. "Tell Stew to call Benny if there's a problem."

Mac grinned sheepishly at Casey. "People"—he'd almost said lawyers—"don't like to accept calls from Asia. I think it's hilarious myself."

"I do too. It's amazing that you got through at all. Are you ready?"

"No. Are you?"

"No, but we have to leave."

He took her in his arms and kissed her again, a long, lingering kiss that spoke of the future.

At Tan Son Nhut, Casey's windowless, patched-up C-130 set down. She tossed the Mickey Mouse bag into the yawning opening in the back of the plane. With ease Mac lifted her onto the cargo ramp. The plane's engines wheezed and sputtered. "You didn't tell me what you want to call your dog," Mac shouted.

As the hydraulic ramp lifted up with a loud whine, and the wind whipped at her hair, Casey yelled at the top of her lungs, "Fred. What are you going to call yours?"

"Gus," Mac bellowed. The ramp slammed shut and the plane taxied off. He waved frantically.

Then Mac checked into the flight operations office, and minutes later boarded a Huey helicopter. He was airborne almost instantly.

Even though they were going in separate directions, they were doing what they'd come to do, trying to make a difference. But they'd also found the love that had eluded them all their lives.

Chapter 6

BACK IN THE world, the Beach Boys topped the charts with "Sloop John B," and the front pages of newspapers carried headlines that Sophia Loren had tripped to the altar for the second time. Those headlines gave way to others when an unmanned spaceship filmed the moon. The populace buzzed anew when twenty-one-year-old actress Mia Farrow, star of *Peyton Place,* married fifty-one-year-old crooner Frank Sinatra. On American campuses, students began to picket, march, and chant, and sometimes riot in opposition to the Vietnam War.

In New York, at the United Nations, Hanoi insisted that the United States must end the bombing in Vietnam before peace talks could begin. Three days later attention turned to the Baltimore Orioles, who swept the Dodgers in the World Series.

The headlines swept back to Vietnam seventeen days later with LBJ's surprise visit to South Vietnam and his unexpected visit to Cam Ranh Bay to salute his troops. "You are fighting a vicious and illegal aggression across this little nation's frontier," he told them. The same troops looked on while the President of the United States awarded General Westmoreland the Distinguished Service Medal for courage and leadership. The Distinguished Service Cross was presented to Captain Mac Carlin, U.S. Army Provisional Reconnaissance Detachment. Their handshakes were firm and manly. Secretary of State Dean Rusk clapped Mac on the shoulder and said in lowered tones, "Mac, your father is going to be so proud of you he'll strut like a peacock."

"Yes, sir," Mac said stiffly.

"I'll give your regards to him."

Mac wanted to tell him not to bother, but he remained silent. He found himself laughing after LBJ turned to the troops as he was boarding his plane and said, "Come home safe and sound."

Mac did his best that day to hitch a ride north on a Huey to see Casey. He had already boarded when he was asked to give up his spot on the plane to two wounded men. After that, he hadn't had much choice but to head back to the Ho Chi Minh trail, his home away from home.

Five days later, on Halloween, Mac received word that he was the father of a seven-pound, three-ounce baby girl named Jenny. He tried to absorb the news, wanted to be happy and elated, but only felt sad and depressed. He didn't even care that Alice hadn't kept her word to name the baby after his mother.

THE ONLY THINGS that interested Mac were Casey Adams and his own safety.

He didn't see Casey again for six months. It seemed an eternity. He did, however, write weekly to her, sometimes only a few scribbled lines, other times, long two-page letters, which she returned in kind.

When word filtered down the Bamboo Pipeline that a Fourth of July picnic was being planned on China Beach, Mac finagled and connived to get a twelve-hour pass to Saigon, where he wasted three whole hours trying to get a call through to Benny at the Pentagon. When he finally heard his friend's voice, he said, "Just listen, Benny, and do what I tell you." He spoke loudly so his voice would carry over the static on the wire. "You got it all?"

"Every word. This is all the way to . . . the top. I saw that picture of you shaking hands with LBJ and Rusk. Rusk is your old man's new best buddy, according to the papers. They played golf when he got back, in case you're interested."

"I'm not. How's Sadie?"

"Misses you. I saw little Jenny. Are you interested?"

"No," Mac said coolly.

"Okay, I can deal with that. Who is this girl, Mac?"

"My destiny, my life. Don't ask questions unless you can

handle the answers. I gotta go, have some shopping to do for the men. I want this done ASAP, Benny."

"Yesterday, old buddy. Take care of yourself."

"You too."

ONE WEEK LATER, as Casey Adams and Lily Gia were peeling off their operating gowns, the chief operating room nurse, Maureen Hagen, appeared at their sides with a sheaf of papers in her hands and a murderous look on her face. "Get your gear together, girls, you're being transferred to Da Nang. According to that chopper pilot, you have about five minutes."

"What?" Casey blurted. "Why?"

"Did we do something wrong?" Lily demanded.

"Ever see this before?" Hagen waved a crackly piece of paper under Casey's nose.

"It looks like a notarial seal. No, I never saw that before."

The disgust on Hagen's face finally registered with Casey. "Someone very high up wants you transferred to Da Nang where you will work in a nice, clean, air-conditioned hospital with trauma patients. You will work nine to five. The same thing goes for you, Gia. There will be accommodations for you, your own apartment with your very own bathroom, and you will have air-conditioning. You'll be able to go to the beach. Enjoy yourselves, ladies," she said nastily.

Casey stood rooted to the floor. "Major Hagen, there must be some mistake. I didn't put in for a transfer. Maybe there's another Casey Adams someplace in Vietnam. I don't want to go. I'm needed here."

"Me too," Lily bleated.

"This is a direct order, ladies. Get your gear and move out." Casey still didn't move. "I don't understand this."

"Obviously, someone you know has a lot of political power," Major Hagen said, her voice less harsh than before. "I didn't think for a minute it was you. Good luck, girls. Think about us up here from time to time."

They scurried like rats across the compound, throwing their belongings into their duffels. Lily was waiting when Casey joined her, carrying the cornflower-blue dress bundled in the cornflake wrappers under her arm. Overhead the rotors of the helicopter whined. It sounded to Casey like *MacMacMacMac.*

"I figured out why you're going, but I don't know why I'm going. It was Mac, right? They can't make me go, can they?" Lily said in a strange little-girl voice.

"The army can make you do whatever it wants. They allowed you to work in our hospitals, so I guess they feel they have a claim to you. If it was Mac, he would want to make sure I had a friend. Oh, Lily, do you think he's at Da Nang now?" Casey asked excitedly.

"Let's go, ladies," the chopper pilot called out. "Straight to Da Nang, no stops along the way."

THREE DAYS LATER, their blanket spread out on the sand, books in hand, Lily giggled, "I can get used to this real easy."

"Me too. Nine to five is wonderful. And two days off. It's almost obscene."

"And all the comic books I want." Lily sighed happily. "I just love comic books."

While Lily's eyes scanned the colorful, tattered comics, she wasn't really reading the captions. She was thinking instead about her friendship with Casey and what it really meant to be here in Da Nang. She was a nurse, trained in the United States to help the sick. She thought of herself as a good nurse, graduating second in her class of sixty. It was right, and just, that she give back a little here in her own country for the wonderful education she'd gotten in the States. She'd done her share, given one hundred percent, just the way Casey had. Now, thanks to Mac Carlin, she had a plum assignment. This was her chance to lead an almost normal life with nine-to-five hours. She had time off. She could go to the Officers' Club and socialize, make new friends. She turned the page of the comic book.

Tomorrow, if she wanted, when she got off duty at three-thirty, she could hitch a ride to Saigon to see her family and Eric, sleep in her own bed, and be back to go on duty at seven. She could take Casey with her if she wanted to. Immediately, she negated the idea. Later, she would invite Casey to her parents' home. She looked at Casey, who was struggling hard over a letter to Mac. She knew her friend would write the letter over and over until it was perfect, long after she herself was asleep. Casey was in love, that was obvious. Lily crossed her fingers the way she'd seen her American friends back in the States do and whispered, *"Don't let anything go wrong for Casey."*

They were so alike. They were the same size, right down to their shoe size. They liked the same things, liked to read the same books, liked the same movies, felt the same way about world politics and religion. They were both dedicated nurses, and both loved totally.

Casey was closer to her than a flesh and blood sister. Sisters rarely confided details to one another about their love life. She and Casey did, in the quiet, sultry nights. They also shared their hopes and dreams, and in the darkness, it was easy to speak of one's humiliations, one's fears. But there was one great difference between them. Lily turned her head slightly, her oblique eyes full on Casey; she knew she would give up anything if she could be an American with yellow hair and blue eyes. If she were American, she might stand a better chance with Eric. If she were American, she wouldn't have to see the shame in her parents' eyes. The thought was so stupid, so shameful, Lily slid down in her beach chair. If she were American, she wouldn't have Vietnamese parents who didn't understand how their daughter could fall in love with a married doctor who was going to leave her behind. But then, if the situation were reversed and she had American parents and fell in love with a Vietnamese, those same parents would toss her out on her ear. Why can't I just be a human being? she wondered.

There were no letters, no messages from Eric in her room. There was nothing for her to read, to hold close to her heart, except a picture of him. In the beginning he'd made crazy promises to her, saying he'd take her back to the States with him. He said his marriage had soured and he would divorce his wife. He'd said he never had an affair, and she believed him. Now, she wasn't sure. If he really loved her, he would have found a way to get word to her, the way Mac had with Casey. Mac had found a way during a war. But then, Mac was an

American and Casey was half American. Maybe that was the difference. It was obvious to her that neither one of them worried about shame, while she herself felt consumed with guilt. Was Eric seeing other women? Honesty forced her to acknowledge that he probably was, as he had an enormous sexual appetite, which needed to be satisfied on a regular basis. She felt like crying when she wondered how many women he'd seen since she'd left Saigon for Qui Nhon. Once she'd asked Casey what she thought about her romance with the American doctor. After Casey hemmed and hawed, she'd said, "In my eyes, marriage is forever. Any man who cheats on his wife will cheat on his mistress. I won't marry until I'm certain in my mind it will work. Marriage is hard enough without having to worry about faithfulness. If you aren't in too deep, Lily, get out before your heart breaks. What will you do when Eric leaves to return to the States?"

"I'll wait for him to return to me," she'd responded.

And then Casey said, "What if he doesn't come back? What if he doesn't get a divorce and decides to stay with his family?"

Lily recalled how blasé she had been when she'd responded, "There is no other man for me. I will love only once. I will simply wait. It is my way."

She'd read pity in her friend's eyes, but it hadn't mattered. Now they didn't talk about Eric anymore because it made Casey uncomfortable. So Lily did what the American girls did—she wrote it all down in her diary and relived her memories in the darkness before she fell asleep. Memories and dreams, that was all she had. And, of course, Casey, and her disapproving parents. That they didn't go together was all right. She'd accepted it and lived one day at a time. Happiness would find her when it was time.

"Lily, listen to what I've written and tell me if it sounds . . . ungrateful. I don't want to hurt Mac's feelings. I'm sure he went to a great deal of trouble to have us sent here."

The Asian girl listened, her dark eyes troubled. Afterward she said, "A bit strong, Casey. Why don't you just be honest and tell him you want to go back?"

"Then I'll never get to see him. Five times we were scheduled to meet, and five times we were—what's that expression?—blown out of the water. I need to see him. Letters and notes aren't enough. I keep telling myself I've packed more into the time I've been here than if I worked in a hospital for ten years. Maybe twenty. We left Major Hagen shorthanded. I feel so guilty when I think of all the parents of those wounded soldiers. I have to go back, Lily," Casey said firmly. "But that doesn't mean you have to go back."

"If you go, I go. We're a team. Will it be as easy as it was to get here?"

"I have no idea," Casey said. "We aren't needed here. If anything, we're resented."

"Then you have made the decision?"

"Yes, right after the Fourth of July picnic. I'm not giving that up. It might be the last time I get to see Mac. I have seven more months to go after the picnic, and the way our luck is running, we'll be lucky if we squeeze one more meeting in. Do you think he'll understand, Lily?" Casey asked anxiously.

"If he's the man you think he is, then yes, he will understand."

"What about Eric?" She counted on her fingers. "It's almost time for him to leave here, isn't it?"

"One more month," Lily said lightly.

"You're going to Saigon this weekend, aren't you?"

"Yes. I've made arrangements with one of the C-130 pilots."

"The blue dress is ready." Casey smiled.

"Oh, no, I can't. You haven't worn it yet. I was to be second, not first. It is not right. Thank you anyway."

"I don't want to hear another word. You're taking it with you. I can't wear that gorgeous creation to a Fourth of July picnic. It's perfect for an evening of dancing and dinner in Saigon. Take notes, I want to hear every single thing that happens. Well, almost everything."

Lily grinned. "That's more like it."

THE BLAZING SUN was so brutal, Mac removed his helmet. He ordered his men to do the same. He had no desire to fry his brain in this godforsaken country. The sky was bluer than he'd ever seen it. His men were tired after two firefights in a row, and he felt as if he might collapse any second. He popped two salt tablets and watched his men do the same. He had a good perimeter now. "Kick back, men, get some rest." He knew it was a joke, but it sounded good even to his ears.

Overhead a squadron of Phantom jets streaked by, followed by a second set. B-52's would follow soon, based on his orders. Today would be no more than mop-up, a welcome release for himself as well as his men. He wanted to relax, to reread the last letter from Casey, but he couldn't—not until his wounded were safely aboard the medevac choppers. And, God willing, there might be another letter from Casey. At least he hoped so; he hadn't heard from her for over two weeks.

"What's taking them so long, Captain?" the medic asked, his hands tight on a pressure bandage. "This ain't exactly a hot LZ," he grumbled.

"Freeze, what's the problem?" Mac shouted, not liking the looks of the medic's patient. He felt his heart thud when he looked down at the young kid, a boy from Nebraska.

"Mortars, sir. The first chopper got hit. There's one on the way. The pilot is that guy Rick. If anyone can get through, it's him."

The relief Mac felt at his radioman's words was so intense, he felt himself momentarily start to black out. Rick had a guardian angel on his shoulder—every foot soldier, every grunt, every officer said so. He himself was a believer. He'd seen the chopper pilot land in LZ's so hot with enemy bullets, the ground smoldered. The guy had some kind of help from on high.

It took eighteen minutes for the chopper to get there. It swirled up such a thick dust cloud when it landed that Mac had to drop to his knees.

Mac swiped at the dust settling over his body as the helicopter took off. His face was black with dirt. He waved, knowing Rick couldn't see him. What the hell would they do without men like Rick? His shoulders slumped. He'd been given a message that the two men didn't make it. He'd known they wouldn't but hearing it confirmed made him so angry, he slammed his helmet on the ground. "Son of a bitch!"

"Easy, Major," Phil Pender said, coming up behind him. "Here, have a smoke."

Mac turned. This was a new Phil Pender, one he'd actually come to like and respect. He was lean now, hard and tough, a man fighting for his life along with the rest of the company. It hadn't happened overnight; in fact it had taken six months before the snappy lieutenant got his act together. When he realized he was on the trail for good, he'd buckled down. Next to Stevens and himself, Pender had the most kills in the outfit. He'd even managed to take two prisoners, a feat headquarters recognized and rewarded. Pender was a captain now, and he himself was a major.

"The perimeter is as tight as a duck's ass, Major. There's a stream over there in case you want to cool off. Stevens found it by accident. Well, actually, the truth is, it's little more than a puddle, but it sure as hell is wet."

"Thanks, Pender." There was no need to give Pender orders. He seemed to know instinctively what was required in his C.O.'s absence.

Mac laughed when he saw the water Pender referred to. He almost hated to disturb the little puddle. He dropped to his haunches. He was about to dip his hands when he noticed, because he was so low to the ground, that the vines and greenery were trampled on the opposite side of the puddle. He'd come down a path that had been hacked by his men. The fine hairs on the back of his neck moved. He found himself looking overhead, sensing danger. He listened, his eyes watchful. It was so still, so quiet, he could hear his own heartbeat. He looked at the puddle again. He had only an instant, which he used to drop to the ground. He rolled back into the thick greenery, whistling shrilly at the same time he opened fire, spraying the perimeter of the puddle. He heard a grunt, a curse, and gunfire. He rolled again before he opened fire a second time, followed by return fire.

When the jungle was silent again, Mac thrashed through, his eyes murderous. "Pender, I'm going to string your ass from the nearest tree! Didn't you check?"

"Yes, sir, I did," Pender grated.

"How many were there?"

"Seven, sir," Sergeant Stevens said. "You got them all. Do we leave them?"

"The VC come back for their dead. Drag them out of here and set up an ambush. Pender, you jackass, this is your detail."

Back inside the perimeter, Mac sat down. He'd lost his cool, something no good officer was supposed to do. For a few brief minutes he'd stared at his own mortality, and he'd reacted. Jesus Christ, was he ever going to get it down to a science? Sloppy leadership, every officer's nightmare. Shit! He had to remember Pender was as green as he was. Still, a puddle in the middle of the jungle should have been suspect, even to Pender. He couldn't blame Pender for the band of VC. The little weasels were everywhere—under bushes, in the trees, in caves and holes. Just because an area looked clean didn't mean it was. This wasn't his turf. He couldn't ever lose sight of that fact.

The idea of going into politics was starting to look better and better. "Bull*shit!*" he exploded, thumping the ground next to him. A snake, whose sleep was disturbed, slithered into the open, rearing its obscene-looking head, poised to strike.

"I got 'im, Captain. Don't even breathe," Pender hissed. A second later the snake's head was airborne, the main body twitching at Mac's feet.

"Good work, Pender," Mac said gruffly.

"Just trying to do my job, sir," Pender said quietly.

Mac moved into the open, but not before he kicked the snake's remains into the jungle, cursing as he did. Twice within an hour's time he'd stared at death. He felt himself shudder. Jesus, did it mean his time was coming close? He was beginning to feel as if he was only one step ahead of the Grim Reaper. If he wasn't careful, he was going to spook his men. He had to get himself together.

"Sir," Freeze said, "an order to stand by for cover fire just came in. Supplies. And some mail."

Mac gave the order to take cover as a Huey gunship perforated humid air. He watched as it circled overhead, then banked, hoping to draw enemy fire. Seconds later, a second ship sizzled in, dropped supplies and lifted off, all within five minutes.

"Stevens, distribute the ammo; Freeze, dole out the C-rations; Pender, sort the mail."

The mood of the men lifted when they heard the word mail. Word from home. How bright and hopeful their faces were. Mac felt a lump rise in his throat. For a little while, until they started on their trek up the mountainous terrain, things would be okay. Letters from home, the cure-all for just about anything.

Pender handed three letters to Mac: one from his father, one from Benny, and one from Alice. He read his father's one-page, large scrawled note first, just to get it out of the way.

Dear Mac,

Dean Rusk stopped by the other day to fill me in on your activities over there. I understand you're well thought of in the upper echelons of the army. (He told me the Distinguished Service Cross you received will look good in the papers when you throw your hat in the ring.)

We're gearing up for your return, eight months or so, isn't it? If you like, I can have you ordered back here so you can be home for the holidays. Advise as to your intentions.

The letter was signed Justice Marcus Carlin, after which his father penned in his initials. Mac snorted. "You know what you can do with all your grand plans, Pop," he muttered.

He ripped at the envelope from Alice written weeks before. A picture of baby Jenny fluttered to the ground. He picked it up, stared at it with clinical interest, and wondered why he didn't feel paternal. He read the short note.

Dear Mac,

I know you're alive, otherwise the army would be knocking on the door. Your father told me you receive mail even though you're in the jungle. So, if you receive mail, why don't you send mail?

I understand it's very warm over there. What do the women wear? Do they know the miniskirt is in fashion, or do they wear some kind of traditional clothing?

I will probably never forgive you for giving Benny your power of attorney. That was a lousy thing for you to do, Mac. A baby certainly costs a lot of money. You should be ashamed to have your wife beg for money.

Jenny is growing rapidly. She eats constantly.

The letter was signed, Your wife, Alice.

Mac looked at the picture of the baby again. She looked like Alice. She was chubby with a full head of hair. He supposed she was a pretty child, but her face was screwed up in a grimace. He imagined she was wearing a dirty diaper, which Alice was too lazy to change. He slid the picture back into the envelope and ripped at Benny's letter, which was as normal as apple pie and hot dogs.

Dear Mac,

How's it going, good buddy? Jeez, I envy you. Not really. Your old man managed to get an article in the *Washington Star* about you after Johnson and Rusk's visit. It read real good. I saved it in case you want to see it when you get back.

Important news. Carol is pregnant. She swears it's going to be a boy this time. Better be, is all I can say. We're painting everything blue. I've never seen Carol so happy. Me too, for that matter. Every man wants a son. I talked it over with Carol, and she agreed to name the baby after you, if you have no objections. We want you to be the godfather. We can do it by proxy for now, and when you get back we can do it all over again.

No luck in tracking Bill. I've got this gumshoe named Snedeker on it. There, for a while, we thought we had a hot lead, but it didn't pan out. We're now working on magazine subscription lists, since Bill was a sports fiend. Something might turn up.

I saw Sadie last week. We spent the entire evening talking about you. She misses you terribly. She's planning a ticker tape parade for you when you get back. Don't laugh, she'll pull it off too, you wait and see.

On the home front—your wife is more than a little per-

turbed with me. I didn't know speech could be as flowery as
hers. She even had your old man call me to loosen the purse
strings. I told them no soap. Before I dole any monies out,
I make her tell me what it's for, and then I ask the world's
best budgeter if it will fly. What that means is I go by Carol.
By the way, she loves tooling around in your Benz. That's
something else Alice didn't like. All is well, so don't worry
about it.

   Your last letter was an eye opener. I knew you could do it,
Mac. I'm so proud of you, I could just bust. You just watch
your butt is all I can say. You and I have things to do and
places to go when you get back, and my kid needs a godfather, one who can give him ritzy presents, because that's the
only way he's going to get them.

   Take it easy, Mac, I miss you. Carol and I include you in
our prayers every day. Carol sends her love, the girls send
kisses, and I send you my best.

                                                      Benny

Mac wiped at his eyes. Goddamn sweat, a man could hardly
see straight. The letters went in his field pack.
   His fingers were careful, cautious, as he undid the flap of a
fourth letter. Rick had dropped it off along with the information about his men. Before Mac unfolded the single piece of
paper, he held it to his nose, his eyes closing as he brought
Casey's image to the forefront of his mind.
   The moment he finished it, Mac pushed his helmet back on
his head. "I'll be damned," he muttered. He felt like standing
up and shouting "Hooray!" for the whole damn United States
Army to hear. She wanted to go back to Pleiku where she was
needed, but not until after the Fourth of July picnic. "Please
understand, Mac," she'd written, "I came here to do what I'm
trained to do, just as you are doing. What kind of person would
I be if I sat here on the beach reading novels when I could be
helping some dedicated doctor save one of *your* men?"
   She was right and he was wrong. Jesus, was he ever going to
do anything right? The nurses and doctors were as vital to this
war as the men who fought it. He laughed then, a sound of

pure, unadulterated joy. His men smiled tiredly. It was good to hear someone laugh in this hellhole. The problem was, how was he going to rectify his mistake? By taking precious time from his visit to Da Nang for the famous picnic all of Vietnam knew about. He'd go to Saigon on foot, if necessary, or maybe he could manage to get a call patched through from Da Nang. Whatever it took, he would do. "She's a winner," he told himself over and over. He read the letter again and again. When he was confident he knew the contents by heart, it too went into his field pack.

He got to his feet and stomped on an army of red ants that were as big and fat as his pinky finger. He winced at the sound his boot made when he crushed them. They left a vicious sting that made a person's eyes water. He could see the men swatting at them as they chewed through their fatigues.

Red ants, bamboo vipers, blistering skies, and VC—all treasures of Southeast Asia.

"Saddle up! Move out!"

Day 487 on the Ho Chi Minh trail.

Chapter 7

WHILE THE SOLDIERS and nurses, along with Red Cross volunteers, prepared the momentous Fourth of July picnic, hoping it would take the brutal edge off the horror of the war, the American populace was attending a free Barbara Streisand concert in New York, and Elvis Presley was tying the knot with Priscilla Beaulieu. Titillation turned to sorrow when Spencer Tracy took his last curtain call at Katharine Hepburn's kitchen table, followed by Jayne Mansfield's tragic death in an auto accident.

Who could blame the Americans for wanting a pleasant memory to take home from Vietnam? Certainly not General Westmoreland, often referred to as Westy by his peers. It was rumored that 446,000 Americans were in Vietnam, and that Westy was asking Defense Secretary Robert McNamara for an additional hundred thousand men, saying, "We're winning slowly and steadily." On hearing the news, those attending the picnic sent up a shout of victory that was short-lived.

"Let's paint this place red, white, and blue and drink to old Westy," a grunt shouted as he wielded a paint brush, intent on painting anything that wasn't moving.

The war wasn't exactly put on hold, but it came damn close when the chopper pilots and the Bird Dog pilots dropped leaflets all over the country announcing the picnic on China Beach. There was no wording on the clever leaflets, simply pictures of men and women reclining on beach chairs with drinks, topped by colorful parasols alongside a beach with a china plate for identification. Word spread faster than a brushfire.

Later, by general consensus, it was decided the Fourth of

July picnic at China Beach was the highlight of the Vietnam War.

Choppers started to arrive an hour past dawn. On the ground hundreds of hands lifted down crates of corn, and cartons of hot dogs and hamburger patties packed in dry ice. Condiments were whisked into tents along with barrels of Budweiser beer and Coca-Cola. Buns, five hundred to the bag, were left sealed to ensure their freshness. The ice cream, which turned out to be chocolate and cherry-vanilla, was still frozen solid, thanks to the Sealtest Company, which packed it in special shipping freezers for the long trip. There was even a sheet cake cut into sections, decorated like Old Glory, along with enough candles to set the beach on fire. Tens of thousands of marshmallows were wrapped in identical bun bags. When the fifth chopper landed, a shout went up from the eager soldiers unloading the plane. "Watermelons! Real goddamn watermelons!"

The sixth chopper was full of entertainers, singers in miniskirts and comics of every description. A small band in glittering, sequined outfits chorused, "Hi, guys, what's new!"

The fifth chopper pilot, his rotors still at high speed, leaned out, waving a clipboard. "I need Carlin's signature on this before I can return to the base."

Mac, in a flowered shirt, straw hat, and canary-yellow shorts, strode over to the pilot. He scribbled his name, a slash that was little more than a scrawl and completely illegible.

"I don't know how you pulled this off, Major, but I'd sure as hell put you up for a commendation. Don't tell me, I don't want to know. Just make sure you get me out of the stockade if some smart-ass general gets downwind of this. There's not a man in this country who will rat on you, Major, so rest easy and save me a hot dog. I'll be back later in the day for some ice cream and corn and whatever the hell else you have."

"You got it," Mac chortled happily.

How *had* he pulled it off? He was grinning from ear to ear when he thought about it. With the help of friends, that's how. If there was one thing Benny liked, it was a challenge. He looked down at the paper he was holding. On the back were two notes, one from Sadie and one from Benny.

Benny's read, "I hope you get gas from all of this! I'll be thinking about you when those fireworks go off. It was my pleasure, Mac."

Sadie's read, "Mac, honey, I had a ball helping Benny with this. Don't eat too much—you'll get sick. We had help from some of the White House personnel. All I had to promise was that I'd put their pictures on the wall. The camera is in the middle of the marshmallows, along with twenty rolls of film. Send them on and we'll make you copies. I have a new board in the bar, just for you and the wonderful people you're serving with."

He saw Casey then, a vision in pink, complete with a cherry-red visored cap and dark sunglasses. Next to her was Lily in white shorts and halter, every bit as pretty. When Casey spotted him, she ran straight into his arms. He hugged her, a devilish grin on his face. A minute after she was introduced, Lily excused herself.

"I missed you," Casey whispered. "Please, you have to tell me you aren't angry with my decision to go back to Pleiku. Tell me you understand."

"Of course I understand. By tomorrow morning it will be taken care of," Mac said, hugging her.

As they walked along they could hear hushed tones, fingers pointing in Mac's direction. "That's the guy. Hebrew National hot dogs. In Vietnam, yet!" Hundreds of times they stopped so Mac could shake hands or get clapped on the back. Rank was left back on the trail. Here, he was one of the guys. Casey loved every minute of it.

Every fifty feet there was a small fire and a phonograph. The Beatles sang "When I'm Sixty-Four" and "Lovely Rita," while further down the beach the Rolling Stones sang "Ruby Tuesday." From somewhere off in the distance a third phonograph was playing the "Star Spangled Banner" over and over.

Laughter, good-natured teasing, frolicking in the water, and gorging on food were the orders of the day. There was no drunkenness, no brawling, no anger of any kind. This picnic was too important to everyone attending. Choppers set down and then lifted off, delivering men who shouted happily as they shed their combat boots and field packs to plunge into the sparkling blue water before accepting beer and hot dogs. Men straggled in from the jungle while others came in jeeps. At one point Mac, who felt like an indulgent father, estimated the body count on the beach to be around a thousand. Some of the guests stayed no longer than thirty minutes, just time enough to have their pictures taken alongside a pretty entertainer and to get something to eat. It was the nurses, dressed in skimpy bathing suits, who arranged the relay races with scoops of ice cream for prizes. They worked in shifts so they too could take advantage of the cool, beautiful beach. Mac and Casey took their turns cooking and pumping beer and snapping pictures. Several times during the day, Mac announced over one of the gerry-built loudspeakers that copies of the pictures would be available at Saigon headquarters in about a month, or as soon as Sadie could send them.

It was a day neither of them would ever forget.

The sun was setting, and the USO show was over, when Casey and Mac handed over their fire tongs to the next shift. Hand in hand they walked down to the water's edge. Off in the distance the sounds of war, which, up till now, had been subdued, with nothing more than an occasional mortar burst from the south, grew more fierce. They looked at one another, and by silent, mutual consent they headed back to Casey's small hooch. She waved airily to Lily, who was about to start off on the one-legged sack race.

"I love you," Mac whispered huskily. "I have to tell you this now, because I don't know when we'll see each other again. I also want to make some kind of plan in case I get sent out of here before you do." The crazy urge to tell her about baby Jenny almost choked him. He bit down on his lower lip, tasting his own blood. If he talked about it to Casey, she probably could figure out why he felt the way he did, but then she would know he was married, and he wasn't ready to divulge that fact just yet.

"I love you very much too," Casey said. "That first day when we met and chased the fog, I knew then. I . . . I thought I was never going to see you again. And now this. Our time over here, even though we haven't seen much of one another, has allowed me to love you even more. Our letters are all that have kept me going. But I am so fearful that one day I'll be staring down at my patient and it will be you. I live with that fear, Mac."

He'd thought the same thing, wondering how she would react if it did happen.

"Hey, look at me," he said, tilting her chin up. "That isn't going to happen." He said it with more confidence than he felt. "Tell the truth," he teased, "I'm invincible. I pulled this off, didn't I?"

"You certainly did. But that doesn't mean I'm going to stop worrying."

Mac laughed. "This is probably the first time in my life anyone has really worried about me." Sadie didn't count. Sadie worried when it rained and he didn't have his fishing boots on. Alice didn't count at all. She hadn't appeared even once the time he'd been hospitalized after a car crash, giving the excuse hospitals made her sick.

"Okay, you can worry about me. So, this is where you live, huh?"

"For another day at least. The bed is soft and dry," she teased.

"Uh-huh," Mac said, the ring of heat around his neck expanding. His ears felt incredibly warm. He felt himself stiffen, a condition he'd been experiencing all day long. It was so unbearable, it was difficult to walk.

They were inside Casey's hooch, each shedding their clothing as if by some silent command. Eyes as blue and hot as the Asian sun stared directly into his own, and what he read there sent his pulses throbbing, echoing through him. A sound escaped his lips, a groan, a plea, as he brought her close against him, crushing his mouth to hers, tasting her, feeling her lips yield to his. When he broke away, he saw the flush in her cheeks, the way her lips parted, lifting once again for his kiss.

Mac brought her closer, aware of the sea's scent in her hair. Her skin smelled like a sunshiny day, and the delicious womanly scent that was hers alone. He felt her arms wrap around his neck, tighter, pulling him down with her to the bed. She was seducing *him*. He thought he would choke on his own desire. A rich sound of pleasure bubbled from his mouth.

Something inside him wanted to rebel, some part of his manhood and his pride. *He* wanted to be the aggressor, *he* wanted to be the one to show her how it could be between a man and a woman.

She lay in his arms, fragile as the first flower of spring. He buried his face in her hair, reveling in the softness and the feeling it evoked in him. He drew back, gazing at her in the dim light of the room. All of his pent-up yearnings, feelings he hadn't realized existed until this day, rose to the surface as he slid down beside her. Her skin was golden as honey, soft as satin. Exhilaration coursed through him.

Once again his lips clung to hers, and Casey's head spun as she felt her body come to life beneath his touch. He was gentle, his hands unhurried, as he intimately explored her. His mouth moved against hers, and her senses reeled as she strained against him, trying to be closer to him, trying to make them one.

With infinite tenderness Mac loved her. He put a guarded check on his growing feverishness, waiting for her, patiently arousing her until her passion was as demanding and as greedy as his own.

His hands seared her flesh as they traveled the length of her, stopping to caress a taut breast, a yielding, welcoming thigh.

His lips left the sweet moistness of her mouth to find the tender place where her throat pulsed and curved into her shoulder. Down, down, his mouth traveled, turning her in his arms, finding and teasing places that brought consummate pleasure and sent waves of desire through her veins. The tawny luster of her breasts beckoned him, their pink, rosy crests standing erect and tempting. Her slim waist was a perfect fit for his hands, her firm haunches accommodating the pleasure of his thigh. He placed a long, sensual kiss on the golden triangle her nudity offered, and Casey gave herself in panting surrender.

The strains of "When I'm Sixty-Four" drifted through the hooch as Mac's lips touched her everywhere, satisfying his thirst for her, a thirst that was deep and raw. The intricate details of her body intoxicated him with their perfection. The supple curve of her thigh, the flatness of her belly, the dimples in her haunches, the lightly muscled length of her legs. But it was always to the warm shadows between her breasts that he returned, imagining that they beckoned him in silent, provocative appeal.

Casey's body cried out to him. She offered herself completely to his seeking hands and lips. And Mac, sensing her passion, furthered her advances, hungry for those secret places that held such fascination for him. He indulged in her lusty passion, which met and equaled his own.

Beneath his touch her skin glistened with a sheen of desire. She slid her hands down the flat of his belly, eager to know him and satisfy her yearning need. She strove to learn every detail of his flesh, touching his rippling, muscular smoothness, feeling the strength beneath. She kissed the hollow near the base of his throat, tasting the saltiness left by the China Sea. And when she cried his name, it tore from her throat, painful and husky, demanding he put an end to her torment and satisfy the craving he had instilled in her.

As if on cue, the galaxy of early stars overhead became one world, fused together by the white-hot heat they created. Together they spun out beyond the moon, reveling in the beauty each brought the other, seeing in each other a small part of themselves. One golden-haired spirit, one dark, came together in their passion, creating an aura of sunlight in the dark, endless night.

They slept to the strains of "When I'm Sixty-Four" and woke an hour later to the same strains. They smiled at one another. "Oh, Mac, I love you so," Casey whispered.

Mac tickled her chin. "I love you more," he said huskily. Once again he buried his face in her hair when a picture of a pink-cheeked, dark-haired cherub invaded his vision. He squeezed his eyes shut so the vision would vanish.

Casey stirred in his arms. With the starlight spilling through the open windows, he realized just how beautiful she was. Her hair gleamed with silver that belonged to the stars alone, her skin smooth and glowing, softer and sleeker than silk. At his touch on her cheek she leaned her face into his hand, eyes closing, lips parting. Wordlessly he smoothed the golden curls, feeling the satiny strands between his fingers, thinking that her hair was like the moon itself, shining and sleek.

When she turned to him, it was to offer her lips to him, clinging softly with arms wrapped tightly around his middle, pressing herself against him. Her appetite for their lovemaking was as intense as his, and that knowledge heightened his desire for her. She was the most exciting woman he'd ever known: soft and lovely one moment, then softer still, but always beautiful.

Casey's emotions found an answering response in Mac as his mouth sought hers hungrily, desperate to satisfy his need for her. Their hands reached for one another, softly touching, rediscovering each sweet caress.

He kissed her neck, tasting the perfumed skin of her earlobe, the gently curving softness of the arch of her throat, that hollow between her breasts which constantly beckoned him. The intricacies of her, the delightful difference invisible to the naked eye, which made her different from all other women. His lips lingered, taking and giving pleasure.

Casey's hands found the smoothness of his back, luxuriating in his warmth and solid physique. Her mouth tenderly nipped at the place where his muscular shoulder yielded to his neck, and she was aware of the quiver of delight that rippled through him.

Mac moved away from her, and when they touched again, his hands slid down her body, adoring her, lifting her into a realm of passion and desire known only to lovers.

His arms circled her, drawing her tightly against him, reveling in the length of her body pressed against his.

Her hands were woven in his hair, pulling it back from his forehead as she kissed him, opening her lips, begging him to enter. Straining against him, her body rose and fell rhythmically, desperately seeking to fill this sudden need that throbbed within her.

Seizing his shoulders, she pressed him backward against the bed. His breathing came in short, rapid rasps, and when she leaned over him, pressing the fullness of her breasts against the fine furring of hairs on his chest, she heard him emit a low, deep growl of pleasure.

Beneath her fingers his skin glistened with a sheen of perspiration, and the long, hard length of him heightened her lusty appetite. Learning her lessons well, taught by him, she tasted every detail of his body, luxuriating in the rippling muscular hardness of him.

Her legs tangled with his as she held herself above him, melting herself to him, rubbing against him, bringing him to the height of his desires. The contact between their bodies was as smooth as satin. She crushed his face into the firm plenitude of her breasts, giving, wanting to give . . . only to give. In giving, she was receiving and being filled with a sense of power that she could evoke this emotion in this strong, rugged man. Bringing him pleasure, pleasuring herself.

She felt his hardness throb between them. His eyes were upon her, delving the darkness, perceiving her with more than his eyes. She was a goddess, golden and fair, bringing the warmth of the sun to his cold, hungry needs.

She mounted him, and the flatness of her belly was hard against his, drawing the aches and the hunger from him. Her breasts were offered to his hands, her mouth as greedy as his own, and he knew there was more between them than finding a momentary respite from the urgency of passion. Love.

IF THERE WAS one thing Mac didn't want to do, it was dress and return to the Ho Chi Minh trail. If he had his choice, he would elect to stay here forever in this little hooch with Casey. He would handle the war and all that went with it. But it was a dream, and Vietnam was no place for dreams, only reality. He kissed Casey, a long, lingering, gentle kiss that spoke of many tomorrows, before he swung his legs over the side of the bed.

"The team is moving to Chu Lai. It isn't that far from Pleiku. We'll manage. Trust me, Casey."

Casey nodded, tears brimming in her eyes. She was up and out of the bed, pulling on shorts and tee-shirt. She wanted every minute possible with Mac. She would walk him to the chopper, kiss him good-bye and not care who saw her.

"They're getting ready to set off the fireworks. I'll miss them," Mac said wistfully. "I knew I was going to miss them, but now that the time is here, I'd like to see them. My mother told me that when I was little she used to take me to see the display, but I don't remember."

Casey linked her arm through his. "Look at it this way, Mac," she said with a giggle in her voice, "we had our own fireworks."

Mac stopped in his tracks. He laughed until his eyes filled. "I'll hold that thought."

"No, don't," Casey said in panic. "If you have our lovemaking on your mind, you won't . . . you could get . . . please don't," she begged.

"Okay, okay," he said, chucking her under the chin. "I'll only think about us when I go to sleep."

"Promise." The worry and concern in Casey's eyes tugged at Mac's heart.

"I promise. Hurry, Casey, I only have two minutes. We'll have to run."

"I'm ready," she said, pointing to her bare feet.

They ran. The last strains of "When I'm Sixty-Four" and "Ruby Tuesday" ended. Mac's face split into a broad grin when he heard the music to "Hail to the Chief." He allowed himself one brief statement before he climbed aboard the chopper. Waving his straw hat, he yelled over the whirling rotors. "Men, on behalf of the President of the United States, I accept your gratitude. Carry on!" he said, saluting smartly. He pretended to catch a kiss Casey blew him. A minute later he was circling overhead. Casey sucked in her breath in awe when she saw the American flag light the sky. She clapped wildly, as did everyone on the beach.

Suddenly Lily was next to her, her eyes as starry as Casey's. Casey winked and Lily giggled.

"Was today as wonderful for you as it was for me?" Casey asked.

"Oh, yes," Lily said dreamily. "We only had a few short hours. Eric left around five-thirty. I've been helping with the food. Everyone is so happy. Mac did a wonderful thing. The fireworks flag was a wonderful send-off, wasn't it?"

"The best," Casey sighed. "How's the food holding up? Is there anything I can do?"

"Help clean up," Lily said, wrinkling her nose. "There's a little of everything left for any stragglers coming in. When the sun was going down we had over two hundred marines, and not a bit of trouble, if you can believe that. If it wasn't for the pilots we couldn't have done it. Come on, time to get back to work."

"Yes, it's time. Life goes on, doesn't it? Oh, Lily, I wish I could stop time and just en—no, I don't wish that at all. What I want is for us all to stay safe so we can get on with our lives."

"We all wish the same thing," Lily said, hugging her friend. "How about a hot dog and some toasted marshmallows? My treat."

"I'd be a fool to turn that down." Casey smiled. Friends were so wonderful.

THREE DAYS LATER Casey leaped from the medevac chopper into a soldier's outstretched arms. The first person she saw was Luke Farrell, sitting on his haunches, staring at what looked like a small garden. "Luke! It's me! I'm back!" Casey cried happily.

"Where's Lily?" Luke muttered.

Casey frowned. She'd expected him to grin and throw his arms about her.

"She . . . she's in Saigon. It was either Saigon or Da Nang. Her parents are in the city, so she elected to stay in Saigon. I thought you'd be happy to see me," she said in an accusing tone. "If you're angry because I didn't say good-bye, there wasn't time. I told Captain Hagen . . . we spoke at the picnic, Luke. I explained all that. Is something wrong?"

Hell yes, there was something wrong. He'd seen her with Mac Carlin at the picnic; his eyes had followed them to her hooch. He'd eaten his hot dog and ear of corn and took off like a scalded cat. He should tell her how hurt he had been. He'd wanted to be the one to go into that hooch with her. He wanted to get up now, to take her in his arms and say, welcome back, but some perverse streak in him wouldn't allow him to stick his neck out for further rejection. He stared at the greenery in front of him. "What could possibly be wrong?" he said sourly. "No pushes. Things are quiet. We only have six patients waiting to be transferred." He poked viciously at a luscious green leaf, careful not to uproot it.

"That's a weed," Casey said tartly. She felt angry and hurt. She'd given up a cushy job in Da Nang to come back here and work at his side, and all she was getting from him was a nasty attitude.

"You can't know that for sure," Luke muttered. "You damn women think you know everything. It's pretty."

"It's still a weed. I know weeds. If you keep watering it, tomorrow it'll be a foot high. Weeds grow fast. You should have planted some flowers. Do you want me to help you?"

"No, I don't want you to help me," Luke snapped. "It made me happy to think this might turn into a flower, and you come along and ruin the whole idea for me. That's shitful, if you want my opinion."

"This isn't about weeds and flowers at all, is it? Look, I had orders, I didn't have a choice, I had to go to Da Nang. I'm back. I didn't belong there. I didn't *want* to be there. So I came back to where I'm needed. What do you want? Do you want me to get down on my knees and beg you to take me back? If that will get you over this . . . this . . . whatever it is you're going through, I'll do it. We're such a good *team*, Luke. Now you've spoiled it all. Water your weeds, see if I care."

Casey stomped off, her shoulders stiff with anger. A few feet across the compound she realized Luke wasn't following her. She thought he would quickly beg her forgiveness. Her shoulders slumped. She dropped her bag and walked back.

"How about a beer, Luke? I'm buying." It was her way of apologizing for whatever it was Luke thought she'd done wrong. She waited, holding her breath, for his response.

"Only if you admit you lied about this gorgeous thing being a weed. Just look at it, for God's sake. It's like green velvet, all shimmery and soft. And look how the water beads up on the leaf. It looks like an upside-down umbrella. I requested flowers, but I guess it wasn't a top priority. I liked those that you planted when you first arrived. I guess I was . . . I wanted things to be like they were before the picnic," he blurted.

"You can't go back, Luke, only forward. You taught me that. Now, how about that beer?"

"I missed you, Casey. I mean, I really missed you."

"And I missed you. God, I couldn't wait to get back here. I thought I'd go out of my mind in Da Nang." Casey stood on her toes and kissed Luke lightly on the lips.

Both of them totally misunderstood the conversation.

TWO WEEKS LATER, across the front page of *Stars and Stripes* blazed a banner headline that read: ARMY HOSTS FOURTH OF JULY PICNIC IN DA NANG. It was a tongue-in-cheek article that claimed the host or hostess of the infamous party was a phantom whose guest list included two hundred marines. The article went on to describe the tons of American food, the fireworks, and the man who thanked everyone in the President's name. The phantom, it read, wore bush shorts, sandals, a flowered shirt and straw hat, the same attire worn by all the guests except the marines, who were in full battle dress.

It was the end of September before Mac received a copy of the article from Phil Benedict, who said in his note: "Your old man called me personally to ask me if you were the phantom. I said, with respect, sir, I work at the Pentagon, how would I know? He said, and this is no joke, that you were making a laughingstock out of him. Not true, old buddy, I heard via the grapevine that the Joint Chiefs thought it was a hell of a feat and they toasted the phantom over drinks the day the paper came out. Onward and upward, old buddy. Stay well."

Mac passed the article around. It was found in December, in the pocket of a dead soldier, tattered and torn, along with his picture of a pretty nurse on his arm, taken at the picnic.

In the real world, December ushered in yuletide festivities the men in Vietnam could only dream about. Another year was drawing to a close, and Americans, if they weren't too busy with holiday shopping, took precious minutes out of their busy schedules to reflect on the year's events. They mourned the death of Louis Washkansky, the world's first heart transplant, paid their respects at St. Patrick's to Cardinal Spellman, and then rushed out to buy the newest appliance called a microwave oven, after which they clucked their tongues in collective approval when the church banned the movie *Barbarella*, starring Jane Fonda.

On December 23, two days before Christmas, the commander-in-chief, Lyndon Johnson, set down at the largest base in Vietnam to confer with, console, and wish the troops a Merry Christmas. Mac stood on the sidelines waiting for a chopper to take him to his appointment in Saigon, where he was to meet and spend the holidays with Casey. He expected to hear the President say he was ordering a lull in the bombing, but instead he said the Viet Cong had met their match and the United States would not "shimmy" in its resolve. He spoke about protesters back home, and assured the troops that slogans and signs could not diminish the pride Americans felt in their fighting men. The applause was restrained. Mac stood, stone-faced, his hands jammed into his pockets.

The death count in the month of December was 365 Viet Cong in the Mekong Delta. Four days later the United States ended its biggest airlift, landing 6500 men in Vietnam. With so many new bodies coming in, Mac and his men could be granted five-day passes for the Christmas holiday.

"Fifteen thousand of our men are dead, with over one hundred thousand wounded," Mac muttered to an enlisted man standing next to him.

"I hear you, sir," the man said quietly. "We're doing our best."

Mac looked at him. Christ, he was so young. He'd probably never shaved yet. Mac felt old and tired by comparison. "I know you are, son. Every man over here has given a hundred and ten percent." He touched him lightly on the shoulder. "Don't forget to write home, soldier," he said quietly.

"I won't, sir. Merry Christmas."

"Merry Christmas," Mac said softly. He ran then. He was in a frenzy to reach Saigon so he could find a church to pray in.

Saigon looked the same, Mac decided, when he checked into

the Princess Hotel. This time he took a suite of rooms. He had the better part of eight hours before Casey arrived. Time to go to church, eat, and do his Christmas shopping. And if it was the last thing he did, he was going to find a Christmas tree so he and Casey could decorate it. This was a Christmas he wanted to remember all his life.

Mac's first stop was the small orphanage there run by French nuns. They escorted him to their chapel, where they told him he could stay as long as he wanted. Nothing, Mac decided, was ever more peaceful than this tiny chapel. He prayed for his men, for all the American men and women in Vietnam. He prayed for Casey, and then he prayed again, asking for guidance in telling her about Alice and the baby. He knew now he must tell her, for he was certain he wouldn't see her again before both of them were rotated back to the States.

"Please help her to understand. Help me to do the right thing," he pleaded in a voice choked with emotion.

He shopped then, going from one store to the next, buying whatever caught his eye. Twice he returned to the hotel with purchases. On his last trip he carried a scrubby pine and a bag of colored tissue paper. He was so proud of himself that he started to whistle as he set the pine in a metal wastebasket he'd filled with water. This was going to be the best Christmas of his life.

He had it all planned. Tomorrow evening, Christmas Eve, he and Casey would go to the orphanage chapel. If there was a service, they would attend; if there was not, they would join the nuns in prayer. Christmas morning they'd share a wonderful breakfast and then go to Lily's apartment to drop off their gifts. Casey, he thought, was as anxious to see Lily as she was to see him. She wanted to see Lily's baby. The thought that Lily might need something prodded him to go out again. According to Casey, Lily was working in the hospital and a mama-san was taking care of the infant, the infant her parents wouldn't acknowledge because he was Amerasian. His own guilt demanded he seek out Lily and hear her story for himself. Casey had been sketchy at best, giving him only the highlights of Lily's sad departure.

He got lost twice before he found the shabby building Lily lived in. He knocked and knocked again. Lily opened the door. She had the infant in her arms. She looked so pretty holding the baby. Mac's throat constricted. "May I come in, Lily?"

"Of course. I'm sorry, my manners are . . . I was just surprised to see you. Is Casey with you?" she asked hopefully.

"No. She should arrive early this evening. Lily, is there anything I can do for you?"

"No, Mac, thank you for asking though. I have my job at the hospital. I can pay my mama-san for taking care of the baby while I work. We have enough food. There is nothing else I need. I appreciate your concern," she said wanly. "Would you care for some tea? It is fresh. I just made it."

"If it's no trouble."

"It is never trouble to fix tea for a friend. Would you like to hold the baby?"

He didn't want to hold the infant, didn't want to know what it felt like to hold a baby in his arms.

"Of course," he said, holding the baby so gingerly that Lily laughed.

"He won't break. He's quite strong actually, and he is a little glutton. He weighed eight pounds at birth," she said proudly.

"He's pretty," Mac said, feeling out of his depth.

Lily laughed again when she set the tea things down on a scarred wooden table. "Girls are pretty, baby boys are handsome."

"I stand corrected. He's a handsome little fellow."

"He looks like his father. Of course, he has my hair color, but his eyes are definitely those of his father."

"Lily, please tell me about it. Perhaps I can help."

Lily looked surprised. "Casey hasn't told you?"

"A little. She's your friend, Lily. She wouldn't think of interfering in your life."

"Casey is the best friend I ever had. I feel like I deserted her," Lily said, wiping at the corners of her eyes.

"Casey doesn't feel that way at all. She wants what's best for you." *This,* he knew, was going to play a big part in Casey's decision when he told her about Alice and the baby.

"I was pregnant before the picnic. I was going to tell Eric that day, but I didn't want to spoil things. I thought I would have more time before he left. He was gone two weeks later. I never got to wear the blue dress," she said sadly. "I did my best to hide my pregnancy from Casey. She did comment a time or two about my weight gain. She didn't pick up on my bouts of nausea either. As soon as I had the baby I wrote and told her."

"If you give me his name and outfit, I can get word to him." He pretended not to see the tears in Lily's eyes. She was so proud he didn't want to offend her.

"He's a doctor and he's married. I knew that in the beginning. We were honest with one another. He already has children. This baby won't make a bit of difference. I know this in here," she said, touching her chest. "I wanted him to love me, and he said he did. For a while I believe he did, when he first arrived. The other nurses told me he was a playboy. But by then it was too late for me, I was in love with him. My parents . . . objected strongly. They love me, but have forbidden me and the child in their home. It is our way, and I understand this. I have disgraced them." Lily cried softly. "My child will suffer all his life for my mistake, and nothing I do can change things."

"Maybe I can change them for you. Maybe I can get you out of here. If I can, will you leave?"

"Oh, yes, yes, Mac, I will leave. This is possible? You could do this?"

"I can try like hell. It may take a while. I rotate out of here in February, so does Casey. If you're willing, so am I. What about your parents?"

"I must do what I must do for my son. Someday my parents will understand this. Now, enjoy your tea and tell me what you and Casey have planned for your holiday."

They talked quietly, so as not to awaken the sleeping infant, until it was time for Mac to return to the hotel to wait for Casey. At the door Lily smiled. "Thank you so much for coming by, Mac. It has been a wonderful visit. I'll look forward to spending Christmas Day with both of you."

It was raining, though the dry season had begun, a steady, gray drizzle that was cold and left Mac feeling raw and half angry. He tried to understand his feelings as he made his way back to the hotel. By the time he reached his hotel he felt chilly, with goose bumps dotting his arms. It was the first time since he'd arrived in Vietnam that he felt anything but hot and sweaty.

He shed his clothes for dry ones before heading for the bar to wait for Casey. His heart was pumping furiously, his adrenaline at an all-time high. Soon he would see the girl he would love into eternity.

OUTSIDE HER TENT the rain fell in torrents, dampening what should have been Casey's exultant mood. She was edgy, overtired, with a headache that wouldn't let up. She'd swallowed eight aspirin in as many hours, with no relief. Her head felt thick, and from time to time she shivered. It never occurred to her that she might be getting sick. She'd been here for twenty-two months and had suffered nothing more than heat rashes. She wouldn't allow herself to get sick, not now, when she would leave within the hour to keep her appointment in Saigon with Mac. In her mind she blamed her overtiredness on five straight days of working eighteen-hour shifts. She was exhausted, but she could sleep on the various hops that would take her to Saigon.

A sudden wave of dizziness overtook her when the chief nurse walked through the open flap of the tent. She shook water from her poncho before she cursed the weather, the VC, and the medical supplies that were already three days overdue. "You still look peaked to me, Casey," Major Hagen said, full of concern. "And you're shivering."

"It's nothing," Casey lied. "I think it's that time of the month, arriving a little ahead of schedule."

"Oh, okay." The relief in Maureen Hagen's voice was so pronounced, Casey had to smile. Hagen inevitably fell apart whenever one of her nurses got sick. She could handle anything else: a soldier's guts steaming in an open wound, amputations, death and more death, but she turned green then white when one of her nurses complained of anything worse than a headache. No one as yet had been able to explain the woman's anxieties.

"I know this isn't the time to speak with you, but I want you to think about what I'm going to ask while you're in Saigon. You'll be rotating pretty soon. I'd like you to think about extending for another six months. The army will send you anywhere in the world for thirty days of leave if you do. You're the best nurse I've ever seen. I honest to God don't know how we're going to get along without you. The doctors came to me and asked me to . . . what they said was you were the finest operating room nurse they ever worked with. So, I'm asking."

Casey pulled on a sweater. "I'll give it serious thought, Major."

"It's all I can ask. Listen, Casey, have a nice Christmas, and say a little prayer if you attend midnight mass."

"I'll do that, Major, and you have a Merry Christmas yourself. Is there anything you want me to bring back from Saigon?"

"A white knight. Barring that, a box of caramels will do nicely."

Casey's face was too white, Hagen thought. And she looked weak slogging through the mud to the chopper pad. Hagen realized she hadn't taken Casey's temperature. What in the hell kind of nurse was she? She'd meant to, intended to. She'd even brought a thermometer with her. But nurses didn't get sick. Nurses cared for the sick. That's all there was to it. "Watch out for her," she whispered in a little prayer.

The first leg of Casey's trip ended in Tuy Hoa, where she boarded a second chopper along with two corporals heading for Cam Ranh Bay. The moment the young men leaped to the ground, the chopper was airborne, its rotors fighting the sluicing rain. When she transferred to yet another chopper in Long Binh, she knew she was sick. She swallowed three aspirins. When she reached Saigon she was so feverish and weak she could barely make it into the airport.

"I'm laying over until tomorrow. I'll help you," the pilot said gently. "Just tell me where you want to go."

Casey debated a moment. Should she go to the hotel or to

Lily's apartment? She didn't want Mac to see her like this, and if she went to Lily's, the baby might pick up her germs. "The Princess Hotel," she croaked. She coughed, her slim body shaking so badly that the pilot held her close.

"I think I should take you to headquarters so a doctor can take a look at you."

Casey shook her head. "This is just a bad cold. Once I get warm I'll be okay. I've been taking aspirins all day. I'll get some fresh juice and some toast and by tomorrow I'll be fine. If I'm not, I'll see a doctor."

"As long as you're sure," the pilot said dubiously.

Casey went through another bout of coughing. Holding her erect, the pilot led her to a waiting taxi and gently helped her into a corner so she wouldn't slip off the seat.

She slept on the short ride. She struggled to wakefulness when the pilot opened the door for her. She tried to get out of the cab, tried to stand on her feet, but her knees buckled. Tears streamed down her cheeks. What was Mac going to think?

Mac stopped pacing long enough to look toward the hotel entrance. A guy carrying a girl. So what. Then he saw the golden head and the Mickey Mouse satchel.

He'd never seen sickness before—death, yes, but not sickness. He saw the tears, heard the apology before he took her in his arms. His eyes questioned the pilot. He was scared witless.

"I wanted to take her to a doctor," the pilot said, "but she said no. She needs a doctor, sir."

"I'll take over, Captain. Thanks for . . . for bringing her here."

"I just need to get warm, Mac. It's a cold. I'm so sorry. I couldn't go back. I didn't . . . I just had this headache when I left . . . the rain . . . I'm so cold. I'm so sorry." She was crying and coughing. Mac felt frightened all over again when he felt the way she was shaking in his arms. "Please," she begged, "don't take me to the hospital. Call Lily, ask her if she'll come over. She might have some antibiotics. I'm out of aspirins. Mac, please."

He could deny her nothing. "Okay," he whispered. In the space of five minutes he'd stripped off her clothing and wrapped her in thick bathroom towels like a mummy. He piled every cover and bedspread he could find in the hotel room on top of her. He turned off the air conditioner and the room started to grow warm almost immediately.

"Do you have any aspirins, Mac?" Casey whispered.

He poured four from the bottle he kept in his shaving kit, then propped her up so she could swallow them with water. His heart fluttered wildly when he smoothed the wispy blond curls back from her forehead. She was burning up. "I have to get you a doctor, Casey. I'll call down to the desk, and then I'll go and fetch Lily."

She knew she was being foolish, stupid even, but she didn't want a doctor, didn't want to be put in the hospital, not on Christmas, not when Mac was here. "No. Just get Lily. Promise me, Mac. If I'm not better tomorrow, we'll call a doctor. This is just a . . . cold that got out of hand. I've spoiled everything, haven't I?" She was crying again, unable to stop.

"Shhh, it's all right. You haven't spoiled anything. I'll take care of you. I'll do whatever you want. Juice, you said you wanted juice. I'll get juice. Yes, orange juice, whatever kind you want. A toddy. You know, tea and whiskey with butter. Or is that rum? I'll get one of those too. That smelly stuff they put on your chest. Some kind of plaster. Vicks salve, Musterol. My mother used to grease me up like a pig when I was little and got sick. I'll do that . . . okay?" he asked anxiously.

"Fine. Yesss," Casey said, drifting into a feverish sleep.

Mac sat next to the bed, Casey's hot hand in his. She looked so sick. God, what if she died? He felt himself growing light-headed. He shook his head and bit down on his lower lip.

He couldn't let anything happen to her. She was part of him now, the reason for his future. If he had to go against her wishes, he would do it and deal with her reaction later. When she was well, she would understand. But first he had to fetch Lily. Lily would know what to do.

He returned to the hotel room with Lily in tow, and she didn't know what to do. Her eyes became fearful when she looked at the thermometer. There was no way she could hide her concern from Mac, so she didn't try. Instead she sent him to the drugstore for homemade remedies she knew wouldn't work.

"Casey, listen to me, please. We have to get a doctor for you. I know how you feel, but this time . . . this isn't going to go away with aspirins and Vicks salve. You need antibiotics. You're a nurse, I'm a nurse, and we both know this is foolhardy. Please, Casey, let me call a doctor."

"Tomorrow if I'm not better. I do feel a little better now that I'm warm," Casey lied. "Not on Christmas, Lily. I've had colds like this before," she lied again.

"Luke Farrell is in town," Lily said quietly. "I saw him the day before yesterday. I can try and track him down. You'd let him look at you, wouldn't you?"

"Luke's here?"

"Yes, and he asked about you. He's on his last week of R and R. He extended. This is the fourth time. He's either at this hotel or the Ambassador. I'll see if I can find him after Mac gets back. A shot, some antibiotics, and by tomorrow you'll be feeling better. Please, Casey, don't be stubborn. Don't put Mac through this. I've never seen a man so upset."

"All right," Casey whispered. "What's my temperature, Lily?"

"One hundred and four."

"I've spoiled everything. Who's taking care of your baby?"

"He's well taken care of. I can stay as long as you need me. As soon as Mac gets back, I'll see if I can find Luke. Try to sleep."

When Mac returned, Lily helped him with the alcohol rubs and the chest plaster. Casey was so exhausted, she fell instantly asleep the moment they wrapped her back in the towels. "I'm going to see if I can find Luke. It might take me a while, so don't worry if I'm not back right away. Just keep swabbing her forehead with the alcohol. If she wakes up, give her more aspirin. When you run out of things to do, decorate your Christmas tree."

"Is she going to get better, Lily?" Mac asked worriedly.

"Of course. Luke will know what to do, and if anyone can talk sense into her, it's Luke."

Mac frowned.

"Don't worry about Luke, it's you she loves."

"Am I that transparent?"

"Only to me. I'll see you in a little while."

How vulnerable Casey looked, how sweet and lovely. And so very tired and weary. How could he fault her for not wanting to go to a hospital? People died in hospitals. She'd probably seen more death in these twenty-two months than a team of doctors back in the States would see in a lifetime. They'd written about it in their letters. In one she'd sworn that even if she were on her death bed, she would fight against going to a hospital. It wasn't that she was afraid of medical treatment. It was simply defined in her mind as death versus life. There was no gray area, no middle ground. She'd even poked fun at herself. He'd chuckled over the whole thing, thinking they were both young and had fifty years or so before either one of them would have to think about going into a hospital. He wasn't chuckling now. He was worried sick.

Mac lost track of time as he changed the alcohol cloths on Casey's forehead. Once he took her temperature. One hundred four point five degrees. He'd started to decorate the skimpy pine after that, but he kept one eye on the restless woman on the bed. When he saw the string of colored lights come alive, he tried to make himself believe that nothing would happen to Casey because it was the Christmas season. Tomorrow was Christmas Eve.

He needed a drink. He called down to the bar and ordered a double scotch and soda. When it arrived, he gulped it down and ordered another. He added two fat, colorful buddhas to the tree and a colorful pin cushion that looked like a Christmas ball. He added a tacky paper fan with a plastic handle he had to bend around a spindly branch. Last to go on the tree were two strings of beads, one crystal and one a god-awful purple. He stood back to view his handiwork. It was awful, but beautiful. "Merry Christmas," he whispered.

He sat down and guzzled his second drink. He thought about Alice and the kind of tree she would have the servants decorate. It would be glittery as hell, and artificial. One year she'd had a white plastic tree decorated with blue lights and blue balls. It was the most ghastly thing he'd ever seen. Another year she'd decorated the same white tree with pink Victorian bows and tiny little crinkly pieces of paper shaped to look like fans. Last year he'd gone out two days before Christmas with Benny and they'd cut down two monstrously large spruce trees. He'd lugged one home and set it up in the living room. He'd wanted to decorate it right then, but Alice said no, it was still dripping wet. When he got home the next day, the tree was outside by the garage and the white one up and decorated with red balls and red lights. It had taken him exactly seventy-three seconds to pick it up and hurl it across the room. Alice had let it stay that way until his father stopped by early on Christmas Eve. All *he'd* done was raise his eyebrows and say, "Another tantrum, Mac?" That year he'd spent the rest of Christmas Eve with Benny, and Christmas Day with Sadie.

His tree, here, was looking better and better. In fact he thought it the most gorgeous thing he'd ever seen.

He ordered another drink and some food, his eyes glued to the most beautiful Christmas tree in the world.

LILY SLOSHED THROUGH the teeming rain, her clothing soaked, her hair plastered to her head, her slippers a soggy mess. She was walking because she'd been too embarrassed to ask Mac for cab money.

She'd left messages everywhere for Luke Farrell. She'd been to Army Headquarters, to the USO on Nguyen Hue, and to every bar along the way. She'd been up and down Tu Do Street three times. She finally found him in a Basque restaurant on Nguyen Hue having a midnight supper. He was also drunk.

"Sweet Lily, is that you?" Luke asked, stuffing his face with yellow eggs smeared with ketchup and honey. "What brings you out at this time of night?" he asked, his eyes full of concern. "It's not safe. Is the baby sick?"

"No, it's Casey, Luke. She came down from Pleiku today, and she's very, very sick. She has a hundred and four fever. It's probably higher now. She refuses to go to a hospital. I've been looking for you for hours."

Luke pushed his plate away. "You left her alone? Didn't you at least get her a mama-san to watch over her?"

"In this weather? I was lucky I found one to watch Eric. Her . . . lover is with her. Will you come?"

"I'm drunk, Lily," he said morosely. "You want me to treat Casey while I'm in this condition?"

"Drunk, sober, it makes no difference. I've seen you cut a man open and put his insides back together when you were just as drunk. Please, you must come, Luke."

"Of course I'll come," he muttered. "Coffee! American!" He fumbled under the table for his thong sandals.

"Where's your medical bag?" Lily asked anxiously.

"At the counter. Is it still raining?"

"Yes. Luke, if you want to take a cab, you'll have to pay."

Luke was suddenly so sober, his eyes so intent, Lily backed up a step.

"Are you telling me you don't have any money? I asked you the other day if you needed anything and you said no. That was a lie, obviously. You've been trundling around in the rain all night looking for me. You're a kind person, Lily Gia. We'd make a good team. Almost as good as Casey and me. Her lover, huh? Is he a stand-up guy, Lily?"

"Yes, Luke, he is," Lily said quietly.

"I'D BET MY medical diploma this is viral pneumonia," Luke snapped. "Lily, call a cab. Major, I'll be the bad guy here. I'll carry her down. She belongs in the hospital. I don't give a shit what she says. You don't ever mess around with viral pneumonia, not over here anyway. We need to run tests."

"Okay, Doctor," Mac said, relieved the decision to hospitalize Casey was out of his hands.

Mac thought his heart would break when he heard Casey whimper and say, "Oh, Mac, it's the most beautiful Christmas tree I ever saw." His eyes were moist when he followed the gangly doctor down the hall to the elevator. She would get well. She had to.

Hours later Luke returned to the hotel, his feet dragging. Lily was right: Mac Carlin was a nice guy and he loved Casey. Any fool could see that. Carlin probably loved Casey as much as he did. Casey loved Carlin too. Jesus, he was always the last one out of the gate. He pitched his medical bag against the wall. Long fingers wiped at his eyes. Raindrops? Tears? Both, he thought glumly.

Casey was lost to him, but then he'd known that for months. Seeing Mac Carlin in the flesh and talking to him convinced him that the torch he carried for his nurse needed extinguishing. God, it hurt.

Luke propped the pillows behind his head and then cradled it in his laced fingers. He stared at the ceiling, which was so blindingly white it made his eyes water.

An instant later he was on his feet. There was no way in hell he could stay here. He walked for hours in the rain, without knowing or caring where he was. He ended up back at the hospital, and had no idea how. Instinct, he guessed. "I look," he muttered to no one in particular, "like something the cat dragged in and then took back out."

Luke spent five minutes observing Mac Carlin sleeping propped up on a leather couch. He wished he didn't like the guy. His shoulders slumped lower.

Satisfied that Casey was resting and in good hands, Luke left the hospital a second time.

It was full light when he threw himself on the hotel bed. He had a pounding headache and he knew he was strung tighter than he'd ever been in his life. The urge to smash something was so strong he pounded his clenched fists into the pillows. A look of stunned surprise crossed his face when feathers mushroomed around the bed.

The scorching anger building in him was directed at himself. "You're stupid, Farrell, a dumb hick from Squirrel Hill, Pennsylvania. Fucking stupid!" he seethed. Luke's clenched fists whacked the pillows again. More feathers took flight. His diagnosis of Casey, rendered at five A.M., was viral pneumonia. It would take at least another day before the diagnosis was confirmed, but he knew, and there was nothing he could do. Not one damn thing. He was certain Casey was in good hands. This wasn't his turf, he had no say. The doctors had been more than kind when they listened to him. Professional courtesy. Casey had Lily and Mac. She didn't need him. She didn't want him.

Jesus Christ, why had he thought . . . He'd hoped. And he'd prayed. Spending all those shifts with another person, be it eighteen hours or six, taking meals, writing letters, spending all their free time together . . . He'd foolishly thought he had a chance with Casey. They'd shared their hopes, their fears, their dreams, with one another. They'd held hands. He'd even told her about Jimmy Oliver. Not once had she mentioned Mac Carlin's name aloud. He knew about Carlin, everyone did. He told himself over and over that if Casey didn't make Carlin come alive, say his name, share the contents of his letters, then he wasn't really in the running. He was so goddamn stupid it was sickening. Fool! His fists whacked the pillows once more, and then the wicker headboard.

He loved her. Stone-cold sober, he'd told her so. He hadn't made a joke of it either. She'd hugged him, kissed him on the cheek, squeezed his hand, and smiled. There were tears in her eyes when she left to go back to her quarters, leaving him alone with tears in *his* eyes. He should have known then, and stopped dreaming about something that could never be.

Luke was on his feet, shaking the feathers off his damp clothing. He threw his clothes into his duffel any old way and called down to the desk for his bill. He was going back to do what he did best.

Ten minutes later he paid his bill. He asked for an envelope and stuffed all his money into it, licked the flap, then pounded it shut so the glue would adhere. He scrawled Lily Gia's name and address across the front. "Have someone hand deliver this," he said to the desk clerk.

On the short ride to the airport, Luke muttered to himself, to the driver's amusement, "You better take care of her, Carlin, or I'm gonna be your worst nightmare come to life."

I SHOULD LEAVE, Mac thought wearily. Instead he lit a cigarette he didn't want or need. The coffee cup at his elbow had been with him for over a day now, filled, rinsed out, and filled again.

At one point he'd counted his refills, but gave up when he reached thirty-six.

Christmas Day. *Silent night, holy night* . . . She could die, they said. Luke said she wouldn't. "Trust me, Major, Casey is not going to die. I won't kid you, she's on the edge, but she isn't going to die." Mac had winced. If pressed, he couldn't say who looked the sickest, Casey or Luke.

"I probably look worse than both of them," Mac muttered to an old mama-san hobbling about the waiting room. Luke loved Casey, but Mac wasn't jealous. How could anyone not love Casey? He knew in his gut that if he called the hotel and asked for Luke, the desk clerk would tell him the doctor had checked out.

Christ, he was tired. He stubbed out his cigarette, stretched out his legs, and leaned his head back against the couch. He wanted to think about the Fourth of July picnic. Instead he thought about Alice and his father—an unholy combination if ever there was one—and Luke Farrell.

The judge was probably in New York City visiting friends. Christmas Day was over. It was December twenty-sixth back in the States. Was it a white Christmas back home? The judge always gave expensive bottles of wine and outrageously expensive cigars to his friends, whether or not they drank or smoked. He also sent out Christmas cards made from hard, shiny paper layered in foil with his name embossed inside the card and on the envelope. He had never, as far as Mac knew, added a single message inside a card. Several days ago Mac had received his. It was blue and white with the word PEACE on the front. Inside, it read, Justice Marcus Carlin. Mac remembered crunching it into a ball.

The card from Alice had eight tiny reindeer on the front. She'd written a note that said, "Merry Christmas, Mac. Your present is under the tree." The third card made him clench his teeth. There was a fat Santa on the front. Inside was a sticky handprint; so sticky, he'd had to rip the card to open it. It was from Alice's daughter, Jenny. The card smelled like strawberry jelly. He'd crunched those two cards into balls too. "Merry Christmas," he said bitterly.

"It may not be merry, Mac, but it is Christmas. Casey's alive."

Mac's eyes snapped open. Lily was standing to one side.

"And Luke is gone," she said.

"Gone?" Mac demanded.

"He sent this," Lily said, withdrawing a fat envelope from her purse.

"What is it?"

"Money," Lily said, an embarrassed look on her face. "Luke knew I would never take it, so he sent it by messenger after he was gone. That's the way Luke is."

Mac's eyes sparked. He should have seen Lily's need and done what Luke did, but he had been so wrapped up in his own misery he'd had no time for anyone else. "You really do like him, don't you?"

"Of course. Luke . . . all the doctors are wonderful, but Luke is special. Did Casey ever tell you he writes to the parents of the boys he couldn't save?" Mac nodded. "He doesn't have to do that. Casey helped him. We all did. Luke got the other doctors to do it too—write the letters, I mean. Sometimes he has to make up little stories—lies, if you will. He's got this . . . this book. He writes down all the names. I've seen him cry in anguish over those letters, and yet he won't stop writing them."

Mac felt his throat tighten. "He sounds like a hell of a guy. I liked him, and I know Casey adores him."

"Like a brother," Lily said softly. "Casey loves *you*, Mac." She squeezed both his hands reassuringly.

"Sit down, Lily, there's something I have to . . . talk about. I need to talk about it."

He talked at length of Alice and Jenny. He needed to confess his lie to lighten his guilt. He wasn't half the man Luke Farrell was, he thought miserably.

Mac pulled his hands free of Lily's grasp. He walked to the window and jammed them deep into his pockets. He didn't want to see Lily's face. He whirled about a moment later when Lily whispered hoarsely, "I know."

"You know! What do you mean you know?" Mac demanded.

"Luke told me."

"Jesus," was all Mac could say.

"One of your fellow officers said something about . . . your wife's whining. It was at the Fourth of July picnic. He was telling someone how you came down hard on him in the beginning. You were such a hero that day, everyone was talking about you and this officer wanted to . . . he didn't know about Casey. Of course neither Luke or myself said anything to Casey. Luke . . . Luke told me to keep my mouth shut. Those were his exact words. I would never have said a word," Lily said miserably.

"I was going to tell her. I've been in touch with my attorney back in the States. I told him to start divorce proceedings. I need you to believe me, Lily. When I came over here, my marriage was over. Even if I had never met Casey, I would still be getting a divorce when I leave here."

"I'm not making a judgment, Mac. Casey . . . I don't know how Casey will . . . take the child . . ." She let her words hang in the quiet hospital waiting room.

"The child isn't mine. I'm sterile, Lily, I'm sure of it. That's something else I never told Casey."

"When she's well, you can tell her," Lily said quietly. "I must leave now, Mac. You should leave too. There's nothing you can do here. You need a shower, shave, and clean clothes."

"I will, later though," Mac said gruffly.

Lily approached him, stood on her toes to kiss him on the cheek. "I'll stop by in the morning before I go to work to check on Casey. Merry Christmas, Mac."

"I don't have a Christmas present for you, Lily. Casey and I were going to shop together. I'm sorry. I wanted something for Eric . . . I'm sorry."

"It's not important. Don't give it another thought. Next year, though, I want two presents." A moment later she was gone.

He was alone again. He groped for a cigarette, changing his mind when the Zippo lighter refused to spark.

The short walk down the corridor to the nurses' station seemed to take forever. He pantomimed his need to see Casey.

The tiny, trim nurse, her eyes full of compassion, led him to Casey's room. Mac reached out to the doorjamb for support. For as long as he lived he knew he would carry this vision of Casey with him. Luke Farrell said Casey wasn't going to die. He had to hold on to Luke's promise. "You better be right, Dr. Farrell, because if you aren't, I'll track you down and cut your heart out," Mac muttered as he stumbled down the corridor and out into the dark night.

IT WAS THIRTY days before Casey was well enough to leave the hospital, and even then she was not well enough to return to Pleiku. Against all regulations, she moved into Lily's tiny apartment.

Alone with the mama-san and the baby, Casey looked around the poor apartment. It was clean and neat but almost bare of furniture. Two old chairs, a round table, and a tiered shelf were all that was in the tiny living room. A fan circled lazily overhead, moving the still air about the room. The bedroom, which was little bigger than a closet, held a wicker dresser and two futons for sleeping. Lily's clothing hung on a rope stretched across the room. The bathroom was tiny, the kitchen tinier yet. She was imposing herself on Lily and she knew it. Somehow, she would have to make it up to her. Perhaps when she was able to get up and about, she could go to Lily's parents and make them see how unjustly they were treating their daughter. How could they not want this beautiful, innocent child? Culture be damned.

Wearily, Casey curled up on the futon and was asleep almost instantly.

LILY GIA LOOKED down at her patient in the sterile white bed. He was old, probably with many grandchildren. A simple farmer, the head nurse said when she handed the man's clothes to Lily. "He will be your patient until he is released. He has given us no information about himself. For now it is doubtful that any family member will come to visit him."

Such an old man, Lily thought, to have so many shrapnel wounds. Obviously he'd been in the wrong place at the wrong time. She wondered vaguely if he'd been wounded by the Americans or by his own countrymen. His skin, she noticed, was a pasty yellow, his lips thin and waxy, but he'd just come out of surgery. He would recover, but what would happen to him? Who was there to care about this old man? Then she looked at his hands and his feet before she pulled the white sheet up to his chin. His hands and feet weren't old-looking at all. The nails were still white. She frowned. He also had a full head of hair that wasn't gray.

She was out of sorts today and was at a loss to explain why. She'd been fine when she awoke and fed the baby. She'd been fine when she shared tea with Casey and felt relieved at the color in her friend's cheeks. She'd been fine when she kissed the baby good-bye and patted the mama-san on the shoulder. From that point on the day had been murky, her mood changeable. She'd walked to work the way she always did, nodding to acquaintances who bowed and nodded respectfully at her white uniform. But the streets were different. Today there had been no familiar faces, no nods or bows from shopowners. Today there had been many new faces in town, young men, probably university students. Quiet students.

With preparations under way for Tet, the Lunar New Year, the streets should have been teeming with shopowners hawking their wares beneath colorful streamers. Tet was the most important day of the year for her people, and it took days, weeks, to prepare for all the festivities. For years she'd taken part in it, but no longer. Not since Eric and the birth of the baby. Now she was an outcast, disowned by her family and barely tolerated at the hospital, all because she'd given birth to an American bastard.

Her patient moved restlessly, his legs thrashing under the thin white sheet. "Shhh, you must lay quietly, your sutures will open otherwise," she said softly. The patient calmed almost immediately. Lily checked the IV in his arm and took his blood pressure and temperature. She recorded both on the chart at the foot of the bed. He was muttering, murmuring names. Poor thing, Lily thought, he probably wants to know if his wife and children are here. In the same calm, soft voice, she said, "Tell me who to get in touch with. What is your name? Tell me your name, sir."

His eyes were open now, and they weren't old eyes. They were dazed, and she knew he wasn't seeing her clearly. "Where do you live?" she whispered.

He was thrashing about again, muttering furiously about the Tan Son Nhut Air Base and destroying the foreign enemy. He was cursing ripely. She bent over to listen. She had to reach for the metal side supports on the bed or she would have fainted. He said something about an offensive, the Tet Offensive.

Lily had her notebook out. She scribbled furiously. The Tan Son Nhut Air Base, the . . . Tet Offensive. She underlined the words Tet Offensive. Times, she needed to know the times or her information would mean nothing. She had so little information. Who was she to tell? Who would believe her?

Two days until Tet. What could she do in two days? Tell Casey. Casey could go to Army Headquarters and tell those in charge. Would they believe Casey, one of their own? Perhaps, until Casey told them where she got her information. Maybe what she was hearing was nothing more than the delirious murmurings of a sick patient.

Confused and desperate now, Lily leaned closer to her patient. "Tell me what time. . . ." She made her voice deep and gruff. "Tell me, I need to know the time of the offensive." But he was asleep. She had nothing.

When her shift was over, she wanted to run home, to tell Casey, but she forced herself to walk the streets, hoping to see something that would give credence to what she'd just heard. So many students. Why weren't they in class? Were they soldiers? Sometimes they walked in groups of three. Hundreds of students. The air base, of course, was off limits to her, but not to Casey.

Lily looked around wildly. Saigon had always been safe. Surely the VC wouldn't open fire on the city. But according to her patient, that was exactly what they were going to do. Two days. Forty-eight hours. It wasn't much time.

Casey knew the moment Lily walked through the door that something was critically wrong. The smile she showered on the mama-san was forced, her full lips stretching into thin lines. *She's lost her job,* was Casey's first thought. Her second was that she'd heard something terrible about her family.

Tea. Tea always made things right. "Sit, sit, Lily, and tell me what's wrong. The mama-san made tea a few minutes ago. We were worried about you. You're late," she babbled uneasily.

"I know. I've been walking about the city because . . . because . . . Oh, Casey, I need your common sense here." She told her everything she'd heard, about how she'd tried to question the sick patient. "His hands were young, so were his feet. Our men tend to look prematurely old, especially the soldiers. It is the sun that does it. But who is going to pay attention to what a patient's hands and feet look like?" she said, wringing her hands in agitation.

"Drink your tea and then we'll talk," Casey replied. "You must relax, Lily. Your anxiety will transfer itself to the baby, and that isn't good. Maybe we can do something about what you heard. At least we'll try."

When Lily had swallowed the last of her tea, Casey said, "Now, calmly, tell me everything."

"This is the Year of the Monkey, and most believe it to be a harbinger of bad luck. The Lunar New Year for us is a time of family reunions," Lily said with a break in her voice, "with all manner of festivities, as well as feasting and fireworks. Probably nothing half as grand as those we had for the Fourth of July, but wonderful nonetheless. Every family will place a matching pair of watermelons on their family altar for good luck and to honor their ancestors. I, of course, will not do this, for I have no altar, so I will remember other times. Do not be sad for me. I have accepted my new way of life now.

"Each year as the New Year begins, thousands of people pour into Saigon. They come on bicycles, by bus, by scooter and sampan. Thousands more come on foot from the various countrysides. This year . . . this year, there will be thousands of others, hidden among the travelers. Most of these others will be Viet Cong. I understand the plan. It will be easy for the enemy to come into Saigon. They will strike on the morning of Tet. It's less than forty-eight hours away, Casey. You must go to the

American embassy. They'll know what to do. We can't use the Bamboo Pipeline, it takes too long. They'll believe us, won't they?"

"I hope so," Casey said fretfully.

"You must be the one to tell them. They will not believe me. Your people say they believe us, but they don't. They will think this is a trick of some sort. That is why I cannot go with you, Casey. I will stay here with my son."

"You're absolutely right, Lily, no one would believe you, and they won't believe me either, because I will have to tell them where I got the information," Casey said wearily.

"You must try."

Of course Lily was right, she had to try. She bent over to put her shoes on. A wave of dizziness swept through her. She took deep breaths before raising her head slowly. The moment passed.

"How do I get to Thong Nhut Street, where the embassy is?" Casey wrote down Lily's directions.

"I'll find it. If I don't make it back before midnight, I'll find a place to sleep until morning. I won't risk the curfew. Now, wish me luck."

Instead, Lily hugged her, tears streaming down her cheeks. "Be careful," she whispered.

"I will," Casey whispered back, a smile tugging at the corners of her mouth. "Why are we whispering?" She giggled.

"Go. This is no time for jokes," Lily ordered. Casey nodded as she slipped through the door.

While Casey was walking through the streets of Saigon, Lily paced the confines of her tiny apartment. She paced for forty minutes before she went to the apartment next door to ask her young neighbor if she would watch the baby until she returned. "I will be gone no more than thirty minutes." The young woman agreed.

Lily ran down the three flights of steps and out into the night; her destination—her parents' home. She was breathless when she arrived. She leaned against the stout, solid iron gate and caught her breath before she rang the bell. Within moments tiny lights beamed upward from the narrow walkway. She recognized her mother's mincing footsteps. She wished now she'd taken the time to change out of her madras shorts and shirt and into more traditional clothing. "I look too American," she muttered under her breath.

Lily bowed low. "Mother, I must tell you something. Please listen to me," she pleaded.

"You should not have come here, daughter, for you have brought dishonor to our family. You must not come here again. Go now before your father comes to the gate and sees you."

Lily heard the sob in her mother's voice, could see the shimmer of tears in her eyes from the yellow glow of the walk lights. She wanted to cry herself, could feel her shoulders start to shake.

"One moment, Mother." Quickly, breathlessly, Lily recounted what she'd heard earlier at the hospital. "You must leave the city as soon as possible. Thank you for talking to me, Mother. I love you very much. I will always love you. Take this," she said, slipping a snapshot Casey had taken of little Eric earlier in the week. "It is all I have to give, Mother, for the New Year."

Lily felt her mother's fingers touch her own through the grillwork of the iron fence, then she withdrew them abruptly. The walkway lights went out.

"Go quickly, Lily, your father is coming down the walk. I will tell him a colleague stopped by, and I will pass on your information. You will always be in my heart, daughter." Lily didn't hear the soft whispered words. She was already melting into the dark shadows.

Her parents wouldn't leave, she'd known that when she rang the bell. They were doctors, dedicated to saving lives. If an offensive did occur, they would be needed. Had she come just to see her mother, to see her face and to pass on the small snapshot? Of course she had. Her mother still loved her in the same way Lily would always love her own child. She cried all the way back to her shabby apartment.

CASEY WAS EXHAUSTED when she reached the Armed Forces Training Center. At the last second she'd changed her mind about going to the American embassy. Something perverse in her insisted she try instead to locate Sue Collins, the woman she had met when she first arrived in-country. She was so tired, she couldn't explain her reasoning to herself, but the gods of Fortune smiled on her. When she entered the building, Collins was on her way out.

"I'll be damned." Collins grinned. "What brings you to Saigon? Don't tell me. Tet. I think everyone and his brother is here for the festivities. Listen, I have to thank you for that great Fourth of July party at Da Nang. I got to see Rick for twenty whole minutes. Your turn." She laughed.

"Can we go somewhere to talk? This is . . . crucial."

"It's something serious, isn't it? Has something happened to Rick?" There was desperation in her voice.

"I'm sorry if I . . . no, it has nothing to do with Rick. It's something else."

Outside in the darkness, Casey repeated Lily's story. "I believe her, but Lily says the authorities, the national police, won't pay any attention. I thought you would know who to go to. I'm willing to go with you. At first I was going to go to the embassy, and I'll still go if you think it will do any good."

"Let's go back inside," Sue replied. "There are phones we can use to call the embassy. I know some of the guys there. Hell, we'll call everybody we can think of. From experience, I think the first thing to do is send word out on the Bamboo Pipeline. It will be better and faster than any communications center."

"Whatever it takes," Casey muttered, wiping the sweat from her forehead. It was wonderful to sit down, to feel the coolness of the building. The tall glass of Tang that Sue handed her was the most welcome thing in the world.

The calls took over an hour. When she finally hung up the phone, Sue looked at Casey. "An economic-commercial officer at the embassy is coming over. He has a pass so he can move about after curfew. I told him to stop at the hospital to check on Lily's patient. He said he would do it, but he could have been humoring me. Thong Nhut Boulevard is within spitting distance of us. It shouldn't take him long."

They passed a few nervous minutes talking about less important things. About snow, the new rage in fashion, the miniskirt, Easter bonnets, and white-shingled houses with picket fences. They spoke of home and family, but they kept their eyes glued to the plate-glass doors.

Sue was nervously pleating the hem of her corded skirt. "I heard this morning when I came on duty that guerrillas in the Central Highlands overran Tuy Phuoc. That town was considered the showcase of 'Revolutionary Development,' the program that was supposed to rid the countryside of Viet Cong. I also heard that Westy has shifted thousands of troops north to beef up defenses. Right after he did that, the U.S. announced the cancellation of a thirty-six-hour unilateral truce, at the same time the VC proclaimed their seven-day cease fire for the Lunar New Year. Something *is* going on, there's no doubt about it." She started to nibble on a nail, her eyes far away.

Casey knew Sue must be worrying about Rick. It was weird, she thought, how both of them were more concerned with their loves than with themselves.

"I was just thinking," Casey said, ruminating aloud. "I don't know where I'm supposed to be. I was discharged from the hospital but wasn't well enough to go back to Pleiku. I have another ten days and a medical checkup to go through before I can return to the hospital. I left word at the hospital I was staying at Lily's. Major Hagen came down to see me, but I don't think I'm listed anywhere. I should be listed," she added fretfully.

"Are you certain you aren't?" Sue said, her face full of concern.

"I'm positive. Major Hagen said the paperwork alone would take a month. Even though I was discharged from the hospital, that's my last known address, for want of a better word. Mac, of course, knows where I am, and he has the address. Major Hagen, bless her heart, can't find her way out of a paper bag. She has difficulty with names over here. I know by the time she got to the airport she'd forgotten Lily's address. I'm just talking, don't mind me," Casey said tiredly.

"No, no, Casey, this is important. If something happens here in the city, if Lily is right, and they open fire, anything can happen. There has to be a record of you, and the hospital isn't going to be good enough. The army doesn't like it when things get flubbed up. In the morning I'll see what I can do. Write down the name of your unit and everything I need to know. Uh-oh, here he comes," Sue said, sotto voce.

Geoffrey Hollister looked like a pompous, overstuffed walrus. He was overweight by a good forty pounds, and his flabby fat jiggled as he walked. He was wearing walking shorts with beige knee socks that sagged around his ankles. His light green shirt was soaked with perspiration, as was his bald head. His brown eyes looked mean and angry, his cheeks puffing out with the exertion it took to walk across the anteroom to where both young women were sitting. Be charitable, Casey warned herself. It's the end of a very long day and the man is probably exhausted. He introduced himself before he sat down on the hard, plastic chair, his thighs hanging over the side. He acknowledged Sue's introduction with a curt nod.

"I hope this is important, Captain," he said, addressing Sue. "I don't like to be out on these streets after curfew. And if what you are about to tell me is army business, I'm going to be very angry," he said irritably. Everyone knew you didn't disturb army brass after midnight. It was okay to disturb embassy personnel though.

Sue told him everything Lily said. Both girls watched the man's fat face for his reaction. When he laughed, Casey felt an adrenaline surge.

"Is this the same Lily Gia who hung around with Eric Savorone before he headed back to the States? Eric was a friend of mine. Did it ever occur to either one of you that this might be a—"

"Don't say it," Casey said hotly. "Don't even think it. Lily Gia is not a liar, Mr. Hollister. We've given you the information, and if you choose to do nothing about it, then it becomes your problem, not ours."

"Exactly who are you?" Hollister snapped.

"I'm the mistress of someone you salute and take orders from," Casey lied. "Do I need to mention names? Of course you can see why this matter must be handled sensitively and discreetly. We thought you were the man to do it . . . But, of course, I'll leave that up to you, Mr. Hollister. By the way, is Hollister spelled with one L or two?"

"Two," Hollister said, flustered. She was pretty enough to be a general's mistress, but a little too scrawny for his taste. In a crazy kind of way, it did make sense. The high, muckety-muck brass had to have everything handled discreetly and sensitively. Then he remembered the patient's hands and feet—the patient in Room 312 who was awake and angry when he'd pulled down the covers to stare at his feet. He remembered the way his heart pounded in his chest at the hatred in the man's eyes. "All right," he said, struggling to his feet. "I'll put the word out."

"What should we do, Mr. Hollister?" Casey asked.

"Do? Whatever you want. Go home. Drink tea. This will be squelched quickly if it proves to be true. The VC wouldn't be crazy enough to *actually* attack Saigon. But that doesn't mean they aren't thinking about it," he added hastily. "Good night, ladies."

GEOFFREY HOLLISTER WAS wrong. Twelve hours later the attack began.

"Do we stay or go to the embassy?" Casey asked Lily. "We might be safer if we just stay here. We have to think of the baby."

The decision was taken out of their hands when a marine rapped sharply on the door and then identified himself. Her eyes round with fear, Casey opened the door a crack. "You're to come with me, miss. Mr. Hollister's orders."

"Get the baby, Lily," Casey ordered. "Where are you taking us?" she demanded of the marine.

"To the embassy. Mr. Hollister didn't say anything about a baby. He said to pick up the blonde."

"An oversight, I'm sure," Casey snapped.

"I already have one passenger, Captain Collins," the marine said uneasily when he saw Lily.

"So what's the problem, Corporal?"

"Room, miss. I have a jeep."

"I'll sit on Captain Collins's lap. The problem is solved. How bad is it out there?"

"It's not good."

The M-16 slung over the marine's shoulder reassured Casey as they made their way down the steps. The baby whimpered in Lily's arms. Casey saw another M-16 propped up on the front seat of the jeep. The .45 caliber pistol in the marine's belt gleamed in the darkness.

He was driving too fast, Casey thought as he careened around a corner on two wheels, one hand on the steering wheel, the other on the butt of his pistol. They were rounding the corner of Thong Nhut Boulevard when an explosion ripped through the night. The corporal slammed on the brakes then threw the jeep in reverse. The .45 was out of his belt in a split second. "Get down!" he ordered. He debated three seconds too long. Automatic weapons fire followed by more explosions ripped through the embassy. In the glaring firelight, Casey saw the great seal of the United States come loose from the embassy wall. Four gaping holes looked like giant eyes. It was the last thing she saw before the grenade hit their jeep.

AT 8:35 IN the morning, the American forces regained control of the embassy compound. The counted dead were seven: four MP's, a marine corporal from Miami, Florida, and two women. A third woman had been airlifted to Thailand with burns over thirty percent of her body and face. The name on the quickly-filled-out tag pinned to the woman's blouse said Lily. It was the medic's mistake when the only identification he could come up with was what the woman whispered: *"Lily, Lily."*

Lily was in truth Casey Adams.

THREE DAYS LATER, when Saigon was back to what passed for normal, Mac Carlin burst through the embassy doors like a human tornado. He demanded answers and cringed when he got them. His hands trembled so badly, he could hardly hold the flimsy piece of paper Geoffrey Hollister handed him.

In a voice that was so deadly calm it made Hollister turn as white as flour, Mac said, "She was safe where she was. Why in the name of God did you order her brought here?"

"Because," Hollister said coldly, "she told me she was some muckety-muck's mistress. Christ, how was I supposed to know it was a lie? I was covering my ass, just the way you would have covered yours, and don't stand there and try to tell me anything different. Look, no one is sorrier than I am. We lost five of our own. Six if you count her. Seven if you count the WAC."

Mac's fist shot out. Hollister went down. Tears burning his eyes, he stepped over the flabby body.

His dream had become a nightmare.

Mac ran then, every demon in hell on his heels, down the air-conditioned corridors, through the doors to the blistering heat outside. He kept on running, his eyes searching for landmarks that would lead him to Lily Gia's small apartment.

Hollister didn't seem to know very much. From what he'd said, five people were dead and two more were missing, and perhaps dead too.

He started to call Lily's name the moment he recognized the building. He thought he was screaming, shouting so loud everyone for miles around would come to offer news of Lily. Only silence greeted him. The building was empty, its doors hanging wide open. Lily's door was closed. He slammed at it with both his hands, pushing inward. Nothing. He called her name again and again as he walked through the sparsely furnished rooms. Lily's things were in the tiny bedroom, a baby's rattle and nursing bottle on the dresser. He yanked at the drawers, looking for the Mickey Mouse satchel, for a sign that Casey had really been here for over a month.

The moment Mac saw the cellophane and wax-paper bundle, he knew what it was. The blue dress. He cursed then, so richly, so ripely, that he stunned even himself as he ripped and gouged at the surgical tape protecting the dress. How soft it felt. He thought he was holding the most beautiful thing in the world. He closed his eyes, trying to envision Casey in the dress. He brought the material close to his cheek. He thought he could smell cornflakes. Casey was going to wear this dress on Christmas Day. It took him all of three minutes to shred it. When he was finished, he was so light-headed he had to sit down.

In the bathroom that wasn't big enough for him to turn around in, he saw the gold bracelet and Cracker Jack ring on a small wicker shelf over the tiny sink. A roar of pain tore from his mouth as both his hands pounded down on the sink. He was jolted backward when the sink came away from the wall, teetered, and then fell. He took the ring and put it in his pocket.

Outside in the hot, still air, Mac looked at the ring. It was all that was left to him. And his memories. His vision blurred for a moment.

Still looking for Lily, hoping he might find her and, through her, a clue to Casey's whereabouts, he went to her parents' house and then the hospital. He wanted to cry when he was told that both Lily's parents were caught in crossfire as they tried to get to the hospital. No one had seen Lily or heard from her.

Mac stood helplessly on the curb, his eyes wild. He bellowed his pain again. No one paid any attention to him.

It wasn't right. Didn't anyone care? Was he the only one in this godforsaken country who cared? He thought about Luke Farrell and all the dedicated doctors and nurses. They cared. Such a goddamn small group. He wondered if he had the guts to send off a note to Luke Farrell. (Did Luke know Casey was missing and maybe dead?) Jesus, what if he didn't? Of course he knew. Hollister would have sent word to Maureen Hagen. Luke knew. Luke had to know. And if anyone could get a lead on Lily and her son, it would be Luke. As for Mac, his tour would be up in three weeks. There wasn't much he could do.

Mac wrote his note at the airport, sealed it in an envelope, and handed it over to a young marine who promised to turn it over to the first chopper pilot to set down at the airport. The pilot did his best to keep his promise to the marine, but he was shot down ten miles from Pleiku. Mac's letter to Luke burned in the dense jungle.

Three weeks later Mac Carlin climbed aboard a Flying Tiger

plane in Saigon on the first leg of his journey. (He'd accepted the fact that Casey was dead and it left him feeling dead inside.) He didn't look back.

It was time to go home.

PART THREE

PART
THREE

Chapter 8

"DOCTOR, DO YOU think she was beautiful?" The voice was soft, cultured, and full of compassion.

"I imagine she was," Singin Vinh said helplessly as he stared down at the patient. He'd managed to stabilize her, but just barely. "Has she said anything?"

From a faraway place she couldn't identify, Casey Adams strained to hear what the voices were saying. She moved restlessly. She must be in a hospital, nothing else would explain the pain she was feeling. Once before, when she was conscious, she thought she smelled hospital odors, but in a second she was asleep. God, where was she? Then she remembered. Her bandaged arms flailed. She was filled with more pain. From a long, dark tunnel she heard a voice whisper. "Shh, you're in good hands, Miss Lily. If you remain very still, I will tell you what we know. You were in Saigon, probably for the New Year festivities. There was an offensive action. The Viet Cong attacked your American embassy. It was quite brutal. We think you were headed for the embassy, since the car you were in was firebombed on Thong Nhut Boulevard, which is where the embassy is located. The driver of the car, a marine, was killed, along with two other women. We were told their names were Casey Adams and Sue Collins. Both women's bodies were so badly burned it was difficult to identify them. We understand there was a child, a baby in the car too. He was taken to an orphanage. This is what was told to us when we called the embassy in Saigon. They made your identification from a small colorful suitcase and Miss Adams's dog tags. The American embassy said they sent a driver to pick up Lieutenant Adams, who was an army nurse. They don't know why or how Sue Collins and the baby came to be in the car, or you for that matter. The little suitcase was thrown clear and so was the child. Fortunately, the little one landed on it when he was thrown from the jeep. The suitcase had half a name tag on it. The marine medic who had you airlifted said you kept saying Lily, Lily, so we assumed that was your name. We did our best to make a proper identification. It seemed logical to him and to us you are Lily Simon. Does any of this sound familiar to you?"

Of course it was familiar. She'd borrowed fellow nurse Nancy Simon's Mickey Mouse suitcase at Christmas time when she'd gone to Saigon to meet Mac. When the marine arrived to take her and Lily to the embassy, she'd thrown underwear and her toilet articles into the bag. Lily had the baby and an armful of diapers in her arms. Did she remember? She would never forget. She herself had been sitting on Sue Collins's lap. She remembered sailing through the air, her body on fire. The baby must have been thrown clear the way she was, while Sue and Lily were trapped in their seats. Lily, because of their likeness in size, had been taken for her. But if that was the case, how did the embassy and the military account for her being here? And what about Lily? Did anyone know if Lily was dead? Was anyone mourning for her? Of course not, no one knew she was dead. The enormity of her situation hit her full force then. Lily's parents didn't know their daughter was dead . . .

"I think she's asleep again," the nurse said quietly. "Will she die, Doctor?"

"No, she won't die, but before she is well again, she will wish she were dead." The doctor closed his eyes wearily when he thought of what the faceless patient was going to endure in the coming months. He couldn't even begin to imagine how many grafts it would take to repair her burned body. "Twenty-four-hour nursing care, Maline."

The tiny nurse's eyes shimmered with tears. "Does this mean you won't be going to Vietnam to help your friend Luke Farrell?" She held her breath, waiting for the surgeon's reply.

"That's what it means," Vinh said tiredly. He'd gone without sleep for forty-eight hours as they worked tirelessly to stabilize their patient.

"Do you realize we missed every New Year festivity, Maline?"

"There will be other New Years. Miss Lily had only this one chance to be made whole again," Maline said softly.

How pretty Maline is, Singin thought. And how very tired. Maline had lost as much sleep as he had. He wondered why he'd never noticed before how pretty she was. In fact, Maline was beautiful. He ran his fingers through his thick, black hair. "Do you have many boyfriends?" he blurted.

Maline didn't blush, didn't stammer, and her color didn't change. Her heart, however, skipped a beat. Long ago she'd given up hope of having Singin notice her, and now he was asking such a personal question. She thought about the question before she replied, and when she did, her response startled her. "Why do you ask, Doctor?"

"I thought it might be . . . nice if we went on a picnic, but I can't very well ask you if you're . . . spoken for."

"I'm a modern Thai, Doctor. If you want to ask me to go on a picnic, then ask me." She held her breath waiting for the invitation. When it didn't come, she wanted to stamp her tiny foot in frustration, but that would have been unprofessional.

"I'll be back in an hour, Maline. I have to see about getting word to Luke Farrell that I'm on hold for the time being. Call me if there's any change at all. I'll be staying at the hospital until Miss Lily is 'out of the woods,' as they say in the States."

He was gone, the door swooshing closed behind him. Maline sat down and let her shoulders slump. She'd been in love with Singin since she was a little girl. When he went to the United States for his education, she went too, but not until he was serving his residency in Seattle. When she finally got up the nerve to call him at the hospital where he worked, he'd been so polite, so reserved, so . . . so . . . she coined a new word—doctorish. He'd worn sneakers and blue jeans and parted his hair on the side. She'd bought sneakers and blue jeans too, and had gone one step further and got a permanent wave, which had been a disaster. He'd teased her unmercifully, until she'd been forced to cut it all off. For the longest time she'd walked around with her hair cut like a boy's.

When she returned to Thailand, with a fashionable hairdo, gold jewelry, high heels, and Western clothes, she'd seen Singin blink in amazement. His neck got red and he said, "Maline, is that you?" It was such a stupid question, yet endearing somehow. She hadn't bothered to respond, simply because her tongue was too thick in her mouth. So she winked and batted her eyelashes before she sashayed down the hall. Halfway down she'd turned and said, "I'll be working with you, Doctor." Even at that distance she could see the red in his neck travel to his face and ears. She'd felt so powerful then. But all that was five years ago, and nothing had transpired since. She still loved him—that would never change.

Her patient stirred restlessly. "Shh," she said. "Please do not move, first listen, Miss Lily. You're in good hands. The best hands in Southeast Asia. You've been in a terrible accident, but you will recover. I'm Maline, Dr. Vinh's nurse. You're safe here. Nothing more will happen to you." She wanted to say more, but her patient was asleep again, full of painkiller.

Dutifully, Maline wrote on the patient's chart, *Fretful for several minutes. I calmed her.* Maline logged the time. Her vision blurred when she looked at the long list of things wrong with her patient. Ruptured spleen, broken shoulder, shattered jaw, broken wrist, fingers smashed, shattered ankle, four cracked ribs. Burns over thirty percent of her body. Face burned, cheekbones shattered, nose broken, damage to eyes.

It could all be dealt with, Singin had said. Reconstructive surgery was his specialty. Skin grafts were the important thing now, and doing every thing possible so the patient didn't develop pneumonia.

DAYS PASSED, THEN weeks, and finally months. It was summer before Casey was able to respond to her surroundings. She wanted to communicate, to tell Maline and Dr. Vinh her name wasn't Lily Simon, but her jaw was wired shut and her hands were heavily bandaged; all her fingers were broken, as well as one of her wrists. She'd tried wiggling her toes as a means of communication, but the Thais hadn't picked up on it. She'd had optical surgery and now had permanent contact lenses implanted. Her eyes hurt and watered continuously, but she could see. For so long she'd been "blind," with patches over her eyes. Now, for a while, she had to wear dark, wraparound sunglasses. Her ribs were healed, her spleen removed. Her ankle was reconstructed, and she would walk, but with a slight limp. She still had many skin grafts to go, and the work on her face would take even longer. At least another year.

Months ago she'd lost track of time, and only when one of the nurses read an American paper to her, her only entertainment, did she know what day or month it was. It was done religiously, at four o'clock every day, on the hospital terrace where she sat in the shade, bundled from head to toe. Each day, as she waited for her reader, she also waited for Mac to find her, or for someone, anyone, to say, "Thank God, we finally found you."

Casey listened to the breeze ruffle the leaves overhead, and to the soft squish of the nurses' rubber-soled shoes as patients were wheeled in and out of the terrace. She loved the clink of glassware and the sounds of birds chittering nearby. Part of her wanted Mac to appear, to take her in his arms and say, "Marry me, I don't care what you look like." The other part of her didn't want him to see her ugliness, and she knew without having to be told that she was scarred and ugly. There was nothing she could do about it but cry behind the sunglasses.

All she did these days was to think. Think and cry, cry and think. Did everyone believe she was dead? What was Mac told? Had he extended his tour of duty or had he returned to the States? He would be out of the army now, a civilian, if he had rotated back home. And Lily? She was dead; Casey knew it, felt it. Sue too. Sue who only lived to see Rick for twenty minutes a month. The child, she seemed to remember, was in an orphanage. Half the time she didn't know what had been said and what was in her thoughts. The drugs they had her on fogged her brain. If she came out of this in one piece, she would never take another drug, not even an aspirin, for as long as she lived. *Oh,. Mac, where are you?*

Sooner or later she was going to have to think about Pleiku, Saigon, Luke Farrell, and all the wounded, but not now. Her heart was too sore and bruised, and she was in constant pain; but the dreams, the cold sweats were the worst.

She smelled Maline's sweet scent before the girl came around her chair to sit opposite her.

"It's a beautiful day, isn't it?" Maline didn't wait for a response but rattled on. "It's the kind of day that is wonderful for a picnic with one's lover. Today is Sunday, Lily. I checked with the office before I came on duty, and no paperwork has arrived in regard to you. Dr. Vinh is staying on top of it. It's taking much too long, but you are not to worry. Your army has other things to concern itself with besides paperwork. You're alive, and that's all that matters. Now," she said cheerfully, "I have two newspapers, and they're only three days old."

Casey leaned back against the soft pillows. This was the best part of the day, the *only* part of the day she liked. She half listened to the words, paying more attention to the soft, musical, cultured voice. It wasn't until Maline said, "The political news is that Major Malcolm Carlin of McLean, Virginia, has thrown his hat into the senatorial ring. There's a picture of Major Carlin, his wife, baby daughter Jennifer, and his father, Supreme Court Justice Marcus Carlin. Everyone is smiling. It says Major Carlin served in Vietnam for two years, and then it mentions all the medals he was awarded." With her eyes riveted to the newspaper in front of her, Maline failed to see Casey's back stiffen and the tears rolling down her cheeks.

Wife and daughter. A child. Mac was married with a child. It wasn't possible. He'd never given any indication of a child or that he was married. At least Eric Savorone had told Lily that he was married. She, Casey, was no better than Lily, and she'd had the nerve to chastise the Asian girl. She swayed sickeningly in her nest of pillows. Married. She felt herself slipping into blackness, powerless to stop what was happening to her. When she awoke, she was back in her room, the nest where she'd been for so many months. She could hear voices coming from a long tunnel, those of Maline and Dr. Vinh.

"Did something happen?" he asked sharply.

"Nothing, Dr. Vinh. We talked about how nice it was today with no monsoon rain. I read the paper to her. It was political news, nothing alarming. Perhaps it was the heat."

"It's not your fault, Maline," Singin said kindly. "I'll feel so much better when we can unwire her jaw and she can talk. Another week or so and she can tell us what happened. Her vital signs are fine now, but I still want her watched carefully. I don't want her left alone even for a moment. Is that understood, Maline?" He knew it was understood. He'd never had to admonish Maline and didn't know why he was doing it now. She was a dedicated nurse, and Lily seemed to grow calm and respond only to her. He was worried though and didn't know why.

Casey wanted to cry, to sob her heart out, but she lay still, sick with humiliation. The beautiful memories, the wonderful notes and letters, were all lies. Her love, like Lily's, was based on a lie. How fitting that they should call her by Lily's name now. She cowered in the bed, tears of shame at her own stupidity sliding down from behind the darkened glasses.

In her drugged daze, Casey listened to the conversation from a faraway place, her humiliation so total, so secret, she wanted to die, until she heard Luke Farrell's name mentioned. She tried to struggle up from her cocoon, but she was powerless to speak, to tell them to get in touch with Luke.

"I heard from my American friend in Pleiku yesterday," Singin said softly. "He says I am needed desperately, and once again I must tell him I cannot accommodate the American forces. I wrote him early this morning and told him about this patient. I feel so guilty, Maline, I don't know if I'm doing the right thing. Lily needs me and so does Luke. I could be helping so many. Instead, I am here trying to restructure this one person's body, because this is what I was trained to do. I can't cast her aside or turn her over to another doctor. I've done nothing but think about this all night long. I've sent a letter to the doctor under whom I trained back in the States, but so far there has been no response. I took liberties and was quite forward in asking him to come here. If he comes, I know Miss Lily will be in safe hands, and I would be free to help Luke. I want desperately to give back to the Americans for giving me my fine medical education, but I cannot do it at the expense of this patient," Singin said sadly.

"Is it possible to send Miss Lily back to the States?" Maline asked quietly. She knew it was impossible, but she felt the need to voice the question aloud.

"Look at her, Maline. If it were you, would you want me to ship you off in this condition? She has no stamina. She is nothing but skin and bones. I think I'd give everything I own to know what is going through her head, to know what she thinks. I haven't heard one whimper all these months. That in itself is amazing. My God, what we've put her through. I must see it through, or I won't be able to live with myself. I couldn't have done all this," he said, waving his arm about tiredly, "without your excellent nursing care. It's amazing how your touch and your voice seem to reassure her. I truly believe she knows she's in good hands. Now, it's time for rounds, Maline," he said briskly, changing the subject.

In the corridor, his patient list in hand, Singin stopped long enough to say, "Will you have dinner with me this evening?"

Maline's eyes sparkled before she replied, and even then she answered his questioning invitation with one of her own. "Will we talk of patients and medicine?"

"No, we'll talk of wildflowers, summer rains, and Hollywood." Singin smiled, his eyes warming at Maline's blushing face.

CASEY DIDN'T LIKE the blinding whiteness of the operating room or the strong antiseptic smell. She knew if she closed her eyes she could pinpoint where everything was, right down to the tongue depressors. She'd lost track of the times she'd been wheeled in here and then wheeled out. In a little while, probably less than an hour, when the anesthesia wore off, she'd be able to speak. Questions would be asked and answers would be expected.

All she'd done this past week was think about what she would say. Just last night she'd finally come up with answers. She knew they were the wrong answers, but she didn't care.

When they asked her if she was Lily Simon, she was going to say yes. She would claim that she couldn't remember anything and that she knew her name was Lily only because they'd been calling her that for all these months. She was never going back to nursing—she'd decided that too. She'd seen too much death, a hundred times more than an average nurse would see in a lifetime. If she ever recovered fully, she wanted no reminders of this time in her life. If she had to sum it all up to someone, to herself, it was simple: she had lost the ability to care. Right now her life as she knew it was over. God alone knew what her future held.

Her future. Was there going to be a future for her? If she mended and was eventually discharged, she would return to Paris and get a job in a shop as a salesgirl. Nicole was banking her money, and there would be more now if the United States government paid off on her death policy. None of that mattered anyway. She was going to be ugly and deformed. All night long she'd dreamed about going to work for the rest of her life wearing a black veil.

It was dawn when a horrible thought struck her. When she was discharged, there would be a hospital bill. Who would pay it? The doctors' fees must be enormous, with all the skin grafts and operations she'd had.

She hadn't wanted to cry, but she had, great gulping sobs when she thought of Lily and Sue Collins. She didn't know where little Eric was now, and if she was going to go through with her plan to pretend to have amnesia, she couldn't ask.

Could she pull this off? She had to, she had no other choice, she decided. She forced herself to relax when she saw Maline at the foot of her bed, hypodermic syringe in hand. "In just a little while, Lily, we'll be able to speak to one another. I've tried so many times to imagine what your voice sounds like. Very American, very soft and gentle, is what I think." The needle shot home. It was a trick every nurse used. Talk to the patient, say something pleasant, and then, pow.

For the first time, Casey fought the drug she'd been given. Maline had said something, something she had to pay attention to, something that could cause her a problem. Her voice, she thought groggily. They wanted to hear her voice. Maline's voice was different too. She's in love with Singin. It was Casey's last thought before slipping into the deep, drug-induced sleep that would allow the surgeon to remove the wires imbedded in her jaw.

AFTER SURGERY, PATIENTS normally awake in degrees, but Casey awoke fully, instantly aware that she was in the recovery room. She knew without opening her eyes that Singin and Maline were at the foot of her bed. They'd already done her vitals. Careful, go carefully, an inner voice warned. Give one-word answers and remember all your English lessons. Don't sound French!

"Today you will have noodle soup, which you will drink through a straw," Singin said softly. "Tomorrow you won't need the straw."

He's in love too, Casey thought. She could hear it in his voice. She wanted to weep. She lay quietly as he prodded her tender jaw with deft fingers. "Tell me your name. Make your jaw work, but do it gently, easily. If it hurts too much, speak around your teeth." She did as ordered.

"Wonderful! Is there much pain? No, that's good. Do you want the noodle soup now? Ah, I thought so. Maline, please fetch it."

"Well what do you think? I think I do good work." Singin grinned.

"Mirrrorr," Casey mumbled.

"No!" Singin said sharply.

"Ugly?"

Singin felt his throat constrict. "Very ugly," he said honestly. "But," he said, holding up his hand, "I'm going to fix that. Do you trust me?"

"No." The horror on Singin's face was so total, Casey would have laughed if she could have. She would never trust a man again. "Ah, I see, it is a joke! Ha ha," he said self-consciously.

Think what you want, Casey thought bitterly.

Maline would try next, but not today. She would try to feel her out, to use her influence, since Casey trusted her, and then report back to the doctor. She'd gone that route herself many times. All in the best interests of the patient, of course.

"As you know, there has been no word from the United States about you. We have filed dozens of reports, filled out many forms, all with numbers on the top. We then make copies of those forms when we file our next report. You are Lily Simon?"

Here it is, Casey thought. She worked the words around in her head before she uttered them. Talking through her clenched teeth garbled the words, but the meaning was clear. "I don't know."

"You don't know if you're Lily Simon? It is a joke, ha ha."

"No joke," Casey said forcefully.

"You don't remember who you are? Do you remember anything prior to the accident? Do you remember the accident?"

Casey waited until she was certain there would be no other questions before she answered. "No."

"You are American? Lily Simon is . . . American-sounding. Over here Lily is a very common name. Much like the name Mary back in the States. Simon is American. If you aren't American . . ." He let the rest of what he was about to say hang in the sterile air. Casey waited. "You are not Vietnamese, you're Anglo. We checked with the Red Cross and none of their people are missing. You must be what they call a WAC. Is this possible?" He didn't wait for a response. "A middle name. Do you have a middle name?"

Did she? What would go with Lily? Nancy, she almost blurted. She thought of the real Nancy Simon and wondered if she was still in Pleiku.

The way the army took its time doing things, she just might get away with this. She waited, every nerve in her body twanging. "Bills," she whispered. She almost blacked out then.

"Yes, yes, the bills are mounting. Lily Simon. I'll have the office start all over and see what can be done. Can you tell us anything about the accident?" At Casey's blank look, Singin backed away from the bed to allow Maline access to the hospital stand-up tray. "You have no recollection of anything until you woke here?"

"No."

Casey tried to listen to the whispered conversation between nurse and doctor, but couldn't make out any of it.

"How awful for you," Maline said, her voice full of compassion. "All these months we didn't know . . . that you didn't know who you were. You are a very brave woman. I would have . . . freaked out. You are familiar with that term?"

"Yes." Play dumb, Casey cautioned herself.

"That is good, Lily. They say that in America. I love American slang," Maline said, fixing the straw between Casey's teeth. "Suck," the nurse ordered. "The noodles are small and fine and will easily go through the straw. Just a little," she cautioned, "or you will get sick. You've been on intravenous nutrients a long time, so we must do this very gradually." Casey sucked greedily. Nothing in her life ever tasted so good. "We must talk, Miss Lily."

She removed the bowl, then wiped Casey's chin.

Casey listened to the nurse's words, she'd heard it all before, from the doctor and from Maline herself. What they wanted now was for her to verify what they'd been told.

Casey's thoughts drifted to Lily, to Mac. Sweet, gentle Lily. Mac. Did anyone know Lily was dead? Did Mac know? The baby, that sweet cherub who Lily loved with all her heart, was he safe and in good hands? Did Lily's parents know? To her mind, Lily's parents didn't love their daughter or they wouldn't have abandoned her. Eric Savorone had abandoned her too. *And Mac betrayed me,* she thought. *No one cares about me and no one cares about Lily. I have to think of myself now. There's no one in this whole world to help me but myself.*

Maybe she wouldn't go back to Paris. Nicole and Danele had probably spent all her insurance money by now. Damn, she couldn't think anymore. All she wanted to do was sleep. But as she drifted off, she made a promise to herself. If the day ever came when she was well and fit to take her place in society, then and only then would she think about setting the record straight. For now she was Lily Simon, and she would stay Lily Simon for as long as it took to get her life back together, if that was possible.

Casey dozed fitfully before slipping into a deep sleep, a sleep invaded by demons of her past. She was in Da Nang, in the sterile white hospital, moving among the rows of operating tables, looking at the faces of the injured men. Every patient looked like Mac. Mac minus a foot. Mac minus an arm. Mac with a deep belly wound. Mac with half his face blown away.

I don't care if you're crippled! I don't care if you're ugly! I love you! Do you hear me? I love you! Luke! Make him whole again. Please. Please make him whole again, for me. If you love me, you'll do this for me. Damn you, Luke, stop whistling. "When I'm Sixty-Four," is my song, mine and Mac's. You have no right to whistle that song. Please, Luke, don't let him die! Damn you, give me that scalpel, I'll do it myself! He's dead. You waited too long. I hate you, Luke Farrell . . .

Chapter 9

MAC STEPPED OFF the commercial airliner at Dulles Airport. He didn't look to the right or to the left but headed straight for the terminal and a taxi. He caused more than one head to turn in the busy terminal. He was so tanned, his skin looked like rich copper. His shoulders were tense and tight, his face grim. He was creased and polished.

He'd returned to the Ho Chi Minh trail, after accepting the fact that one of the six burned and mutilated bodies at the embassy had been Casey, to go on a killing rampage. He'd been a one-man army, taking unnecessary risks, without caring if he lived or died.

It was over now. In just two more days he would be a civilian. He'd hang up the uniform, shove the medals in a drawer, along with the pictures of the Fourth of July picnic, and never look at them again.

"Seventeenth and Pennsylvania Avenue," Mac barked to the cab driver.

"Yes, *sir*," the cabbie said, easing the cab away from the curb.

"And I don't want any conversation."

"You got it, sir."

Mac leaned his head back against the seat. This wasn't the way it was supposed to be. He was supposed to be happy. His first stop should have been his attorney's office to check on the divorce proceedings, the second stop Sadie's, where Benny would be waiting. He'd show them pictures of Casey and invite them to the biggest wedding Washington ever saw.

Burned beyond recognition. Jesus Christ, he didn't even

know where they sent her body. The day would come when he'd *need* to go there, to see that final place, but not now, not when he was so raw and bleeding.

He'd wanted to die back there on the trail. He'd done everything to get himself killed, yet here he was, sitting in a taxi in Washington, D.C. Thank God he'd had the good sense not to involve his men in his crazy stunts. He'd been invincible, every nerve in his body tuned to danger, and still he'd survived. Behind his back his men called him Captain Marvel. They also called him crazy, but they backed him up to a man. Even old fuckface Morley had tapped him on the back and said, "Well done, Carlin," which was as close as the man ever came to an apology in his life. Mac had wanted to deck him on general principle, but he hadn't. He'd suffered through the handshake and back slapping.

If he hadn't been so devastated, so dead inside, he would have preened like a peacock when he heard one of his men say, "They don't come any better than Carlin, man. He's all army." He had all their addresses. Hell, he had everyone's address in Vietnam, and he had promised them all to throw a bash equal to the one he'd thrown on the Fourth of July. "When I get my shit together, men," was the way he'd said good-bye. He would too. It was a promise he meant to honor.

This just wasn't right, he thought, staring at the neon sign in Sadie's window. Casey was supposed to be with him. He was going to show her off. They were going to walk through the door together and Sadie was going to close the bar. How could she be dead? Only young soldiers died ahead of their time, not vibrant, lovely young women who saved lives in the operating room. Not Casey, never Casey. He tried to swallow past the lump in his throat.

He opened the door because that was what he was supposed to do.

Sadie was dressed to the teeth, standing behind the bar. Benny was on a bar stool, a glass of orange juice in front of him. They looked at him. He looked at them. And they knew.

Together they held him, his best friend and the closest thing he had to a mother, while he cried great, manly, gulping sobs.

Their tears mingled with his and not one of the three cared. He thought he was going to die when he heard the platter drop on the Wurlitzer. He dug down to the last ounce of his reserve when he heard the words to "When I'm Sixty-Four."

"You okay, buddy?" Benny said gruffly.

"Of course he's not okay, he's hurting," Sadie said tearfully.

"I can handle it," Mac said hoarsely. "I'm hungry, Sadie. Let's go upstairs."

"Hungry? Well, you certainly came to the right place. I'll fix you the grandest meal you've ever had in your life. If there's one thing I know how to do, it's cook," Sadie babbled happily as she led the two most important men in her life up the stairs to her apartment.

"It's the same. Why did I think it would be different?" Mac said quietly as he sniffed the popcorn-scented air.

Both men ate heartily. When the plates were slipped into the soapy water, Sadie took her place at the table.

"So what are my options?" Mac asked wearily.

"This isn't the time to do *anything*," Sadie said carefully. "You have the rest of your life to make decisions. You need to mourn, honey. You need this time to think about your life and what you really want to do."

"What do I do about Alice and the child?"

"Why don't you try the truth? Tell her what you told us, that you've been sterile since the age of fourteen when you had the mumps and there's no way you could be the father of baby Jenny. You should have told her long ago, Mac. That's just my opinion, of course," Benny said miserably.

"It's mine too, Mac, honey," Sadie said sadly. "This isn't the time though. Why don't you and Benny go off together on a fishing trip or something. You know, just hang out with nature. Bill always used to do that, and he would come back full of spit and vinegar. It might help, Mac."

"It's been great seeing you both. I . . . talked about you to Casey, and I always told her what you wrote in your letters. She couldn't wait to meet both of you. Look, I'm going home. I don't know why because I don't want to go there. I might even stop and see my old man. It's something I have to do. I'll be back. Thanks, it was wonderful, Sadie. Benny, thanks for being here. I'll give you a call."

When the door to the bar closed, Sadie laid her hand on Benny's. "You can't go after him. He has to handle this in his own way. We're here and he knows that. It's all we can do. He'll be all right, but it's going to take a while. That business about him being sterile, I didn't know that. Did you?" she asked in an accusing voice.

"Yeah, I knew. It's not the kind of thing men rush to explain to people. No guy wants to admit to that. I sure as hell wouldn't. Hell, I don't even think his old man knows. Just us."

"But . . . that was so long ago . . . Isn't it possible he could have . . . what I mean is, is the sterility . . . forever?"

"Jeeze, Sadie, I don't . . . it wasn't something we discussed in detail . . . I've heard of cases where . . . shit, I don't know," Benny groaned. "I just know that he doesn't deserve this, Sadie."

"God never gives us more than we can handle," Sadie said quietly. "Mac can handle this. He's not the same, Benny, surely you noticed that. He's his own person now."

"Yeah, guess you're right. He's gotten hard, Sadie. I hate to say this, but he reminds me of his old man." Benny shrugged, his round, homely face worried. "I'll call you, Sadie," he said, crushing her to him. He wondered how it was possible for her always to smell the same, always just right. He had to remember to ask Carol, who always smelled like Johnson's talcum powder. God, he couldn't wait to hug Carol, to look at the kids asleep in their beds, to pull up the covers, to bend down and kiss them good night. He wanted to make love to his wife, to have her hold him, to have her tell him what they had would last forever, and when forever was over to have her tell him they would meet in eternity. That's all he wanted, all he ever wanted out of life.

"THIS IS GOOD enough," Mac said to the taxi driver and handed him two bills. He wanted to walk the rest of the way up the long, curving drive. This was *home,* that wonderful place everyone in Nam thought about and talked about. His home. He'd never talked about it, but he had listened, his heart sore when he listened to the stories his men told. Home. Family. Parents. Pets. Friends. One out of five was all he had. All that counted.

The house was lit. Alice had a thing about making the electric company rich. It looked the same, and why shouldn't it? They certainly paid enough to gardeners and maintenance people. Still, he thought, there should be *something* different, some small change, but there wasn't, at least not any he could see. Unless you counted his father's car in the driveway. That was new. Usually his father had his driver waiting. Marcus Carlin never drove himself because he was a terrible driver, unable to concentrate on the road. Yet, here he was, the Mercedes 560 SEL with the government license plates.

Something perverse in him made him ring the doorbell. A woman with a coronet of braids atop her head opened the door. He'd never seen her before. She was all in gray, from her gray hair to gray uniform, complete with gray ruffled apron. She even had on gray shoes. "Who should I say is calling?" she asked in a guttural accent Mac took to be German.

The perverse streak was still with him. "The man of the house," he said coldly. He wasn't amused when he heard the woman repeat the words twice as she walked away.

He stood in the foyer, the light at his back, more commanding than any general, as he surveyed the two people walking toward him, both their faces registering shock. He watched as his wife's step faltered and his father's eyes narrowed.

"Mac!" they said in unison.

"The prodigal son," Mac said tightly.

My God, Alice thought fearfully, this person can't be Mac, not with such cold eyes and dark skin. Her heart fluttered in her chest. Thank God she'd had her hair done today.

Marcus Carlin's jaw dropped. He had it in place a second later. This was trouble, he could feel it oozing from Mac's pores. Who *was* this steely-eyed man standing in front of him. Certainly not the young man he'd said good-bye to at the Jockey Club twenty-four months ago. For the first time in his life, he felt fear and wasn't sure why. He didn't need anyone to tell him there was a new game in town and it was called Mac Carlin.

"Mac, boy, it's good to see you," Marcus said, holding out his hand. "You should have called us. We'd have rolled out the red carpet and hired a band. You deserve a hero's welcome."

"I'm no hero," Mac said curtly as he suffered through an arm's length embrace from his wife. "I see you got your hair done today."

"You noticed," Alice said.

"What's this you're saying about not being a hero, boy?" the judge said playfully as he poked at the ribbon bars on Mac's duty uniform blouse.

"These," Mac said, ripping at his jacket, "belongs to you, not me. It was what you wanted, and now you have it." He wadded up his jacket and tossed it at his father. The elder Carlin had no recourse but to reach for it. "I gave you ten years and now I don't owe you a thing."

"What's wrong with you, Mac? We had a deal. Ten years and then politics. You can't welsh on me now. It's all set to go. I expected a certain . . . change. After all, you just came out of a war. You'll need time to get acclimated again. We have time. We'll talk in a few days. I'll leave you lovebirds alone now," the judge said, stepping out of the way, his face flushed with controlled anger.

Mac didn't bother to reply. Instead he turned to Alice. "What's the name of the maid this month?"

"Why, it's . . . Olga. Yes, it's Olga," she said fretfully.

"Olga!" Mac roared.

"Yes, sir," the maid spoke up.

"I want the guest house cleaned. Now! I want my things moved there. Now!"

"I was about to serve dinner, sir."

"Dinner can wait. My father won't be staying. Mrs. Carlin has lost her appetite and I ate at a bar and grill. Now!"

Alice bristled. "What's gotten into you, Mac? You certainly are not staying in the guest house. What will people think? Marcus, talk to your son," she pleaded.

Marcus was about to open his mouth when Mac swiveled to face him. "Don't interfere," he said coldly.

"I wasn't about to. She's right though, it isn't going to look good."

"That's rather amusing since this is a fifteen-acre site and there are no neighbors. Unless of course you were planning on a press conference. It's either the guest house or Sadie's apartment."

He stared his father down. The judge's eye twitched. Mac smiled.

Alice seethed when Mac picked up his bag and headed for the door. "Don't you even want to see the baby?"

"No," Mac said curtly, walking back out into the dark night. He heard the door of his father's car shut then saw the headlights spring to life. He didn't look back.

He liked the guest house, had always liked it. It was a brick building that looked deceptively small from the outside. Inside, it was spacious, with a living room, a dining room, a study, two full baths, and three bedrooms. The study was Mac's favorite room, with a huge fieldstone fireplace that stretched all the way to the ceiling. Bookshelves lined the other three walls and were full, from floor to ceiling. It had central heat and a fully equipped kitchen that would be stocked before the night was over. Tomorrow he would ask Sadie to hire him a housekeeper who would live in one of the three bedrooms, a motherly person who would take care of him, feed him, and iron his clothes. He wanted someone like his mother's old companion, Maddy, not some cold-eyed fish like Olga.

"I'll be back in a few hours. Air out the house, make a fire, and have coffee ready," he ordered the housekeeper. "Build a fire in the bedroom too. After today you won't have to concern yourself with this building. You do know that I'm the one who pays your salary, don't you?"

The German stared at him with a blank face. She didn't know any such thing. She'd assumed the elderly gentleman paid her wages, and until this evening, she hadn't known the man now standing in front of her existed. She nodded.

While the housekeeper busied herself, Mac rummaged in the

hall closet for his riding boots and a heavy sweater. He'd long ago moved some of his belongings here because Alice said his boots and riding clothes smelled up her scented closet.

His horse, Jeopardy, welcomed him the way a lover would, nuzzling Mac's hands, and neck, and whickering softly. "Hi, fella, hope you missed me. I sure as hell missed you." The gelding whickered again, his tail swishing furiously. Mac could feel the animal tremble when he saddled him. A man and his horse. God!

The moment they were out of the paddock, Mac gave the horse his head. He raced like the wind, faster than the wind, huge clumps of soft earth flying upward from his stampeding hooves.

"Go, boy, go," Mac shouted, and Jeopardy heeded his master's voice. They were neck and neck with the elder Carlin's car and then they were ahead of it until finally they were so distanced from the Mercedes that Marcus Carlin pulled over to the side of the road.

He knows, the judge thought fearfully. He knows and he's going to make me pay. His shoulders sagged, then righted and sagged again when he saw the powerful gelding and its master silhouetted in the moonlight. His brother-in-law Harry's face rose like a phoenix in front of his car. Marcus cringed against the luxurious leather seat. "You told him," he hissed. "I'm glad you're dead, you bastard! Glad! Glad! Glad! Rot in hell!"

From her position at her bedroom window, Alice watched her husband fly across the field. She saw the huge clumps of earth scatter backward. She was afraid of the horse, and more afraid of the man riding it. She trembled with that fear the moment she realized Marcus Carlin was afraid too. She'd seen it in his eyes this evening, and it had stunned her. The tables were turned now and Mac was in control. The realization brought a second wave of fear. Would Mac really divorce her? He'd already moved out of the house, and he'd been back less than an hour. "I'm not giving this up, I'm not!" she muttered.

It was after ten when Mac returned to the stable. He rubbed down the gelding, then brushed him. He talked affectionately as he worked. Jeopardy whickered softly and snorted his approval of his master's brisk strokes. He chomped down on the crisp apple Mac withdrew from the bin at the end of his stall, and sugar cubes brought a soft whinny of pleasure.

"We'll do this again and again, big fella," Mac crooned softly, his face against the huge animal's head. "Casey would have loved you. You would have liked her too. She'd have been like a feather on your back . . . you'll never know now. It's all gone, and I can't get it back. I wanted it so bad. It wasn't too much to want, to expect. Everyone has the right to a little happiness. I don't even know where they . . . where they sent her. I need to know. She didn't have anyone either. What do you think, Jep, will I ever get over this? Will I ever be whole again?" He felt the gelding's warm breath on his cheek as the huge animal reacted to the sorrow in his master's voice.

"See you tomorrow, Jep. We'll head out right after breakfast and make a day of it. I have a lot of thinking to do."

The guest cottage was ablaze. Obviously Olga liked light as much as his wife.

The closed-up, musty odor was gone, replaced by a fresh citrusy smell that was pleasing. The fire was in need of another log. The fresh smell of coffee mingled with the scent of pine-cones popping in the fireplace. This was cozy, this was real. This, he decided, was as close to a home as he was ever going to get. He liked the worn leather furniture, the shabby rugs, the old-fashioned kitchen. When his new housekeeper arrived, he would ask her to get some green plants and maybe some flowers that would bloom indoors. He was going to get a dog too, first thing tomorrow. Man, horse, and dog. It sounded right. He headed for the stairs, but not before he shot the security bolts home on both doors. The only way anyone was going to cross the threshold of this house was by invitation.

Fresh from his shower, dressed in an old terry robe and slippers, Mac made his way to the kitchen, where he poured out a huge mug of coffee for himself. The refrigerator was stocked as ordered, right down to the mustard for his ham sandwich. He carried everything back to the study, flipping on the television before he sat down. He finished the sandwich and coffee. Then he cried. He ached to have someone hold him, ached for someone to tell him it was going to be all right, ached for someone to reassure him that time would heal him.

If it was possible to lose one's soul before death, Mac Carlin lost his in that moment, for he offered it up to the Supreme Being. "Take care of her," he pleaded brokenly.

Bullshit, he was not going to wait till tomorrow to get a dog. In five minutes he was dressed in jeans, shirt, and shearling jacket. He knew where the pound was and he could be there in fifteen minutes. He climbed into a Jaguar in his garage and wondered who it belonged to. Probably him. It smelled like perfume and hair spray. He rolled down the window. He laughed all the way to the pound, but it was a hurt, bewildered sound. As if a dog could ever take Casey's place. "It's a god-damn place to start," he muttered as he swerved into the lighted gravel parking lot.

Inside, lights shot to life as dog after dog barked furiously. An intruder was in their midst. A grumpy little man with a bald head opened the door as he struggled to fit the arms of his eyeglasses over his ears. "Whatcha want at this time of night, mister?"

"A dog."

"We close at six. We open at seven. Come back then," he said, preparing to shut the door.

"Wait, you don't understand. I *need* a dog. I need it now. I'll pay whatever you want. Two dogs, two is good. How about if I take two? Can I get them now?" he asked desperately. He wasn't going home without a dog. He must have conveyed that message, because the grumpy little man opened the door wider.

"What kind of dog do you want? You said two. What kind, mister?"

What kind. Hell, he didn't know. "A man's dog," he said stupidly. "A buddy, a dog I can be pals with."

"You said two," the little man said spiritedly.

"Okay, two. Dogs who will respond to the names . . . Fred and Gus." The little man raised sharp eyes. He'd caught the catch in the man's voice, saw the mist in his eyes.

"Got just the dogs, mister. Two golden retrievers. Five months old. Eight to the litter, no one wanted these last two.

Five hundred bucks, papers and all. AKC registered. Beauties."

Mac dropped to his haunches when the dogs were led out of their pens. They eyed him warily before he fixed leashes to their collars.

"They're frisky little devils. Never been outside the run, so they'll take off on you if you don't use the leash. You gonna take care of these animals, mister?"

"I think it's the other way around; they're gonna take care of me. Don't worry, I'll give them a good home."

Money changed hands.

The dogs yipped and whined all the way back to the house. Once he thought he heard a trickle of water, but refused to confirm the sound.

It took almost an hour before the dogs calmed down enough to eat the food Mac prepared. While they ate he went around cleaning up their puddles. He definitely needed a housekeeper.

They were curious, he noticed, poking and sniffing everything, finally flopping down by the fire, their golden heads between their paws, their eyes unblinkingly on him. "You, on the left, you're Fred. You're Gus," Mac said pointing to each of them. At least one part of the dream was coming true. Casey had said she would name her dog Fred. He'd said he'd call his Gus.

Done.

It was two in the morning when he walked up the steps to the second floor, both dogs at his heels. He undressed, added a log to the fire, and climbed into bed. Two pairs of eyes watched his every movement. Five minutes after he turned out the light and settled himself, he felt first one thump and then another. He laughed into his pillow.

He had someone. It didn't matter that they were animals. They were his, and they were part of the dream. His and Casey's dream.

For the first time since learning of Casey's death, Mac slept through the night.

Two days later Mac left the United States Army. At ten o'clock in the morning he was Major Malcolm Carlin. At eleven o'clock he was Malcolm Carlin, civilian.

Two things happened the afternoon he turned civilian. His new housekeeper, an amazon of a woman, arrived. She towered over him by a good two inches. She also outweighed him by forty pounds. She said her name was Yolanda Angelique Magdalena Consuela Chavez. "Call me Yody," she said, emitting a deep belly laugh that frightened the dogs.

"What shall I call you?"

"Mac will be fine, Yody."

"These animals, they are trained, yes?"

"No, they aren't. I just got them the day before yesterday. I'm working on it." Mac grimaced as he thought of all the puddles and crap he'd cleaned up.

"Tomorrow they will be trained," Yody said firmly. Mac believed her. The dogs slunk out of the room to pee in the middle of the kitchen floor.

"Miss Switzer said you wished some plants and flowers. I can do this. What else do you wish me to do?"

"Cook, shop, iron. I don't like to do dishes. I like clean sheets. I'll try not to be under your feet. For the time being, I'll be here. Take whichever bedroom you like."

"Señor Mac, would you object if I had my trailer moved here? I do not like to stay in my employer's house. I wish to sleep in my own bed. I snore quite loudly and I have two . . . cats. I cannot give them up. I like to be among my own things in the evening when the day is done. Is this a problem?" she asked quietly.

"No, not at all. When can you start to work?"

"I have already started. I am here. My trailer will arrive in a few hours. One of my cousins will hook up the electricity and water. The cats will be no problem for your animals. They are indoor animals, and they are declawed."

"Is the salary agreeable?"

"Yes, very agreeable. But I do not like to do dishes either."

"Hell, I can eat off paper plates. Don't we have a dishwasher?"

"I don't know, Señor Mac. Do we?"

"Guess we don't. We'll buy one. Today. Call up someone and tell him to deliver it."

"My cousins can do this. Then it is arranged?"

"Yes." Mac waved his hands about. "Just look till you find what you want. Do you need money?"

"I will keep a book for the expenses. I wish to be paid at the beginning of each month. Medical insurance is provided and Social Security?" Her tone of voice said it damn well better be.

"Well, sure. If that's what you want. If there's nothing else, I think I'm going for a ride. On a horse," he said. He whistled for the dogs, who came on the run, skidding to a stop in front of Yody. .

"No, they do not go. They stay with me until they learn what every animal must know—they do their business outside." One long arm shot out, the index finger pointing toward the kitchen, into which the dogs, whimpering, slunk on their bellies.

He was curious as hell in the days to come, but Mac refused to ask Yody how she trained both dogs in one day's time. Obviously she hadn't mistreated them in any way, for they adored her. But all she had to do was point with her long arm and she had instant obedience. In the barn he'd tried the same thing, but all the dogs did was lick and jump all over him.

Yody was the second best thing that ever happened to him.

The next thing that happened to him that day was he met the child who carried his name. That's the way he thought of her—*the child.* He purposely waited until he heard the sound of his wife's car leaving the garage before he walked to the house. This time he didn't ring the bell. He used his key and climbed the winding staircase. The child's room was at the end of the hall, the room that had been his nursery when he was a small child. The child was a girl so he expected that the room had been redecorated in pink with frills and ruffles. He felt a momentary pang when he realized that all the toy soldiers scampering up the wall would be gone. His mother had painted them, allowing him to dip his own small brush into the little pot of red paint so he could add his personal touch to the high-topped hats. He wondered how many coats of paint it took to cover them up. Had his childhood toys been thrown out or moved to the attic? Surely thrown out. By Alice. There wasn't a sentimental bone in Alice's body.

Mac changed direction and headed for the attic door at the opposite end of the hall. He wanted to know before he walked into the strange new room to see the strange new child.

The attic was wonderful, full of things he'd considered treasures when he was a child who'd played alone. Rusty lamps with tattered shades were sentinels guarding his domain; the huge trunks that held outdated clothes contained make-believe gems and pieces of eight. He remembered pushing and tugging till he had all the brass-bound trunks in a half circle, his fort for fighting off Apaches with broom handles and knobby-topped canes. On snowy days he'd picnicked with his wooden soldiers who were taking a break from the war.

The attic looked just the same, the way an attic is supposed to look. Perhaps there were more cobwebs, but the half-moon windows were exactly as dirty and dusty as he remembered them. The trunks were set in neat rows, and the rusty lamps were rustier, with shades full of spiderwebs. He walked up and down the small aisles created by the trunks and cartons. He looked for his Flexible Flyer with the broken runner, and his stout wagon which he'd carted all the toy soldiers to war in. There was no box full of roller skates and hockey skates. His skis were gone as well, and so were his model planes and ships. He searched for his books, those treasures he'd read far into the night, but he couldn't find them either. Everything was gone. He might as well have never lived here, he thought sadly.

His hands in his pockets, Mac descended the steps to the second floor. He had to remember to get the box of books he'd brought into Sadie, which his mother had left him. They would fit into the guest house the way he fit in. It was all he had.

He saw it all at once, the frilly, beribboned room, the nanny sitting in a stout wooden rocker, the child in a wooden-slat playpen. She was just sitting, slapping at her pudgy knees with her pudgy hands. She had golden curls just like Alice's. In the room was every toy ever made, he thought. Rocking horses of various heights, little plastic trikes, and a real one with fat rubber wheels. Three toy boxes were filled to overflowing. Shelves with stuffed animals covered every wall. The closet door was open, revealing hundreds of outfits on little hangers.

He recollected Lily and her baby and the mean little apartment. Their belongings wouldn't fill a paper sack.

The nanny saw him at the same time the child became aware of his presence. Mac stumbled then, his eyes wide and disbelieving. Those same eyes questioned the nanny, who looked at him inquiringly. For a single startled moment he was back in Vietnam, on the trail, and seeing for the first time the bamboo cages hanging from trees with half-dead GI's inside—the VC's way of keeping prisoners. His eyes swiveled from the playpen to the crib, which had the same kind of slats. In the far corner there was a youth bed with rails, rather like a child's small hospital bed. He thought of Lily again and the futon she and Eric slept on. His throat constricted.

"Mr. Carlin, is something wrong?" the nanny said, rising to her feet.

He ignored her and dropped to his haunches to stare at the child. She wasn't his, he had to keep remembering that. "She's . . . a . . . Mongoloid," he said in a cracked voice he barely recognized as his own.

"Yes, Jenny has Down's syndrome. You didn't know?" the nanny said, her eyes filled with horror.

"No, no, I . . . I didn't . . . know."

The nanny sniffed as though to say she thought as much. Mac continued to stare at the child, trying to fathom what he was seeing. He was sterile, three doctors told him so. Yet . . . he'd had an aunt who was severely retarded, his father's sister, whom the family had kept institutionalized. He'd seen her once. It was a memory of pure horror. Later, his mother had explained who the woman was and why she did the things she did. He couldn't remember her name. She'd spit on him and slapped him. She'd slobbered all over herself. He remembered that and he remembered how she'd tried to hug his father, her brother, and the way his father had shoved her away, revulsion on his face. His mother had cried. He'd cried too, not understanding. People had carried her out the door, kicking and screaming. She'd never come back. He had to remember her name. Peggy, that was it, but his father had called her Margaret. Aunt Margaret.

Mac leaned over the playpen. His arms reached out, but the child backed away from him, sliding into the corner.

"You're strange. She doesn't know you," the nanny said quietly. "She's very lovable, Mr. Carlin. She responds well to affection, and she certainly gets enough of that, between Mrs. Carlin and myself. Mrs. Carlin plays with her for hours at a time. She won't let anyone bathe her but herself. It's lovely to see them together. Your wife is a devoted mother."

Chapter 10

MARCH BLEW IN and out, then the April rains came, and Mac, for all his intentions, did nothing more than eat, sleep, and ride the fields with Jeopardy, while Fred and Gus ran alongside. He read in the afternoons, spoke to Sadie and Benny on the phone, and when he was finished with what he called his busy hours, he walked to the house to see baby Jenny. She knew him now and held out her arms to be picked up. He played with her on the floor, building blocks made from sponge and colorful cardboard. He played horsey with the little girl on his back, and she held on to his neck for dear life. Her squeals were full of joy. Jenny made him smile.

On a rainy, gray day at the end of April, Alice walked into the nursery and smiled. She dropped to the floor, her face full of something Mac had never seen before. He almost toppled backward when he saw Jenny tug on her mother's hair and ears. "I love her so much, Mac. I've been to every top doctor in the country, and she'll always be what she is now. We take it one day at a time. But I will never, *never* put her in an institution. She's bright. Every day I work with her. She's still a baby, but she responds so well. I truly believe she's educable. I don't know if it's wishful thinking on my part or not. If she's not, then I will have to live with that. Do you have any feelings on the matter?" she asked carefully.

He realized he too loved the little girl, even though he was certain in his heart she wasn't his flesh and blood. He couldn't turn his back on a retarded child. A child was a child, and it didn't matter if she was whole or not. These days he needed all

266

the love and affection he could get. It was so easy to return love to the chubby little girl with the round face.

"Do you, Mac?" Alice asked quietly.

"We need to talk, Alice. Let's go downstairs."

"Very well," Alice said, handing her daughter over to the nanny, "but I have to be back here in half an hour to give Jenny her bath. I like to do it at the same time every day. We have a routine," she said proudly.

Downstairs in *her* chrome and glass room, Alice reverted to the old Alice, her hair smoothed down, her voice snide and cool. "Are you comfortable in the guest house?"

"Very comfortable. I'm not coming back here, if that's your next question."

"But Jenny . . . I thought . . . you seem to . . . what is it with you, Mac? Did something happen to your brain when you were in Vietnam? You're not the same person. You aren't working. You don't appear to be interested in anything but your dogs and that damn horse. You don't call your father, you don't talk to me." She lit a cigarette and blew smoke toward his face. "The only thing that makes any sense at all is that there must be someone else. That's it, isn't it?" she said spitefully. "And another thing . . . that . . . that person who works for you . . . Where does she get off telling me I can't go into the guest house? She looks like a convict. Where *did* you get her? She told Olga what you pay her, and now Olga wants a raise. Damn you, Mac," she said, blowing a second jet of smoke in Mac's direction.

Mac held up his hand. One by one he ticked off the answers to the questions she asked. "Nothing happened to my brain in Vietnam. You're right, I'm not the same person. I am a better person. You're right about me not working too. I may never work again. Fortunately, thanks to my mother's side of the family, which is where all the money comes from, I don't have to work. I love my animals, they love me unconditionally, and they're loyal, which happens to be a word you know very little about. I don't call my father because I have nothing to say to him. I do not like my father. I have never liked my father. You, Alice, backed the wrong horse. As for talking to you—what is there to say to a woman who at one time professed to love me, when it was all a lie? You see, Alice, I don't love you either. Jenny is not my daughter, as much as you would like me to believe that she is. Shhh, don't sputter like that. It's unbecoming. I'll tell you how I know she isn't my daughter. I'm sterile. I have been since the age of fourteen when I had the mumps. I have three different medical reports that will bear this out. I know I misled you. And I'm not proud of that. It was vanity on my part because I thought it made me less than a man. I always told you to use your diaphragm because I didn't want you to know. Now it doesn't make any difference. You've given your child my name, and I won't take that away from her. I'm fond of her. Her disability makes me love her all the more. As for my housekeeper, the less you say the better, or you will find yourself without Olga to boss around. I pay the bills around here, and I suggest you remember that. Yody is not a convict and she doesn't look like a convict. She is a warm, loving, compassionate woman who has worked hard all her life. She's taken over in the care department, and I will be eternally grateful. Besides, she plays a hell of a game of gin rummy. There is no one else in my life but Benny and Sadie. No one," he said coldly. "Did I leave anything out? Yes, yes, I did," Mac said mockingly. "The family money is *all* mine, not my father's. Oh, he has a handsome salary and a few stocks and bonds. He gets dividends. He owns a few properties. But the *real* money is mine— left to me by my aunt Rita, my mother, and my uncle Harry. No one," he said savagely, "bothered to write and tell me Uncle Harry died! That was your job, Alice, and you didn't do it. That money is tied up six ways to Sunday, so you weren't quite accurate when you said I've been doing nothing. Taking care of one's money is a full-time job. There is no way you will get your hands on any of it. I'll take that one step further—there's no way my father will get his hands on it either. I'm going to use it to set up a foundation for children with Down's syndrome and another one for Amerasian children. What do you think of that, Alice?"

"I think you've lost your mind," Alice snarled. "Jenny is your child. She has . . . has your ears."

Mac laughed. "No, she isn't mine. I can show you the medical reports any time you want to see them. Now, shall we talk about a divorce?"

"I'll never give you a divorce. You can't do this to me. Your father won't allow it. Why are you doing this?" Alice asked imploringly.

"And if you think you can threaten me with a scandal, don't bother. I personally don't give a good rat's ass about anything you do. Do you get it, Alice? I don't care!"

"This was supposed to be a wonderful new beginning for us, and look what you've done, you've gone and spoiled it with your lies about Jenny. Damn you to hell, Mac!" she shouted. She was still shouting when Mac let himself out the front door.

The rain was cold, but he barely noticed it. What he did notice was the cheerful lights shining out from the guest house. He knew there would be a fire to take the dampness out of the house, and delicious, tantalizing smells would waft from the kitchen. He continued on to the back of the house. When he was abreast of the kitchen door he whistled sharply and was rewarded with two taffy-colored streaks heading straight for him. It had been Yody's suggestion to have a doggie door cut into the kitchen entrance so the dogs could let themselves in and out. One of the little secrets of her training, he supposed.

Mac walked, his hands stuck into the deep pockets of his shearling jacket. He was oblivious to the rain as the retrievers trotted alongside him. The pain at his circumstances was so overwhelming, he stopped in his tracks, his face raised to the pelting downpour. The dogs growled softly as they nuzzled his legs. "What do I do? Point me in the right direction," he begged. There was no bolt of lightning, no lessening of the rain, no clout on the head. The rain continued, the dogs kept growling, and he kept walking until he came to an eight-foot drainage ditch, at which he turned around to retrace his steps. Delighted, the dogs ran ahead, stopping from time to time to see if their master was following.

"You can always find your way home, fellas, if someone cares enough to put a light in the window. In our case the back porch light is on, so we'll make it," Mac mumbled as he slogged in his wet sneakers up to the back porch.

Yody's chocolate-dark eyes showed concern. "A hot bath," she said sternly, "two aspirins, and a glass of juice. If you don't care about yourself, Señor Mac, think of these two soaking-wet dogs. You at least had on a heavy jacket." She clucked her tongue while she toweled the dogs briskly. "Go, señor, quickly, before you catch a chill. Sickness bothers me. I am no good with ther-momb-beters."

"I'm gone," Mac said, delighted with the concern in her voice. She was right, a hot bath and some aspirins would make him feel better. "What's for dinner? It smells wonderful."

"Chicken noodle soup, roast chicken, mashed potatoes, gravy, peas, and a salad. Fresh dinner rolls and a peach cobbler. Go, go," she admonished. "One hour till dinner."

When Mac entered the den forty minutes later, he burst out laughing. Both dogs were wrapped like newborn babies in fluffy yellow towels. They woofed softly from their position by the fire. He laughed harder when he saw the two empty bowls. Yody had given them chicken soup. He also noticed his own glass of juice and three aspirins on the little table next to his chair. He swallowed them dutifully. "I think," he said, dropping to his haunches, "we're all going to get real used to this kind of care and attention." The dogs woofed but made no move to get up. Yody put them here, and here they would stay. Mac swore he saw steam coming out of the yellow towels.

"Dinner, Señor Mac, is ready."

There were flowers on the table, Mac noticed. He asked what kind they were.

"Spring flowers. Daffodils, tulips, and the purple ones are iris. I thought they would cheer you up. Spring, señor, is a beautiful time of the year. Everything comes to life at this time. It will be a beautiful life again for you. Time does not stand still for any of us. I do not wish to know," she said, when she thought Mac was about to explain his feelings. "My cousins tell me I am in-toot-tiv. I know it is possible for one's heart to break. I also know it is possible for one's heart to mend. There will be a scar, but that is life. Now, eat, Señor Mac, for I have cooked all day."

He ate. More than he should have, but he didn't care. The coffee, when Yody served it, was so delicious Mac asked for a second cup. "What did you put in this?"

"Vanilla, Señor Mac. Sometimes it is better than a dessert."

Mac tipped back in his chair, coffee cup to his lips, when Yody clapped her hands softly. Seconds later the dogs were in the kitchen, each dragging a towel. She set down two plates loaded with the same food Mac had eaten. They wolfed it down in minutes. "Ah, they think I am a good cook too. I am," she said imperiously.

"How is it you aren't married, Yody?"

"Oh, but I was, Señor Mac, four times. I buried all four husbands. I don't wish to marry again. Funerals are too expensive."

"Oh." It was all Mac could think of to say. He stared at her. She wasn't beautiful, but she wasn't ugly either. Her best feature, Mac thought, was her huge dark eyes. Her skin was the color of molasses, and she had the whitest teeth Mac had ever seen. She also had more teeth than he'd ever seen, and he saw them a lot because Yody wore a constant smile. The only time he'd ever seen shoes on her feet was the day she'd arrived. She refused to wear an apron, saying she paid a lot of money for her skirts and blouses and she didn't want to hide them. Her hair, he knew, was down past her buttocks, but he only knew this because she told him so. For the most part she wore it tied in a huge knot at the back of her head. He laughed, remembering the day Alice came to the door and opened it. For a large woman, Yody moved like greased lightning, and met Alice at the door, her huge arms crossed over her breast.

"No visitors," she'd said, showing every one of her teeth.

Alice had insisted on entering. Yody insisted that she would not. Yody had finally picked Alice up and turned her around to face the walkway.

"No visitors unless Señor Mac invites you," she repeated.

Alice had retaliated by shrieking that Yody's trailer was a rusty eyesore and tacky to boot. Yody had slammed the door, muttering obscenities Mac had never heard before. He grinned. By God, it was time someone put Alice in her place.

A few days later his father had tried the same thing. The minute the door opened his father had said, "I'm Justice Marcus Carlin and I'd like to see my son."

To which Yody replied, "I am Yolanda Angelique Magdalena Consuela Chavez. No visitors unless invited." Bam, the door was shut in the judge's face. Mac had hooted his glee in the kitchen, where he was having apple pie and coffee.

When the phone rang, it was Yody's job to answer it. He was in to anyone but his father and Alice. When they called, which they did almost on an hourly basis, her answer was always the same. "We will call you when we wish to speak. No calls."

He knew he was carrying the thing with his father too far. He'd settled Alice for the time being. He was going to give himself one more week before he started to make decisions. For now he needed time to himself. He'd earned it, and no one was going to take it away from him.

Tonight he was going to write letters to every organization he knew of to ask for help in finding Lily's baby. He'd already placed two calls to Eric Savorone, Lily's lover, but neither had been returned. A letter was called for now. He had to give careful thought to what he was going to say and how he was going to say it. He also wanted to spend some time thinking about his uncle Harry and the trust Harry had left him, along with the Charleston mansion.

While he was in Vietnam he'd written one letter to his uncle, but there had been no return letter. He hadn't expected one, and that was okay. Now he was glad he'd taken the time. He'd written all about the Ho Chi Minh trail and the guys in his company. He'd gone into detail about the Fourth of July picnic. He'd even touched on Casey, not knowing if his crotchety uncle would approve or not. He'd done it because he needed to acknowledge Casey in some way to the outside world.

The night was long, his mind full of memories, his heart aching unbearably, as he wrote all of his letters on a typewriter that was as old as his father.

Out of the corner of his eye, as he pecked away at the keys, he could see the retrievers playing with one another, tugging and fussing with a length of clothesline Yody had tied into huge knots. Every so often in their frenzy they would catapult over one another. Their yips of happiness made Mac smile. Things were getting back to normal.

At ten-thirty he licked the last stamp. At 10:35 he carried the stack of letters out to the mailbox at the end of the drive, the dogs loping ahead of him. The rain, he noticed, had let up, but there were no stars in the sky. Tomorrow wasn't going to be any better than today in the weather department. The thought depressed him. Sunshine, no matter where you were, was preferable to this dismal grayness.

As he loped up the cobblestone walkway, the dogs growled. The signal the phone was ringing. He raced inside, his greeting breathless.

"Hello," he said.

"Eric Savorone, Mr. Carlin, I'm returning your call. Sorry about the late hour, but I've been in surgery all evening, an accident case. Do I know you?"

"No, Doctor, we never met. I'm calling about Lily Gia."

"Lily?"

To Mac's ears it sounded like "Lily who?" He bristled, his voice sharp when he said, "I thought you might like to know I believe she's dead. She was caught in the Tet Offensive, but I have no concrete details. I also believe that your son is in an orphanage in Thailand."

"Now hold on here, Mr. Carlin. I don't know what you're talking about. Yes, I knew Lily. It was what it was, nothing more. I don't like this talk about 'my son,' so let's knock that off right now. Wait a damn minute here. I know who you are. I read about you in the papers. It sounds to me like you're trying to stir up trouble for me. I can't allow that. I have a respected position here, and as far as I'm concerned, I have no son. If Lily was pregnant—and I'm not admitting she was—it's not my problem. I'm sorry if she's dead. I can't do anything about that either. I don't want you calling me again, Mr. Carlin. Do we understand each other?"

He understood all right. Poor Lily. "Decency demands I tell

you I am going to try to bring that child here to the States. Lily was a friend of mine. She was ostracized from her family, but then you know that, don't you, Doctor?" Not waiting for a reply, Mac continued, his voice hard and brittle, "Somewhere, someplace in Vietnam, there's a birth certificate that has your name on it. I'll find it if it takes me the rest of my life. If you don't want the child, that's okay too. I called only to tell you you had a son and to give you what little information I have on Lily. The fact that you are so uninterested is your problem, not mine, Doctor. I won't call you again, although other people might."

"That sounds like a goddamn threat, Carlin. Listen," Savorone hissed, "they all opened their legs, and if you were one of those puritanical do-gooders who didn't take advantage, that's *your* problem."

"You son of a bitch!" Mac swore at the pinging receiver before he slammed it down. The retrievers stopped their play long enough to stare at him, their ears flattened against their huge velvety heads. He didn't waste his time thinking about Eric Savorone.

Afterward, he sat in front of the fire, the dogs snoozing contentedly at his side. He was warm, the fire burning brightly with a mixture of cherry and cedar logs with a sprinkling of pinecones that gave off a heady, intoxicating aroma that vied with Yody's pot roast. A bottle of Budweiser beer and his cigarettes were at his elbow. The television set was on, the voices muted.

Mac reached for a cigarette, his eyes on the letter next to his ashtray. It had arrived two days ago. At first he wasn't going to open it, but his curiosity as to why Phil Pender would write him finally got the best of him. He'd read the letter so many times over the past few days, he could recite it verbatim. He read it again:

Dear Major Carlin,
    Guess this letter is a bit of a surprise. I'm kind of surprised myself to be writing but the guys insisted, so read on, Major.
    By the time you read this I should be stateside and selling

used cars. Freeze, Stevens, and myself will be the last ones to rotate out of here. Colonel Morley left this morning amidst cheers and catcalls. I felt like crying yesterday when I saw the first batch of new guys. Your replacement is a little thick around the middle and his feet are plastered full of Band-Aids. Freeze refers to the new guys as whipper-snappers. The term makes me feel old.

I guess I should get on with it. We all took a vote, and as you can see by the attached list, everyone in your command, plus a few others we rounded up, signed it. We all know about your background and all those political people you're buddies with, so we kind of thought you'd be the perfect guy to go to the U.S. Senate and take care of us guys. We're gonna need someone like you on our side when this is over, someone who can wade through all the bullshit and red tape. I've had some feedback, so have the others, from guys who rotated home a year ago. They're being treated like lepers. Who can these guys go to? Who's going to understand? Not those fat cats on the Hill, that's for sure. Freeze said he's embarrassed to go home. Shit, Major, that's not right.

Something has to be done about the babies our guys are leaving behind. Aspacolas did his best to try and get his girl and baby out. No luck. Miles of red tape and bureaucratic bullshit. We took a vote and decided the Senate is a good place to start.

I did what you said, I put the word out on the Bamboo Pipeline about Lily Gia's son. So far nothing. I've clued in my replacement and he's agreed to pass any info back to me in the States.

Word came down the Pipeline ten days ago that a memorial service was held for Lieutenant Adams. The word is Dr. Farrell read the eulogy, then got so drunk he busted up the makeshift Officers' Club and then worked a twenty-two-hour shift.

The third piece of paper will tell you where Lieutenant Adams's remains were sent. I thought you would want to know. I really did some digging and called in a lot of markers to come up with this. I was told that a Nicole Dupre, Lieu-

tenant Adams's friend, claimed her body. I've enclosed Miss
Dupre's address. I'm sorry, Major, if this opens any wounds.

I hope you're enjoying civilian life, Major, and if you ever
need a *good* used car, look me up. Best of Luck.

Phil Pender

Mac stuffed the letter back into the envelope. His eyes burned
hotly when he stared at the long list of names scrawled on the
yellowed paper. Hundreds of names, maybe as many as a thousand. Most of them he recognized, some he didn't. Pender, he
knew, would have gone to a hot LZ to get names if he thought
it would help.

The dogs, sensing a change in their master's mood, raised
their heads in unison. Mac scratched behind their silky ears.
"It's okay, fellas, I just had a bad minute there. I think Pender
just solved my problem. He's right, you know. The political
climate back here in regard to Vietnam stinks worse than the
country itself."

Could he run for the Senate and win? He had the background, the political connections. Did he want to do it? He'd
never liked politics, especially his father's brand. Could he do
a turnaround and work at something he detested? He admitted
he didn't know. He did know that he was capable of working
tirelessly, twenty-four hours a day, for something he believed
in. And, by God, he believed in everything Pender said. He
closed his eyes and tried to picture himself in the Senate cham-
ber. His eyes snapped open. Hell yes, he could see himself there.
The dogs woofed softly. Mac closed his eyes a second time, the
vision behind his closed lids that of himself in the governor's
mansion with his father sitting at a desk behind his own. "Hell
no!" he exploded.

The dogs leaped from the couch, the satiny hairs on their
sleek backs on end. They pawed his legs and arms, growling
deep in their throats.

"Hey, fellas, it's okay. Everything is fine. Come on, I'll give
you some root beer. Yeah, yeah, I know all about the root beer.
I saw Yody sneak it to you. She gives you root beer and you do
whatever she wants. That's how she damn well trained you.

You like those bubbles in your nose. Don't worry, I'm not going to let on I know," Mac muttered as he splashed soda pop into two round yellow bowls.

He had a purpose now, a reason to get on with life. He knew in his gut, because he knew himself so well, that sooner or later he would have come to this very same conclusion on his own. Pender just speeded up his mental processes, jerked him out of his complacency. Thank God for Pender.

The root beer finished, the dogs inched close, their wet noses pressed tight into Mac's thigh. He scratched their heads, grinning when they growled with pleasure. Such a little thing, a touch really, and the animals were happy. That's what *he* needed, a kind word, a touch, and it would all be bearable.

He sat through the evening programming and the late news, content for the moment. When the newscaster signed off for the evening, Mac knew it was time to make some decisions.

Eleven-thirty wasn't too late to make a phone call. Benny was a night owl, rarely going to bed before one-thirty or so. He dialed the number from memory. Benny's voice was alert, but not the least bit enthused to hear from Mac at such a late hour. "I didn't wake you, did I? The kids and Carol, how are they?"

"Everyone is fine. The family is sound asleep. The breadwinner is sitting here trying to figure out how he's going to pay his bills this month and who is going to get a letter of apology instead of a check. What's up?"

Mac had long ago given up asking Benny if he could help out. He didn't ask now. "I want to throw something at you from left field. Think about it and call me tomorrow with your answer."

"Hey, it's almost tomorrow now." Benny laughed. "Shoot."

"You know my old man's plans are for me to run for governor of this fine state. I don't want to be governor, and I'm not sure I could even get nominated. But what I do want is to make a try for the United States Senate on the Democratic ticket. I want to help make law. I might have a chance at that. I'd like you to be my campaign manager. I know you have to talk it over with Carol, and that's fine. The pay is good, and you won't have to send out letters of apology every month. It's not charity, Benny, you know me better than that. You'll earn every cent I pay you. We can even put Carol on the payroll. She can stuff envelopes at home—they do that in campaigns, I think—if she has the time or is even interested. If I don't make it, we'll go to Chula Vista and open a hot dog stand. What do you think?"

"Jesus, it sounds great. It really does." Mac smiled at the excitement in his friend's voice. Then he laughed out loud, startling the dogs, when Benny said, "Have you given any thought to the fact that I know diddly-squat about politics?"

"Hey, we'll be starting out even. I don't even know how many members there are in Congress or the Senate. That's how green I am. I'm going to learn though."

"What's your father going to say?" Benny demanded.

"Plenty. I plan to . . . go over his head."

"Alice?" Benny asked hesitantly.

"Alice is very busy with her daughter. For now I'm going to let sleeping dogs lie, and the longer they sleep, the better for everyone concerned. We'll work on that angle. For now we need some powerful people who will endorse me."

Benny whooped with laughter. "Are you thinking the same thing I'm thinking? All those wonderful pictures on Sadie's bulletin board? All those glossy, shiny pictures? Did Sadie tell you or did you notice that there are only two spaces left on that board?"

"You're kidding!" Mac said in awe.

"Would I kid you about something that important? Sadie has been dithering for months now between the Attorney General and some guy named Nebermyer, a cabinet member. That's for the number-two spot. God and Sadie are the only ones who know who gets the number-one spot. She may never fill it. There's something about that last spot. The list for that spot, my friend, is miles long. Someday," Benny said thoughtfully, "I want someone to tell me how that little bar and grill got to be so popular with the power elite." Benny cleared his throat. "Okay, boss, when do you want to get started?"

"As soon as you resign. I'll wait for you, Benny. You want out by five tomorrow, you're out. The paperwork might take a little while, but you'll be *out*, I guarantee it. All it takes is one phone call."

"Day after tomorrow is fine with me. I still have to talk to Carol. Listen, how about if I go wake her and call you back? Yeah, I'll do that. Wait right there, Mac."

Twelve minutes later Mac's phone rang.

"She said okay on one condition," Benny said happily.

"What's that?"

"That I leave her the car."

"What's wrong with the one I left with you?"

"Don't you want it back?" Benny asked stupidly.

"Nah, she can use it. There's a Jag in the garage here. I can use that. Alice has her own car."

"Okay, it's settled. I want to be a civilian by five o'clock . . . today. Can you work that kind of magic?"

Mac looked at the clock on the mantel. It was two minutes past midnight. "You got it. I'll meet you at Sadie's at five-thirty."

"I'll be the guy in the flowered shirt." Benny cackled glee-fully.

"Good night, Benny."

It was the first day, Mac thought, of his *new* life.

Chapter 11

THE KITCHEN WAS flooded with sunshine. The dogs lay in the biggest patch of light forcing Yody to step over them. She smiled indulgently when she set down plates of scrambled eggs and Canadian bacon next to each of them. "If it's good enough for me, it's good enough for them, eh?" Mac laughed.

"That's what you said, Señor Mac. You said they were to eat what you eat. It is good nutrition. Your father called while you were in the shower. He said it is," she had to think about the word she wanted for a moment, finally coming up with, "*crucial* that you call him as soon as you can."

As he ate his breakfast, Mac thought about all the *crucial* times he'd waited for his father to get back to him. One time it had taken him three months, and even then there had been no apology.

"Señor Mac, I won't be here all day. Today is—"

"Bingo day. I know. We'll manage." He reached into his pocket and peeled off a ten-dollar bill. "Play the round-robin for me, and if I win, you get half."

Yody giggled. He'd never heard her giggle before. It was a wonderful sound. Marathon Bingo, Yody's reason for living.

"*Do* you ever win, Yody?" Mac asked curiously.

"Sometimes. If no one wins today, the jackpot next week will be one thousand dollars. I think, Señor Mac, next week I will be lucky."

"Good luck, I'll clean up here. You don't want to be late."

Yody threw her arms around Mac. As one, the dogs stood up, their ears alert, their eyes curious. "You do not mind that you will have to eat leftovers?"

280

"I won't be home for dinner. Don't worry. The dogs will be fine. Go get 'em, Yody!" He felt indulgent, as though he was sending off his mother, instead of his housekeeper, to play Bingo.

Mac decided that he liked this kitchen. It was quiet and bright. He barely heard the radio playing softly on the counter, the radio Yody kept on twenty-four hours a day. Everything was old: the refrigerator with the big cooler on top, the stove with legs, the chipped porcelain sink. Even the tables and chairs were old, from his mother's time. He liked the curtains with their red tie-back bows, which allowed a breeze when the windows were open. The little pots of chili peppers, mint, and thyme on the white windowsills added a certain homeyness, as did the braided Mexican rug in front of the sink. The rug was Yody's. It pleased him that she would bring something of her own into his house. *His* house. How good it sounded.

Mac looked down at the scattered granules he'd spilled when he spooned sugar into his coffee. He was attempting to count them with the tip of his knife when the phone next to the refrigerator rang. His father, of course. He continued to count the granules of sugar. He was on 125, and the phone was on the fourteenth ring, when he picked up.

The judge didn't identify himself; he never did. "All right, Malcolm, enough is enough. We need to talk. You can't hide forever behind that Prussian general you call a housekeeper. If you don't want me in your . . . in the guest house, I'll meet you out by the stable. I'd like to remind you that I deeded that house to you, so technically it's still mine, and you have no right to bar me from the . . . guest house."

"The law says it's mine. A man's home is his castle. This is my castle. If you aren't invited, you don't cross my threshold. You can move into the main house if you want, but you don't come here." He was losing patience, Mac thought. In his life no one had ever talked to Marcus Carlin the way he was talking to him. How long, Mac wondered, before the arrogant, austere judge lost control? Not long, he decided.

"You are your mother's son." It was not a compliment. "I'll be there by noon. Don't keep me waiting, Malcolm. I won't tolerate it." The connection was broken before Mac could respond.

It was amazing, Mac thought irritably, as he made his way to the stable, that his father could still get under his skin. He'd thought he was past all the hatred, but obviously he wasn't. The first goddamn thing he was going to do was to take his father to task over his uncle Harry. He should have made a list to wave under his father's nose. He didn't feel childish or superior in any way with what he was about to do. Long ago he'd learned that anger wasn't his answer, but anger was all he had to strike back with. Now he knew where to hurt the old man: in his pride. No man liked to be made a fool of.

It wasn't until he was racing across the field on Jeopardy that he realized he was acting just like his father. He laughed, the sound carrying across the barren fields.

Mac didn't time his ride; in fact, he lost all track of time as Jeopardy streaked across the fields, but some inner mechanism brought him back to the stable at five minutes before noon. His father was waiting in a Savile Row suit, Bally shoes, and Rolex watch.

"At least you're punctual," the elder Carlin snapped irritably, then added disapprovingly, "You look like a ranch hand."

Mac chose to ignore the remark. He concentrated on the gelding's sweating flanks. The dogs, he noticed, had created a perimeter and were stalking the judge, their tails between their legs, their silky ears flat against their heads. They didn't like him.

"You're here, I'm here, so let's get to it, Father," Mac said quietly.

His eyes on the circling dogs, the judge drew himself to his full height. He felt out of his depth. He felt at a disadvantage, and he didn't like the feeling. "This is ridiculous," he snapped. "We should be sitting down in an atmosphere conducive to serious talk, with a drink in our hands. What the hell's gotten into you, Malcolm? I've taken everything into consideration— the war, what you've gone through—but it's all behind you. You're home now with your family. Life goes on."

"It doesn't work that way," Mac said coolly.

"It does if you work at it. I didn't say it would be easy. You have a family, commitments, and I expect you to honor them. I want to know why you're living here in this guest house instead of in the main house with your wife. And before you can say it's none of my business, it *is* my business. You asked me to look after your wife while you were gone, and I did as you asked. Now you come home and refuse to live in the same house with her, not to mention the daughter whom you refused even to see when you arrived. You forbid either Alice or me entry to the . . . the abode you're living in, and you refuse to tell us why. This is not the behavior of a rational man, Malcolm. I want an explanation and I want it now. In the meantime, call off these dogs."

"That sounds to me like an order," Mac said, rubbing industriously at the horse's sweating back. "I'm a civilian now. I don't take orders. Since I'm over twenty-one, I don't have to give you or anyone else an explanation of how or why I do things." His nonchalant voice was in direct odds with his churning stomach and the tremor he felt running through his body. "As for the dogs, they know you don't belong here."

"Then I have to assume by your attitude that things are not right between you and Alice. Well, Malcolm, you will have to make them right. We can't have you running for governor with a sour-faced wife and retarded child, although Jenny will give us a lot of media attention. There are no divorces in the Carlin family, as you well know, so don't start down that road," the judge said ominously, his eyes on the dogs.

"I've changed my mind about running for governor. I'm sorry if this upsets your plans. I told you when I left that we would discuss politics when I got back. I promised you ten years in the army, and I delivered. You demanded I come back a hero, and I did that too, according to the army. The way I see it, I don't owe you anything. I'm a free agent now. Thanks to Mother's side of the family, I don't ever have to lift a finger again, except to write the checks to pay Alice's bills. That's a feat in itself, *sir*."

"Now, just a damn minute," the judge blustered, then thought better of it when the circling dogs moved closer, so close he could feel their breath on his legs. "It's all set. Everything is ready to go. We have tremendous support. I've been lining up that support since the day you left for Vietnam. We're ready to announce! You cannot do this, Malcolm!" The edge in the judge's voice was so sharp, the dogs stopped in their tracks, their eyes glued to his tall, imposing figure.

"You acted prematurely, Father. It's not what I want. I'm sorry, I can't help you. As far as I'm concerned, the issue is history. But there's another issue that needs to be cleared up. Why didn't you tell me Uncle Harry died? I had to find out from my lawyer. That's a hell of a thing. You could have had your secretary type the letter, for Christ's sake. I can't forgive you for that."

"Alice said she would write you. I thought she had. I'm not her keeper. You can't blame me for that. Harry was an old man, it was his time to die. What could you have done? Nothing."

"That wasn't for you to decide. In fact, you will never make another decision for me. I don't like you, Father, and you don't like me. We tolerate one another. What you *do* like is what you think I can do for you. Even you should know you can't live through me, but then that's not what you had in mind, is it? If I won, you'd be 'the man' behind the man. All your cronies would know it, and I'd be your puppet. The answer is an unequivocal no! If there's nothing else, Father, I have things to do."

The judge changed his tone to the one he used when he wanted a favor from one of his powerful friends. "What changed you, son? Was it all the killing? Maybe you should talk to a psychiatrist. There's a very competent fellow at Georgetown. No one need know."

Mac laughed bitterly, harshly. "If I do that, I'll have to dig way back in my childhood; you know the way head doctors love to blame their patients' problems on their parents. Aunt Margaret will come out, and so will the way you treated Mother. Uncle Harry figures in this someplace, so I'll have to talk about him. The doctor is going to want to know why Mother is buried in Charleston and why you have a plot here

in Virginia. And of course he'll ask me what kind of a relationship we had. You know, did we play ball, did we go fishing, did
you tuck me in, did you ever clap me on the back? You know,
the bullshit stuff."

The judge's face blossomed with color. The dogs continued
to stalk him. "That sounds rather like a threat. I suggest you
tread very carefully. I can be a terrible enemy; I think you
already know that, Malcolm."

Mac pretended to think about his father's remark, to the
judge's annoyance. "I think, Father, in one way or another,
you've always been my enemy. Or do you mean something
different?"

The dogs were still completing their dizzying circle, to the
judge's dismay. He was furious, but he was also afraid, Mac
noticed. He felt a momentary pang of guilt at the way he was
acting toward his father.

"It means you are making a fool of me. We had a deal,
Malcolm, and you are reneging. Carlins don't renege."

"I gave you my answer. I won't change my mind. So what
will it be? Enemies? Or just plain father and son?"

"We're past that stage, Malcolm. We're equals. We could
eventually control Washington, you and I. It was not in my
plan to have you stay on as governor forever. You could be
another Jack Kennedy. I can have all those stories squelched.
Alice and Jenny. The public will eat that up. It's all there,
Malcolm."

"What stories?" Mac asked in a dangerous voice. The dogs
stopped their frantic circling, Fred in front of the judge, Gus in
back.

"Do you take me for a fool, Malcolm? As soon as you started
writing all those letters, making all those phone calls about that
Vietnamese woman and her son, word got back to me. I can
cover that up. There's a lid on it right now. If you back out of
our deal, that lid isn't just going to come off. It's going to
explode in your face."

Mac's jaw dropped, his eyes almost bugged out of his head.
Surely he wasn't hearing his father correctly. "Are you talking
about Lily Gia?"

"If she's the one whose child you've been trying to bring over here, then yes, that's the one. I thought more of you, Malcolm. First you father a retarded child, and then you . . . you shacked up with some . . . and weren't smart enough to use a condom. I can put two and two together. There are times, and this is one of those times, when it does not pay to be noble. There will be no slant-eyed children in this family. One retard is enough. What were you going to do, bring the boy over here and you and Alice and the Mongoloid live happily ever after?"

Mac's face drained of all its color. How stupid he'd been. Of course his father would find out about all the inquiries he'd made. He hadn't tried to keep it a secret. Now he wished he had. He looked at his father and stared him down. Any feelings he might have had for him died in front of his eyes.

"I will not discuss this with you except to tell you you are all wrong. I think you should leave now, Father, and please, don't come back," Mac said hoarsely.

Judge Carlin stared at Mac's balled fists, then met his eyes one last time before he walked over to his car. Mac watched till it was out of sight, then led Jeopardy into the dim barn, the dogs at his heels.

The barn felt like a sanctuary, with its warm, pungent, earthy smells. For a few moments he was reminded of Vietnam. He allowed himself to shake and tremble, for tears to burn his eyes. He felt more alone than he'd ever felt in his life. He likened it to his devastated feeling when his mother left him, or when he had to accept Casey's death. He'd been a little soldier the first time, a grown-up soldier the second. Now he was a big ex-soldier, and it hurt in the same way. He'd almost struck his father, actually meant to strike him, and would have, but the dogs would have joined in and he hadn't wanted that to happen. The intent was bad enough, something he was going to have to live with.

"We're a hell of a team, the four of us," Mac said, craning his neck backward to include Jeopardy. "The four of us against one old man. I do believe we just made an enemy."

With an energy he didn't know he possessed, Mac mucked the horse stalls, all twelve of them. He seethed and fumed, cursed and moaned his circumstances. He was a man, the army said so, his birth certificate said so. He was a married man whose wife said he was a father. He dug the pitchfork into a bale of hay with a vicious thrust. All he wanted, all he had ever wanted, was to belong, to be loved. For a little while God smiled on him. Because it was wrong, it was snatched from him in the blink of an eye. How was he supposed to live with that? Did it mean he was supposed to return to Alice and pretend her infidelity didn't make a difference? That would be living a lie too. "What do You want from me?" he cried. "Tell me and I'll do it. Just help me get through this," he pleaded.

Jeopardy whickered softly, alerting the dogs to their master's strange new behavior. They nudged him, begging to be stroked, which he did. He squatted down, and the dogs pressed close. They felt warm, silky. "Okay, if this is all I get, I can learn to live with it," he muttered.

MAC ENTERED BILL'S Bar and Grill at fifteen minutes past five. His eyes took in the three senators, two congressmen, and one cabinet member at one table. At a second table three truck drivers from the Sealtest Dairy across the street munched on pretzels and draught beer. The volume on the jukebox was low, but he could still hear Hoagy Carmichael's rendition of "Stardust," Sadie's favorite song. The bar was crowded. He sat down next to Nelson Rockefeller, who was in town for the day, and discussed the weather for ten minutes until Benny arrived.

Mac held up his draught beer to toast Benny's vividly flowered shirt.

"I'm all yours," Benny said, throwing his arms out to indicate he was a free man. "Snap me up, buddy, you might not get a second chance."

Mac downed his beer. "I thought I snapped you up last night."

"Yeah, yeah, yeah, and you also said you were going to wear a flowered shirt. I know silk when I see it." Benny guffawed. "You're forgiven. I'm a communications expert, so why don't we start to communicate?"

Sadie took that moment to enter the bar, a vision in her

salmon-colored dress, which swished against her knees. She waved airily to the patrons, but she threw her arms around Mac and Benny. "Do you want to go upstairs or sit at your table?"

Mac's eyebrows shot up questioningly. "It's your call. You're going to run this show," he said to Benny.

"The table. I think better with noise. The kids and all," he muttered. "I can't think when it's quiet."

"Dinner?" Sadie asked. "Bill's favorite, corned beef."

"Sure," Mac said. Both he and Benny hated corned beef, but if they didn't eat it, Sadie threw it out with tears in her eyes.

"Didn't you find out anything on Bill?" Mac demanded as he fired up a cigarette.

"I think old Bill's six feet under," Benny said under his breath. "You sure you want those private dicks to keep on with this? It's costing a damn fortune."

"Yeah, I do. I don't care what it costs. Goddamn it, *I* want to know now. It's getting personal with me at this point. I thought you said you had a lead."

"The last report said there were four possibilities. Two haven't panned out. The dick is working on the third as we speak. It doesn't look good. It's personal with Dominic Snedeker, that's the dick's name. His business claim is he always finds his man. His reputation is at stake. I'm telling you, old Bill isn't on this earth."

"I think he is, and when we finally do find him, I'm going to bend him into a pretzel. When I'm done doing that, you can straighten him out."

"I'll be back later. Call me if you need me," Sadie said, setting two corned beef dinners down on the table. Her smile was all-encompassing as she walked about the room, touching one man's shoulder, bending to whisper something in another's ear, asking about family, always smiling. The patrons preened.

"Okay, let's get to it," Benny said, washing the hateful taste of corned beef down with the last of his beer.

They talked far into the night.

Two weeks later, the *Star* carried the banner headline: WAR HERO TO TRY FOR VIRGINIA SENATE SEAT.

Those in the know in the nation's capital drew in their collective breaths and immediately chose up sides.

The owner of the *Star*, whose picture was third from the right in the second row of Sadie's picture board, swung his paper's support to Mac. It was whispered among the power brokers that Marcus Carlin considered the man's support of his son an act of treason to their friendship. They never spoke again.

The smart money, and there was plenty of it, was on Malcolm Carlin, who was running against an old Democratic warhorse in the primary.

Mac pulled up his socks, tightened his belt, squared his shoulders, and looked the public square in the eye. "If you send me to Washington," he told the voters, "I will never lose sight of the fact that by voting for me you trust me to do what's best for our state. I won't let you down."

IT WAS A warm summer day in early June with blue skies and fluffy clouds when Alice Carlin waylaid her husband as he was backing his car out of the garage. "Mac, I need to speak with you."

She looks pretty, Mac thought as he cut the engine. "Yes?" God, they were so polite to one another.

"First of all I want to apologize to you for not being at your side when you announced. Even though your father . . . said some . . . He started talking about Jenny and how children like her don't live long . . . oh, he said so many things, none of them worth the breath he used to utter them. I just want you to know I would have been there that day, regardless of your father, but Jenny was running a very high fever. I couldn't leave her. You probably don't care, but I had to tell you. He's done a complete turnaround, Mac. He's your enemy now. You ripped his world apart when you refused to run for governor. Then when you thumbed your nose at him and announced for the Senate .'. . he's not accepting it gracefully.

"I'm on your side, Mac, whether you believe it or not. I can't campaign with you because of Jenny. She takes too much of my time, and I won't neglect her. I've agreed, if you're willing, to do one interview with pictures the day after tomorrow. It's scheduled for eleven o'clock, right before lunch. Is that okay, Mac?" she asked anxiously.

"Why?" Mac asked suspiciously.

"Because I don't trust your father. I feel . . . he intimated . . . he has . . . I don't know," she said miserably. "I think it would be better for you and your campaign if I align myself with you. Not for me, but for you. It's the truth, Mac."

For some strange reason, Mac believed her. "What can my father do now? Nothing, it's too late. He can bluster and blow smoke, but that's about it. He's my father, for God's sake. I think you're overreacting with that enemy business." There was no need to tell her he'd thought the same thing not too long ago. "I'll do the interview with you, and yes, it will help. I appreciate it, Alice."

"There's no need to say you live in the guest house, is there? I don't want to be humiliated, Mac."

"I'll be at the house in plenty of time. I won't say anything. How's Jenny?" he asked coolly.

"Fine. She's doing fine, Mac. Thank you for asking about her. She asks about you all the time. Of course, I'm the only one who understands what she's saying. She loves the red ball you bought her. She . . . she isn't coordinated enough to . . . to catch it. Yet. Someday she will be," Alice said positively. "I work with her every day. I'm sorry, Mac, I've kept you long enough. I know how busy you are. They say that every night on the news. I'll see you on Wednesday then."

"Okay." Mac pretended not to see the tears in his wife's eyes. Guilt washed through him. Alice's offer was so sincere, so genuine, it was hard not to like her. The thought jolted him. They were acting like *friends. That* thought jolted him more. He continued to back the car out of the garage. He found himself smiling into the rearview mirror. Imagine being friends with your wife.

WHEN MAC WALKED into his busy campaign office on Thursday morning, Benny and his volunteer workers, most of them Vietnam vets, were holding copies of the *Star*. "This is great!" Benny chortled. "This is better than great! How'd you get Alice to do it? This is a wonderful interview. This picture of you holding Jenny in the air is . . . it's nice, Mac. It's good copy. It's *real* copy. There's a difference." Noticeably absent from the interview was a quote or statement from Supreme Court Justice Marcus Carlin, who, according to the paper, was unavailable for comment.

Benny immediately started to pick apart the interview, looking for the pluses and minuses. "I love this one where you say your three weeks of intense jungle training was spent in San Francisco due to a military snafu. I imagine the army's face is going to turn several shades of red and purple. I can't find one negative in this whole interview, and, man, they gave you some serious space here. Will Alice mind if we spread this about, you know, use it over and over again?"

"I don't think so, but she only agreed to do this one. I think the reporters understood. She let them know she was behind me one hundred percent, and that was all they wanted to hear. My father now . . . they pretty much glossed over that. One of them said sotto voce, 'Judge who?' "

"You're gonna win the primary, Mac. I can feel it in my bones," Benny said gleefully. "Your father . . . he'll come around. Better to have a son in the Senate than one clipping coupons. A governor is just a governor. Lighten up, Mac, it's all going to work out just fine. Trust me, buddy."

"The primary is just the battle, Benny. I have to win the war in November," Mac said quietly.

"You will," Benny said confidently. "It's time to go to work. Big smiles everyone!" He was pleased at what he called Mac's shit-eating grin. He *was* going to make it.

WHILE MAC AND his campaign workers were rejoicing over the news coverage, Judge Marcus Carlin was ringing Alice's doorbell. He stomped his way inside and said to Olga, "Get Mrs. Carlin and then get lost." His tone was so imperious, so arrogant, the dour-faced Olga ran up the steps to the second floor and rapped sharply on her mistress's door.

"Tell him I'm busy," Alice snapped, "and there's no need for you to get lost. My husband pays your salary. Never mind," she said angrily, throwing on a gold-colored robe. She tied the sash so tight, she gasped. "Stay here, Olga," she called over her shoulder.

"What is it, Marcus?" Alice snapped. "I don't like it when you come here and interrupt my day. I'm due to take Jenny for a hearing test, so let's make this quick."

"I thought we were allies, Alice. After all I did for you," the judge said ominously. "I didn't like that article in this morning's paper. You swore to me you could bring Mac around to our way of thinking. He's made a laughingstock out of me. And you permitted it. You swore to me you could bring him into line, and what happens? He comes home and moves into the goddamn guest house. So much for your wiles, Alice. Why didn't you tell me you weren't woman enough to hold Mac?"

Alice was speechless. "You're blaming *me*!" she cried out shrilly when she finally found her voice. "It was *you*! He hates you! You hate him! I'm not a miracle worker. *You* told me he would step into line. Those are your exact words, Marcus. You're the one with the power. Do something for yourself and stop bothering me. Get it through your head, I have no influence over Mac. He damn well does what he feels like doing. It was my idea to do the interview, not his. I owe him that much support."

"You owe me, Alice," the judge said.

"This is getting us nowhere, Marcus. Mac is running for the Senate. Someone else is going to be governor. Cut your losses. Throw in with Mac now before it's too late."

"After the fact? That's not my style, Alice. I'd rather see him ruined. I can do that you know."

"You wouldn't! He's your son! How can you talk like this?" Alice cried wretchedly. Overhead she could hear Jenny wailing. Alice hated pressure of any kind. He looks insane, she thought fearfully.

"Did Mac tell you about the Vietnamese woman's son, whom he's been trying to bring over here?"

"What are you talking about, Marcus?"

"Are you all going to live together, Alice? Will she be your housekeeper? Will the little slant-eye play with Jenny? That's rich, a retard and a gook."

"I— How dare you! I think you should leave, Marcus. I don't want to hear this. You'll do anything to get back at Mac. That makes you a sick man, Marcus. Sick!" she screeched. Overhead Jenny wailed louder. Damn, now she was going to have to cancel the child's hearing appointment. Once Jenny got upset, there was no controlling her.

"Really. Take a look at these. Or if you don't want to read them, I can tell you what's in them. While Mac was still in Vietnam, he started on the paperwork to bring a woman named Lily Gia and her son Eric here to the States. The woman is dead now, but Mac still wants to bring her son here. It's all there, read it. If you aren't too stupid, you should be able to put two and two together and come up with the right answer. You came in a poor second, Alice. That doesn't say much for you, now does it?"

"What do you want from me? What do you plan on doing with this information?" Alice demanded, a sick feeling settling in her stomach.

"I want what I always wanted, for Mac to be the governor of this state. It's not too late. Tell him to withdraw from the Senate race. He can still make a run for the governorship. I have the political power to pull this off," the judge barked.

"Go to him yourself. You tell him." Mac and a Vietnamese woman. A child, a boy. Men always wanted sons. Mac wouldn't care if the boy's eyes weren't Western. Mac had loved someone else. The thought was so horrendous, she thought she was going to throw up. While she didn't physically want Mac, the idea that he'd wanted someone else left her feeling sick.

"You'll do it, Alice. If you don't, I'll . . ."

"You'll what, Marcus?" Alice asked, trembling so badly she could hardly stand. "Don't you understand? He won't listen to me!" She was losing control, screaming at the top of her lungs.

"I'll tell him you welcomed me into your bed, and you did. I paid for your favors."

"You got me drunk. You seduced me. Then you blackmailed me. I never went to bed with you willingly. Not once. You're an old man, Marcus. Why would I want you? You wait right here. I have something to show you. Don't leave, Marcus. I will not allow you to blackmail me, not now, not ever," Alice screeched.

Her satin robe billowing out behind her, Alice raced up the steps to the second floor. She ran down the hall to the nursery, where she grabbed Jenny. She whirled and ran back downstairs, her breathing harsh and ragged. "Here," she said, "is the result of what you did. Jenny is your daughter, not Mac's. And you know what else? Mac knows she isn't his, but he allowed me to give her his name. They have blood tests, Marcus. I can prove that Jenny is your daughter. You have a sister just like her. Now, what do you have to say, you son of a bitch!"

The look of revulsion on the judge's face repulsed Alice. She cried brokenly as she hugged Jenny to her breast. "Get out of my house! Mac's sterile!" she shrilled, the child's cries just as shrill.

The judge was halfway to the door when Alice plopped Jenny down on the floor to run after her father-in-law. She snatched at his arm, a maniacal look on her face. "If there's one thing we both know, it's that Mac is no liar. Leave him alone. If you tell the press about his . . . what you found out, then I will tell Mac you are the father of this child. Your silence for mine, Marcus. And support for Jenny in the form of cash. Once a month. And don't ever set foot in this house again. Your word, Marcus. Now!" Alice threatened.

"You wouldn't dare! You would never give up this comfortable life. Where would you go with a child like Jenny? Even if you divorce, no man will want a brat like that. So don't threaten me, Alice," the judge said, his face a hateful purple. A huge vein in his neck bulged.

Once, Alice would have buckled, crying and whining to get her way. But now she was different, a mother. She stood her ground and said, "Try me. *I* have nothing to lose. You, on the other hand, have everything to lose. Remember what I said about a blood test? Shall my attorney get in touch with your attorney, or will you do what you and I both know to be right?"

She didn't expect an answer, and none was forthcoming. She watched as her father-in-law slammed his car into gear and careened down the driveway, taking half an azalea bush with him. Obviously, the judge needed glasses.

Alice slammed the door shut. She bent over, taking several deep breaths before she ran to Jenny and gathered the child in her arms. Jenny wiped her tears and slobber on the sleeve of her mother's dressing gown.

"Shhh, everything is going to be all right. Mama is going to make things right for you. Let's go upstairs and play with that pretty red ball. Please don't cry, Jenny. I'm doing my best."

The child cried harder and louder, until Alice thought she would go out of her mind.

"I'll take her, Mrs. Carlin," the nanny said.

"No," Alice said sharply. "It's my fault she's upset, so it's up to me to calm her." *I have to do this as punishment for the lie I'm living.*

NO ONE IN the political arena was surprised when Malcolm Carlin won the primary, which gave him the right to run against the Republican contender. He campaigned vigorously, day after day, sometimes for eighteen hours at a stretch. Over and over he told himself he was meant to do what he was doing. In the Senate he would get himself appointed to as many committees as possible. The Armed Services Committee, The Near Eastern and South Asian Affairs subcommittee—of which George Mc Govern was chairman—the Senate Foreign Aid subcommittee. He was going to plan his strategy just the way he did when he was on the Ho Chi Minh trail.

He thought about the pile of telegrams on his desk from *his men.* To a man they said, "Don't let us down. If you need us, get on the horn." By God, he'd die before he let even one of them down. When he allowed thoughts of Casey, Lily, and her son into his head, he knew he'd made the right decision.

On October 4, months after winning the primary, when Mac felt he had the election sewn up tight, three things happened in rapid succession. The morning edition of the paper announced that Cambodia had opened its doors to provide sanctuary to the Viet Cong; the private detective Benny hired to find Bill Trinity called to say he'd located the elusive and reclusive Bill in Perth Amboy, New Jersey; and the evening edition of the paper carried a front-page article saying that Malcolm Carlin, the Virginia Democratic contender for the Senate, was rumored to have a mistress and an illegitimate son in Vietnam, both of whom he was trying to bring to the United States.

While Mac, Benny, and Sadie tried to come up with a solution to the devastating news story, Alice was trying to figure out how she could elude the newspaper reporters camped out at the end of her driveway so she could drive to her father-in-law's house in Georgetown. In the end she knew there was no way she could leave the house. The reporters would follow her. Her face a mask of fury, she dialed the judge's home.

Alice immediately launched into her tirade. Her voice dripped venom. "You went back on your word, Marcus. I told you what would happen if you did that. Right now there must be thirty or forty reporters outside this house. How dare you! You had no right!"

"Get ahold of yourself, Alice," the judge barked. "I didn't tell anyone anything. I'm not a fool. If I found out about . . . the woman and child, what makes you think other people wouldn't find out the same thing? Nothing is sacred in a political campaign. What surprises me is they waited so long to spring it."

"With just thirty-four days to the campaign it could destroy Mac," Alice shouted angrily.

"Why, Alice," the judge said mockingly, "I didn't think you cared. Why the sudden change of heart? After all, Mac has moved out of your bed, and if what you say is true, he was finished with you long before I tasted your . . . charms."

"You are nothing but a dirty old man, Marcus. My skin crawls every time I think of you. Damn you, I'm trying to make up to Mac for what I did, for what you made me become. And now this. Mac doesn't deserve this . . . this kind of press. If that child were his, he'd be here with Mac now, and we both know it."

With his reputation at stake, the judge knew he had to make Alice believe it. He did know it, that was the trouble. He hadn't leaked the story to the press. The only way he could do that was to issue a statement, something he had not wanted to do. It was all going wrong. Everything in his life was wrong. A vision of Jenny rolling and screaming on the floor made him wince.

"I'm coming right over. I want you dressed appropriately, with Jenny in your arms. Together we'll issue a statement."

"I told you not to come here ever again," Alice said icily.

"Then, my dear, I suggest you handle it yourself."

"All right, we'll give the statement by the front door, and as soon as we've finished, you will get in your car and leave." Alice had had to back down, knowing the judge was right. This time.

JENNY WAS IN a good mood. She clutched an all-day sucker with a soft, curled stem in her chubby fist. Alice had her attired in a red velvet dress with a round Peter Pan collar. She herself was dressed in a simple skirt and blouse, with a sweater over her shoulders. She looked every bit the mother and housewife. The judge, when he arrived with the reporters he'd invited, looked staunch and stalwart, just the way a Supreme Court justice was supposed to look.

"It's preposterous!" was the judge's comment.

"My husband is a wonderful husband and father, and how dare you terrible people say such terrible, wicked things about him," was Alice's comment.

"Are you saying the story is untrue?" a middle-aged reporter demanded.

"I'm saying it's preposterous," the judge replied coldly. "It's a last-ditch effort by the Republicans to try and sway votes. Malcolm would never compromise his family in any way."

"Mrs. Carlin, is there anything else you wish to say?"

There was plenty she wanted to say, but she held her tongue. "Just that I believe in my husband implicitly, and I know in my heart Malcolm would never bring a scandal upon this family. Family is sacred to Malcolm."

Afterward the judge said, "You carried it off, Alice," his eyes glued to the mess Jenny was making of her dress. His eyes, Alice noticed, still expressed revulsion.

"Go to hell, Marcus," she spat. "I told you I don't want you here, so get out."

His eyes were still on the child, who was trying to stick the sucker in her ears. "I'll leave when I'm certain the reporters are all gone," he said in a sick-sounding voice. "I kept my word, I did not leak this story. With the threats you made, what would be the point?"

"How do I know you didn't tell someone else, and that's the one who leaked it?"

The all-day sucker landed on the judge's snowy-white shirt. He brushed at it as though it were contaminated. "Again, what would be the point? Look, Alice, I simply didn't do it."

Alice snorted, a very unladylike sound. "No, I guess you didn't. I can see the fear in your face, Marcus. If I ever find out you had anything to do with this, in any way, I will keep my promise. Believe me, I will."

Jenny, too big to be in her mother's arms, squealed to be set down. She yanked at Alice's hairdo with sticky hands.

"She belongs in an institution," Marcus said through tight lips.

"That's one place she will never go, and don't ever say that to me again. Say good-bye to your daddy, Jenny," Alice taunted.

The judge slammed the door in both their faces. "Come along, sweetie, I'm going to clean you up, and then we'll play with your new doll house. Mama loves you," Alice crooned as she took Jenny upstairs to the nursery.

At his campaign headquarters, Mac made a statement on the evening news. It was a short, complete denial. In a voice shaking with compassion, he explained who Lily Gia and her son were. He ended with a plea. "Lily Gia is dead. She was a nurse who took care of your sons, saved their lives, and then had the misfortune to fall in love with an American doctor who refuses to acknowledge the child he gave her. The boy deserves a better life than an orphanage can give him. I was prepared to adopt him, and I still am, if that is possible, since his real father wants no part of him. That's all I have to say, ladies and gentlemen."

Beyond his news appearance, Mac refused to comment. "It's up to the voters who they believe," he told his campaign workers. "I'll take my chances with them."

"That's good enough for me," Benny said.

"Me too," Sadie agreed, her eyes alight with pride.

"Benny, can I see you a minute, in private?" Mac said as soon as Sadie was out of earshot.

In a tiny room filled with stacks of campaign literature, Mac told Benny about the phone call he'd had earlier from the private detective.

"He honest to God found him!" Benny yelped.

"Found him and he's goddamn alive," Mac hissed. "Where the hell is Perth Amboy, New Jersey?"

Benny shrugged. "He's alive! We should kill him, Mac, for what he's done to Sadie. We're going there, right?"

"Just as soon as we can scare up a map of New Jersey, square things away here, and get something to eat. It's almost midnight now. If we drive all night, there won't be much traffic, and we'll be there when he wakes up. What do you say?"

"Listen, I'm game. I can't wait to see this guy. I've got this picture of Bill in my head of what he looks like now. How about you? I never thought they'd find him. Do we bring him back with us?" Benny asked anxiously.

"Even if we have to hog-tie him."

"They call that kidnapping, buddy. Since you're a public figure, maybe I'd better do the hog-tying."

THE CAMPAIGN WAS forgotten, as was everything else, when the two friends set out for New Jersey in Benny's Land Rover. They drank coffee and ate sandwiches Carol had prepared at the last minute as they tooled along the turnpike. Their conversation consisted of ways they could torture the still-faceless Bill. When they ran out of possibilities, they tried to guess what Sadie's reaction would be when they marched Bill into the bar.

Six hours later, Benny pulled the Land Rover into a service station.

"We're in Perth Amboy," Mac said as they waited to have the tank filled at a Texaco station. "Ask this guy where we are and how close we are to Elm Street."

"Well, boys, you're just a spit away from Elm. This is Market, so's all you have to do is go down three blocks and make

a right. Elm runs both sides. Who you looking for?" the attendant asked.

"Bill Trinity. Do you know him?" Mac asked, holding his
breath.

"Yep, gets his gas here. Just seen him yesterday. Won't do
you no good to go to his house. He opens his bait and tackle
shop at five-thirty."

"Where's the shop?" Benny demanded.

"Down on Water Street. Make a left out of here, go all the
way down to High, make a right and follow it to the end. Bill's
shop is right there. Can't miss it."

Now that they were within, as the attendant said, a spit of
where old Bill was, neither man knew quite what to do. "We
can't just barge in and snatch him," Benny said.

"Yeah, and what if he's married?" Mac fretted. "Do we
snatch him anyway? Jesus, what if he yells for the cops?"

"Listen, this whole thing was your idea to begin with,"
Benny grumbled as he pulled out onto Market Street.

"Shit, let's just tell him we came to renew his subscription to
what the hell is the name of that magazine? Better yet, let's tell
him he won a prize. A thousand bucks. Yeah, that should do
it. Then we tell him we have to take him back to Washington
so we can take his picture. Whatcha think of that, Benny? I'm
open to any and all suggestions here," Mac said sourly.

"What if he doesn't remember Sadie? What do we do then?
Maybe this isn't such a good idea after all."

"It's a good idea, we just failed to come up with a good plan.
I say we go with the prize and picture bit. The dick said he had
a subscription for twenty years. That in itself is worth a thousand bucks. Do you agree?" Mac asked anxiously.

"Yeah. It's as good as anything I can come up with. This is
High Street. Make a right."

It was a tidy, little, smelly place. Bill was just as tidy, dressed
in clean coveralls with a black and white plaid shirt. Wizened
was too kind a word to describe him, Mac thought. The man
had a stringy body, white hair and beard, and eyes the color of
his coveralls, pale blue, though bright and alert.

"Coffee smells good. Bet Mrs. Trinity taught you how to make it, huh?" Benny said, believing he was being clever.

"Made it myself, young fella. Never been a Mrs. Trinity. Got close a couple of times, but couldn't bring myself to take that final step. A man has to be real careful who he gives his name to."

"I always say that too," Benny babbled. "You say that too, don't you, Mac?"

"Yeah. Do you do a good business here, Mr. Trinity?" he asked, looking around. He had no idea what all the paraphernalia was. Something fishermen used, he supposed.

"Make a living. My customers keep coming back. Satisfied customers are what make a business work. 'Course you always smell like fish. Where are you fellas from?"

"Ah, Virginia. Just visiting. We're leaving today as a matter of fact. We, ah, what we do is we . . . sort of have this bar and grill. Real good money in bars," Benny said, tripping over his words.

" 'Spect so. Men like to drink. Women too. I don't drink. Used to, but then I got this ulcer and, well, I drink a lot of milk."

"Uh-huh," Benny said brightly.

"Can you eat popcorn?" Mac asked.

"Used to. Used to do a lot of things. Don't do them anymore."

"You should have gotten married, then you'd have someone to take care of you," Mac said, in what he hoped was a burst of insight. "Plenty of good women out there looking for good men. Isn't that what your wife Sadie always says, Benny?"

"Yeah, that's what Sadie always says." Benny grinned.

"What can I do for you fellows?" Bill asked, failing to pick up on Sadie's name.

"It's like this, Mr. Trinity," Mac said candidly. "We, ah, we're friends of an old friend of yours. We've been looking for you for a few years now. We finally tracked you down through your magazine subscription. Sit down, Mr. Trinity, this is going to take a while.

*   *   *

"So you see, Mr. Trinity, we have to take you back with us," Mac said as he finished his story. "We're . . . we thought we were prepared to hog-tie you if necessary. After you see Sadie, if you don't want to stay, you can come back. We'll have someone drive you back here, that's a promise."

"The old girl's still alive, eh? Would have thought she hated my guts. A shrine, you say," he said, preening like a peacock. "How's she look?" he asked craftily.

"A real looker," Benny said truthfully.

"Salt of the earth," Mac said.

"Has powerful friends."

"And she's rich. A hell of a cook. Always smells good. Sadie, I mean," Mac babbled.

"What do you say, will you come back with us?" Benny asked anxiously.

"Guess I can take off a day or so. I'll have to make a few phone calls though. It's pretty early in the morning to be making decisions like this. I'll have to go back to the house to pack my dancing shoes and pick up some duds. Sit down, boys, while I make some phone calls."

Benny and Mac listened, their mouths hanging open, as Bill called first one business and then another. "And you thought I just ran this bait shop, eh?" He chuckled. "Got two apartment houses, a bakery, a sandwich shop, a quarter interest in the yacht club, and I own a Buick dealership. I'd appreciate it if you didn't mention my assets to Sadie, though."

"Our lips are sealed," Benny agreed happily.

"I'm ready. It will only take me a few minutes to pack my duds, and I live five minutes from here."

Bill was as good as his word. It took him fifteen minutes to change his clothes and pack his bag. He still smelled like fish. Mac drove with the windows down all the way to Washington.

"Well, here we are," Mac said brightly as he pulled the Land Rover to the curb.

"I'll be damned," Bill said, eyeing the neon sign. "You boys weren't putting me on. Wasn't sure for a while back there."

"It shouldn't be too crowded now. Lunch is almost over," Mac said as he got out of the car. "Are you excited, Bill?"

"A tad. You boys look more excited," he said, nervously fingering his red tie. "She's going to tell me I'm dressed all wrong and to cut off this beard. Bossy woman. Well, open the door, son, and let's see what time has done to Sadie. If she turned out half as good as I did, we might have something to talk about."

Mac wrinkled his nose as he opened the door to the bar. He saw Sadie talking to a smiling congressman. Even from where Mac was standing, he could smell her scent. She was wearing something the color of burnt orange, and as always, her skirt swished when she moved. She turned and looked at the three men. When she spoke she sounded so calm and matter-of-fact that Mac's jaw dropped. So did Benny's.

"Hello, Bill."

Confused, Bill backed up a step. He'd anticipated something a little more ecstatic.

"Hello, Sadie," he mumbled.

"Where have you been, Bill?"

Mac thought it sounded like she didn't give a hoot where Bill had been all these years.

"Perth Amboy, New Jersey. You look good, Sadie," Bill said sincerely.

"You look old, Bill." Sadie smiled.

Mac and Benny both groaned.

"Bar's closed," Sadie announced to all the patrons. The burnt-orange dress swished angrily.

"Why's that?" Bill asked. "First rule of business is you never close your doors if there's money to be made."

"Why? Because I'm going to strangle you, and I don't want any witnesses. Mac, honey, snap the lock on your way out."

They snapped the lock.

Benny smacked his hands together in glee. "We do good work, Carlin."

"The best. Couldn't have done it without you, Benny. She won't kill him, will she?" Mac asked anxiously.

"You kidding? She's probably loving him to death as we speak. He was ready, I can tell you that."

"You know what scares me, Benny. I *can see* Sadie in that bait shop wearing a coverall just like Bill's."

"Nah," Benny said.

"Ten bucks," Mac said.

"That's a sucker bet, and I'm no sucker. Buy me lunch instead."

"You got it," Mac said happily.

Over lunch, in a coffee shop down the street from campaign headquarters, Benny unfolded the paper he'd snatched off Sadie's bar, while Mac gave the order for two bowls of chili. Benny found an article, the headline of which read: FRIENDS AND FAMILY SPEAK OUT FOR VA. SENATE CONTENDER. "I think you're going to like this, Mac. Aside from the fact that your father finally got around to issuing a statement, your wife backed you up again, one hundred percent. But wait till you hear this. This reporter said that as the paper was going to press, a rash of telephone calls from men who had served under you started to come in. You were national on the eleven o'clock news, by the way, so I guess that's how these guys knew. They all claim to know the father of Lily Gia's son, and they said it ain't you, Mac. Pender, Freeze, Stevens, Aspacolas, and three or four others whose names I can't even begin to pronounce. Captain Pender, who now works for IBM, said he was willing to give out the name of the copter pilot who personally ferried the father, and that's in quotes, back and forth in-country to see Lily Gia."

"Pender said that?" Mac said in awe. "Let me see that, Benny. I'll be damned. He's talking about Rick, that crazy chopper pilot I was telling you about. His girl was . . . she was killed with . . . when . . ."

"I know, Mac," Benny said softly. "It's great, your father and Alice coming through like this. And I don't for one minute believe your old man leaked the story. He knows that sooner or later those news hawks would come up with his name. He wouldn't risk that, don't you agree?"

"No, I don't think he did it either. Cover your ass, is my father's credo. They flushed him out though. He gave a statement. That bothers me. He doesn't like to lose, Benny. As far as I know, he only came out on the bad end of a deal once."

MAC AND BENNY left the restaurant with their eyes watering and their throats burning.

"That chili was so hot, I think I scorched my vocal cords," Benny complained. "Hey, that's Alice, isn't it? Uh-oh, that guy swooping down on her is from the *Herald*. Should we head him off?"

"Why? If Alice has something to say, I guess she has the right. You go ahead, Benny, I'll catch up to you later. She's here for a reason, so I might as well find out what it is."

At first, by the look on her face, Mac thought his wife was in pain. She was strapping Jenny into her car seat. Mac climbed into the car next to Alice.

"Is something wrong, Alice?"

"No. You got a letter marked urgent from the Bureau of Asian Affairs, so I thought I would drop it off. It looks . . . important. I had to take Jenny to the doctor for her checkup, and this isn't out of my way. I saw the news last night. I want you to know I never . . . I don't believe any of it. I know if that child were your son, he'd be here already. I know you better than you think. Your father didn't leak the news, either. He swore to me he didn't, and I believe him. He was absolutely livid. I have to get back before Jenny starts to get cranky. Feel free to *use* me any time, Mac," she said bitterly.

"Alice, I didn't . . . I made no demands on you. I didn't ask you to give out any interviews. I'd be a fool if I said they weren't important. You've really helped me. However, I can't help wondering what it's going to cost me," Mac said just as bitterly.

"At one time, probably a pair of diamond earrings. Now, nothing. I wish you'd given me a chance to talk to you when you got back. I wanted to tell you that I'm not like that anymore. Yes, I was shallow; yes, I was selfish; and yes, I was a lousy wife. I know all that. But yes, I also finally came to my senses. Jenny . . . Jenny made me stop and look at myself." She lowered her hand from the steering wheel. "Jenny needs a father, and I appreciate any time you do give her. I also want you to know that if you are successful in bringing Lily Gia's son to the United States, I am agreeable to having him live with us. That's if you decide not to get a divorce. I won't fight you if you decide to go ahead with it. I don't want Jenny traumatized in any way. That's all I have to say, Mac."

This wasn't the Alice he knew. He noticed her hairdo for the first time. It was short now and feathered softly about her face. She wore hardly any makeup and no jewelry of any kind. She almost looked like Benny's wife.

"You cut your hair," he said stupidly.

"And my fingernails and toenails. I also gave up on what you always called my manicured eyebrows. I guess you could say this is the real me. It's because of Jenny. She takes all my time. I just don't have time or energy to do all those personal things anymore." She laughed. "I don't shop either."

Too little too late, Mac thought as he turned to chuck Jenny under the chin. "Are you being a good girl for your mommy?" He wiped at her drooling mouth with a tissue from the front seat.

He was about to close the door when Alice spoke.

"What does Lily Gia's son look like?" Her voice was so wistful, Mac's throat constricted.

"He was just a baby when I saw him last. He looks more American than Asian. He was a sturdy little guy. Thanks for bringing the letter by. I appreciate it." He backed away from the car, Jenny slapping at the windows. Alice would be a physical wreck by the time she got home. *Too little too late.*

THE VICTORY PARTY for newly elected senator Malcolm Carlin was held at Stone Acres, Mac's Virginia home, the Saturday after Thanksgiving. The list of invited guests read like *Who's Who*. It was hinted that the power and the money in one room alone could have sustained a third world country for twenty years. The ordinary people, as the press referred to them, mingled with the high rollers. Mac's personal friends, his army buddies, and his old pals from West Point, claimed most of his attention, which just went to prove, one reporter wrote, that Carlin was "a regular guy for regular people."

The obligatory toast at the start of the festivities was made by Justice Marcus Carlin. Only Alice correctly interpreted the anger and hatred in his eyes as she took her place next to Mac. "To Senator Carlin—long may he reign in office—and to his lovely wife, Alice."

"Congratulations, Mac. If Jenny was capable of understanding, she'd be very proud of her daddy," Alice said softly.

The camera caught Mac looking down at his wife, a smile on his lips.

He had a new life now.

Chapter 12

IT WAS THE Monday after Thanksgiving, Singin and Maline's day off from the hospital. Casey was invited to dinner, her first outing away from the hospital since the day she'd been admitted. Maline, Singin said, was preparing a belated Thanksgiving feast for the three of them, the same kind of dinner they'd had in the United States when they both were students there.

"We will have one other guest for dinner. He arrives by taxi as we speak. I wanted you settled comfortably," Singin said quietly as he expertly maneuvered the small car through traffic.

Casey started to tremble. She was out of her cocoon, exposed to the outside world. And she was deathly afraid of what Singin's visitor would have to say. His name was Alan Carpenter, and he was the reconstructive surgeon Singin spoke of constantly, his beloved teacher. Together, the two surgeons would decide how best to proceed in regard to restructuring her face. She'd been permitted to see it just one week ago. She'd known it was bad, but nothing had prepared her for the horror she saw in the mirror. If Maline hadn't been holding her, she would have fainted. "There's no way you can fix this," she had croaked hoarsely. "Don't even try."

"You're thinking about your face," Singin said, interrupting her thoughts. "I can feel your horror, Lily. No doctor gives guarantees, you know that, but I feel that Alan will agree that we can do it, if you're game. It will be another year, possibly two, out of your life, and I think Alan will want to take you back to the States. We have a modern hospital here, but not like the facilities Alan has at his disposal. I feel you should take full advantage of their help. It's a small matter to have all your

308

records transferred back to the States, and you're well enough to travel now. Maline and I want this for you. You have a whole life ahead of you, Lily. So please, have an open mind with Alan. Then, when you're well and beautiful again, Maline and I want you to be in our wedding. We will wait for your recovery. It's that important to both of us."

"You want me to get on an airplane where people will *see* me?" Casey whispered. "Children will be frightened." Tears rolled down her cheeks.

"It's the only way for you to get back to New York. You can, of course, wear a veil."

"A veil will be . . . yes, a veil. I'm so afraid, Singin."

"I know. I probably would be too. You must think of the future. You will want to marry someday and have children. If you hide away and refuse to go through with this, you will always regret it."

What husband, what children, what *life* was he talking about? How was she to earn a living? Should she rise up from the dead now and say who she really was? To what end? Two years was such a long time. One hundred four weeks. Seven hundred and thirty days. Hours and hours of operations and pain. More skin grafts, more very painful skin grafts.

"I'd be very happy to be in your wedding," she said, "but I don't think you should wait. Marry Maline now."

"No. It is not time for us to marry. We have just come to terms with our feelings for one another. It will be a short two years. You must view it the same way."

"When . . . when would I leave?"

"In five or six weeks. Alan is prepared to stay this long. We discussed with him your leaving right after New Year's. Providing everything goes . . . well. You understand?"

Of course she understood. As the chopper pilots used to say, it was a crapshoot.

The skies opened in a burst of rain. If there was one thing she hated about Thailand, it was the monsoon rains. She clamped her lips tight. She was certain it was an omen of some kind.

They rode in silence, each busy with their thoughts, until Singin said, "Here we are."

It was a modest building, and the apartment even more modest. She swayed sickeningly at the smell of roasting turkey. She allowed herself to be hugged by Maline, who was attired in Levi's jeans and a tee-shirt that said NEW YORK YANKEES on the front. The shirt and jeans had been laundered many times. On her tiny feet Maline wore Keds sneakers. Another concession to Americanization.

"Welcome to my home," Maline said shyly.

"It's lovely," Casey said honestly. She was about to say that the open, airy feel of the place reminded her of a California house. She caught herself just in time. How could she know what houses in California looked like if she was pretending to have amnesia? It was true that amnesia patients remembered all manner of strange things and events. But it was better to continue as she was, so she didn't make a mistake. The decor was Eastern, right down to the pillows, which were made of violet, red, yellow, blue, and green fabrics. There were chairs set up around a folding card table—another concession to Casey, who couldn't squat and bend without pain. They were being so wonderful to her.

"When I was in your country, I fell in love with fireplaces and snow. I always said when I had my own place I was going to decorate it the way Americans decorate their homes, with many trinkets and mementos, but here, it didn't look right. Here, because space is so limited, one must not . . . clutter. Do you really like it?" Maline asked anxiously.

"Yes. It reflects you, Maline. I love the colors of the cushions."

Casey continued to walk around the tiny apartment, which was really one large room serving as living room, dining room, kitchen, and bedroom. The strategic use of lacquered screens as partitions made it all possible. If she herself lived here, she would prepare only sandwiches, as more than one pot or dish in the kitchen area would make the room look cluttered.

"We have many things to drink," Maline said, playing the perfect hostess. She motioned for Casey to sit on a Western-style chair that Casey was certain had been borrowed for the occasion. She sank down into the softness gratefully.

"Fruit juice, soft drinks, beer, or gin?"

"It doesn't matter, anything will be fine."

"Let's have beer," Maline said sprightly. "I even have pretzels. Oh, dear, Lily, I hope they're not too difficult for you to chew." Her eyes implored Singin to help her take her foot out of her mouth.

"On the contrary, it is time for Lily to experiment a little more. She must start to chew."

It was a habit they had—talking around her like she wasn't there, or at least didn't count. Making decisions for her. She felt a head rush that passed as quickly as it had arrived. "She has to try harder." Try? Did they have any idea how painful it was for her to chew, even now, months after the wires were removed from her jaw?

"Will she be able to enjoy this meal?" Maline asked anxiously. "I wish I knew if she remembers what Thanksgiving is. If it's just another meal, it will be spoiled for all of us."

"Nonsense," Singin said sharply. "We will explain it in detail. Besides, Maline, Thanksgiving is past. It really *is* just a dinner. The object of this meal was to get Lily away from the hospital and to meet Alan in a more relaxed atmosphere."

He was doing it again, talking around her, but in a kindly way. They must think me an idiot, she thought. She was instantly ashamed of herself for thinking it. Maline and Singin were the kindest, most wonderful people she'd ever met. In the early days, when she had lost track of her life and could only tell time by light versus dark, they'd sat with her, comforting her. More often than not it had been in the evening—that much she did remember. Maline always made a point of mentioning the date and the hour. Casey knew it was to give her a sense of reality.

Casey realized for the first time that there was music in the room, soft music, something that sounded like a flute and a harp with bird and waterfall sounds. The same kind of music they played for her at the hospital. It was relaxing, soothing, a balm. She felt herself start to relax.

"It is cold," Maline said, handing over a glass of orangy-pink melon juice.

The hours passed pleasantly enough, with the turkey cooking and conversation about living in the United States. Casey found it interesting, and loved the fact that both of them were willing to share their experiences with her.

When the knock they'd all been waiting for finally came, just as Maline was mashing the potatoes, Casey spilled her juice. She turned her head the moment she heard the strange voice. Tears burned her eyes. This man, according to Singin, was supposed to be her savior. In her heart she hoped he was, but she didn't really believe it.

"This is our friend and our patient, Lily Simon. Lily, this is Alan Carpenter, the doctor I spoke to you about."

Lily raised her eyes, certain she would see revulsion, dismay, hopelessness. She was stunned when the man smiled at her and offered his hand.

"I've heard a lot about you, young lady. I'm pleased to finally meet you. Ah, I see I arrived in the nick of time. Dinner is being served. Please, allow me to lead you to the table." He held out his arm, which Casey took gratefully while he continued his running conversation. "It looks like Thanksgiving. I just had a dinner like this a few days ago and managed to put on five or six pounds."

He looked like someone's father, or at least the way she'd always wanted her own father to look. He was round, but not fat. His face, by contrast, was angular. He was older than Singin by a good many years. Early sixties, she decided, with the kindest, warmest, most compassionate eyes she'd ever seen. He was right up there with Luke Farrell. But his eyes twinkled; Luke's didn't. He was almost bald, his lack of head hair in direct contrast with his incredibly bushy eyebrows. She thought she could come to like Alan Carpenter.

Halfway through dinner she nearly dropped the cranberry sauce from her fork when she heard Alan say, "It's not hopeless, we can fix it. And I think, Singin, that you have lost your American ways. What have you been doing to this man, Maline?"

"Loving him," she said boldly.

"I see. Is a wedding in the offing?" He chuckled.

Casey's heart fluttered in her chest. Not hopeless. Her face could be fixed. She ate the cranberries.

"When Lily is well and ready to be in our wedding party. Perhaps we will come to the States and have the wedding there."

"Great idea. We'll have it at my house," Carpenter said, digging into his turkey. "What do you think, Lily?"

"I think it's a wonderful idea, but I told them they shouldn't wait."

"Oh, why is that?" he asked nonchalantly.

"Two years is a very long time. Many things can happen. I think," she said, her voice slightly frantic, "I don't know how I . . . why I . . ."

"Don't worry about it. You're right. Get married now," he said to Singin, "and then we'll marry you again in the States. See," he said blithely, "the problem is solved."

Casey accepted her slice of pumpkin pie. That's what she'd been drinking—pumpkin juice. She felt as though she'd solved the problems of the universe. "It's pumpkin juice," she blurted. Three pairs of eyes stared at her.

"You didn't know?" Maline asked in surprise. "Why didn't you ask?"

Casey shrugged. "I need to find these things out on my own."

"Rightly so. I'll have a big slice, Maline," Carpenter said, holding out his plate. He had beautiful hands, Casey thought, with long, slender fingers and bluntly cut nails—surgeon's hands, a pianist's hands. She thought about Luke Farrell again. Did he believe she was dead? She would probably never know.

The moment the meal was over, Maline ordered her guests to go for a walk. "I must tidy up, and then Lily must be taken back to the hospital. A short walk." It didn't occur to any of them to object. With a doctor on each side of her, holding her arms, they walked down the length of the short street and then back again.

"I think, Lily," Alan Carpenter said, "that we can be successful as long as you are prepared to gut it out. Can you? I need to know now. Tomorrow I'll go through all your files, run some additional tests, and make my decisions. I plan to return to the

States right after the first of the year, on the second or third. We'll start your paperwork now. It will take that long."

"I don't understand. You've barely looked at me. I can . . . gut it out, as you say. I think I am capable of doing whatever it takes to . . . to become whole again. It doesn't matter to me when we leave, as long as I can wear a veil."

"Then we're in business. You're wrong about me barely looking at you. I observed you all during dinner. Don't forget, I know everything there is to know about you. I've studied the pictures Singin sent on to me. We're a team now, if that's agreeable."

"Yes," Casey said breathlessly. "Oh, yes."

"Oh, by the way," Carpenter said, "I brought along a copy of yesterday's *New York Times*. You might like to read it this evening. Who knows? Perhaps you might see something that will trigger a memory. These things happen," he said kindly.

THINGS HAPPEN ALL right, Casey thought as she read the paper. She felt the blood drain from her face when she saw Mac staring up at her, smiling. She tried to swallow, to shake off the wave of dizziness. It was a long time before she felt her strength return. She read the gossipy article slowly, her finger running along under each word. She stared intently at the picture of Mac's wife, Alice, and their child. Senator Malcolm Carlin. She didn't cry—there was nothing to cry for.

The hospital was asleep, for it was after midnight when Casey walked down to the nurses' station to ask for a pair of scissors. "I wish to cut something from the newspaper. I'll return them as soon as I finish." The nurse didn't think anything of it and handed over the scissors. She did mention it to the day nurse when she came on duty, who immediately reported to Dr. Vinh, who in turn reported to Dr. Carpenter. The waste basket in Casey's room was confiscated and the paper sent to the doctor's quarters, where both surgeons stared at the cut-out section of the paper.

"We won't say anything about this to Lily, Singin. When I get back home, I'll check out the paper in the library and see what she cut out. If she brings it up, we can discuss it. If not, I don't think we should mention it. Agreed?"

Singin nodded.

THE INTERCONTINENTAL JET from Thailand set down on American soil on January third at the same moment Malcolm Carlin was being sworn into the United States Senate, his wife and daughter at his side.

PART
FOUR

PART
FOUR

Chapter 13

CASEY SETTLED INTO Alan Carpenter's house on Beekman Place easily. She hunkered down for what she knew was going to be a grueling, gut-wrenching time in her life. The end result, Alan said, would be worth her while. That was six months ago. So far all Casey could see was disfigurement. "A small matter," Alan said quietly. He said the same words every day, until she thought she would scream and go out of her mind.

She fought him every step of the way, right up to the moment she was given anesthetic, and again when she came out of recovery. She cursed him, herself, and anyone else who came to mind. But when she was alone, she whimpered and cried into her pillow. She knew she was being unfair, but she seemed unable to stop herself. She wasn't the same person any longer. She didn't care if she lived or died, didn't care about anyone or anything. She *did* care about having her face made whole again, and didn't know why. In her heart she didn't believe Alan Carpenter could do it, and she'd called him a liar. His face had turned crimson, and her own had burned with shame. She apologized instantly, but the words rang false. They both knew it.

Casey stretched her legs out on the ottoman, a cup of herbal tea at her elbow. Maybe it was the dreams, the god-awful dreams that left her sweating and sleepless, so that she spent most of her nights staring at the ceiling. And while she stared at the ceiling, she thought of Mac Carlin and his family. When those thoughts and memories became too unbearable, she thought about Lily and Luke Farrell. She no longer cried though. She gulped at the tangy tea, draining the contents of the cup. Alan said this type of tea would relax her. That was a lie too, she thought in disgust. If anything, it made her jittery and cranky.

A light breeze wafted through the window, stirring the curtains so they danced. She got off the chair to pin the sheers against the window frame..How good the summer air felt on her skin. She wanted to touch her face, to run her fingers up and down the scars that crisscrossed it. "Don't do it," Alan said. She clenched her hands into tight fists.

"God help me, please," she prayed aloud. "Make these terrible dreams go away. Give me some measure of peace, and please, please, help me to rid myself of this anger. Help me to be kinder to Alan. He's a gentle, wonderful man, and I am an ungrateful, silly, stupid female, a nurse who should know better." She almost blubbered then, but bit down on her tongue.

She'd had such good intentions when she arrived here from Thailand. Alan hadn't minimized a thing. If anything, he had made it all sound worse than it actually was. Gut it out, that's what she'd promised to do, and she'd done it so far. She hadn't agreed not to get angry and belligerent. Damn it, she was trying. Then try harder, an inner voice chided. Alan doesn't deserve to be treated the way you're treating him. "I know, I know," Casey mumbled. If she could just get a good night's sleep, she thought, things might be different. She might be able to cope better. Just one good night's sleep. Speak to Alan, the voice pleaded. Tell him about the dreams. Talk it out. "Sure, so he can tell me I need a psychiatrist," she said aloud. "No thank you. I'll work out my own problems." She knew Alan had enough on his mind without her adding to his burden. If he knew about her headaches, he'd probably ship her to some hospital for brain scans.

Thoughts of doctors and hospitals always conjured up Luke Farrell's name and face. Where was he now? What was he doing? Did he ever think of her? What had been his reaction when he'd heard that she was dead? Casey kicked out at the ottoman. Pain shot up her leg. "Damn," she seethed. "I probably broke my toes. Oh shit!" She hobbled to the chaise and flopped down to massage her aching foot. She swore then, with every word she'd ever heard Luke Farrell and the other doctors use. It didn't make her feel any better.

Luke. Gentle, caring, wonderful Luke. If she could just talk to Luke for a minute, she knew she would be all right. Right now, this very minute. Why not? the inner voice queried. There's a telephone two feet from where you're sitting. Pick it up and call him. I dare you! "No, no, I can't do that." Sure you can.

Casey continued to argue with herself until her head began to pound so badly she wanted to bang it on the wall for relief. She knew the sweats were going to come on any second. She leaned back against the chaise, the soft pillows cushioning her head. When she started to shake, she moved from the chaise to the phone, where she dropped to the floor to hug her knees. Call him, talk to him. Tell him you're alive.

Casey blinked past the headache, her teeth chattering when she reached out a shaking hand for the phone. In a hoarse croak she asked the operator to put through a call to Luke Farrell, saying, "I don't know the number operator, but I know he practices medicine and lives in Squirrel Hill, Pennsylvania. Yes, I'll hold." Casey was trembling, her eyelids were twitching, and her head was pounding worse than before. Spasms, worse than any she'd ever experienced, coursed through her as she waited.

"Dr. Farrell here. Hello. Is anyone there? This is Dr. Farrell. Mom, is that you? Speak up, I can't hear you. Is anyone there?"

I'm here, Luke. Luke, it's me, Casey. God, you sound so wonderful. Luke . . . help me . . . I can't go through whatever this is I'm going through alone . . . I've prayed until the prayers stick in my throat. I'm trying . . . I'm scared . . . Luke, oh Luke . . .

"Guess there's no one there. Must be gremlins on the line." Luke Farrell chuckled. "Feel free to call me anytime. That's what I'm here for."

Casey replaced the buzzing receiver in the cradle. She swiveled around, stunned to find her headache gone, and the twitching and trembling diminishing with each ragged breath she took. The spasms and the sweats were gone too. Wearily she closed her eyes as she made her way back to the chaise. Luke.

Luke was her Band-Aid. Luke could help her get through this. For a moment she felt shame and guilt. Back in Vietnam Luke had said, time after time, "You do whatever you have to do to get through this. It's the same principle as saying you kick ass and take names later." Right or wrong, she now had something to hang on to. "Someday, Luke, some way, I'll make this up to you. I don't know how or when that will happen, but I'll find a way."

The tension eased and she slept dreamlessly, then fitfully, thrashing about on the narrow brocade chaise, running in her dream, faster than a sprinter, with a white surgical bag in her hand. She stopped, bent over to pick up an ear, a finger, a foot, another foot, a hand. "Wait! Wait!" she screamed. She unzipped the body bag, trying desperately with surgical tape to attach the contents in the white surgical bag to the lifeless bodies in their plastic bags. "Help me!" she shouted. "Give me a chance to fix it! Please help me!

"Stop it, Casey, you can't fix it," Luke Farrell said. "We tried, don't you remember? We did our best. We can't do more than our best. Let them go. You have to let them go."

The pasty, blue-white hand with its chewed-off fingernails fell into the surgical bag.

"Atta girl," Luke crooned, stroking her hair. "It's all right. We get another shot at it today. Incoming wounded. Shake your ass, Adams!"

Casey rolled over, muttering in her sleep. She curled into the fetal position, her arms clutching a thick, fat pillow against her stomach. "It's a parade," someone shouted. "Attention!"

"Soldiers?" Casey looked to the right and then to the left. She was back in San Francisco at her father's house, in the green and yellow bathroom with the ceramic frog on the windowsill.

"The parade starts here and goes to the Savoy Hotel, where Mac stayed. Get in line, Lieutenant Adams. That's a goddamn order!"

"I can't. All these boxes are in the way. Can't you see them?"

"I gave you an order, Lieutenant Adams. Get in formation!"

"I'll have to jump over these boxes. I can't do it. Move them, please move them."

"They aren't boxes, Lieutenant Adams, they're coffins, and I can't move them. If you'd done a better job, there wouldn't be so many."

"I did my job. Luke did his job. We all did our jobs. You're the one who didn't do his job. You sent these young boys out to kill and . . . and we did our jobs, damn you! Luke writes letters—he doesn't have to, but he does. He makes up . . . what he does is he . . . he tells parents their son's last words were . . . about *them*. I can't do anymore. We're doing our best!"

"That's not good enough! You have to do better. Much better. I'm waiting, Lieutenant."

"I'm not climbing over those . . . boxes. I'm not! You can't make me!"

They were moving then, the long line of boxes, slipping and sliding out of the green and yellow bedroom, through the living room and out the front door.

Traffic on Lombard Street stopped. People sneered and jeered as the boxes trundled down and around the corners on their way to the Savoy Hotel. *Oh say can you see by the dawn's early light . . .*

She was running, her nurse's cap falling over her left ear. She jerked at it, tossed it in the direction of the brutal voice ordering her to lead the parade.

"I won't do it! Where's Luke? Where's Mac?"

"They can't help you. This is your punishment. I told you it would come to this. Now do you believe?"

"Sister Ann Elizabeth!"

"Yes, Sister Ann Elizabeth. This is all your fault, Casey Adams. All these boys are dead because you couldn't save them. I knew you would come to a bad end!"

"No! No!"

"Yes!"

"Go to hell, Sister!"

Casey woke then, her entire body bathed in sweat. She felt calm for some strange reason. She lay quietly, her eyes closed, trying to make sense out of her dreams. She felt normal. Tired perhaps, but she felt the call to Luke, hearing his voice after so long a time, was really going to help her. Knowing, making the decision to pick up the phone to call him, was going to make all the difference. She could call him anytime and listen to his voice.

She *was* going to get through this. With Alan and Luke, she would mend, physically and mentally. All she had to do was work at it.

Chapter 14

OUTSIDE THE BRIGHTLY lit brownstone building on Beekman Place, the world was dark as a womb. Only a medical doctor, such as himself, would use such a description, Alan Carpenter thought. Inside, where it counted, the rooms were brightly lit. A six-foot twinkling Frazier fir added even more light. It was Christmas Eve, the first holiday in seventeen years that he'd actually celebrated as such. It wasn't that he simply ignored holidays. More than that, he slept through them, because there was no one he cared to celebrate them with since the death of his wife. They'd had no children.

This year, however, he'd been as excited as a child, shopping through Saks, Bloomingdale's, and every other expensive store in New York. He'd buzzed through Van Cleef and Arpel, Tiffany, and Cartier like a man with a mission, secreting the gaily wrapped presents in his wall safe. The box from the furrier, along with the brilliant red and silver boxes from Bergdorf and Saks, were hidden in his closet.

The whole day, until this very minute, had been an exercise in secrecy. With the aid of his housekeeper and butler, they'd smuggled the tree into the house. They'd decorated it and wrapped presents for Casey until all three of them were so tired they had to break for a toddy at five o'clock. It was done now, in the study, his favorite place in the twelve-room brownstone.

The room looked the way a room is supposed to look on Christmas Eve. The scent of the fir and the pinecones in the fireplace had a dizzying effect on Alan. He sniffed appreciatively. He didn't want this night ever to end. But, of course, after tomorrow this idyllic time would be just a memory. Tears burned his eyes.

Alan Carpenter, M.D., who would go back to his ordinary life the day after Christmas, had committed the cardinal sin of falling in love with his patient—he, a man of sixty-five with a paunch and balding head. How he'd always guffawed whenever a colleague fell in love with a younger woman. May–December marriages never worked. But if someone asked him right now, this very second, what he wanted most in life, he would say Casey Adams. He knew exactly the minute he'd fallen in love with her, because his aging heart had skipped two beats when she confessed her identity. "Because I love and trust you," she'd said. He'd kissed her, and she'd returned his kiss with an ardor that surprised him. He remembered the date too—November 27, 1969. Thanksgiving. It was the anniversary of the first time they'd met in Maline's apartment in Thailand. At first he told himself she was just being grateful that, yes, she did love him, but she wasn't *in love* with him. When his heart skipped the second beat, he told himself he didn't care.

This whole past year they'd lived as man and wife, sleeping together in the same bed when her surgery permitted. Now she was well and it was time for her to leave. He'd waited until now, hoping the wonderful holiday would make it easier. A new life for Casey, a life he was providing. He wanted her happiness more than he'd ever wanted anything in his life. He'd had his moment in the sun, now it was Casey's turn. He thought it a corny analogy, if it was an analogy at all. He couldn't seem to think this evening. He drew a deep breath, inhaling the pine-scented air. He swayed dizzily. Only this time he knew it wasn't because of the fragrant air. Six months ago his cardiologist had said he was a walking time bomb. He was going to correct that problem the day after Christmas when he would be admitted to Columbia Presbyterian for bypass surgery. In more ways than one, this just might be his last Christmas. He'd decided long ago, when Marie died, that his life and death were preordained.

Casey loved this old house, which he'd painstakingly re-stored. She loved returning after a bout of surgery at his private clinic. He loved having her in the house, hearing her call his name, seeing the smile that was just for him. *Grateful.* He knew Casey would never leave, if he agreed to it, but he couldn't do that to her, couldn't shackle her to him out of gratitude. Yes, part of him wanted to do just that, but the other part of him, which he called his conscience, wanted to see her soar and fly. He'd taken care of that too. He'd taken care of everything, right down to the last detail.

He was not without influence and connections. He'd operated on some of the richest, most powerful people in the world. He'd finally come to terms with everything, and had secured Casey's future. Tonight, right after midnight, when it was actually Christmas Day, he was going to present her with her new life, right after all the packages were opened. He was going to tell her it wasn't possible to gift wrap a new life, but he would hand her a big, red, silky bow.

There were other things he was going to tell her too. The first and most important was that the United States Army now knew there were two Lieutenant Simons, one with the first name of Nancy and the other Joyce. Nowhere, they said, in any of their records, was there a Lily Simon who had served in Vietnam. He'd handled all the paperwork through his attorney, when the army denied all claims, refusing payment. Lily Simon no longer existed. Casey Adams was listed as dead. Casey herself wanted it kept that way.

A second lawyer, with connections on the other side of the law, had helped him secure a new identity for Casey, right down to a Social Security card and a passport. She had a driver's license even though she didn't know how to drive, something she was going to have to remedy rather quickly.

On December twenty-seventh Casey would start her new life as Mary Ashley, assistant to the producer of the noonday news at CXT with a salary of $13,000 a year, along with an apartment on East Seventy-ninth Street. The apartment, which Alan Carpenter owned, had been refurbished and furnished. He would tell her he was going to retire to Spain and close up the brownstone. As far as he could see, his plan was foolproof. He would have his surgery, come back to the brownstone to recover, and then go to his Spanish villa, where he would live out his days. *If* he was lucky.

He gazed at the beautiful Christmas tree, holding back his tears. Would it be so terrible, he wondered, to cry? He'd always been a sentimental man, and sensitive as a child. Now, in the twilight of his life, he wished for family, for blood ties, but there were none. Not even distant cousins. He was alone with thousands of acquaintances and perhaps a dozen close friends. And several thousand grateful patients and their families. It hadn't been a terrible life; in fact he'd thought it quite wonderful until Casey came into it. He had then realized that his life had merely been content. Her appearance turned it to wonderful. He had no regrets. He would have retired this year anyway. He was just moving things ahead of schedule.

Last week he'd called his old friend Marcus Carlin in Washington to ask his advice about drawing up a new will and voiding his old one, in which he left his fortune to various medical schools. And he did have a fortune: this brownstone, the villa in Spain, a ski lodge in Aspen, a small house in the Cayman Islands, and, of course, his stocks and bonds. He'd told his old friend a conservative estimate of his fortune was close to three million dollars. "All of it goes to Mary Ashley."

"Who's Mary Ashley?" Marcus demanded.

"My illegitimate daughter," Alan had snapped. "It's not important for you to know everything about my life, Marcus. I'm sure there are things in your life I don't know about, even though we go back fifty years."

"Are there records? Documents that can substantiate her identity?"

"Of course," he'd responded irritably. The sleazy lawyer on the Lower East Side had provided every document known to man. "I want no problems for the girl, when it comes time to claim my estate. I'm sending several pictures on to you along with a sample of her handwriting. Look it over, Marcus, before I pass it on to my lawyer here. Make sure there are no problems. Give me your word."

Marcus, however, refused to be satisfied with pictures and handwriting. He was driving to New York tomorrow to have dinner with Casey and Alan. At some point tonight, Alan was going to tell Casey about the judge. He knew she would balk about being called his daughter, but in the end she would do as he asked, simply because he asked.

Alan listened to the Bavarian clock in the wide, central foyer strike the hour of six. Casey would be coming downstairs in half an hour. They'd sit on the deep, sea-green sofa and have cocktails, their shoulders touching, and talk about the extensive, complete physical she'd undergone during the day. He'd known at four o'clock that all her tests were negative. She was in perfect health. He'd heard her come in and go to her room. She had to be exhausted, but she would take the warm bath and nap he'd ordered earlier in the day. Not once during the last two years had she complained about or refused him anything he wanted. Christ, he loved her. He ached with love, carried it like a suit of armor. The doctors who would treat him were fools, he thought. You can't mend a shattered heart. Let them try, he didn't care anymore.

Alan's eyes kept going to the Frazier fir standing in the corner and the huge mountain of gifts underneath. It all looked so festive, so real. The whole room was beautiful, with the poinsettias and garlands of evergreen roped along the mantel. A huge basket next to the fireplace held hundreds of Christmas cards. He hadn't sent a single one this year. The furniture was old, shabby really, but so comfortable he wouldn't give it up. Casey loved snuggling in a cozy corner of the couch with her feet curled under her, book in hand. He was going to miss her reading aloud from the mystery stories she loved. He'd always figured out who the villain was by page fifteen, but not Casey. She would squeal her displeasure and say, "I never guessed it was so and so." He loved their four o'clock ritual of hot chocolate and brownies. He loved sharing the *Times* with her before dinner. There wasn't one thing he didn't love about Casey.

She was so fit these days, thanks to his expertise. Every day he thanked God for his surgical talents. Every day he thanked God for *everything*.

A day and a half with Casey was all that was left to him. He wanted eternity. He felt a tear trickle down his cheek. He hadn't cried in years, not since he was a boy. Now he cried silently. He didn't bother to wipe the tears from his cheeks.

His life was ending, and Casey's was just beginning.

ONLY HERE, IN the privacy of her mauve- and champagne-colored bedroom, would Casey allow herself a cigarette. Alan had forbidden her to smoke, so she allowed herself to lapse only in secret. She sucked on mints, but he always knew. She wasn't fooling anyone but herself. She'd wanted to quit and had tried, but cigarettes were such a perfect pacifier. She'd given up everything else, but she needed this one last thing. It wasn't that she smoked much, three or four cigarettes a day at most. And it was something to look forward to. She puffed greedily, knowing when she stubbed out the cigarette it would be time to go downstairs.

She smiled. Christmas Eve was going to be wonderful. She'd bought a load of presents for Alan, anguishing over this and that, uncertain if she was making the right choices. She was going to tell him tonight that she wanted to marry him, to spend the rest of her life with him. Right after they opened their presents, when the Christmas glow was still with both of them. It was the only way she could think to repay him for these two wonderful and hateful years. She'd gutted it out the way he'd asked her to. She'd done everything. It had all been carefully orchestrated, and now she was better than new. Thanks to Alan. In her lifetime she knew she would never, ever meet as wonderful a human being as Alan Carpenter. She loved him with all her heart. He was her lover, her father, her brother, her uncle, her cousin, but most important, he was her friend. He was her whole life, her reason for being. She'd been *in love* once, and once was enough. What she felt for Alan would endure. She would make him happy. She'd work at it twenty-four hours a day. He loved her, he said so. Said he was *in love* with her. She'd responded in kind, but she'd seen the shadow in his eyes. He hadn't believed her. There were times, like now, when she wished she'd been entirely truthful with Alan. The only thing she'd held back was the name of the married officer with whom she'd had an affair. To this day she couldn't bring herself to say

Mac's name aloud. Mac Carlin was as dead as Casey Adams.

It was all over now: the operations, the recovery time, the days and weeks when she couldn't move about. All of it was behind her. In another week it would be a new year, and a new life with Alan. The thought was pleasant. She could see herself catering to him, waiting on him the way the Japanese women waited on their mates. She wanted to do it, needed to do it.

Everything she owned, she owed to Alan's generosity, right down to the underwear she had on and the food she ate. She owed him, she thought, her very life.

For this evening she had a new dress, and for tomorrow another. She looked down at the crushed burgundy velvet she'd spent a fortune on. She could hardly wait to see the approval in Alan's eyes. It was important to her that he approve of *everything* about her. She felt festive. Tomorrow, after church services, she would change into the hunter-green A-line dress she'd purchased only yesterday. Faux pearls would be her only jewelry.

Her color was high this evening, she thought, peering into the mirror over the dressing table. She stood, mesmerized for a moment as she stared at her new face. It had to be a miracle, no other explanation would suffice. With God's help and Alan's hand she was whole again. Different, but whole. Her nose was shorter, more defined, to compensate for the surgery on her shattered cheekbones. Her jaw at first glance looked the same, but it too was different, thinner somehow, to match her other new features. Nicole and Danele would never recognize her. She hardly recognized herself. The implanted contact lenses which turned her eyes from blue to aquamarine had made the greatest difference. Luke wouldn't recognize her either. Alan said she was beautiful. Impishly, she stuck her tongue out at her reflection. She didn't know if she would agree to the beautiful part, but she was different, pretty, attractive. Luke would say she was a head turner. She tweaked a stray curl, working it so it fell artfully over her forehead to cover the red scar along her hairline. Wisps of hair that looked so casual were actually camouflage to cover scars around her ears. Someone named Kenneth had come to the brownstone to study her for hours before he finally came up with a hairstyle both Alan and she approved of. His fee had been outrageous, but well worth it. The other scars on her cheekbones, sides of her nose, and chin were covered with a special pancake makeup Alan had created just for her. When it was removed, the scars were blatantly visible. Alan predicted that in time they would lighten, but they would never disappear. Twice a day, before she applied her makeup and when she removed it, she would run her fingers along the scar lines and stare at herself, remembering the way she looked at Maline and Singin's Thanksgiving dinner. Then she'd been deformed and disfigured. Ugly. Now she was whole, healthy, and alive. A few scars didn't matter. Nothing mattered but Alan.

Today had been grueling, but now she was relaxed. Carolers would come by, Alan had said. He'd also said it would take all evening to open her presents. Her eyes lighted. His wouldn't take that long. She made another face at herself in the mirror.

Life was worth living again. *Are you happy? Do you ever think of me?* She wondered what would happen if she walked into his Senate office on some pretext or other. Would he sense something? Her heart thudded in her chest. Maybe she would do just that someday. Someday when her heart was healed. Just one more look so she could drink her fill of him before she buried him once and for all. She deserved a last look.

Casey took one last look around the room. It was exquisite, done by a decorator during her first series of facial operations. When she'd returned from the clinic, she'd gasped. First at the beauty and then at what it must have cost. Alan had beamed. It was a creamy confection, a bonbon. The long narrow windows were draped in mauve with scalloped valances that matched a quilted bedspread of the same delicious color. The carpet was champagne to match the silky, scalloped skirt of her dressing table and chaise lounge. Today, while she was out, creamy white poinsettias in baskets with huge satin bows had been delivered. The fireplace, in which a log always glowed, was gas fueled to keep the room clean, Alan said. The log was for decoration. They'd made love here in front of her fireplace, and it was a slow, lazy, satisfying love, but only for Alan. She tried to respond, tried to feel something, wished for it, prayed for it, but it didn't happen. She pretended. It was enough for her to snuggle, to feel Alan's arms about her, to sleep in the crook of his arm. She vowed to work harder at her feelings, and if that didn't work, she would seek out a competent doctor or therapist for help. All in the new year.

She was loved. Someone cared about her. She wiped at the tears forming in her eyes. She couldn't let them trickle down her cheeks, for if she did she would have to reapply the pancake makeup.

"He loves me," she murmured as she glided out of the room. It was twenty-nine minutes past six on Christmas Eve when she descended the steps to ask Alan Carpenter if he would marry her.

Chapter 15

ALAN, FORBIDDEN DRINK in hand, eyes on the door to the library, felt his heart lurch in his chest as Casey paused a moment, her eyes on the shimmering Christmas tree. Her hands flew to her mouth to stifle her exclamation. She ran to him and threw her arms about him. "Alan, it's so beautiful! Did you do it all? Oh, it's so . . . so. . . . *us*." She kissed him warmly. "Thank you, Alan, for all this," she said, waving her arms about.

"Do you like the smell?" Alan asked anxiously. "I heard somebody say, just recently, that Christmas trees don't smell like Christmas trees anymore. People spray scent from a can. This smells," he said, awe in his voice.

"We could get drunk on this scent. At least I could," Casey said happily. "Alan, who are all these presents for?" She ran to the tree and dropped to her knees. She was being the little girl she'd never had a chance to be, poking and probing each gaily wrapped gift. When she shook a small box, trying to guess what was in it, Alan beamed with delight.

"Who do you think they're for?" Alan asked fondly.

"The housekeeper, the chauffeur, the gardener, the cook. Is there one here for me? Which one? Does it have my name on it? Alan, there are no cards on these. How do you know who gets what? Oh, I see, by the color scheme: red, gold, silver, green. How clever of you. It's all so wonderful! Quick, tell me now, which one is mine? I must shake it!" she babbled.

In his life he'd never been this happy, Alan thought. The look of pure rapture on Casey's face was almost more than he could bear. She *would* be satisfied with just one present. His tongue

334

felt thick in his mouth. How he loved this wonderful young woman. "They're all for you!" he said huskily.

"All of them!" Casey gasped. "You're joking, aren't you, Alan? As a child I never got more than one present. One Christmas I didn't get any at all. Are we going to hang up our stockings, Alan?"

"Dear girl, they're already up, how could you have missed them? They're filled too," he said proudly. Thank God I remembered, he thought.

"For me!" she repeated again. "How . . . when . . . why?"

"Because you deserve every one of them. I wanted to buy out the stores for you. I want you to have . . . everything life has to offer."

"I already have that. I have you. Alan, this is all so wonderful. But you didn't have to do all this. I don't know what to say," Casey said, tears brimming in her eyes.

Alan's voice was husky, just as choked as Casey's. "I did it for myself too. It's been years since I celebrated Christmas. It used to be my favorite time of year. I wanted to do this, I needed to do it. For both of us. It's done, so let's just enjoy our evening. Dinner is at seven-thirty."

"Are we having plum pudding and all that?" Casey teased.

"Not on your life." Alan laughed. "There is nothing traditional about our dinner this evening except maybe the silver and china. We are," he drawled, "having your favorite dinner. Pizza, egg rolls, tacos, and hot dogs. Banana splits for dessert."

"No!" Casey squealed.

"Uh-huh." Alan grinned. "Cook's having a hissy fit, but she agreed. Tomorrow is our real dinner, but no plum pudding."

Casey dropped to her knees next to Alan's chair. She looked up at him adoringly. "I love you, Alan," she whispered. *Ask him now. This is the right time, the perfect time. Tell him you want to spend the rest of your life with him. Do it.*

"How can you love an old man like me? I'm overweight, almost bald, have a terrible disposition, and you hate my smelly cigars." I'm entitled, he thought, to hear her answer. He needed to *hear* her say the words.

"Yes, you are overweight, and I'm going to personally see

that you lose it. Age is a number, Alan, one I have never paid
attention to. I will never pay attention to it. I love your shiny
head. Hair doesn't make a person. We'll have to work on the
cigars though. Will you marry me, Alan? I want it more than
anything. Please, Alan, don't look at me like that. You said you
were going to retire and perhaps do a bit of consultation work.
We could spend all our time together. I can make you happy.
Alan? You aren't saying anything. You . . . you said you loved
me. Were you just . . . did you say that so I would . . . please
say you meant it," Casey pleaded.

"Darling girl, I love you as much as life. I think we should
wait awhile and discuss this when we aren't so emotional. This
evening is going to our heads. Later, we'll talk. After midnight,
when it's Christmas Day."

"See, you're doing it again," Casey teased. "You can twist
me around your finger. Am I so pliable?" She giggled, laying
her head in his lap, certain everything would be fine.

Alan stroked her hair. It felt as soft as corn silk. His chest felt
heavy. He hadn't expected a proposal, never dreamed she
would want to marry him. Maybe what he was contemplating
was wrong. Of course, his inner voice chided, saddle her with an
invalid. She means it when she says she'll take care of you. Out
of gratitude. She deserves more. She's young, healthy. She'll
want children someday. She has to get on with her life, and you
have to get ready to die. You know what the odds are of your
surviving this operation. You can't do that to her.

"I have an idea," Alan said brightly. "After dinner how
would you like to go caroling? Just the two of us. I think I
remember 'Silent Night.' And I can do a robust 'Jingle Bells.'
How about you?"

"Oh, Alan, I would love to go caroling, but I thought you
said carolers would come here. How will that work if we aren't
here?"

"I'll have the cook and butler offer them toddies and they can
offer the donation for the church as well as I can. Let's do it!"
he said exuberantly.

Casey clapped her hands. "I am so very happy, Alan. For
such a long time I didn't think I would ever be happy again. I

wouldn't be if it wasn't for you. I want to ask a favor of you. I have no right, I know that, but . . . if we get married, I want us to be completely happy. We will be, I know that, but a child . . . how much money do I have left, Alan? Is it enough to start a search for Lily's son? Can we bring him here? You have so much love, Alan. That little boy, he's three now. I think of him all the time, alone, with no one to love him. We could love him, Alan. You have enough money to support us, don't you?" she asked anxiously. "If you don't, I can go back to work. Part-time. One little boy won't cost much. Can we . . . would . . . do you object?"

Alan fought the head rush he was experiencing. A package. A family. What he'd always wanted. He could love a little child. But time was simply running out for him. He felt the urge to bellow like a bull. It could have been so perfect.

"Of course I have enough money left," he said. "Tomorrow . . . I can bring up the subject . . ."

"That's right, you said your friend was very influential. You never did tell me his name, Alan. Is he powerful enough to set the wheels in motion?"

"Dr. Carpenter, dinner is served," the housekeeper said from the doorway.

"Marcus Carlin. He's a Supreme Court justice. We've been friends for years." He reached out for Casey's arm, but she toppled sideways, her face bone-white. His arms around her shoulders, Alan held her close. "What's wrong?" he asked hoarsely.

"I . . . I guess I caught my heel in the hem of my skirt. I thought I was . . . going to fall on my . . . on my face . . . You know how paranoid I am about hitting myself. I guess it was a combination of the heat and the pine scent. I'm fine now, Alan," she said shakily.

Mac's father. He would sit at the Christmas dinner table. He would probably mention Mac's name. Her step faltered, but Alan's grip on her arm was secure. She tried to smile. The concern she read in Alan's eyes made her try harder.

Alan squeezed her arm. "Good. The color is back in your cheeks."

"Oh, Alan, the table is beautiful," Casey sighed.

It was beautiful, Alan thought. Colorful was the second thought that popped into his mind. The cook had set the table with Christmas plates, bone china with delicate poinsettias in the center. The napkins were fine red linen tucked into fragile pale green crystal wineglasses. The linen tablecloth was appliquéd around the hem with miniature red poinsettias with tiny pearls set in the middle. He wondered where it had come from. Probably one of those things his wife Marie had bought and saved for a visit by the Queen of England. Marie had always referred to things like the tablecloth as "the good stuff." There were trunks of good stuff in the attic. The centerpiece was just right, a wire-shaped Christmas tree filled with small poinsettias. His eyebrows shot upward when he saw the cook wink at him. In all the years she'd been with him, he'd never once thought of her as a romantic. Why, he wondered, was he finding out all these things now, when it was too late?

"I'm going to eat everything . . . at once," Casey babbled. How could she even think of food now? She felt sick to her stomach. She did her best to pull herself together. She wasn't about to spoil all of Alan's efforts because of Mac's father.

She stuffed herself.

Alan picked at his food. Casey didn't notice.

She was halfway through her banana split when she laid down her spoon and said, "I think I've changed my mind about Lily's son. For now. Later, when things are more . . . stable, I'll . . . I have to start to curb my impulsiveness. I just didn't think it through. Please, don't say anything to your . . . friend tomorrow. The time isn't right. Promise me, Alan."

"Of course, if that's what you want." He felt relieved. He hated the thought of asking Marcus for a favor. Marcus was such a shit when it came to using his influence. He would have done it for Casey though. There was nothing he could refuse her.

"Is coffee by the tree all right with you?" he asked her.

"Absolutely," Casey said, glad to be able to move, to try and get her nerves under control. She could hardly wait to get outdoors and walk. Marcus Carlin coming here.

She forced a lightness into her voice she was far from feeling. "How is it you never mentioned Mr. Carlin before? Most people would brag if they claimed a friendship with a Supreme Court justice. What's he like, Alan? How should I act around him?"

Alan laughed. "He's a bit pompous, but a good friend. We try to see each other at least once a year, and of course we go back to Yale for homecoming when we can. I've heard others say that we belong to the Good Old Boys' Club. There were five of us. Dennis Melnic is CEO for some big rubber company in Ohio; Clyde Barrows owns a string of hotels; Frank Simpson is a pediatrician; and of course, Marcus. We send Christmas cards. Frankly, I didn't think you'd be interested in my old college friends."

"Alan, I want to know everything about you, and that includes your friends. When we come back from caroling, I want to sit by the fire and hear all your war stories about your college days. After all, I told you all about me."

"We weren't wild and wicked, if that's what you're thinking. We were a rather boring group as I remember. As a matter of fact, when we met in later years we didn't seem to have much to say to each other. The others finally started talking about their children, and I didn't have any."

"You poor thing," Casey teased. "That means you had to suffer through the pictures of the kids and the dogs and cats. How many are there all together? Children, I mean?"

"Let's see," Alan said, ticking off on his fingers. "Dennis has five, Clyde has four, Frank has three, and Marcus has a son, Mac. I think he's the most successful. He's a United States senator. Lovely little wife. Their child has Down's syndrome. I've met Mac, but none of the other children."

Something strange and alien clutched at Casey's heart. "It sounds as if you're fond of Mr. Carlin's son," Casey said quietly.

"I don't know if fond is the right word. I've only seen him five or six times. He's quite likable. Handsome young man. I seem to recall him being an unhappy youngster. Something to do with his mother's breakdown and her return to her girlhood home. I always thought Marcus was too strict with the boy, but then I never had children, so I don't know if my opinion is worthy or not. I was surprised when Mac got married. No, that's not what I meant to say. I think I was surprised at his choice of bride. They were like oil and water. Marcus liked her, but I . . . I decided to reserve judgment. In any case, he came back from Vietnam a real hero. Marcus puffed up like a walrus. I suppose I would have too if it was my son." Alan sat up and clapped his hands. "I think it's time to get our coats. What will it be first, 'Silent Night' or 'Jingle Bells'?"

Casey giggled. "If we get stuck on the words, we can keep saying 'Jingle Bells' over and over. No one will know the difference. Is that okay with you?"

"Wonderful," Alan said, holding Casey's coat for her. The last thing in the world he wanted to do was go caroling. His chest felt so heavy, and the cold air wasn't going to help. The singing would probably bring him to his knees. At that moment he realized how old and sick he really was. He wished he could renege and sit in front of the fire with Casey curled up alongside of him. Just thinking about going outdoors made him shiver.

"Oh, Alan, it's snowing!" Casey cried excitedly. "Look, it's staying on the ground. You knew! You knew it was snowing and that's why you suggested we go out. You are the most wonderful man on this earth! This is so perfect, I don't ever want it to end. What could be more beautiful than a white Christmas?"

Now my feet are going to get cold and wet, Alan thought as they gingerly walked down the steps of the brownstone. He had galoshes, but he had no idea where they were. Galoshes were something old, feeble people wore. People who were careful about their health.

Their caroling lasted two full hours. Both Casey and Alan were hoarse when they retraced their steps for home, declining four offers of hot cocoa.

Inside the warm brownstone Casey headed for the upstairs bathroom. Alan marched on cold, numb feet to the bar alongside his desk. He gulped two fingers of Jack Daniels in two swallows. For a split second he thought his chest was going to rupture. His watch told him it was ten minutes past ten.

"Look," Casey said, holding up socks and his slippers, lined with shearling wool. "If your feet are as cold as mine, you need these. Sit down and I'll undo the laces," she ordered. It didn't occur to Alan to protest.

When at last they were snuggling on the comfortable couch, their feet stretched toward the fire, Alan drifted off to sleep. Casey closed her eyes wearily. Both of them were trying so hard. Why? It hit her like a bolt of lightning then. Alan hadn't accepted her proposal. Waiting till after midnight meant he was going to say no. She'd expected an exuberant yes, had expected to make immediate plans. She inched away from her kindly benefactor. She felt shame at her blatant proposal. First Mac and now Alan. Let's not forget your father while we're doing this soul-searching, an inner voice taunted.

Tears scalded her eyes and trickled down her cheeks, smearing the medicinal makeup. She didn't care. If her intuition was right and Alan rejected her, what was she going to do? He'd taken care of her so long, made all her decisions, that she no longer knew what she was capable of doing. What a fool she'd been, thinking this would go on forever. Fool, fool, her mind shrieked.

Alan stirred, a strange grimace on his face. Casey wiped at her tears with the back of her hand. Poor dear, he probably had indigestion. The tears trickled again. He'd suffered through dinner, eating things she loved just to please her.

Christmas Eve. Where was Mac? What was he doing right now, this very minute? Decorating the tree with his wife so their daughter would think Santa did it when she awoke in the morning. What sort of gift would he give to his wife? Diamonds? Gems of some kind? Perhaps a bracelet with matching earrings. And the little girl, what would Santa give her? Dolls, picture books, toys that made noise and music? Mac's wife, what would she give Mac? A cashmere jacket, gold cuff links. Something monogrammed. Mac said he played the piano. They were probably singing carols around the piano now and drinking Christmas cheer. Mac would be tall enough to hang the Christmas angel on top of the tree.

"Merry Christmas, Mac," she whispered.

Chapter 16

MAC CARLIN LOOKED at the calendar on his desk. December 23. Two days until Christmas. Hands jammed into his pockets, he got up and walked over to the window. The day was bleak and gray, with weather forecasters predicting snow for Christmas. He didn't believe a word of it. He hated Christmas. Hated it with a passion. Somehow, he'd managed to get through the holidays in the past, mainly by sleeping through them. The memory of his last Christmas in Vietnam was still with him. He'd been able to live with it during the year, but the moment the season arrived, he was unable to concentrate.

He hadn't even shopped this year, nor had he in past years. Benny's wife, busy as she was, said she would do his shopping for him. Alice had requested a shearling jacket. He'd been surprised at her simple request. She'd explained that she needed to be warm when she tramped the fields with Jenny. Jenny, she'd said, wanted a stand-up doll that was supposed to be lifelike and as tall as she was. For his father there was a humidor he hadn't bothered to even look at. Carol, bless her heart, had wrapped the presents in bright red paper with huge silver bows. All three presents were locked in the trunk of his car.

He was antsy, every nerve in his body twanging. He wandered aimlessly around the office, touching the flag, staring at a fern whose tips were brown. The coffeepot was clean. Everyone was gone—but him. The offices looked empty even though they were filled with furniture.

As he walked down the long corridor of the Rayburn Building, he thought of himself as the loneliest man in the world. And the unhappiest.

God, how he hated Christmas.

He drove expertly, his eyes keen, his shoulders taut, his mouth grim. Holiday traffic was terrible, the worst he'd ever seen. Everywhere he looked he saw smiling faces and brightly colored shopping bags. Mostly women, shopping for their families. Alice ordered from catalogues these days. The queen of the shoppers had fallen off her pedestal.

A long time later, hours really, Mac pulled his car to the curb. Jesus, what in the fucking hell was he doing at the airport? He gave himself a mental shrug and climbed out of the car. He turned once to look back at it. How long would it take before it was towed? He remembered the Christmas presents in the trunk. *What was he doing here? What was this consuming anger coursing through him?*

"Hey, do you have a minute?" Mac called to a gangly youth with a backpack. "You going or coming?"

The young man laughed. "Depends. I'm waiting for a buddy of mine to come over here with fifty bucks. The ticket was more than I expected. Had a few too many parking tickets to settle up at school before I left. Why?" he asked curiously.

"I'm Senator Mac Carlin and I . . . I need someone to park my car in the lot and arrange to have some presents in the trunk delivered. It's worth three hundred bucks to me. You can put the key under the mat. I have a spare. What do you say?"

"I'm your man, Senator. Cash?"

Mac was already peeling bills from a money clip. "Leave a note at the information desk telling me where you parked the car. Have a nice holiday, son."

"You too, Senator!" the young man said, exuberant over the sheaf of bills in his hand.

Mac walked slowly to the ticket counter and got into line.

IT WAS EIGHT o'clock when the DC-10 set down at Orly Airport. An hour was used up going through customs, a second was required for a car rental and the Christmas Eve highway rush. Mac's watch said it was twenty minutes after ten when he knocked on Nicole Dupre's bright blue door. The girl, who was every bit as tiny as Casey had said she was, spoke in rapid-fire

French. Mac understood none of it, but when he introduced himself, he saw tears glisten in her eyes.

"What took you so long, Monsieur Mac?" she said in stilted English.

"I couldn't . . . I wasn't ready. I don't know if I'm ready now or not," he whispered hoarsely. "I need to know where . . ."

"St. Gabriel's. You can walk from here if you wish. I cannot go with you. I have a house full of guests. Are you sure, monsieur, that you want to go now? The morning—"

"I need to go now. I'm sorry for taking you from your guests. I'll find it. Casey . . . Casey spoke of you often. She loved . . . the blue dress. She never got to wear it."

"One moment, monsieur." She was back a moment later with a long-handled flashlight. "It is to the right of the third walkway. The stone is simple, one Casey would have approved of. When I can, I take fresh flowers. So does Danele. We have not forgotten her. Good evening, Monsieur Mac." The blue door closed quietly.

Mac walked slowly, his hands jammed deeply into his pockets. It felt, he thought crazily, as though he'd been here before. He looked upward to the gray steeples. Casey had gone to church here, been raised in the orphanage. It looked cold and austere. How was it possible, he wondered, for such a place to give comfort?

It didn't take him long to find the grave. Anger rose in his chest at the simplicity of the stone. Casey deserved something better, larger. She should have something . . . *noticeable*. He said so, aloud.

Mac dropped to his knees. He was holding his breath and didn't know why. "I'm here," he whispered. "A day doesn't go by that I don't think of you. I fill up my days. I got the dogs, and I live in the kind of house we said we would have someday. It's the guest cottage, and I have a housekeeper. I would have gotten a divorce. It was in the works. I didn't betray you. I'll never stop loving you. Never." He talked then, slowly at first, his voice gentle, and then the words tumbled out. He spoke of Jenny, tried his best to explain about the child and Alice.

"The thing I'm most proud of is this idea I have to set up a foundation for Vietnam vets. I can do it too. It's going to take awhile. Every time I try to do something, I get stonewalled. But I'm going to do it. I wish I could say I like politics, but I don't. I'm not going to quit though, at least not for a while. The day I realize I can't do anything positive for people is when I'll pack it in."

He was on his haunches now, more comfortable, as he continued. "I've been trying to get information about Lily's son. I've written so many letters, I've lost count. I've come to the conclusion Lily is dead, but that her child is alive. I feel that. I won't give up on it either. I made a promise to Lily, and I intend to keep it."

He spoke then of his trip to the little apartment and finding the blue dress, and the Cracker Jack ring. "It's in my pocket, on my key ring. It's all I have left. Sometimes when I can't sleep, which is most of the time, I take it off the ring and hold it in my hand. In the morning the palm of my hand is green."

Mac's breathing grew harsh, his eyes wild, as he leaped to his feet. "I don't *feel* like you're here. I should feel something. Comfort perhaps. A feeling of peace. But it doesn't feel like your spirit . . ." He wiped at his eyes with the back of his hand.

He was cold, his feet numb, but he didn't move. He was finally at Casey's final resting place. Perhaps it was good that she was here. If she'd been buried in Arlington or California, he'd spend all his time buying flowers and visiting. Before he walked away, he promised himself to return once a year. He looked back once, and waved. "Wait for me," he whispered in a choked voice. He swiveled and ran back, vapor puffing from his mouth when he said, "Merry Christmas, my darling."

As Mac walked along the path, he was aware of small groups of people and the sound of carols coming from the church. He looked at his watch. Midnight mass. He took a seat at the back of the church just as a line of nuns filed down the center aisle. Mac's eyes narrowed. Which one was Sister Ann Elizabeth? As soon as this mass was over he was damn well going to find out. He counted them. Twenty in all, two of the sisters in wheelchairs.

It was a pretty church, he thought, looking around. Larger than it looked from the outside.

He was warm now, his feet thawed, his hands back to normal. He looked around at the small families, their children half asleep at this late hour, probably daydreaming about what they would find under the Christmas tree when they awoke in the morning. He thought of Jenny and the life-size doll. He was half asleep himself, remembering his visit to the cemetery. Did Casey ever sit in this particular pew? His eyes popped open as he counted the pews, both sides and then the center pew. Maybe later, after he spoke to Sister Ann Elizabeth, he would come back here and sit in each and every pew until he felt something.

After the last carol had been sung, the last parishoner had gone, and the robed priest was no longer visible, Mac approached the first nun in the parade to leave the church.

"Can you tell me, Sister, which one is Sister Ann Elizabeth?" Mac asked quietly.

"Why do you wish to know, monsieur?" the old nun asked softly.

"I must talk with her about a student, one of the children who resided at the orphanage. Please, may I? It's very important. I've come all the way from Washington, D.C."

"Very well, monsieur, it is Christmas Eve so I will permit it. Do not be long. Sister isn't well. She suffers from cataracts and heart seizures. We will wait in the vestibule for you."

Mac approached the nun in the wheelchair. Even in the yellowish light of the church he could see the thick white film in her eyes. She must be blind, Mac thought. He wondered exactly what a heart seizure was. Was a seizure the same as a heart attack? He realized he didn't care what it was.

"Sister, my name is Malcom Carlin. I'm a senator from Washington, D.C. I came over here today to . . . to pay my respects to a former student of yours. Casey Adams. Do you remember her?"

The voice was feeble-sounding, fretful and yet defensive. She understood him and replied in English, spoken without hesitation, but with a soft accent. "Yes, I remember her very well. Did

I hear you correctly when you said you came to pay your respects? Is the child . . . ?"

"Dead?" Mac said coldly. "Yes, Sister, she is."

The nun blessed herself. Mac noticed how crippled and deformed her hands were. "I'm very sorry, monsieur. It is always sad when a young person dies. God should have taken me instead."

"Why didn't he?" Mac blurted.

"One never questions the Lord," Sister said quietly. "What is it you wanted to ask me?

"Did you ever . . . hug or kiss Casey? Did you ever pat her on the head or sing her a lullaby? Were you ever *truly kind* to her?"

It was several seconds before the sister could marshal her response. "I tried to explain to Casey the day she came to see me, and I thought she understood, but to answer your questions, monsieur, no. It was not permitted."

"Permitted!" Mac was outraged, his voice ringing in the quiet, still church. "Are you, a woman of God, going to sit here, in this church, and tell me you weren't allowed to show affection and love to a child?" he thundered.

Tears gathered in the old nun's eyes. "It was for their own good. Mother Superior said so. I didn't always agree, but I had to obey my orders. She was a scrapper, a defender of the underdog. When she was ten, she told me to my face—mind you, to my face—that she was going to be a nurse someday, and if I ever came into her hospital she would refuse to nurse me. At the time she meant every word of it. But the time did come when I had to have surgery and Casey *was* my nurse. I think she was the finest nurse the hospital ever had. It isn't easy for the children here. It's harder when they leave. We have to prepare them for how hard it is. Mother says we build character here and that's how the children survive in the outside world."

"Oh yeah, well what about the goldfish in the cracked cup?" Mac said belligerently.

"The fish was dead, monsieur. It already smelled. I had to get rid of it. A child doesn't know . . . she thought because it was floating on top of the water that it was still alive. The cup was cracked. She could have cut herself."

"You have an answer for everything, don't you?" His tone was still belligerent.

"No, monsieur, I don't. Is Casey buried here at St. Gabriel's?"

Mac's rage was total. "Do you expect me to believe you don't . . . how could you not know? Of course she's buried here. Nicole, one of your other less fortunates, saw to it. Now I suppose you're going to tell me no one goes there to pray for her."

"I was ill for a very long time, monsieur, and in the hospital. Perhaps Mother thought I would be unduly upset if they told me. I did not know."

"And would you have been upset?" Mac roared so loud, the Mother Superior came on the run, her black habit floating behind her in the draft she created.

"Monsieur, what is going on here? Why are you upsetting Sister? Why are you here, what is it you want?"

"Want? Want? It's too late to want anything. I hope, Sister, if you ever get to Heaven, that you have a suitable explanation for . . . the way you . . . for your . . . you make me sick, the lot of you, and if your God is going to punish me for my tongue, so be it. At least I can live with myself. I do have one more question though. Just one. How many children have ever come back here after they left?"

"Casey was the only one who ever came back," Sister Ann Elizabeth said spiritedly. "The only one. They hated us. Why would they come back?"

"Sister!" the Mother Superior said virtuously.

"You should have told me the child is buried here. I had a right to know. Why did you keep that from me? I wish to go there now. This very minute."

"Sister, I forbid—"

"Forbid, Mother? I don't care. I'm old, I'm almost blind, I'm ill, I'm in constant pain, and I will die soon. Do you think I care now if you forbid me? This is Christmas Day and I wish to go to the cemetery. Monsieur, if you don't mind, do you think you could . . . is it too much to ask?"

"Not at all, Sister. Are you warm enough?" Mac said, stunned at this turn of the conversation.

"It doesn't matter, monsieur. I suppose I am warm enough."

"Sister, I absolutely forbid you to leave this church," Mother said angrily. "Don't force me to call Father Adrian."

"Hurry, monsieur, she will do as she says."

Mac hurried, the old nun muttering nonstop as he pushed the awkward wheelchair over the rough cobblestones and then onto the frozen ground of the cemetery.

"Casey always said she was going to have a little house with ruffled curtains that she would sew herself. She was going to hook the rugs too, when she came home from the hospital on long winter evenings, while the children lay by the fire doing their schoolwork. She said she was always going to have oranges in her fruit bowl because they smelled so wonderful. A pet too, maybe several. The goldfish *was* dead, monsieur. It never occurred to Casey or Nicole to ask where the goldfish came from. Nor did you ask, monsieur. From me. I found it at the market and hid it in my pockets. It was in a very small jar that leaked. You see, I always listened to their hopes and dreams and prayed they would come true. Many times, monsieur, I climbed from my bed in the middle of the night to check on the children. No, I did not kiss them, nor did I hug them, but I did touch them. I made the sign of the cross on their little heads and I cried for them and I selfishly cried for myself that I couldn't do more. You must have loved her very much, monsieur."

"Very much, Sister."

"You should leave now. There's no need for you to witness a scene with Mother and Father Adrian. I will pray for Casey. Go, monsieur. I wish to be alone, and I will make my confession to God instead of Father Adrian."

"Are you sure, Sister? It's very cold out here." Over her objections, Mac slipped out of his topcoat and spread it over her shoulders. He bit down on his lower lip when he saw her struggling with her rosary, her gnarled hands losing their grip on the slippery beads.

Mac left then, because it was what the sister wanted. His step was lighter as he made his way out to the rental car. He spent the entire day sitting in a restaurant in the airport, unable to walk the short distance to the ticket counter. He felt like his life's blood had been drained from his body. He thought about his past and his future until he grew bleary eyed. He missed three flights and returned home the following day, when Christmas was over.

Chapter 17

ALAN AWOKE WHEN Casey added a log to the fire. It sent a shower of sparks upward as a half-burned log dropped with a thump to the bottom of the grate.

"What time is it?" he asked sleepily.

"Five minutes to midnight. Almost time for Santa to arrive. Guess he'll have to come to the front door and ring the bell," she teased.

"Why did you let me sleep like that?" he asked crossly. "I slept for almost two hours."

"We both did. I just woke myself when the log dropped," Casey lied. "I do believe, Alan, that we are like an old shoe and an old sock. We belong in bed at ten o'clock. We're now two hours past our bedtime."

"Are you sorry we decided not to go to midnight mass?"

"Not at all. Morning mass will be fine. Please, can we open our presents now?"

"Of course. That's what Christmas is all about." Alan smiled as he slid down onto the floor next to Casey.

Alan ripped and gouged at his packages shamelessly. Casey neatly unwrapped each one, folding the paper neatly and saving all the trimmings.

"How wonderful! Such loot! I never expected . . . you didn't miss anything. How can I ever thank you, Alan? This has been the most wonderful Christmas of my life. A mink coat! In my wildest dreams I never thought I would have something so luxurious. Diamond earrings? They must be at least two carats each."

"Three." Alan laughed.

"Good lord, what if someone steals them off my ears? I'll be afraid to wear them."

"Don't be. They're insured. I want you to enjoy everything."

"I have enough new clothes . . . luggage . . . shoes . . . underthings . . . a coat, a jacket, and the keys to a brand-new car. Alan, why? Why did you do this? It's almost as if you're preparing me for something. That's it, isn't it?" The fear in her eyes tugged at Alan's heart.

He reached for both her hands and drew her to him. "I want you to listen to me very carefully. Let me talk until I'm finished, and then you can speak. You must hear me out."

He held her eyes with his, leaving nothing out except his operation. Tears streamed down Casey's cheeks. Twice she tried to jerk free of his hold, but he held tight. "Listen to me, Casey. I'm doing this for you. You have a whole life ahead of you. If I didn't love you, I wouldn't be able to do it. I want to hear you say you believe me. These past two years have been the happiest of my life. Nothing is forever, my dear. It's best, Casey, for both of us."

She didn't understand, would never understand. He didn't want her anymore. He was going to Spain to retire, and he didn't want her along to clutter up his life. She felt instantly ashamed of the thought and cried harder. He had done what Singin asked of him, and now he was going back to his own life. He'd given her two precious years, made her whole again so she could laugh and be happy, to live again. She could deny him nothing, not even this, even though her heart was breaking.

"I understand. I'm so . . . ashamed, Alan. I misinterpreted your feeling for me. What must you think of me for asking you to marry me? I . . . how can I look at you without feeling shame?"

He wanted to cry himself, just the way she was crying, but he held the choking sobs back. Didn't she know what this was doing to him?

"I don't like the name Mary Ashley," Casey said belligerently.

"You will have to grow to like it, my dear. It was you who

354 Fern Michaels

said you wanted a new identity. I've provided it. Tomorrow your new life begins."

"Yes, without you. I can't do it, Alan. I'm not ready," she said in the same belligerent tone.

"You must. You've been well now since October. The longer you stay, the harder it will be for you to take your place in the world. You'll love your new apartment, and I know you're going to like your new job. You'll make friends. Friends, Casey, are very important." Alan said gently. "I want you to get a cat so there will be someone to welcome you when you come home from work."

"A cat is a pretty poor substitute for you, Alan," Casey said sourly. "And another thing, Alan. Don't think for one minute I'm going to pretend to be your illegitimate daughter tomorrow when your friend arrives. If you're ashamed of me, I'll stay in my room. I'm not ashamed of loving you. What do you have to say to that, Doctor?" she snapped.

"I say you're absolutely right. I'll say you're my mistress who is heading for greener pastures tomorrow. How's that?" he asked, his eyes twinkling.

"I think that stinks too. You've broken my heart, Alan. You can't mend a broken heart, even with your skill."

And what about mine? he almost asked. "Time, my dear, heals," he said. "Doesn't it?"

Casey nodded miserably.

"Let's have a toast before we turn in. To your future, and to my life in the sun." Alan clinked his glass against hers. Both glasses smashed simultaneously in the huge fireplace. "Merry Christmas, Mary Ashley."

He felt meaner than Scrooge, the worst villain in the world. God, how he loved her. Casey had gone to the adjoining room, tearful. He'd wanted to bring her here to his bed, one last time, but he knew he would weaken, wouldn't have the courage to send her away. He had to think now about what he was going to tell Marcus Carlin. First, he would say the illegitimate daughter explanation was a joke in poor taste. Damn it, why did he have to explain anything? So there would be no problems for Casey later on. The truth, he thought—always opt for the truth and nothing will go wrong. Marcus didn't need to know details. Casey was his friend, his lover, and he was leaving his estate to her. He wondered, as he dropped off to sleep, if he would regret what he was doing. Suppose the operation proved successful? He could have as much as fifteen years left to his life. Of course he would regret it but that was the price he would pay for Casey's happiness and new life.

CASEY AWOKE, TOTALLY and instantly aware of where she was and what had transpired during the previous hours. She was also aware of how light and bright the room was. She'd been so devastated, she'd fallen into bed without bothering to draw the drapes. The blinding whiteness from outside turned the champagne-colored furnishings to alabaster white, the mauve spread and carpet a pale off-white. She blinked before she buried her face in the pillow.

It was Christmas Day. She squinted at the bedside clock. Nine-thirty. She buried herself deeper into the cocoon of warmth. She didn't ever want to get out of this bed, to face the day. How was she to look at Alan? She felt so humiliated. And Marcus Carlin, how was she to sit at the table with him and carry on a normal conversation? God, what if he and Alan started to talk about Mac? Would she be able to cover her emotions, or would she run screaming from the table? Thank God she hadn't mentioned Mac's name when she had revealed her identity to Alan.

One long leg stretched out and immediately jerked back up at the feel of the cold sheets. She loved sleeping with Alan. He was so warm and toasty, like a teddy bear. But soon he'd be gone. It was obvious she didn't know nearly enough about men. She'd botched up twice so far. Nicole would wring her hands in despair.

She was probably botching up the rest of her life too. Why she was persisting in this new identity was, so far, beyond her. She got dizzy each time she thought about it. But when that dizziness passed, as it always did, she took a hard look at reality. As Casey Adams she'd been a royal bust. Her father didn't want her, didn't love her. Mac had lied to her. And the army said she was dead. If you were dead, you stayed dead. Perhaps as Mary Ashley she would have a chance at happiness. She didn't really hate the name. She'd just said that to Alan in anger. Alan must have gone to a great deal of trouble to fix everything—to be rid of her, she thought miserably. She wondered tearfully what he would do with all her medical records.

Mary Ashley. The name had an Old World sound to it. "I can get used to it," she muttered.

The knock on the door was soft, tentative. "Come in," Casey called, thinking it was the housekeeper.

"So, you are awake," Alan said cheerfully. "I thought we could have our morning coffee by the window. It's so beautiful outside, it takes your breath away. There's not much snow, perhaps two inches or so, and most of it will melt in a few hours, so you'd better hop out of that bed and enjoy it. Hurry, Mary," Alan said deliberately.

Casey swung her legs over the side of the bed. Tying her robe as she went along, she padded in her bare feet to the window. "Ohhh, Alan, it's gorgeous. Look, there are icicles on the window. As children, Nicole and I used to pick them and lick them. Once one stuck to Nicole's tongue and pulled the skin off. She was miserable for weeks and had to go around with her tongue sticking out so it would heal. When it finally did, Sister walloped her bottom soundly."

For a moment she was silent and played with her fingers in her lap. "I'm so sorry about last night. It wasn't my intention to embarrass you and myself. I'm so very grateful, and if I gave you the impression I'm not, I'm sorry. No, no, Alan, let me speak. Since I'm leaving tomorrow, I want to clear the air. I want us to be able to see one another again. In this new job you have arranged for me, they will give me a vacation at some time. If it's all right with you, I'd like to visit you in Spain. Please don't take that away from me. I'm going to need something to hang on to, something to look forward to." Her gaze came upon the snow-filled limbs of the tree outside her window. A maple, she thought, or was it an elm? In the spring and summer it had wonderful big green leaves, which shaded her bedroom like a bright canopy.

"Of course you may visit. It will give me something to look forward to also, as I write my memoirs—which no one but you will ever read." He reached for Casey's hand. "Darling girl, I am not banishing you from my life. We'll be in touch. I cringe now when I think of the telephone bills I'll run up." He hoped for a smile, and when he saw it, he smiled too.

"Okay," she said. "That makes me feel better."

"It's what's best for you, Casey," Alan said softly. "Ah, can you smell our dinner? A feast fit for a king." He laughed, a gentle heartbreaking sound to Casey's ears. "Marcus will view it like that. He rather envisions himself a king. Sometimes it's amusing."

Casey's heart fluttered. "It almost sounds as if you don't care too much for your friend."

"I suppose it does," Alan said ruefully. "However, we go way back together, so I've learned to accept him with all of his faults. I'm sure he feels the same way about me, though I have never been able to see beneath Marcus's surface. He's very easy to like. He's charming, urbane, world-traveled. Women are enamored of him. Or is that an old-fashioned word?"

Casey shrugged, wondering what he would confide next. She was sitting on the edge of her chair, waiting to hear Mac's name. To her disappointment, he changed the subject.

"Tell me, are we still going to St. Patrick's for mass?" he asked her.

"If you like. I forgot to call to see what time mass was. If we miss it, we can sit quietly in the back and light a candle. It's up to you, Alan."

"I think I'd like to go. When we get back, before Marcus gets here, I'd like to put in a call to Singin. He adores Christmas. I sent him a package, and I want to see if he got it in time. It may take me all day to get through. Usually the circuits are busy on holidays. We should have done it last night."

"We'll get through," Casey said soothingly. "Scoot. I'll be ready in thirty minutes." She reached over to kiss Alan lightly on the cheek. "Merry Christmas, Alan, and thank you so much for all the lovely gifts. You didn't tell me how you liked what I gave you," she teased lightly.

"I'm wearing the muffler and gloves when we go to church. I stayed up for a little while last evening to read the book of Keats's poetry. It was beautiful, Casey. I will treasure it. The foot warmer we'll try out this evening after Marcus leaves. He won't stay past five o'clock; he never does. And look," he said, pointing down to his socks. "I'm wearing the argyles you knitted. How long did it take you to make these?"

"Since August. You were right, Alan, knitting has helped my fingers considerably. Typing helps too. They aren't as stiff now. You were right about everything." Casey linked her arm with his as she walked him to the door. "Thirty minutes."

When Casey walked into the study a half hour later, dressed in the hunter-green designer dress, Alan thought she was a vision. To go out she wore the mink coat and covered her golden hair completely with the matching hat. He recalled her depression and her tears when he first met her. His very own Pygmalion.

"I know what you're thinking, Alan," Casey said as they walked down the steps. "You're thinking you created me. Am I right?"

"I never could fool you," Alan said, holding the car door open for her.

"I'll try never to disappoint you. If I falter, it won't be intentional."

"I know that, dear girl," Alan said gently. She was taking the whole thing better than he'd expected. For some reason, he thought more hysterics would be involved. He wanted to hug her close, never to let her go. If it wasn't for the chauffeur, he might have.

Inside the huge cathedral, they knelt and prayed, Alan for life and Casey for happiness. Because they missed mass, they walked up and down the aisles savoring the atmosphere of holiness. Alan dropped bills into every basket and box. They lighted candles in the back and pressed more bills into the small opening.

"Do you really believe lighting candles helps God make decisions?" Alan suddenly said during the ride home. "That's what it boils down to, isn't it?"

Casey did her best to explain her belief. They'd never discussed religion, and now she wondered why. She told him about the votive candles at St. Gabriel's when she was a child, and he immediately promised himself that he would light every single candle at the cathedral tomorrow before he went to the hospital.

Casey was out of the car in a flash, her gloved hands scooping at the snow near the curb. The moment Alan climbed from the car, she pelted him, laughing and giggling. Snowballs in hand, they circled each other warily, laughing shrilly, to the delight of the chauffeur. They were covered with snow, their shrieks of delight echoing up and down the quiet street, when a chauffeur-driven limousine pulled to the curb. Neither Casey nor Alan paid the slightest attention until Marcus Carlin said, "Merry Christmas, Alan." Casey's arm froze in midair as she whirled to see where the voice was coming from.

"Marcus, you're early," Alan said, dropping a snowball to grasp the judge's hand.

"Actually, I'm a half hour late, but obviously you've lost track of the time. It is beautiful out, isn't it? We didn't get any snow in Virginia."

"I'd like to introduce you to my houseguest. Mary, this is my old friend, Marcus Carlin. Marcus, this is Mary Ashley. Come along, let's go inside where it's warm," Alan said in a voice Casey had never heard before. Poor dear, she thought, he's actually flustered.

The whole house smelled like evergreens, Marcus commented.

Casey smiled and excused herself. "You two must have a lot to talk about, and I have some things to attend to." Her voice was as flustered as Alan's.

She closed the door behind her, saw that the maid had already made the bed and carried away the coffee cups. She was trembling so badly, she could hardly light her cigarette. Mac's father here in this house. The odds of that happening had to be one in ten million. And yet it had happened. At some point during his visit, he was bound to mention his son and family. Unless, of course, Alan got all of those questions out of the way before she made her appearance. No, of course not, that was in her past. Why would he think about her at all? She inhaled deeply and blew a steady stream of smoke toward the window. Casey Adams was dead.

How long could she stay up here? she wondered, as she lit a cigarette from the stub of the old one. An hour? Two? More like an hour and a half. Dinner was scheduled for three o'clock. Alan would serve drinks first. That would take at least half an hour. Dinner would last an hour and a half. Coffee would be served in the study. That would take another thirty minutes, possibly forty-five. Another fifteen minutes to say good-bye. By five-thirty Marcus Carlin would be on his way to the Waldorf-Astoria, where he always stayed when he was in New York.

She could get through these next few hours. All she had to do was smile and speak when she was spoken to. She hoped she would remember to respond to the name Mary.

How was she to spend her time until it was the right moment to go downstairs? She'd read all the books on the shelf. She could look through the packet of papers Alan had given her last night. She could go through the mountain of boxes the maids had carried to her room while she was in church. The suitcases had to be packed. That would take some time. The packet beckoned. She lit another cigarette and withdrew the thick sheaf of papers from the manila envelope. The word dossier flashed through her mind. "Hello, Mary Ashley," she said with a sob in her voice. How could all these things be phony? They looked so real. She knew without a doubt her passport would pass muster anywhere in the world. Even her picture was a good one. She noticed the stamps on the first several pages: London, Zurich, Greece, Rome, Paris. Mary Ashley liked to travel. Mary Ashley was a United States citizen. Her home base, when she wasn't traveling, was New York City. She was a graduate of New York University. She looked at her degree with clinical interest. Her birth certificate said she was born in Barnesboro, Pennsylvania. Her family moved to New York City when she was seven years old. She had a small inheritance. She also had tax returns. If she interpreted them correctly, the Internal Revenue Service owed Mary Ashley thirty-seven dollars and twelve cents. She looked at her Social Security card, memorizing the numbers. Her driver's license said she wore glasses. She didn't know how to drive, but as of last evening, she owned a car. The Ford Mustang was listed on the car insurance policy. Alan had thought of everything. Except, she thought wryly, what she'd done for a living. She flipped through the tax returns to see if she had a job description. She burst out laughing when she saw the words teacher and waitress. She'd done that too, back in France. It was really funny. Mary Ashley went through four years of college and waited on tables *after* she graduated.

"I feel like a criminal," she muttered. It's not too late, she told herself, you can still get out of all this. But to what end? So she could be Casey Adams again and confront Mac and call him a liar, tell him he was of the same ilk as Eric Savorone? To pick up her profession? She never wanted to see a hospital again. If she did tell the truth now, it would take years before she could get her army pay, and she'd have to pay back the money they'd paid Nicole on her insurance. There was no reason at all to resume her real identity. Alan had taken care of everything. As of tomorrow morning, she was Mary Ashley.

Casey crossed her fingers and whispered, "Let Mary Ashley be better at handling her life than Casey Adams was at hers."

IN THE STUDY, with the lights of the Frazier fir twinkling festively, Alan sat behind his desk. Marcus sat on the other side. "I don't understand why you're giving me such an argument, Marcus. I'm simply substituting one name for another on this will. It's five minutes out of both of our lives. I want this done *now*. Mary knows nothing about this. My housekeeper and butler and you will be the witnesses. Furthermore, it's not necessary for you to understand *why* I'm doing this. I'm doing it, and that's the bottom line. As you can very well see, I'm in my right state of mind. It's what I want, Marcus," Alan said coolly.

"Very well, Alan, but it goes against my better judgment." He was about to say more until he saw the chiseled look on his old friend's face.

"I want your word, Marcus, when the time . . . comes, be it three days from now or three years from now, that you won't give the girl one speck of trouble. This is to be airtight, and if it isn't, make it that way, *now*."

"You and I know that *I* drew up this will, Alan, though your lawyer will add his signature to it. It's as airtight as it can be. I take umbrage at your statement," the judge said huffily. "What in the world has gotten into you? First you tell me Mary Ashley is your illegitimate daughter, now you tell me she's a good friend and you want to provide for her. This is your business, and I wouldn't be a very good judge or lawyer if I didn't point out to you certain . . . elements. We've said enough. The sooner we get this done, the sooner we can enjoy our holiday. By the way, what are we having for dinner?"

"Duck."

It took exactly twenty-one minutes to change Alan's will. A phone call brought Noah Richards, Alan's lawyer, to the brownstone. He quickly read over and approved the judge's handiwork, intimidated by the presence of a Supreme Court justice. He signed the will, and then the housekeeper, the butler, and Marcus Carlin signed their names, as witnesses, their faces solemn. Richards left immediately afterward.

"Done," Marcus said curtly. "The bequests to the servants stayed the same. All we changed was the principal beneficiary. We're attaching a photo of Mary Ashely to the will. You can rest easy now, Alan. Just out of curiosity, is this why you invited me to have dinner with you today?"

"Of course not," Alan said tartly. "We've been doing this for years. Your coming here merely saved me a trip to Washington. Now, let's you and I have a stiff drink, and you can tell me what's going on in the nation's capital. By the way, how's that son of yours? He must be enjoying his holiday. Children make all the difference. How is it that you aren't playing grandfather today?"

If Alan hadn't turned then to replace the wine bottle on the small bar, he would have seen the scowl that crossed his friend's face as Casey entered the room. When he did turn, what he saw was a look of hopelessness.

"Jennifer gets overexcited. Alice plays down Christmas. One day it's the tree, the next day a big dinner and a present a day. It seems to work well for everyone."

Casey smiled. Alan smiled. The judge remained sober-faced.

"So what did Santa bring you?" Alan boomed.

At first Marcus was tempted to lie. He forced a smile. "Mac gave me a humidor; Alice gave me a new bow and a box of arrows for my collection, and the gift that had Jennifer's name on it was a box of cigars. How about you, Alan?" he asked curiously.

"Absolutely wonderful things. Take a look at these," he said, holding out his foot. "Mary knitted these for me. A book of Keats's poetry that I read until almost dawn. Thoughtful, wonderful presents."

"And you, Miss Ashley, what did Santa bring you?" Marcus asked, sipping at his wine.

"Bonbons." Casey smiled wickedly.

Conversation was easy, even friendly, Casey thought. Over dinner, they discussed the white Christmas, the state of the world, the glamorous Washington parties for which Marcus said he had no stomach.

"How's Mac doing?" Alan asked. "Did he take to Washington politics the way you thought he would? I never did understand why he changed races. Thought he was all set for the governorship. It was an eleventh-hour kind of thing, wasn't it?"

"You know Mac," Marcus said lightly. "He's really into Asian affairs. I'd say he's doing well. He doesn't smile much anymore, if that means anything. Politics leaves very little to smile about," the judge said smoothly.

"I saw the change in him when he got back. I was at the victory celebration, remember? It must have been terrible for him. How's Alice?"

"Wrapped up in Jenny and her husband. Neither Alice nor Mac are into the glamorous social side of Washington you read about in the papers," Marcus said quietly.

"You sound disappointed, Marcus," Alan said.

Alan's needling him, Casey thought in stunned surprise. And, he doesn't really like him. The thought bothered her.

Until this very moment she'd thought Alan didn't have a devious bone in his body. Her stomach lurched. Surely he didn't . . . how could he . . . her stomach lurched a second time. *My God, does he know about Mac?* Did she babble while she was coming out of her numerous bouts of surgery? The thought was so devastating, she dropped her fork on the fine china plate. The sound was like thunder in the quiet dining room. Two pairs of eyes stared at her, one set full of . . . dear God, it wasn't pity, was it? The other set full of . . . speculation and suspicion. She forced a huge smile as her stomach lurched yet again. It *was* pity she read in Alan's eyes. Pity for her. She was convinced he knew. She forced the smile even harder. "Carry on, gentlemen," she said brightly.

"I would like to see Mac more visible, but I think it's safe to say he's leaving his mark. He's dedicated, and that's the backbone of any good public official. Why all this concern about Mac, Alan? It almost sounds as if you're preparing to write a book."

"Actually, I am. I'm going to do my memoirs. Oh, I didn't tell you about my retirement, did I? It starts officially tomorrow. Perhaps memoirs isn't the right word. I rather thought I'd sort of work it in, if you know what I mean. Ah, that doesn't make sense either. I'm going to compile a list of my more memorable patients and do a little history on each of them. You know, my observations, family reactions. I don't expect it to be a runaway best-seller or anything like that. I may never even publish it, but I am going to document it. Take Mac now. When he was in that car accident, and I did the surgery on his ear and eye. I gave that boy a new ear, so, naturally, aside from our personal friendship, I feel a . . . certain closeness to him. I did find it rather strange that neither you nor his wife visited him in the hospital. That's the kind of thing I'm talking about. I want to understand the circumstances of my patients. After the fact, of course. My findings might help some other doctor. Like my student, Singin, in Thailand. We discussed this not too long ago, and he's the one who suggested I do it. I haven't been this excited about a project in a long time," Alan said spiritedly.

"Have you given any thought to the legalities of such a project?" the judge asked tightly.

"Quite a bit, as a matter of fact." Alan beamed. "I expect you'll be the first one who sees the finished product. A definite challenge, wouldn't you say?" Alan pushed his plate away.

You sly old dog, Casey thought. Later, when she was alone, she was going to spend a lot of time thinking about this conversation to try and put the pieces together.

Judge Carlin pushed his plate to the side. He sipped daintily at the fine wine in his glass, his eyes on Alan. "Life is one challenge after another, don't you agree, Miss Ashley?"

"Please, call me Mary. Yes, all of life is a challenge. I, for one, wouldn't have it any other way," she said cheerfully. "Tell me about your granddaughter. I adore little children."

"Early in my career I made a promise to myself not to discuss my family with the media or . . . anyone else for that matter. I'm sorry if that offends you, Mary."

"Not at all. Children have a way of perking up a conversation. This one," she said sprightly, "seems to be getting intense. It is Christmas, after all, and shouldn't we be discussing sugar plums and Broadway plays?"

"I wish I could, but I'm afraid I'm going to have to pass on dessert, Alan. I made a prior commitment to meet a retired colleague at the Algonquin. I don't get here that often, and I try to cram all I can into each visit," the judge said, sliding his chair back from the table.

"And here I thought we'd have hours to visit," Alan said dejectedly.

"Another time." The judge was standing, staring down at Casey. She immediately rose to her feet. She hated to be towered over. The man was imposing enough when he was sitting.

The judge's sudden leave-taking was awkward at best. Something had gone on here, something only Alan and the judge understood. They were both smiling and shaking hands. She was reminded of a shark and a barracuda, but she didn't know which was which. She offered her hand to the judge and was surprised at the limp response. She smiled.

"I wonder if he gave his chauffeur a Christmas present,"

Alan said when the door closed. "Do you believe the man has been sitting out there in front of this house the whole time? It's Christmas Day, for God's sake," Alan said sourly.

"He's your friend, Alan," Casey called over her shoulder. "Let's have dessert and coffee by the fire."

With her legs curled under her on the sofa, she turned to Alan. "Whatever possessed you to invite him here today? It's obvious you don't like him." She hesitated. "You know the truth, don't you? About me, I mean."

Alan nodded, his face full of misery.

"How long have you known?"

"A year, possibly a little longer. With what Singin told me and what I surmised, I was able to put two and two together. You tend to babble when you come out of anesthesia."

"Why this charade, Alan? If you'd asked me, I would have told you everything. He lied to me the same way Eric lied to Lily. I was so gullible. It wasn't that I was trying to protect Mac. It was simply too painful for me to talk about him, and there was no point to naming names. He thinks I'm dead. Tell me why, Alan."

"I was never good at subterfuge. I've been doing my best to do what's best for you. You wanted a new identity. Somewhere, somehow, this will all get out. I feel it in my gut. Marcus can be a very mean adversary. As long as he thinks and believes I'm going to include his family in my memoirs, he'll leave well enough alone."

"This goes beyond me, Alan. How could he possibly . . . he doesn't even know about Casey Adams, and if he did, what could he do? Mac isn't going to announce it to the world. He's probably forgotten all about me. People are generous in their forgiveness of manly indiscretion," she said tartly.

"Mac is very active in Asian affairs because of Lily. I've made it my business to read the papers. I don't know what he hopes to do. I don't know if it's a crusade or guilt. I don't know Mac all that well, as I've told you. I'm sorry, Casey. I've just tried to do what you said you wanted."

"Yes, and I do thank you. This is all wrong, I know it. I'm not Casey Adams anymore. It's that simple. If things fall down around my ears at some time, I'll stand and take my punishment, whatever it may be. You said you understood that I have to start clean and new. I need to hear you tell me you still understand."

"Yes, my dear, I do," Alan said gently. He put his arm around her shoulder, reveling in the warm closeness of her.

Casey snuggled against him. She could talk about Mac now. She could open her heart and let it all pour out. If she wanted to. But wouldn't that just perpetuate the pain of the past? Alan was giving her the means to move on, to begin a new life. She made an instant decision, because she cared dearly for the man sitting next to her. "I'm glad, Alan, because it's been over for me for a long time. I came to terms with it months ago, and I will always be grateful for your support. Now, tell me about those memoirs you're going to write. I want to hear it all."

Alan felt something alien squeeze his heart. He was so grateful for her life. She was everything he thought she was: fine and good and caring. He smiled sadly. "I have to warn you, it's pretty boring stuff."

"I don't care, I still want to hear it. While you're in Spain, I will think about you writing, and feel like I'm close to you."

"Dear girl, I shall never forget you."

"Nor I you, Alan. Everything, don't leave a thing out."

"Let's see, I was twenty-eight when I . . ."

Chapter 18

THE POLISHED BRASS numerals and letters above the double plate-glass doors read 440 PARK AVE. SOUTH. On the doors themselves the gilt lettering read TSN STUDIOS. A bitterly cold wind surged through the naked branches of the trees that lined the street before it rushed at her, almost catapulting her backward. She reached for the huge, polished brass door handle when the marauding wind struck her a second time, pushing her against the glass doors. She whirled to see if it was indeed the wind or someone's hands. There was no one in sight. An omen, she thought. She stepped backward just in time, as the left side of the door swung open and a gaggle of people swept out to the sidewalk. The wind attacked a third time. The girls, three of them, squealed and grasped for the one young man who'd exited the building with them. She was spooked now, uncertain if she should enter the building or not. She wished Alan were here to give her a pep talk, but he was on his way to JFK Airport. She was on her own now for the first time since she'd been injured in Vietnam. Alan would say there was nothing to fear but fear itself. With a burst of confidence she palmed the door and strode through, grateful for the warmth of the lobby.

The black and white register said that TRI STATE NEWS was on the ground floor—101. The polished brass arrows pointed to the right. It seemed simple enough. The buzzer was loud and long. When the door opened, a petite redhead smiled. "May I help you?"

"I'm Mary Ashley," Casey said without a moment's hesitation. "I have an appointment with Steve Harper at ten o'clock."

"I'll ring him." The redhead smiled. "Take a seat. I'm sure he'll be with you in a minute. Would you care for coffee?"

"No, thank you." Casey looked around the small reception area. It was blinding. The walls were hospital white, the chairs black leather and chrome. The small round table was black lacquer with glossy, well-thumbed magazines and a white plastic ashtray sitting on top. Black and white pen-and-ink drawings of the New York skyline dotted the walls. The floor, when she looked down at it, made her dizzy with its black and white squares. She could see her reflection when she bent over. Obviously this was not a room for one to get comfortable in. Waiting rooms, as a rule, were restful places decorated in pale earth tones. This room made one's eyeballs stand at attention. She couldn't wait to get out of it.

Casey felt a head rush when the shiny black door opposite her opened. The man who came through it was bigger than life, she thought, a giant with a Neanderthal face that would frighten little children. His eyes twinkled and his smile was engaging. One paw-like hand shot out. She'd seen tree limbs the same size as his arm. His voice was low and deep, just the way she thought it would be. She felt completely intimidated.

"I'm Steve Harper. Obviously, you're Mary Ashley. I like the name Mary. My mother's name is Mary. I have a cousin and a sister named Mary too. Good name," he said, bobbing his monstrous head up and down. "Come along, Mary. I bet you can't wait to get out of this horror we call a waiting room. We decorated it this way on purpose so people wouldn't want to hang out here." He was through the door before Casey could get off the chair. She had to run down the long corridor to keep up with him. When he stopped, he actually created a breeze. Casey felt a smile tug at the corners of her mouth.

"What's so funny?"

"I don't think I ever saw anyone as . . . tall as you," she blurted.

"Then I'll have to introduce you to my father. Come along so I can go through the formality of interviewing you. You'll be working for me, you know." Casey nodded.

Casey looked around the forty-by-fifty-foot room with a

mixture of horror and awe. It seemed made of three ingredients: part circus, part jungle, and part Steve Harper. She walked around, careful not to disturb the sawdust on the floor. The longest wall of the room was dotted with real banana trees in huge tubs of dark brown soil. A chimp swung from tree to tree, doing flips and somersaults in midair before he secured his perch, all the while making ear-splitting sounds. He wore a red vest and a gold chain around his neck. The color matched the red plumage of the parrot who had her own perch between the last two banana trees. She squawked her disapproval as the chimp shimmied down the last tree to land on a crate of bananas in various stages of ripeness. The opposite wall was filled with colorful posters from Barnum & Bailey. There was a stuffed elephant, and a stuffed giraffe that had its nose pressed into a high wire, on which was a make-believe aerialist in pink tights and satin ballet shoes.

The sound of a motor broke the stillness. Casey looked around wildly, aware that she was standing on a set of tracks that housed a motorized miniature car driven by a stuffed clown.

"Watch this." Harper cackled.

Casey watched as colorful red balls shot up from the bottom of the car. The chimp scurried about trying to catch them, while the parrot screeched, either in happiness or misery.

"It's all mechanical," he said, waving a small black box for her to see.

She nodded before her eyes found the giant fish tank set amid flora and fauna on the smaller wall. Hundreds of fish swam about lazily in the warm, well-lighted water. The matching wall at the opposite end of the room held a small desk, a chair, and two filing cabinets, all of which were practically hidden behind a red-and-white-striped awning with colorful tassels. The miniature car still circled the room, red balls popping in every direction.

"Well, what do you think?" Harper asked, his voice curious.

"It's . . . interesting," Casey said honestly.

"That's the usual reaction. You see, I produce the *Noonday News*, which is depressing. Drugs, crime, murder, you name it.

This is New York City, so we have it all. Don't get me wrong. I like producing; it's what I do best. But it gets to me, so this is, well, I guess you can call it my lair. By the way, the chimp is Izzy and the parrot is Gertie. Izzie can fetch, rub my feet, and he never leaves this room unless I take him on a leash, which I do twice a day. Animals need fresh air. You'll be working in here. I'll scrounge up another desk for you from somewhere.

"All you need is a few of your own plants and a picture or two on the wall and it will seem like home," Steve went on. "You'll be doing mostly legwork and research. Later I'll find an application for you to fill out." He looked around vaguely, as though he thought it would materialize out of thin air. "Alan Carpenter told me pretty much what I need to know. Great guy, isn't he? So, Mary Ashley, tell me about yourself."

She was on, as they said in show business. Everything she rehearsed on the way to the studio flew from her mind. She felt a warm flush creep up her neck into her cheeks. "I take direction well. I'm willing to learn, and I'm dependable. I don't mind working late."

"No, no, I know all that. Tell me about you. You've seen who I am." He waved his arm to indicate the room. "Tell me about Mary Ashley. What do you like? What are your hopes and dreams? What do you do when you get off work? Do you like to cook? We're going to be working together, and it will help if I know something about you."

For some reason she wanted to tell this big, burly man the truth. She searched her mind for the facts Alan had written out for her. She spoke softly, her eyes on the twinkling ones assessing her. She wondered how she was measuring up. "I'm a fair cook. I'm partial to French food. I like kitchens and bathrooms. Decoratingwise, I mean. Someday I hope to have my own house with a yard, and a beautiful kitchen with herbs growing on the windowsill, and a hanging green plant in the window. Maybe a window seat so I can watch the rain. I like rain. Fog too," she said with a catch in her voice. "I really like fog. Once . . . I . . . tried to catch some. I guess that sounds kind of silly."

Harper grinned. "Not to me it doesn't. I try to catch it all the time. You're talking to the biggest kid I know."

Casey smiled and immediately felt at ease. "I didn't have . . ." She'd been about to say the happiest of childhoods, but that was part of her real background. This wasn't going to be as easy as she thought. "Too many friends growing up. I tend to snuggle in at the end of the day. I haven't really made any friends here in this city. I'm sure Alan told you I've been pretty much out of it for the past two years, since my accident. That will change, of course," she said confidently. "I like music—the Beach Boys and the Beatles. As for my hopes and dreams, well, right now, I'm just glad to be alive. I hope to be the best at what I do, whatever that may be. As for dreams, I've found that dreams have a way of turning into nightmares. One day at a time is the way I'm living these days. If that bothers you . . ." She let the statement hang in the air.

"Not at all. You don't think I arrived at all this," he waved his arms about the room, "overnight, do you? It took awhile. I think we'll get on just fine. I've got to leave you now. I have to get the feed-in ready for the news. This is the busiest time of the day for us. I'll introduce you to Danny, and he'll show you the ropes. I do want you to watch the show today. You can stay, can't you?" She nodded. "Alan explained about the salary and everything, didn't he?" She nodded again. "We have a good benefits package," he called over his shoulder. She nodded again, forgetting Harper had his back to her.

The rest of the day was a total blur. When Casey walked out of the studio at five-fifteen, she felt like she'd done a full day in a MASH hospital. In the taxi ride uptown to her new apartment, she leaned back and closed her eyes. All the new terminology she'd learned today ran together in her mind. She'd taken notes and had them in her purse to review later in the evening. She thought about all the people she'd met, all friendly, all hurried, all generous with their expertise. Steve was the executive producer, Morey Baker the producer. There were also directors, editors, a graphics chief, and assorted aides, at least a half dozen of them. She still didn't know how everything was so synchronized. Everyone seemed to know what they were doing except the anchorman, Matthew Cassidy, who was a study in slow motion.

The computer terminals confused her, as did the news wire-service printers. She'd never seen so many telephones in one area. She couldn't remember now what a voice-over or a show-and-tell story was. What she did remember was that she didn't like Matthew Cassidy. At all. Throughout the program, she kept one eye on him and one on the monitor. She thought him a stuffed shirt. Pompous, with an inflated ego. He was good, though, with the TelePrompTer; he hardly seemed to look at it. He really did appear to stare out directly at his audience. One of the aides told her the pages of copy he constantly turned over were just a precaution in case something went awry with the TelePrompTer. She probably could have handled Cassidy, and would never have given him a second thought, if she hadn't overheard him say to one of the writers, "What is she, another one of Harper's charity cases?"

She'd fled to the bathroom and with shaking hands smoked a cigarette. That's *exactly* what she was—a charity case. And she would remain a charity case until . . . what? Until she proved herself indispensable. Work hard, work hard, work hard, work hard, her mind shrieked as she paid off the taxi driver and headed for the elevator that would take her to her new apartment on the sixteenth floor. This was hers, compliments of Alan. As long as she paid the rent. In order to pay the rent, she had to keep her job.

This was her first look at the apartment. She knew that the housekeeper and butler had brought all her things over in the morning and had probably unpacked them. The housekeeper and butler were staying on in the brownstone for a few extra days, according to Alan, to close up and put dustcovers on all the furniture. She assumed, although he hadn't said, that they would join him in Spain. Where else would they go? They were old, and Alan did like his comfort. He wouldn't look at it that way though. He'd want to take care of them. They'd been together for years and years. They all belonged together. She missed him already. She would miss him more in the days to come.

She did look around now and was pleased with what she saw. The apartment was of a nice size, and if one didn't look out the windows to see other windows and rooftops, it would be fine. The couches that formed a half circle were wheat-colored, deep and comfortable; the two recliners and ottomans on each side of the window overlooking the rooftops were the color of dark café au lait. A small entertainment center that held a television, stereo, radio, an assortment of books, and a deep brown center carpet completed the living room. It looked spacious because it was uncluttered. She closed the sheer basket-weave draperies, but could still see twinkling lights in the distance.

The bedroom was neat, almost spartan, the only color added by a flowered spread and matching drapes. The floor was polished wood, the closet doors hung with mirrors. Again, no clutter of any kind. The second bedroom was empty and painted a soft shade of blue. The bathroom and kitchen were neat and clean, but archaic. The three security bolts on the entrance door pleased her. She was safe, cut off from the outside world, while she was here.

She poked around, opening closets and drawers. There were blankets and linens in the closet, along with soap and cleaning supplies. The dresser held her personal things, the closet all of her clothes. Her luggage was piled on the top shelf of the foyer closet. In the refrigerator were juice, milk, eggs, bread, and coffee. The cabinet overhead was filled with soup, crackers, tuna, assorted canned vegetables, and several boxes of macaroni. On the kitchen table was a receipt for the garage rent as well as the keys to the new Mustang. Her bankbook showed a three-thousand-dollar balance and a note from Alan saying she could stay rent free for a full year. The note was to be given to the company that managed the building.

Everything was taken care of.

It was day one of Casey's new life as Mary Ashley.

Chapter 19

VALENTINE'S DAY. HER *real* birthday.

Casey looked around her jungle-circus-television habitat with watery eyes. She was almost used to the huge room now, after six weeks. She wished she had somebody to share the day with, somebody to talk to. Somebody besides Izzy, who perched on her desk with a fat red crayon and colored in his Maggie and Jiggs coloring book. Or Gertie, looking on with sharp eyes.

Izzy was coloring within the lines now, thanks to her patience. He'd calmed down a lot since she moved in, bringing her Coca-Colas from the small refrigerator, depositing his banana peels in the trash instead of on the floor, and remaining always close to her. Together they watched the noon news so she could observe Matthew Cassidy. It was mandatory, Steve said, for her to familiarize herself with the on-camera show.

Izzy didn't like the dapper, slick newsman. The monkey hopped about, yanked at his ears, hid his eyes when the camera moved in for a close shot, and spit angrily when the effeminate-looking face smiled into the camera. Casey herself was reminded of a young shark with too many teeth. Whenever Casey grimaced or laughed at something the newsman did on camera, Izzy would hop on her desk, scratch his hairy belly, and screech. Then he would throw both long, hairy arms around her neck and kiss her wetly on the cheek.

Izzy was her friend, her only friend. She would have taken him home with her at the end of the day, but Steve forbade it. Secretly, Casey suspected the producer might be jealous of her affection for the chimp.

Casey looked at her watch. Five minutes to airtime, time to turn on the television. She pointed to the set and waited for Izzy to go through his usual routine. First he put the red crayon back in the coffee can, closed his coloring book, buttoned his tartan vest, then made his way to the set in the corner. He showed his teeth in displeasure when Cassidy appeared on the screen. Casey lowered her head to hide her smile. She raised her head when she heard Cassidy say, "Today over twelve thousand South Vietnamese troops who had gathered in the northern province of Quangtri crossed into Laos. Some were transported in the early phases of the attack by United States helicopters."

She hated to hear him discuss Vietnam. She knew his off-the-air views. She continued to listen, her eyes filling with tears. "Supported by American planes and artillery, thousands of South Vietnamese troops crossed into Laos in an attempt to cripple the line down the Ho Chi Minh trail." His words were like a slap in the face, reminding Casey of all the letters and notes Mac had sent her from the trail.

Cassidy's voice droned on, and Casey's tears dried. He did an update on the Los Angeles earthquake that killed fifty-one persons. From the quake he swung into a short bio of J. C. Penney and the effect his death would have on the sixteen hundred retail stores he'd founded. Before he signed off on the weather, he smirked into the camera and invited his listeners to Alexander's on the sixteenth of the month, when he would judge a "hot pants" contest. Casey gagged. Izzy kicked the television before he turned it off.

"The guy's a jerk," Casey muttered as she opened the brown paper bag she carried her lunch in. She set out a ham sandwich, an apple, two cupcakes, and candles. Izzy would get half the sandwich, half the apple, and a whole cupcake. Today was special. Normally, she didn't share her lunch with Izzy, because he'd discovered the licorice sticks she kept in her drawer, and now he always refused other food until she handed one over. He was company; it was that simple.

She felt relieved now that the television set was off. She'd view it again later, right before she left work, and make notes.

Now it was time for her lonely birthday party. She was lighting the candles on the two small cakes when Steve walked in. A flood of guilt raced through Casey as she wondered how she was going to explain the cake and candles.

"Your birthday is today, Valentine's Day?" Steve asked, his jaw dropping.

"No." The lie came to her lips so easily, she felt guilty all over again. "I stopped by the bakery this morning and they were giving them away. I thought . . . Izzy would enjoy the candle . . ."

"I always thought it would be neat to have a birthday on a holiday," Steve said boyishly. "Imagine being born on Christmas. Do you suppose you'd get double the presents or get left out?" he asked, his face full of concern.

Casey laughed. Izzy blew out both candles. They watched as he peeled the wax paper from the cupcake. He stuffed the entire cupcake in his mouth, then clapped his hands. "Probably double. I'd want all of mine wrapped in Christmas paper though." Casey smiled. "Red and green, silver and gold paper," she said with a catch in her voice, remembering the past Christmas. "How about you, Steve?" They were friends now, on a first-name basis.

"I'd want my birthday presents wrapped in blue paper, with sailboats, and maybe red with trains on it. I'd want to know the difference. Just in case the relatives cheated me. Terrible, huh?"

Casey shrugged. She liked this boyish side of the big man. She always felt good when she was around him, and over the past few weeks she'd been gravitating toward him at every chance she got. There was something warm and wonderful, safe and secure about Steve Harper. For days now she'd been diddling with the idea of inviting him to her apartment for dinner, but so far she hadn't gotten up the nerve to actually ask him.

"How'd Cassidy do today?" he asked curiously. He asked every day, and paid careful attention to her response. Izzy belched loudly and then preened much the way the anchorman did. "Duly noted," Steve said, rubbing the chimp's head.

"Is he really going to judge a 'hot pants' contest?" Casey asked, trying not to giggle.

"It was his idea. He said his viewers need to see the . . . human side of him." He guffawed then, so loud Izzy leaped into one of the banana trees, chittering a mile a minute. "It's a piece of fluff and the women will eat it up. We're giving him two minutes. Look, the guy can be a charmer. Personally I think he looks like he's embalmed, but women like his type of looks for some reason. As you must have noticed, we go by the sure thing around here. By the way, how'ya doing, Mary? Is it getting any easier? Is this place big enough for you? You don't mind Izzy, do you?" Steve asked anxiously.

Casey cut her cake in half. Someone was sharing her birth-day, even if he didn't know it. "Fine. Yes. Yes. No."

"Jeez, now I can't remember what I asked you. In other words, everything is okay?"

"Everything is fine, Steve. I hope you're satisfied with my work?"

"Satisfied! You work like a Trojan. I don't know what I did before you got here. Listen, are you busy for dinner? There's something I'd like to run by you. It's probably a cockamamie idea, but I like to think I hit on something good once in a while. Cassidy hates my ideas," he said forlornly. "I'm just the boss around here."

Busy for dinner? She thought about Campbell's soup and tuna sandwiches, her usual dinner. Tonight she'd planned on washing her hair and giving herself a manicure, the single girl's idea of a fun evening in New York City. "I'm not busy. I'd love to have dinner with you."

"Great!" Steve said, smacking his huge hands together. "Let's leave from here. I won't keep you out too late, and I'll put you in a cab to go home. I know this great Mexican restaurant not far from the studio. They put beer in their chili. Meet me in the lobby at seven, okay?"

Casey nodded. She had a date. She smiled. "Okay."

She was nice, Steve thought, but then he'd thought her nice the first day he'd met her. She was a hard worker, something he required in all his employees. Mary worked harder than most, and she was usually the last one to leave. She always tidied up and made sure Izzy was secure for the night. He hadn't realized until just a few days ago how much he had come to depend upon her. He made a mental note to drop Alan a note to thank him for sending such a fine person.

He'd wanted to ask Mary out for a long time, but every time he was about to approach her, he had changed his mind. There was something in her eyes, something he wasn't ready to deal with. It was stupid, he knew, but he felt Mary Ashley was nursing a broken heart, and he had his own bruised and battered heart to deal with. If there was one thing he didn't want, it was to ask a woman out and then commiserate all evening about past loves.

He'd almost married Julia last spring, and he would have if she hadn't called it off at the eleventh hour. Julia had called him at three in the morning on their wedding day to tell him she'd decided she couldn't spend the rest of her life with a man who was so *totally* boring that she wanted to scream. *And*, she didn't want to have hairy children. Boring he could handle. Hairy children he couldn't.

The day of the wedding, he'd gone to a pet store and bought Izzy and had then driven to Julia's house. Like a fool he'd demanded his ring back and said a whole bunch of stupid, asinine, sophomoric things, all the while holding Izzy in his arms. She'd gasped and gargled and spit and snarled at him. Finally, she threw his ring in the bushes. Izzy found it and handed it to him. He'd looked at the chimp and said woefully, "You don't ever judge a book by its cover." Julia was a jerk, and he was a jerk for going with her and tying up three long years of his life.

Since then he hadn't been able to get back into the dating pattern. Girls were and always had been a mystery to him. Mary Ashley seemed different. At least she hadn't turned him down for dinner. Of course it wasn't a *real* date, but more of a business meeting.

She liked Izzy too, and Izzy liked her. Right there was half the battle. He felt good until he caught sight of himself in one of the glass partitions. He was too big, too ugly, too . . . *hairy*. "Shit!" he said succinctly. Jesus Christ, it was just a business meeting and getting a bite to eat. If it was a *real* date, he'd take her someplace fancy like the Russian Tea Room, not some dumb Mexican restaurant where they put beer in the chili.

God, he hated working on Sundays. But news was news, and it didn't matter what day of the week it was. He had to remember to ask Mary how she felt about working on Sundays. He wasn't sure, but he thought she worked seven days a week just the way he did, the way they all did. Jesus, had he told her she was supposed to rotate her days, to take time off during the week? For the life of him, he couldn't remember. No damn wonder Julia what's-her-name had dumped him. What the hell kind of husband would he have made? He would never be home to see his hairy children, much less get to know them.

Steve sat down and reached for his eleventh cup of coffee. It tasted like the eleventh cup in the pot too. He grimaced and pushed it away.

"Matt, would it do any good for me to kick your ass right now? How many times do I have to tell you not to smirk on camera? You look like a real asshole when you do it. Your timing was off. Your tie was crooked, and your goddamn nose was shiny. I don't want to hear any of this crap about today being Sunday. You have a fucking contract, and it's all spelled out. And your voice wasn't serious enough when you reported on the Vietnam situation," Steve exploded.

"No one watches Sunday noon news," Cassidy whined. "They're either out to brunch or reading the Sunday paper. Every Sunday you pick on me, and I'm getting fed up with it."

"*Really*," Harper said, leaning across the table. "Why don't we take a vote here and see if the others agree with my assessment of today's newscast. Am I on the money or not?" There was a chorus of ayes. Cassidy tried to shrink into his seat. "We're a team here. Just because you're in front of the camera means diddly to the rest of us. There are thousands of pretty faces out there who would kill for your job. This is the last time I'm telling you, Matt. Get with it. We do it my way, or I take my marbles and go home."

"The ratings," Matthew Cassidy bleated.

"Fuck the ratings," Steve muttered. "So we fall off, lose some money until we build up a new face. You are expendable, Matt.

You're too much of a prima donna. The papers are taking jabs at you, in case you haven't noticed. Now, let's get down to business. I have an idea . . .''

It was a cellar restaurant. It smelled delicious, Casey thought, as Steve helped her off with her coat.

In a voice that was as big as himself, Steve whispered, "The owner of this place looks like Pancho Villa. Great cook. It's small, but cozy. You can't beat the food, and they give you so much you can't eat it all. I come here every couple of weeks. It takes that long for my insides to heal after a meal.''

Casey sat down on a spindly chair at a table covered in red-checkered oilcloth. She giggled when Steve set the plastic rose covered with dust under the table. "What's that smell?" Casey asked.

"Frying chili peppers. Great, eh? Makes my mouth water . . . Two bottles of beer," he called across the room to no one in particular.

A pretty waitress with an off-the-shoulder white blouse and a flowered skirt sashayed over to their table. Her skin was the color of honey, her teeth pearl-white, her eyes dark and inviting. "Ah, señor, you bring a guest . . . finally, to my father's restaurant. It is an honor for us. Is it some special event? My father says your newsman today looked like the back end of his grandfather's horse.'' She laughed gaily, her white teeth showing off her bronzed skin to perfection.

"Tell your father he's right. No, this is not a special occasion, but while we're on the subject, when are you going to get engaged?" To Casey he whispered, "She takes liberties with our friendship. She's pretty, but no man would want her. She's too fresh.''

"Señor Harper, the men are lining up around the corner for my hand. My father says none of them are good enough for me. What am I to do?" She giggled.

"Keep right on sneaking out and down the fire escape the way you've been doing for the past three years." Steve laughed.

"My thoughts exactly.'' Elena laughed.

"Aren't you going to take our orders?"

"Why? We only serve one thing. My father already knows you are here so it will be out in a minute." To Casey she said, "I think he's trying to impress you. This is a humble restaurant." She flashed another wide smile.

"Yeah, right. And they own half of Sutton Place," Steve teased.

"I never had Mexican beer before," Casey said. "Is it strong?" Steve shrugged. Elena set down a pitcher of ice water and glasses. A moment later she was back with two bowls of chili sprinkled with chopped onions.

It was ten o'clock before Casey's tongue, teeth, and lips returned to normal. She'd made six trips to the bathroom, to Harper's amusement. She alone had consumed the first pitcher of water. He'd lost track of the glasses of beer both of them put away. He was feeling no pain; in fact, he was having a hell of a good time. Mary Ashley was a great dinner companion. He hadn't had this good of a time since Julia had dumped him.

"It's getting late, Steve. You said you wanted to discuss something with me." She waited, not knowing what to expect. She'd actually celebrated her birthday, first with Izzy and then with Steve. She felt giddy, half drunk.

Steve slapped at his forehead. "That's right, I did. I've been having such a good time, I almost forgot. We'll have to do this again. Well, what I mean is, we'll go out to dinner again, but not necessarily here. You know, a . . . date." He held his breath waiting to see her reaction.

Casey smiled. "I'd like that."

"You would?" Steve asked, feeling suddenly stupid.

"Uh-huh."

"Ah, great. We'll . . . ah, I'll check my schedule and we'll . . . *do it*."

"Okay." Casey smiled.

"Yes, it is okay." Steve grinned. "Listen, remember the piece we did back in January, right after you came to work for us? The one on Coco Chanel? I think we did it January eleventh, the day after she died? For our 'Show-and-Tell' segment."

"I remember. It was quite good. She once made a dress especially for me. I never got to wear it. It was a beautiful sapphire-blue color. She was a true trendsetter," Casey said quietly.

"The station had so many calls after we aired, I couldn't believe it. Wherever did you come up with that bit about her calling her perfume No. 5 because a fortune teller told her it was her lucky number?"

Nicole had told her that, and without thinking, she'd added it to the research she'd compiled for Steve's "Show-and-Tell" segment. Of course, she couldn't tell him that. Palms up in the air, she said lightly, "Who knows, someplace in all the research I did on her. I thought it was a good piece too."

"Well, what do you think about this, then? Two minutes, three times a week. A 'Show-and-Tell' about newsworthy and noteworthy people who are alive, not dead. Six minutes total. One film clip of Cassidy and the person, a thirty-second clip. Along those lines. I thought we could compile a list of possible candidates. I want you to do the research. I'm prepared to hire a part-timer to assist you if you agree. A good profile is what I'm looking for. You know, meaty, with a script that crackles. Something that will make people want to tune in and stay tuned. What do you think, Mary?"

"It sounds . . . like a lot of work. I think the idea is wonderful. I like hearing about famous people."

"That's just it, Mary, I'm not sure I want famous. If some guy grows the biggest tomato in the state of Pennsylvania, I want that. If some kid rides his bike a hundred miles and doesn't get a flat tire, I want that. *Real* people. I guess what I'm trying to say is I want people who in some way make a difference. I *don't* want movie stars. I realize it's going to be a lot of work in the beginning, but once segments start to air, we'll get all kinds of leads and possibilities. Then it will be a simple matter of weeding out the prospects and doing the interviews. I want you to think about it and we'll talk tomorrow. No, we won't. You're off tomorrow. Tuesday. Lunch. I'll bring some hot dogs from the vendor on the corner. Izzy loves hot dogs. Is that okay with you?"

"It sounds good. I think I should go home now. The beer is making me sleepy."

"I'll put you in a cab. I enjoyed this evening, Mary. You're sure you think this is a good idea?"

"I think it's a wonderful idea. Don't the others think so? What does Mr. Cassidy say?"

"I haven't told the others. I wanted your reaction. I'll spring it on them at next Sunday's meeting."

Casey blinked at the size of the tip Steve left for Elena.

"It's for her trousseau," he said with a wink.

What a kind man he is, she thought. Just like Alan, in many ways.

"I'll see you on Tuesday," Steve said lightly as he closed the door of the cab.

"I enjoyed dinner. Thank you, Steve."

All the way home she hummed the birthday song under her breath. All in all it was one of her nicer birthdays.

Chapter 20

OUTSIDE THE APARTMENT on Seventy-ninth Street, the wind howled and rain sluiced against the windows. It was Wednesday, March 24, Casey's day off.

Casey liked having a day off in the middle of the week, it broke up the long work hours. She was now putting so much time in at the station that she had no time to call her own. It was a good thing, she thought, that she wasn't involved in a relationship. Even the dinner date with Steve hadn't materialized. He had less free time than she did, and she knew for a fact that he often slept at the station on a folding cot kept in the office closet for emergencies.

Her day had been planned. She was going to shop for some new spring clothes, fill her pantry, dust up the apartment, and if time permitted, after she took a nap, take in a movie. Now, however, with the rain, none of her plan would work out, unless she wanted to get soaked and catch cold.

Every lamp and overhead light in the apartment was lit in her attempt to keep the darkness outside. She cringed when an angry slash of rain slapped against the living room window. She remembered the monsoon rains in Vietnam. She started to shake. She clasped both her hands in an effort to regain calmness. Sometimes it worked when she talked to herself or dialed Luke's number. It was almost a game now, calling Luke after one of her bad dreams, listening to his calm voice. She could tell that Luke was intrigued by the things he said to the silence on her end of the line. Sometimes he talked for as long as three minutes before he hung up. She always wrote down what he said, immediately after replacing the receiver in the cradle. In a

minute she would reach for the sheaf of papers and read them
over and over. Actual phone calls were for bad dreams. The
notes were for second-hand comfort during the bad times, when
something triggered a painful memory. Her head was pounding, and for a second she thought she was going to throw up.
She grappled with the papers in the desk drawer. She took a
huge, deep breath. Damn, it wasn't working. She ran to the
bathroom, but she managed to keep down the coffee and toast
she'd eaten earlier.

She paced. It had been three years since her ordeal in Vietnam. She shouldn't be feeling like this. If only Alan were here
to talk to, but he hadn't seen fit to answer any of her letters.
She'd sent one every week. She was out of his life now, and she
simply didn't want to be bothered, she told herself.

Lately she'd toyed with the idea of calling the foundation
Mac Carlin had set up for Vietnam veterans. She'd read about
it a few months ago. The Vietnam Veterans Foundation. She
had called information for the telephone number and had even
drafted a letter, but she hadn't carried through. She remembered so clearly writing the letter and then shoving it in the
desk. At that precise moment she'd said aloud, "I should go
back. Maybe if I go back all of this will go away." She'd gone
into such an unholy tizzy then that she'd actually blacked out,
but when she came to, the thought had still been with her. Since
then the thought was always with her.

She thought about Alan again. She ached with rejection.
How could he cut her off so completely? She tried to make her
mind understand that Alan had done his job. He'd saved her
life, made her whole again, and moved on with his life.

At the station they had constantly spoken of the "bottom
line." Everyone, they said, had a bottom line. Hers, she knew,
was the open acknowledgment that she needed someone. On
that last day, Alan had told her to get a cat. She hadn't gotten
the animal, but now she wished she had.

She continued to pace, circling the apartment, staring at the
few possessions she'd accumulated in the past few months, little
things to brighten her new home. In an antique store she'd
spotted a fat, happy buddha made from teakwood. Every time

she looked at the silly expression on its face, she smiled. Now it rested in one of the dark corners on a pedestal next to a luscious green fern that she watered and spritzed every Sunday. On her coffee table a music box that played "As Time Goes By" rested next to a potted Japanese garden. She watered the small garden once a month and played the music box every day. It always made her sad. In a fabric store on Second Avenue, she'd purchased a pile of pillows in rainbow colors, just like Maline's back in Thailand, to add color to the quiet living room.

On her days off she'd scoured art galleries until she found, she thought, the duplicate prints of the Moulin Rouge pictures that were in her father's house. She had three now. They hung on the wall over the sofa; the vibrant colors of the flower stalls were the same as those in her pillows. Home.

It was still too quiet, even with the rain lashing and gouging at her windows. She turned on the television and the stereo. Now she had too much noise, but she didn't care. Tears rolled down her cheeks. She sniffed, blew her nose and wiped at her eyes. Anger at her situation engulfed her, raging through her until she couldn't think. She lashed out with her foot, kicking at the coffee table, toppling the music box and the Japanese garden. She flung the colorful pillows in every direction, and sobbed as she threw ashtrays across the room and heaved magazines at the television set. When her anger was spent, she dropped down to the floor and cried great, hacking, gulping sobs. She wondered if she was having a nervous breakdown, if this strange behavior would continue, and for how long.

She was calm now, her tears gone. She reached for the telephone directory, and in the Yellow Pages found a long list of psychiatrists. How was she to choose? She closed the book.

Fear drove her as she searched in the hall closet for her raincoat, plastic boots, and umbrella. She was on the street heading for First Avenue, her destination, a pet store. She thought she was crying again, but she couldn't be sure if her face was covered with tears or raindrops.

She turned out to be the only customer in the shop. The owner sat behind a desk with a sheaf of papers in front of him. He waved lazily to indicate she should look around. "Call me if you need me." His voice, Casey thought, was as lazy-sounding as he appeared.

Casey bypassed the tropical fish tanks, the bird cages, the racks of dog, and cat and bird toys. Then she came to the animal cages. She peered into each one, searching for what she hoped would be the perfect animal to comfort her. Tiny pink tongues licked at her fingers. Soft yips of pleasure pleased her. Three times she walked up the puppy aisle. She walked up and down the kitten aisle four times. Cat or dog? Both? Two? Yes, two, she decided, for they would be lonely while she was at work. She craned her neck to look over the rack of animal toys.

On her sixth trip up and down both aisles, she finally made her decision. She motioned to the owner. "What do you call this dog?" she asked.

"She's a Yorkie Poo. Six weeks. She just came in yesterday, and she'll be gone in a few days. She'll make a wonderful pet. I always recommend female dogs for women. You probably won't believe this, but Yorkies are great little watchdogs." Casey nodded.

The moment the dog was placed in her hands, she knew she had a friend. She was so tiny she could fit in Casey's raincoat pocket. She cradled the dog to her cheek. She felt so warm and so *alive*.

Holding the puppy against her cheek, she meandered down the kitten aisle until she came to the last cage, where four kittens romped with a ball of string.

"That one," she said, pointing to a yellow tiger cat.

"Good choice." The owner beamed. The Yorkie licked at the kitten, who playfully swiped at her with one tiny paw. "They'll get along, contrary to what you may have heard about dogs and cats. The kitten is just five weeks old, so the Yorkie will be boss, you'll see. What else will you need?"

Casey shrugged helplessly. "I never had an animal before. You tell me."

"Two kennels, two beds, leashes, food, a few toys, their own blankets, litter box and litter. It's almost like outfitting a room for a new baby," the owner said happily.

"Can you deliver?" Casey asked anxiously.

"Of course. If you like, I can drive you home with the animals. I'll close the store for a little while. Do you live close by?"

"Seventy-ninth, around the corner really. I appreciate it. By the way, do these animals have names?"

"Of course. That's the first thing I do when an animal comes in here. To me they aren't real until they have names. The Yorkie is Samantha. Sam, for short. I thought the name would make up for her size, which, by the way, won't go past eight pounds. The kitten is Gracie. Of course if you want to change the names, you can, but I found that once an animal responds to a name, it's hard to get them used to a new one. It's up to you. These little beauties are going to give you many hours of pleasure," he said. He selected rubber toys and leashes from the rack.

With the animals in their respective kennels, Casey wrote out a check for nine hundred dollars. She blanched at the amount but somehow managed to keep her hand steady when she wrote the check. The Yorkie, the owner said, was a pedigree and worth seven hundred dollars.

It took the owner, Casey, and the doorman to carry everything to Casey's apartment on the sixteenth floor.

The moment Casey was alone with the animals, she let them free of their kennels. They yipped and squeaked as they streaked about the apartment, to Casey's delight, piddling every time they stopped to catch their breaths. Casey felt like an indulgent mother as she cleaned up mess after mess. At five minutes to noon both animals collapsed one on top of the other in sleep. Casey thought it the cutest thing she'd ever seen. Her good mood soured when she wondered if the two pets would exclude her from their affection. Not likely, she decided, since she would be the one who fed them.

Casey was on page seven of the dog manual she'd purchased when Matthew Cassidy's face flashed on the screen. "And now the *Noonday News!*" She listened with half an ear, her eyes on the manual, when she heard Cassidy's voice turn somber. "We've just learned that in the face of heavy communist resistance, South Vietnam was forced to end prematurely its military operation against enemy supply lines in Laos. The withdrawal comes only forty-four days after South Vietnamese troops, supported by American air power and artillery fire, swept into Laos in an attempt to disrupt the supply line, known as the Ho Chi Minh trail. We're told that at the height of the operation, more than twenty thousand South Vietnamese troops were in Laos. South Vietnam suffered heavy casualties, one thousand, one hundred forty-six killed. The United States lost eighty-nine helicopters, and fifty-one Americans were killed . . . In London, Sir Laurence Olivier takes his seat today in the House of Lords . . ."

The despair was back again, so deep and dark, Casey thought she would black out. Would it ever be over? Would people ever understand? Would *she* ever understand? She didn't stop to think, to rationalize. She dialed the long-distance operator and asked to be connected with Dr. Luke Farrell, in Squirrel Hill, Pennsylvania, person to person. "My name is . . . Mary Ashley, from TSN News in New York," she said.

Dear God, his voice was the same. So sane-sounding. So very, very real. She almost sobbed in relief when she heard him say, "This is Luke Farrell, Miss Ashley, what can I do for you?"

In the space of time it took for her heart to beat three times, Casey made her decision. "Luke, this is . . . Casey Adams. I need to . . . oh, Luke, I need someone! Luke, I think I'm losing my mind. Can you . . . will you come? I can meet you at the airport. Please, say you'll come. I'm this new person—Mary Ashley . . . I thought I . . . Will you come, Luke? I'll meet you wherever your flight lands, La Guardia or Kennedy. Please, Luke. New York, Luke. I'm in New York City," she said tearfully.

"Casey! Jesus Christ, they said you were dead. I believed them. Son of a bitch, you're alive! I'll leave now. Christ, you're alive. Goddamnit, I should wring your neck for letting me think you were . . . ah, shit." His voice was so happy, so joyous, Casey laughed in spite of her tears.

"Call me from the airport when you know the time of your flight. I'll meet you. I can't wait to see you, Luke. You're all right, aren't you?"

"I'm fine. I'm really fine. You bet. Couldn't be better. Jesus, I can't wait to see you. Hang up for God's sake so I can get to the airport. I have to go to Pittsburgh, you know. Are you gonna hang up?"

"I don't want to, but I will. 'Bye, Luke."

It was an asinine thing she'd just done. "I don't care," she said so forcefully that both the puppy and kitten awoke simultaneously. She scooped both animals into her arms, her tears falling on their silky heads.

"He's nice, you'll like him," she crooned as she dabbed at her tears. She talked to the animals then, her voice rising and breaking from time to time. They appeared to listen, content in the cradle of her arms, licking at her face, her hands and arms. As one, they leaped from her arms the moment she laughed at their antics. They stopped long enough to listen to her voice.

"We need a routine. I'll get the litter box ready and put down the paper for Sam. That's how we're going to do things until you're ready to walk on the leash, which won't be for a few months, according to the manual. Come along, ladies, while I get things organized, and I bet you're hungry." She filled dishes with the greenish-gray pellets that looked terrible and smelled worse. The Yorkie looked at her dish and backed away. The kitten pawed her dish of dry food but wouldn't eat it. Both animals lapped at the water in a small red bowl she set on the floor. "I don't blame you, it smells shitful. I'll make something." They watched her movements, their heads cocked to the side, their eyes never leaving her striding form as she opened tuna and scrambled eggs. "This probably isn't good for you, but until I can get to the store for some canned food, it's all we have." She squatted on the kitchen floor to watch them wolf down their meal. Immediately she placed the kitten in the litter box. She and the Yorkie watched as Gracie scratched around before she did what she was supposed to do. The minute Casey praised her and lifted her from the box, Sam hopped in and did her thing. "I don't think it works that way, but I'm open to anything that doesn't cause a mess." She gurgled with pleasure when she lifted the Yorkie from the box, calling her a good girl. "Now, go play," she said, putting the rubber squeak toys into a small wicker basket. "This is yours," she said, wagging her finger. "You don't chew anything else."

She continued to laugh as she stepped over and around them while she straightened the kitchen, fluffed the pillows, and prepared the coffeepot for Luke's arrival. As soon as he called, she was going to brave the rain again and run to the supermarket and liquor store for food and wine. Beer too. Hopefully, she would have time for a quick shower.

Hating to tie up the phone, Casey placed a call to the studio and asked for Steve Harper. When his voice boomed on the wire, she lied and said she was sick and would be out for a few days.

"You sound terrible," Steve said, which made her *feel* terrible. "Stay in bed and drink lots of juice, and whatever you do, don't go out in this rain. It's supposed to be like this for the next few days. April showers ten days ahead of schedule. We'll make do around here. Izzy is going to miss you." Sam took that moment to yip at her feet. "Is that a dog I hear? You didn't tell me you had a dog," he said in an injured tone.

"I have a cat too. Sam and Gracie. You never asked me, Steve."

"Yeah, I know. I meant to ask you to dinner too, but I didn't. We'll do dinner when you're feeling better. Take care of yourself. If you need anything, give me a call." She promised she would.

When the phone rang twenty minutes later, Sam leaped into Casey's arms. Gracie arched her back and circled Casey's feet. She whispered soft words as she picked up the phone to say hello.

"Meet me at Kennedy, three-ten. I'll be the guy with the stupid grin, and I'd know you anywhere. Gotta run." Casey stared at the phone. He'd never recognize her, not in a hundred years. She smiled. It might be fun to fool him.

Casey smiled all the way to the supermarket and was still smiling while she showered and applied her special makeup. "Oh, Luke, it's going to be so good to see you." Tears brimmed in her eyes. She refused to allow them to drop below her lashes. She'd cried enough. There would be no more tears. Unless, of course, both she and Luke wanted to cry on one another's shoulders.

It was hard to pick the right outfit. She wanted to look special for Luke, so she finally chose a soft white wool skirt and a periwinkle-blue sweater. She brushed her hair till it shimmered, adding small pearls to her ears for the final touch.

She spent another full ten minutes instructing her new roommates on apartment living. She explained that things were tidy and she liked them that way. She led them to the pantry to show them the litter box again and the thick wad of paper strategically placed.

"It might be a good idea if you took a nap now until I get back." Two sets of eyes stared at her. The Yorkie yipped, the cat purred. She tickled their bellies one last time before she let herself out of the apartment. She could hear them scratching at the door as she walked down the hall to the elevator. Luke was going to like Sam and Gracie. Oh, they had so much to talk about. She could hardly wait to see her old friend.

Casey almost ran down the concourse. Only ten more minutes. The monitor said his plane was on time. She had it all planned. She would be waiting right at his gate but wouldn't say anything until he walked past her. Then she would call him by name, he would turn, gasp, and then they would hug each other.

He looks the same, she thought giddily as she watched the tall doctor shoulder his way through the slow-moving passengers. His eyes were searching for her, that much she could see. They locked with hers before they moved on. She smiled and let him get a little ahead of her before she called his name. He whirled, his eyes searching for the voice and a familiar face. He stared at her again. "Luke," she said softly.

"Casey?" His face crumpled into something that was supposed to be a smile. His tears matched her own.

"Don't make me cry, please. If you do, this special makeup will rub off and my scars will be visible," she whispered.

"Who gives a damn," he said, crushing her to him. "I'm just so glad you're alive, Casey. So very glad." He buried his face in her hair, hugging her so tight that she squealed.

"Jeez, I'm sorry. Come on, let's get out of here. I only brought this carry-on bag. How'd you get here?"

"Taxi," Casey mumbled. "I own a car, but I don't know how to drive."

"That figures. Who wants to drive in this crazy town anyway," he said, linking his arm with hers.

"Luke, thank you for coming. I can't tell you what it means to me to have you here. I've missed you, everyone . . ."

"Yeah, I know," Luke said softly.

"NICE DIGS," LUKE said as he entered Casey's apartment. "Sure is quiet. I always leave the television or radio on. I like noise," he said flatly. "Oh, *my* God!"

There was no way to describe the living room except to say it was a total disaster. The rainbow-colored pillows were torn and shredded with colorful strips of fabric dotting the floor and the backs of the sofa and chairs. The plants were upended, bits of greenery were strewn about, and dirt was everywhere. In the hallway, in the bedroom, bits and pieces of toilet tissue littered the floor. For a moment Casey was reminded of Vietnam. One look told her that Luke had the same feeling. She reached out to clutch at his arm, which felt tight as a ripcord.

"Guess this will teach you not to unroll the toilet paper," Luke said in a choked voice. "Reminds me of those pamphlets the VC used to drop."

"Where *are* they?" Casey groaned, glancing around for the puppy and the kitten.

"Probably worn-out with all the work they did." He was his old self again, Casey thought in relief. She felt better too. It was just that one intense bad moment. She motioned for Luke to follow her as she searched out her new roommates. When she finally found them, she had to clap her hand over her mouth so she wouldn't laugh. The Yorkie was curled comfortably in one well-worn slipper, the kitten in the other. Both were sound asleep. Luke, Casey noticed, was grinning broadly.

"At least you were smart enough to go out and get pets. I meant to do it, wanted to do it, but never got around to it."

"I just did it today when . . . when I couldn't handle it

anymore," Casey said quietly. "You can still do it. It's the silence and the quietness I can't adjust to. Like you, I need noise. We need to talk about this, Luke."

"I'm ready. Actually, I've been ready for a long time, but it had to be with the right person. No one understands. Sometimes I don't understand either. Unless you were there . . ." He left the rest of what he was going to say hanging in the air. Instead he started to clean the litter.

"Listen, why don't you start that dinner you said you were going to cook for me, and I'll make a stab at cleaning up this mess."

It was seven o'clock when Casey slid the steaks from under the broiler and onto heated dinner plates. They toasted each other with their first glass of wine, and then they talked. They were still talking when the clock in the kitchen said it was midnight. At three o'clock they adjourned to the living room, where they settled themselves on the floor. As the first streaks of dawn crept up over the windowsill, Luke's expression became distant. "Rick crashed and burned a few weeks before I rotated back to the States. I think of that guy every day. I tell myself he couldn't make it back here. Flying dead and wounded was all he knew how to do. I heard scuttlebutt that he was going to be forced to come back home. I wonder if he—"

"Shhh," Casey said, placing her finger on his lips. "Don't even think it."

Luke started to shake. Casey put her arms around him. "It was so damn . . . it was the heavy rains . . . that chopper . . ."

"Was put together with spit, glue, and Silly Putty. He made the choice, Luke. It's okay to cry." She sobbed. "I think that's half our problem. We didn't get a chance to grieve. We had no one to grieve with. Now, we have each other. Am I right?" Casey asked in a choked voice. Luke continued to shake. She held him tight, bringing him as close to her as she could. She stroked his head, he stroked hers. She kissed his wet cheek, he kissed hers. They touched and whispered between sobs of anger and frustration. Together they punched and gouged the ruined pillows until they fell against one another, exhausted.

Casey's lips trembled as she leaned down to kiss Luke on the lips, her arms cradling his head against her chest. It was a sweet kiss, full of sadness and relief. Moments later she whispered, "No, no, I don't want you to see . . . I have so many scars. Please, don't look at me. I can't bear it. Oh yes, yes, I do want you, but my body is so ugly, I can't bear it, Luke."

"Shhh, it makes no difference. How can you even think . . . don't cry, please don't cry. I loved you from the first moment I saw you. Shhh, don't cry, Casey, please. It's all right for me to love you, and I do. I can accept anything as long as I know you're alive and well." Casey cried harder, her sobs muffled against his chest. He kissed away the tears and tasted his own on her lips.

"I want to make love to you," Luke whispered hoarsely.

"Oh yes, Luke, yes, yes," she whispered against his cheek.

The gray day with the driving rain against the windowpanes turned to night. Only the rustling of their bodies against the remains of the rainbow-colored cushions, and the soft sound of their murmuring, broke the silence. She nestled against him, burrowing her head into the hollow of his neck, the silky strands of her pale blond hair falling over his shoulder. She breathed the scent of him, mingled with the fragrance of her own perfume. Her fingers teased the light fur of his chest hair. Her leg, thrown intimately over his, felt the lean, sinewy muscles of his thigh.

They were like light and shadow—she silver, the color of moonlight, and he dark, like the night. He held her, his gentle hands soothing her, promising silently all the things lovers promise.

One moment his arms cradled her, the next they became her prison—hard, strong, inescapable. She felt the wildness and loved him for it. She felt a sense of power to know she could arouse these instincts in him. She yielded to his need for her, welcoming his weight upon her, flexing her thighs to bring him closer.

His hands were in her hair, on her breasts, on the soft flesh of her inner thighs. He stirred her, demanded of her, rewarded her with the adoring attention of his lips to those territories he wished to claim. And when he possessed her, it was with a joyful abandon that evoked a like response in her: hard, fast, then becoming slower and sweeter.

She murmured with pleasure and gave him caresses he loved. Release was there, within their grasp, but like two moths romancing a flame, they played in the heat and postponed that exquisite instant when they would plunge into the inferno.

He held her then, soothing her back down from erotic heights.

It was the best of all times, this moment after lovemaking, when all barriers were down and satiny skin melted into masculine hardness. This closeness, Casey thought, was the true communion of lovers who had brought peace and satisfaction to one another.

Casey burrowed deeper into the nest of Luke's arms. He drew her closer and she smiled. She didn't want the moment to end. This man who came to her out of nowhere when she needed him the most. Right now, this very second, if he asked her to die for him, she would. He seemed good for her in every way, understanding her, accepting her, even to the scars she would carry for the rest of her life.

"Do you want to talk about Mac now?" Luke asked quietly.

"He betrayed me, Luke, he lied to me," she said quietly. "There's no need to talk about Mac, not now, not ever. There's no place in my life for Mac, and there isn't a place for me in his. Let's leave it at that and not spoil what we have."

"You're the boss," Luke said lightly. He recoiled a moment later in mock horror when two fur balls pounced on the mound of pillows.

Casey thought she'd never been happier than in that moment as she watched Luke tussle with the Yorkie and the tiger cat. The animals loved his long arms as he gently pushed and shoved them, trying to teach them to roll over. "Treats for everyone," he shouted boyishly as he walked naked back to the kitchen for cookies. Casey watched him and wondered if she had the nerve to stand up, to expose her nakedness and her scars to this man who had just made love to her. She made her decision the moment Luke walked back into the living room, the prancing puppy and kitten trailing behind him. She stood up, a look of panic on her face. He smiled.

"They don't matter," he said gently. "Haven't you learned anything from me?"

"More than you'll ever know. Last one in the shower stinks!" she called gaily.

They scrubbed and soaked one another, touching and kissing under the pelting water, but they didn't make love. "Later," Luke said against her cheek. "Later, we'll do it like normal people, in a bed with covers where I don't freeze my ass off. Don't you have any heat in this goddamn apartment?"

"It was cold out there, wasn't it?" Casey giggled.

"Damn right." He pushed her gently out of the shower. "Get dressed and make breakfast. And feed those animals before they tear this place apart again."

When the bathroom door closed, Luke leaned against the shower wall, the steam and driving spray covering him like a dense gray fog. He took great, heaving gulps of steamy air into his lungs as he cringed against the wall. She'd said scars. Nothing in the world could have prepared him for the ravages of her young body. He could have killed for what was done to her, but anger was useless now. He'd learned that the hard way.

Luke stepped out of the shower into the steamy bathroom. He'd found her again. How was he going to walk away, go back to his empty life in Pennsylvania? Their lovemaking had been a spontaneous thing that grew out of their need to draw something from each other. Now, what was he supposed to do? Stick around and . . . what? Go back and . . . what? Was this a "fling" for both of them? He'd heard his sister use the word once. He didn't like the sound of it. It didn't have any notion of permanence in it. Another day. He'd stay another day, maybe two. They still had a lot of talking to do. He wanted to tell her about the support group he started in Pittsburgh and suggest that she start one here in New York. He'd offer to help.

As he dressed he could hear music. "As Time Goes By." He didn't like the title any better than he liked the word fling. It was the music box. Was she trying to tell him something? His insecurity started to eat at him. What they had . . . what they shared was a moment. Mac Carlin, no matter what she said, would always be between them.

His jeans were so worn they felt like soft cotton. He did a hop and a skip, settled his rear end into the back, then zipped them up. His sweatshirt, which was just as worn and soft, felt as comfortable as a security blanket. He wondered what he would do when they finally wore out. Some things could never be replaced, he thought sadly. Just like some people could never be replaced. Christ, he was stupid. Come to think of it, he'd always been stupid. "What you gotta do, Farrell, is get your shit all in one sock and . . . Fuck it," he mumbled, as he pulled on his socks.

The day was wonderful, the evening better, the night stupendous. "I have to go back today, Casey. I'm giving a speech at the Rotary tomorrow. It's one of those brunch things. I can't get out of it."

"I understand. Can you come back? I don't mean right away, but sometime soon. Or I can come and visit Squirrel Hill."

"Well, sure. Whenever you want. I'm not going anywhere." He could feel her draw away from him, grow rigid. "Ma Bell is a wonderful thing, Casey. Even in Squirrel Hill we have telephones. I want us both to think real seriously about what went on here. Speaking strictly for myself, I've never been happier . . ."

"But . . . What's the but, Luke?" Casey asked coolly. She'd known it. God, how could she have been so stupid? First Mac, then Alan, and now this . . . this doctor who said he didn't care about her scars. Like hell he didn't.

Luke leaned up on one elbow. "There is no but. What's wrong? What the hell did I say?"

"It's what you didn't say. This was all . . . all therapy. Well, I don't need it, and I don't need you either," Casey said, leaping out of the bed.

"Wait just a damn minute. Therapy? Where did you get that notion? I don't get it. Is this your way of booting me out of here? Jesus, all you had to say was go and I'd have gone. I thought . . . Come back here," he said. "That's an order, Casey."

She was in her robe now, her scars invisible when she perched on the side of the bed. "Look, maybe I am touchy, a bit insecure, but I have good reason to be. I asked you if you would come back here. I offered to visit you. 'Well, sure.' *That* was your response?"

"Listen to me, goddamnit. I'm not up on the social ways of lovers. It's been a long time for me. The plain damn truth is I don't know how to act. I've been afraid of saying the wrong thing. You're vulnerable, and so am I. This might be hard for you to believe, but I've never been in love before. If I screwed up, I'm sorry. And furthermore, I won't be a stand-in for Mac Carlin, no matter how much I respect the guy. Yeah, what he did was shabby, but you're forgetting I saw him and witnessed what he went through that Christmas when you were sick. He loved you, Casey. He's not out of your system, and by going on with this . . . this new identity thing, you can never resolve it. Both of us need time to think about all this. I meant it when I said I loved you. However," his voice turned cool and aloof, "I didn't hear you say the same thing to me. No, no, don't say it now. Get my point. There's a possibility that somewhere down the road we might be able to salvage this in some way, but not now. I think I should leave and give you some breathing room. Call me a cab, Mary Ashley."

"You're disappointed in me. I can see it in your face. Can't you at least try to understand why I did it?"

"It takes guts, *Mary*."

"That's all I've heard for two long years. Guts. Guts and then more guts. I'm a person. I hurt, I cry, I feel things. I did what I thought was best for me at the time," Casey said bitterly.

Luke gripped her by the shoulders and drew her to her feet. "How in the hell did something so wonderful turn so sour in a matter of minutes?" he demanded. "I love you. You care for me. We were both spooked, and by mutual agreement we joined together. Now I'm getting dressed and I'm going back home. I'll always be here for you. All you have to do is call me the way you did the other day. And the reason is that I've loved you from the first. This is the end of it. Keep in touch."

Fifteen minutes later he was gone.

Chapter 21

MAC CARLIN LOOKED at the small calendar on his desk. He crossed off the date. April 30, 1972. It was spring again. He tried, but he couldn't remember where he was or what he was doing at this time last year. Existing. He opened a drawer to pull out last year's calendar to see if he'd made any notes. He was disappointed. There were none.

He'd had four invitations to various brunches and dinners today, but, as always, he had declined. He preferred to spend his weekends in his guest cottage going over his mail, taking care of his investments, riding, and hiking with the dogs. It was a shitful life, he told himself over and over again, and he was no closer now to finding Lily's son than he had been when he first started. If there was one thing he hated in life, it was dealing with a foreign government.

Outside in the crisp spring air he could hear Jenny laughing as her mother held her on a bicycle held up with training wheels. He leaned closer to the window. He didn't see much of Alice these days. In fact he'd hardly said more than a dozen words to her in as many months. She'd been so grateful when he turned over the records to the foundation he'd set up for children like Jenny. That's where she and Jenny now spent most of their time. It was good for both of them. He knew his mother would have been pleased at the way he'd been using her legacy.

Mac's pencil tapped on the desktop. Sundays, he thought, were days of reflection, not that there was much to reflect upon, but he did it anyway. He thought of his father and how they'd grown even farther apart. Just this past week he'd heard a rumor that Marcus was retiring. He didn't believe it for a minute. The rumor circulated periodically when something didn't go his father's way. The old man would hang in there till the day he died.

Thoughts of Sadie and Bill always made him smile. He hadn't seen either of them for several months. They were busy handling the bar during the week, and spending weekends in Perth Amboy, where they worked in the bait and tackle shop. Sadie admitted that she wore a bib coverall, but it was a silky blue creation bearing a designer label. They were delightfully happy, as were Benny and his little family. Which left only him. He wasn't *unhappy*. He'd managed to have several discreet affairs that meant nothing but sexual release for both himself and his partner.

Mac's arm shot out to remove the screen from the window next to his desk. He called to Alice, who waved cheerfully. Jenny squealed, pedaling as fast as she could. It looked to Mac as if they were having a good time. He watched as Alice helped Jenny from the bicycle and, holding her hand, walked over to his open window.

"It's too stuffy to be indoors today, Mac."

"How would you and Jenny like to have dinner with me tonight?" Mac asked.

"I think that would be nice. Do you mean going out . . . or up at—"

"Here. In my kitchen. Spaghetti," he said, pointing to Jenny, who giggled.

"Like lots," the little girl said, smiling widely.

"She does. That and jelly sandwiches. Maybe one for dessert. What time?" she asked.

"I know Jenny likes to eat early. Six is okay with me."

"All right. Thanks, Mac. Jenny will enjoy it, I'm sure. She's always asking if she can come over."

"You never told me that," Mac accused.

"What was the point? You said no one could come here unless they were invited. It's all right, really it is. Jenny is easily distracted. Ah, Mac, I think I should tell you she makes up stories about this little house to the aide who works with her at the foundation. She thinks you have rooms full of balloons and all kinds of all-day suckers in red jars. She tells the aide you have butterflies on the walls and that you color pictures for her of happy-faced clowns. They think she has a wonderful imagination. She can cut pictures out of books now and paste them in other books. It's such a wonderful place, Mac. She's made friends with the other children, and there are days when she doesn't want to go home. I was going to talk to you about . . . is there any possibility that we could add another wing?"

"Whenever you want, Alice. You're in charge. Do whatever you think should be done."

"Really, Mac, it will be all right?" Alice beamed. How pretty she is, Mac thought. So womanly, and she smelled wonderful. His wife. "Thank you, thank you very much. I guess I'll see you at dinner then."

"Six o'clock. Don't get dressed up, okay?"

"Okay," Alice called over her shoulder.

Mac's shoulders slumped when he closed the screen. They had their own life now, he thought with a tinge of jealousy. The only thing either Jenny or his wife needed from him was his money, which he gave gladly and willingly.

Mac's thoughts took him to Lily's son, Eric, who would now be four years old. Jenny was five. Where had the years gone? His eyes went to the special box he kept on the edge of his desk. In it he kept all his correspondence concerning Lily and her son. Last Christmas he'd received his first real news about the child in a letter written to him by a nun in Thailand. He'd stuffed it into his suit pocket back in the summer, and Yody had found it a week or so after New Year's. He'd written right away, but the letter had come back on Valentine's Day. The orphanage or the nuns had moved on. For months now he'd been sending letters all over Thailand and Vietnam trying to track down Sister Anna Marie. She had to be easier to find than one small boy among thousands. Yesterday a letter had finally arrived from Sister Anna Marie saying she knew where the boy was and that he was well. She said that when it was possible, she would see about having his picture taken and would send it on to Mac. He wasn't certain the boy had been in Thailand to begin with. One letter had said yes, another had said no. The American embassy said he'd been airlifted with his mother, but a letter months later had claimed that Lily Gia was dead. He no longer knew what to believe, what was real, what was pure guesswork. It seemed inconceivable that a nun would lie. Mix-ups occurred. All infants looked alike. What would make Lily's son stand out and be remembered? Think positive and believe, he cautioned himself. Always believe.

The dogs followed Mac as he made his way to the kitchen. Yody was stirring a bubbling pot of red sauce on the stove, and tantalizing smells circled the room. "We're going to have two guests for dinner, Yody," Mac said, clearing his throat. "Ah, is there any way we can have some balloons and a few . . . some other kinds of decorations?"

"That would depend, Señor Mac, on what you have in mind. I myself can go to the drugstore and buy balloons. Today is Sunday," she said quietly.

"Well, Jenny seems to think this house is . . . magical. I know it sounds kind of silly, but she's just a child. Her mother casually mentioned that Jenny . . . has made up these little stories, and she doesn't want her to be disappointed." He realized he was speaking a lie the minute the words were out of his mouth. *He* was the one who didn't want to disappoint the little girl.

"Very well, Señor Mac, I will see what I can do. Who is to blow up these balloons, señor?" she asked, untying her apron and reaching for her purse, which she kept on a shelf over the sink. It was a straw affair, with colored flowers woven in it, and huge as a satchel. It also appeared quite heavy. As always, he was curious about its contents. Jenny would love it. Alice said she had fourteen different "purses," which she daily stuffed with treasures.

"Sometimes," Alice had said, "she can play for hours just taking things out and putting them back. I think," she'd gone on to say, "it's the same principle as a child playing with the cardboard box instead of the toy."

Today, Mac decided, was a good time to vent his curiosity in regard to the purse Yody carried. "It looks heavy," he said, handing Yody a ten-dollar bill. "If I'm not being too nosy, what do you carry in there?"

Yody looked at Mac for a long moment. "Yes, señor, you are being nosy, but I do not mind. *My things* are in there. If I am not back in one hour, stir the sauce so it doesn't stick to the bottom of the pot."

Mac nodded. He popped a bottle of beer before he returned to his study and the piled-up mail he had to contend with. He spent the next hour going through everything, writing two letters—one to Sister Anna Marie, the second to Phil Pender.

He fished a letter from the box, the last one he had to respond to. He'd received it at the office more than two weeks ago. He'd postponed answering it because it meant he would have to speak to Alice and get her views. It was personal and yet not personal. He looked at the return address on the crisp gray envelope. Tri State News, 440 Park Avenue South, New York, New York. The letter was from the executive producer of the *Noonday News* and addressed to Senator and Mrs. Malcolm Carlin. He'd heard about Steve Harper's "Show-and-Tell" segment. In fact he'd caught it a time or two when he was in New York. He rather liked the show. At first, when he had read the letter, he'd been annoyed, but the annoyance turned to flattery when he realized Harper wasn't interested in his senatorial politics, but in the foundation he'd set up for children with Down's syndrome and his Vietnam Veterans Foundation. He wondered how the producer got wind of his plans to turn his mother's old home into a summer camp for children like Jenny. His other camp, as he now thought of it, would also be in the South. It would be for vets with no place else to go, and staffed with doctors. It was a monstrous undertaking, but he was damn well going to do it. Today he was going to discuss the children's summer camp with Alice. He thought she would be all for it, but the problem of who would operate the facility and see to the renovations was something he himself had no time for. He would be busy with his plans for the Vietnam vets. Alice, he knew, had very little free time. It was something he needed to explore very carefully before he made any concrete decisions.

Mac read the letter again. Six minutes of airtime for the Down's Syndrome Foundation, and a second segment for his Vietnam Foundation. Clips of him, Alice, and Jenny at home;

one at the foundation; one with the children, whom the foundation helped; and one at his mother's home. The last shot was to be of himself, Alice, and Jenny walking into the Senate gallery. Good copy.

This was like manna from heaven. Thank God for people like Steve Harper. Jenny and the children would be well taken care of, thanks to Alice. Just the thought of what he could do for all the vets excited him. He felt alive and in control. He was goddamn well going to pull this off, and he didn't care what it cost. He was tired of batting his head against the stone wall of the Senate, tired of wading through bullshit. If you want something done, do it yourself, was the motto to which he now subscribed.

Mac was satisfied with himself these days. He'd rolled forward his project for the vets. Alice had beamed with pride when he had first told her about it. They now had something in common, she told him. They were each doing something worthwhile and worth caring about. "If I can help in any way, just ask," she had offered. By God, she'd meant it too. Alice was . . . Alice . . . was *okay*.

He had decided he would not get any more involved with his wife and her daughter than he already was. Still, the sound of their shrill, joyful laughter ate at him. He should be out there with them. He'd promised to take Jenny down to the stable and harness a docile pony, named Pee Wee, to the bright red and blue pony cart. Jenny liked the cart but was scared of the pony. Jenny's explanation was that Pee Wee had too many feet. Perhaps they could do it after dinner. No, that wouldn't work either, Jenny was afraid of the dark. *She wasn't his daughter,* he told himself again. She was Alice's daughter; let Alice work on the pony cart. Today he'd promised himself he was finally going to go through the box of his mother's books that his uncle Harry had given him.

He'd brought the cardboard box down this morning from his room. Before he made a final decision to turn his mother's old home over to the foundation, he needed to tie up this last loose end from that old life.

When he opened the box, it smelled old and musty inside. He sneezed. His hands, he noticed, trembled as he reached for the first book. There were five of them, and they weren't merely books. They were diaries. They were all alike in size, with soft burgundy Moroccan leather covers embossed with the word DIARY in gold letters in the center of each book. Down at the bottom, in gold script, was his mother's name. Patches of ugly charcoal mildew spotted them. He was almost afraid to open them, for fear the brittle pages would disintegrate at his touch. He wondered if he had a *right* to read them.

The books seemed to be in order, commencing with the first, written when his mother was ten, in square, boxy letters. The second and third were written with a smoother hand, the fourth and last in beautiful flowing script. The pen had been fine, the writing slanted and tiny. He was going to need his reading glasses. As much as he didn't want to do this, he felt he had to. He carried the box over to his easy chair and fixed his reading glasses on the end of his nose in preparation.

The first two diaries made him chuckle. They dealt mostly with Maddy, the old Negress, and various animals on the plantation. He laughed aloud when he read one section that dealt with his mother sneaking out of bed to catch Saint Nick on Christmas Eve. "Just because Maddy has a belly like Saint Nick," she wrote, "they must think me a fool not to recognize her dark face. I pretended not to notice. P.S. Dear Diary, Maddy told me on Christmas Day she wasn't supposed to turn around because Daddy knew I was on the staircase. They all think they fooled me." Mac rubbed at his throat to ease the lump he felt building.

The third and fourth diaries dealt with wistful looks taken from under bonnets at young boys in church. Tea parties under the angel oaks, secrets among friends. "Today, Cassie told all of us in the azalea garden she let Billy Asher kiss her on the cheek. She said she's never going to wash her face again. I'm jealous. All the girls are jealous. Cassie said she's going to let Billy kiss her again and again, and maybe next year let him kiss her on the mouth. Ohhh, we're all so jealous. I like Adam Ellis. He looks at me all the time. Tomorrow I'm going to wink at him." Mac guffawed aloud. It was wonderful. When he closed the book, he realized his mother had been sixteen when she wrote those entries.

The fifth, and last, diary was obviously presented on her birthday. It was different, Mac noticed. A whole year and a half had passed before it was written in for the first time. The diary started in July, when his mother was seventeen and a half. All of it was devoted to Adam Ellis. "He's so good-looking," she wrote. "He has a dashing smile, and he's a wonderful dance partner. He kissed me. He really kissed me. He asked my father if he could court me. My father said yes, if Maddy chaperoned us. Maddy turned her head so he could kiss me under the big old angel oak in the back of the stable, but she tied my corset tight because, she said, no young buck was going to untie it if she could help it."

Further on he read: "I leave for Miss Adele's school for young ladies. I don't want to go. I don't want to leave Adam. He says he will write. It's only for a year, Maddy says. I cry all the time. Adam says he cries too."

There were no entries for the next year, until his mother's return to her home from Miss Adele's school for young ladies.

Adam is seeing someone else. Maddy says he got too heartsick waiting for me. He's coming for tea this afternoon to tell me he's promised himself to someone else.

"You bastard!" Mac exploded, feeling his mother's pain. Mac continued to read, often seeing blurred spots on the small pages of cramped writing. His mother's tears. What else could it be?

Mac continued to turn the pages, his eyes devouring the small, cramped writing. There was more to write now, more secrets, and the space allotted was too small. Words were written sideways in the margins, powerful, unbelievable words. So powerful and unbelievable Mac didn't hear Yody come in, didn't hear her hammer the butterfly and clown pictures to the wall next to him. He didn't see the dogs get up, and didn't hear Jenny's and Alice's laughter. Yody watched him out of the corner of her eye.

The books were placed back in the box. The string tied. Only the last diary remained on the desk.

His steps were jerky, lopsided, when he walked from the study, down the hall, out to the kitchen and then outside. Yody called to the dogs to stay inside. They sat on their haunches, panting after their master. She watched as Mac ran, not for the barn and Jeopardy, but out across the fields. In unison the dogs howled. The fine hair on the back of Yody's neck prickled. After what seemed like a long time, she heard a sound she'd never heard before. She squeezed her eyes shut, willing the sound to stop.

It did. Finally.

Yody blew up the balloons and tied them to the backs of the chairs with butcher's string, then she set the table. She fed the dogs leftover roast beef because everyone knew spaghetti wasn't good for dogs. She filled their water dishes. She took the cherry cobbler out of the oven, and still the fine hairs on her neck were on end. She fixed the coffeepot and made a jelly sandwich with strawberry jelly, which she wrapped in wax paper for the little girl's dessert. She watered the plants and then blew up the last three balloons, which she tied onto the door handle. "It looks as if we're having a party," she said to the dogs.

She heard him before she saw him. She turned when the dogs did, her ears every bit as keen as theirs.

"I'm hungry, Yody," Mac said tightly. "It's almost six, so I'll wash up. I have to make a phone call. Call me the minute Alice and Jenny get here." He smiled. Yody could feel her body go limp. The dogs laid down in the middle of the floor. Whatever the crisis was, it was over.

Yody drained the water from the spaghetti.

It was seven-thirty when Alice said good night. "We really enjoyed dinner, Mac. I know I did, and I never saw Jenny eat so much. She's almost asleep on her feet. Perhaps we can return the favor one of these days. I'm glad you invited us. Whenever you want to do the interview with those people, just tell me. I'd like at least a day's notice, if you can manage it." She reached up and kissed him lightly on the cheek. "Thanks, Mac. You made Jenny very happy tonight. She loves the balloons."

"I'll walk you over to the house. How about a piggyback ride?" Mac stooped down while Alice helped Jenny climb onto his back. The long strings of balloons were fastened securely onto her wrist. He galloped like a horse across the lawn and up the hill to the main house, with Jenny astride him.

"What you're doing at the foundation is wonderful, Alice," Mac said sincerely.

"I couldn't do it without your help, Mac. It's you who should be proud. What you're doing is wonderful. I'm very grateful, Mac, I just want you to know that. And again, if there's anything I can do . . . if you need me for anything . . . just ask."

"I will. Sleep tight, don't let the bedbugs bite," he teased Jenny. The little girl laughed when he tweaked her cheek.

He was alone.

Again.

Chapter 22

THE FRONT DOOR was made from the finest mahogany, and the brass doorbell shined so that he could see his reflection. Fresh paint, white, of course, permeated the air around him. All about him azaleas bloomed. Bees buzzed in the warm spring air. He could tell by the sweet earthy smell that someone had mowed the acres of lawn recently. He could hear the swish of the lawn sprinklers behind him. He looked for a leaf, a twig, a speck of dirt on the old veranda but could find nothing. In the South, people rose early and did their chores before the heat took over.

Mac rang the bell a second time. The wicker chairs were the same as those at his mother's old home, only in better condition. The owners probably sipped lemonade and mint juleps out here. Maybe coffee. He wasn't up on the ways of the South these days.

He was a nice-looking man, Mac thought when the door opened to reveal a gentleman as tall as himself, dressed in snowy-white shirt and khaki trousers. Distinguished, Mac thought. Silver hair, plenty of it, brushed casually to the side. Handsome. His smile was warm and welcoming, his eyes bright and curious.

"Mr. Ellis?" Mac asked.

"Yes."

"My name's Malcolm Carlin. I believe you're my father."

The smile stretched from ear to ear. "They said they would never tell you. Come in, come in . . . son."

"They didn't. My uncle Harry gave me my mother's old

411

diaries a long time ago. I'm sorry to say I didn't read them till yesterday."

"Let's go back in the kitchen. I hate sitting in this parlor. We can have some coffee or lemonade and talk man to man."

"Fine with me," Mac said.

He was a good host, setting out fine china and silver spoons along with linen napkins. The percolator was silver and electric. Mac could see his reflection in it. He raised his eyes to stare at his father, a stranger.

"I always wondered about you. I heard you came back to the cemetery a while back. Met Harry in the post office and he told me. Harry more or less kept me informed. Not that he knew much. You see, Harry didn't give his promise to keep everything a secret, the way your mother and I did. Harry simply wouldn't do it. And your grandfather Ashwood couldn't make him. Harry was the oldest boy and a real hellion. In the end the old gentleman backed down. I couldn't marry your mother, son, even though I loved her as much as life. I was promised to another wonderful woman who did become my wife. Things are different here in the South, as you well know. Matilda's father and my father struck up a bargain, and this plantation is the end result. Money changed hands, that kind of thing. That's the way it was done back then. Your grandfather Ashwood didn't think my family was good enough for the Ashwood bloodline. His loss, I might add," the old man said sprightly.

"If you were promised, then how did you manage to get my mother pregnant?" Mac snapped.

"In the usual way. You're being cheeky, so you deserve such an answer, young man," Ellis said sharply.

"That's not what I meant and you know it," Mac retaliated.

"Humor me, son. Having you sit there across from me isn't the most comfortable of situations for me. I loved her. She loved me. I had the freedom to go out in the evenings. Your mama would arrange with Maddy to go for a walk, and we'd meet. Maddy would go off for a little while and we'd be alone. Neither one of us knew anything about stopping babies— what's referred to as birth control today. We took a chance and we lost. When your mama came to me and said she stopped perking, I was wild. I didn't know what to do. Excuse me, stopped perking means she stopped menstruating. Southern term. Both of us knew your granddaddy would have strung me up from the nearest oak tree and kicked out the bench. It was your mama's idea to go after the man who . . . Marcus Carlin, who was in town visiting. She set her cap for him, and when he fell for her, she went and told your granddaddy she was pregnant, but she wouldn't tell him the father's name. He was a staunch southern aristocrat with so much money he would have choked a dozen mules to see this northern Yankee's father who had pissed in his poke. They struck up a deal, and as Marcus said later, many, many times, he had bought damaged merchandise. Your mama never loved him. She did it for me, so I wouldn't get hung by my neck and so there wouldn't be an Ashwood scandal.

"Bet you never knew we kept in touch through Harry, did you?"

"No, I never knew that. Did . . . Marcus Carlin know?"

"I'm not sure. When he sent her back here, we thought for sure he knew. It was his way of tormenting us both. I had a wife and family then, and she had no one. We saw each other in church, but that was it. I went to her funeral. We never got to talk about you face to face. Marcus got a whole lot of money for marrying your mama. Actually, his father got it. Same difference. Her dowry, they called it."

"I hated him. I still hate him. I'll always hate him. When I came of age, you should have told me. I'm the one who told my mother about . . . *his* infidelity. I will never forget the look on her face," Mac said miserably. Adam patted his hand reassuringly.

"It's no longer important, son. We should have done a lot of things, son, but we didn't. That's all water under the bridge now. Can't make up the past to you, but the future is just around the corner. Your mama said you were going to turn out to be a fine man, and, by gad, she was right. I was real proud when you took your seat in the United States Senate. What would you think about coming here and working for us? We could use a bright young senator like yourself. I'm not without influence around here." He grinned.

Mac snorted. Where had he heard those words before?

"Do you have children?" he asked curiously. If he did, that meant he would have half brothers and sisters.

"Four girls. My wife died the same year Harry died. I live alone here. A woman comes in to clean and cook. My two oldest daughters live in Columbia, and another one lives in Summerville, and the fourth one lives up north in New York City. Got eleven grandchildren. Guess that makes you an uncle of sorts. I imagine this is all a bit overwhelming now that you've heard it. We gave our word, Malcolm. No true southerner ever goes back on his word. You wait here, one minute," Ellis said, getting up from his seat at the table. "I have something I want to show you."

Mac wanted to cry, lash out. How many goddamn kicks in the gut was he going to have to endure? His eyes were moist when he looked up at his father. In his hands he had a stout wooden box with a padlock.

"I guess you could say this is the story of your life, the only life I knew. Of course, everything stopped when your mama came here, but we still managed to get news of you one way or another. Harry was real good about it. He paid out a lot of money to detectives to snap your picture. See this one? You were going into a moving picture show with a friend. I was at your graduation from West Point. I wouldn't have missed that for all the cotton in the South. Harry was with me. We, both of us, went to the cemetery when we got back here and told your mama what a fine young man you were."

"I don't know what I'm supposed to do now," Mac muttered.

"What is it they say in the army? Fall back and regroup, something like that."

"Yeah, something like that.

"I need to know why my mother didn't . . . she didn't write, call me, or get in touch."

"Harry told me she was afraid of what Marcus would do to you. She knew Harry would tell you some day, and you'd forgive her. She did what she had to do, you'll just have to accept that. She loved you as much as she loved me. Maybe more," Ellis chuckled, "but I was never jealous, because I loved you too. I want you to believe that."

"I do. I can feel it," Mac said in a choked voice. "I'd like to get to know you better."

"I'd like that too, son. When you're ready. Is it true what I hear about you turning the Ashwood homestead into a summer camp for retarded children?"

"News does travel fast, doesn't it?" His father nodded and Mac continued. "There's a lot of land here, more than the Down's Syndrome Foundation can use. I've been thinking about starting up something else down here, for Vietnam veterans. Hell, I'm not getting anywhere in Washington. I went into politics thinking I could do some good. Christ, I tried, but no matter what I do, I get stonewalled. I hate to say this, but our country doesn't give a shit about the guys who fought in Vietnam. So I'm getting out when my term is up. Maybe sooner. I don't want you getting the idea I'm a quitter. It's just that I think I can do more good down here. And thanks for the offer of southern politics, but I have to say no. Those people you mentioned, you said you weren't without influence . . . do you suppose they'd . . . give me some support, or are they as narrow-minded as the people back home? I've got to warn you, this is one hell of an undertaking."

"Son, I'd consider it an honor to do whatever I can." His eyes twinkled happily.

"Then we have a deal." Mac didn't know it, but his own eyes were twinkling. Jesus, he had a *real* father.

"By the way," his father went on, "the tail end of my property links up with yours way back at the end. If you find yourself in need of a few more acres, I would be more than glad to share. The decision is yours. No money will change hands. You think about it."

"I'll do that, sir. If you don't mind, I think I'll drive by the old house and pay a visit to the cemetery. I'll be back. I'm not sure when, but I will be back."

"I'll be here, son."

They shook hands—father and son. He wasn't ready for anything else.

Not yet.

* * *

MAC DID HIS best to digest the past few hours. He had a *real* flesh-and-blood father. The kind of father, he thought, had they lived together, who would have taken him fishing, taught him to drive, gone to sports events with him. A kindly man. A man who loved his mother but, due to circumstances, was prevented from having a family life with her. He understood now, and felt he was capable of putting it all in proper perspective. A father who really did care about him. His mother had truly loved him and had done all she could. The ache in his heart eased when he swung the rental car onto Route 26.

He had decided not to go to his mother's old home or to the cemetery. He had plenty of time for all that. The rest of his life.

So it turned out that he'd been bought and paid for like a bale of cotton by Marcus Carlin. And then he and his mother had continued to pay for the rest of their lives. His real father had told him all about it. The Carlins of Virginia had fallen on hard times, and the Ashwoods of Charleston had bailed out the old northern family. The house in McLean really did belong to the Carlins, but Ashwood money had restored it. Well, he would give it back—lock, stock, and barrel, as they said in the South.

"It's my turn, you bastard," Mac muttered through clenched teeth. "It's finally my turn."

"Carlin's homestead was falling down around his ears," Adam Ellis had said. "Your mama wrote to me and said it was no better than a big old chicken coop with broken windows, cracked floors, bad plumbing, and rotted electrical wires. The roof leaked, the walls were crumbling, and the chimneys were clogged. The first year, the year you were born, there was no heat. Your mama bore it all so you wouldn't be born in disgrace. It was a terrible life she had there in Virginia. She told me she lived for my letters. If it wasn't for my own family, I would have come up there and snatched both of you away. God knows I wanted to. I think what stopped me was the knowledge that your mama wouldn't have come with me. She made a bargain and she stuck to it."

Mac sat up straighter in the rental car. His shoulders felt light; a feeling of buoyancy swept over him.

He was free.

His jaunt was steady, almost a strut, as he made his way through Charleston's small airport. He knew what he had to do now.

The plane ride was short and uneventful. The trip to McLean from the airport was slightly more eventful. He stopped at his bank and a sporting goods store before he finished the last leg of his trip. He pulled alongside of Alice's car, which was heading out to the main highway. He rolled down his window and motioned for her to do the same. "I'd appreciate it if you'd follow me back to the house. I have to talk to you about something. It concerns you and Jenny."

Fear fluttered in Alice's stomach. "All right, Mac," she said quietly. So, she thought, he's finally made the decision to get a divorce. Well, she couldn't blame him. It was all her own fault. She wasn't going to fight him in any way. "You should have given me a second chance, Mac," she whispered to herself. "I would have given you one."

Steeling herself for the words she knew were about to come, the words that would rock her world, she asked, "What is it, Mac?"

"Come inside the cottage, Alice. Yody can entertain Jenny while we talk. This is important. Mainly to me, but to you too."

Alice listened, her face registering shock and disbelief. When she held the diary in her hand, her eyes filled with tears. "What do you want me to do, Mac?"

"Take all your things out of the house. Jenny's too. Whatever you think you can't live without. I'm going to finish out my term, then move into an apartment. I'll pension off the servants. You can move to the plantation in Charleston. I'll join you when my term is up."

"But what about the foundation? I . . . Mac, I don't know if I can leave . . . It's become my life, mine and Jenny's. I understand everything you said. It's just that . . ." She shrugged helplessly.

"I'm not giving up on the foundation. We'll build an extension in the South. You can be in on it from the beginning. On the way home I made the decision to go ahead with the plans for the summer camp. My . . . my real father has offered us the use of some of his land. Combined with mine, we can make a difference, Alice. You have to decide *now*. Right now."

"Does this mean you and I . . . are we going to live together or separately? I need to know, Mac. I'll . . . I'll do it regardless, but I need to know."

Mac's empty life flashed before him. He closed his eyes, trying to visualize his future. It was just as bleak and empty. "Yes, I'm willing to try if you are. We'll take it one day at a time. Is that all right with you?"

"Oh, yes. Yes, it's fine with me." She made eye contact with Mac when she said in a clear, firm voice, "Marcus is Jenny's father."

"I suspected that," Mac said in the same clear, firm voice. "I've suspected it for a long time. But a child shouldn't be punished for its parents' mistakes. I remember Aunt Margaret. We'll never mention it again. I would never have brought it up if you hadn't. As far as I'm concerned, she's our daughter."

"Thank you for that, Mac. I . . . I'll do my best." She wanted to go to him, to touch him, but the time wasn't right. He still had things to do before he could make her part of his life. "I'll take Jenny to the foundation and come back here. If you want, you can start taking Jenny's things from her room. I won't be taking that much. I'm glad we're leaving, Mac. I always hated this house."

"You never told me that."

"I never told you a lot of things. You set the rules in the beginning. I did what I thought you wanted. We were both wrong more often than we were right. We'll talk again when I get back."

He watched her leave, her hand in Jenny's. His wife and the little girl to whom he'd given his name. His daughter. He smiled at Yody, who was staring at him as if he'd sprouted a second head.

"It's going to be all right, Yody. Listen, how would you like to move to South Carolina and live in a big plantation house and take care of all of us?"

"Señor Mac, are you serious? I have many relatives, many cousins."

"Bring them along," Mac said magnanimously. "There will be plenty of work for everyone. Will you think about it, Yody?"

"Certainly, Señor Mac. Will Mrs. Carlin and the child be dining with you this evening?"

"Yes, Yody, and they'll be staying on here for a few days."

Yody's broad face broke into a smile. "The child is enchanting, Señor Mac. She has much love to shower . . . I forget, it is not my place. Tell me, Señor Mac, is there Bingo where we are going?" Her tone was so anxious, so woebegone, Mac laughed.

"If there isn't, Yody, we'll start our own. Would you be amenable to leaving with Mrs. Carlin? You see, I'll be moving out of this house very soon."

"Whatever you wish, Señor Mac."

Mac walked outside. He sat down on the top step, the dogs at his side like two sentinels. For the first time in his whole life, he felt at peace. His arms shot out to encircle the dogs. "I finally know who I am." It wasn't a silent thought, he realized, when the dogs whined comfortingly at his side. "I have sisters who have husbands, and I have nieces and nephews. I have a father who has warm eyes and a voice to match, and whose handshake is sincere and genuine. He'll welcome Jenny, but he'll *know*. He'll understand.

"He said he'd take me coon hunting," he said to the dogs. "Of course we'll let them go once we catch them. We'll go fishing. We might even take Jenny and teach her how to bait a hook. You guys can chase any and all poachers. We'll take Jeopardy down there too, of course. I'd say this is the beginning of a wonderful life for all of us." He fondled the dogs' silky ears.

Twice Yody brought him coffee while he waited for Alice to return. The dogs were on their feet long before he heard the engine of her car. He set his cup and ashtray on the side, got up and stretched every muscle in his body.

"I'm ready," Alice said quietly, a curious look on her face. "Did you speak to the servants at the house?"

"They're packing as we speak. I have their severance checks in my pocket. I called my attorney, and he'll start the paperwork for their pensions. Yody is going with you and Jenny, if that's all right with you."

"That's fine, Mac. Jenny likes her. I like her too. Before, what I said about her, that was just—"

Mac held up his hand. "Before isn't important. Past is past, okay?"

Alice smiled, her eyes lighting with happiness. "I guess I better get started."

"Alice?"

"Yes, Mac?"

"Why did you throw out my things? I can understand giving Jenny my old room, but . . . I looked for my old treasures in the attic and couldn't find them. I need to know why," he said quietly.

"I didn't, Mac. Marcus came over one day right before I had the baby and asked which room was going to be the nursery. I chose your room because it was sunny and had lots of closet space. I thought your things were moved to the attic, but Olga told me Marcus trashed them. He . . . he just had one of his people come and dump everything in barrels by the garage. I went out and packed up everything myself in cartons. It's all in the garage, up over the overhang. I can't believe you thought I would just discard your memories. You and I have to take the time to get to know one another," Alice said with a catch in her voice. "Why knows? We may end up liking one another."

"Who knows?" Mac said softly. He had a slight edge, he thought. He actually *liked* Alice already.

It was four o'clock when the last load of personal belongings was deposited in Mac's living room. "A lot of her things are at the foundation. I thought that, because we spent so much time there, it was better for her. She's learning to share and to interact. She has a little friend named Pamela. I agreed to let her spend the night. If there's anything else you want me to do, tell me now before I start to pack these things," Alice said briskly.

"Have a cup of tea with Yody. I have something to do," Mac said cheerfully.

Both women watched as Mac loped across the front lawn, down the slight incline to cross over the pavement outside the garage, and up the hill to the big house. Their eyes met once when Mac opened the trunk of the car to remove a baseball bat. Alice's hands flew to her mouth. Yody blessed herself. When Mac was out of sight, Yody said, "I will make tea now. I have cinnamon cookies."

"Yes, cinnamon cookies," Alice said, following Yody to the kitchen.

THERE WAS NO faltering in Mac's step as he walked through the open front door. He didn't bother to close it. He stopped a moment at the foot of the steps to look around. Once the house had smelled good, like apples and peaches. The upstairs always seemed to have a powdery smell, clean and fresh. Now all he could smell was furniture polish and Lysol. He hated the smell. Hated the house. Hated everything in it. He took a deep breath and walked up the steps, his back ramrod stiff, his shoulders square.

He liked the feel of the baseball bat in his hands. He took a practice swing and liked the feel even more. He headed for the room at the end of the hall, the room that had once been his father's. He kicked open the door. It was a clean, spartan room, with nothing of his father's remaining. He moved slowly, purposefully, the bat raised to shoulder height. He swung, his upper body moving as professionally as that of any star baseball player's. He was rewarded with the sound of smashing glass as the windowpane and frame split, showering the floor with glass. The antique dresser, armoire, and commode all came under the bat. He toppled lamps, smashing Tiffany glass into millions of tiny shards. The bed fell under his wrath. From his pocket he withdrew the pocketknife his uncle Harry had given him one Christmas, when he was around six. The knife had been dull then. Now it was razor sharp. He sliced and hacked, gouged and ripped. When he was finished, the bat ravaged the old bed, shredding the dry wood to little more than wood shavings. He grinned when he envisioned an army of antique dealers crying for months over the devastation he was wreaking.

He moved on, room by room, until he came to the banister

overlooking the first floor. He eyed the two-hundred-year-old chandelier with clinical interest. His military mind shifted and coalesced. The baseball bat wasn't going to work. He turned on the light for effect. Thousands of tiny crystals winked at him. He saluted smartly, then turned to the long, low, cherrywood table against the wall. Next to it was a cherrywood chair with a petit-point seat. It was heavy too. He picked it up and walked to the end of the wide center hall. He ran then as if he were going to throw the shot put and heaved the chair into the winking mass of light. He loved the sound of the crystal smashing onto the tile floor in the foyer. "Damn, you do good work, Carlin." He laughed.

The stairway and banister, which were built of solid oak and polished to a high sheen, were his next targets. He sat down on his rump and kicked out at the carved spindles. One after another they splintered, until the entire banister weakened. Two wild, powerful swings sent what was left of the banister crashing down on top of the chandelier. He did the same thing again as he slid down the steps, his back to the wall, his feet lashing out at the old dry wood. Once again he congratulated himself as he stood in the foyer to observe his handiwork.

He moved through the rest of the house destroying everything in his path. When he reached the huge kitchen that he'd loved at one time, he stopped to look around. He wasn't breathing hard yet. "That's because you enjoy what you're doing, Carlin," he told himself. He eyed the monstrous refrigerator and freezer, the new shiny appliances, and the old Virginia brick on the walls and floor. He laid the bat down on the butcher block table and walked out the back door, his destination the toolshed. He found the sledgehammer immediately. He was whistling when he made his way back to the house. It took a full thirty minutes for him to smash the ancient brick his father's ancestors had installed—his father's ancestors' slaves, was more like it, Mac thought in disgust. He wiped his hands on his pants. It would take a construction crew months to repair the damage he'd just done to the house.

Carrying the sledgehammer, Mac walked through the devastation in the foyer to the front door. He swung until the door hung drunkenly on its hinges.

Satisfied with his afternoon's work, Mac walked out to the garage and climbed behind the wheel of his car. He turned on the radio full-blast, backed the car out on to the road, then lit a cigarette. He puffed contentedly.

It was eight-thirty and already dark when Mac rang the doorbell of his father's house. A tired old colored man who'd seen too many years of service motioned him inside.

"I know where he is, Elias," Mac said quietly, patting the old man on the shoulder.

The elder Carlin frowned when Mac barged into his private study. By God, he was going to finally fire that old fool Elias. He set aside the legal brief he was reading. He was on his feet in a second. Mac looked threatening somehow, with a cigarette dangling from his lips, and a baseball cap set at a cocky tilt on his head. The cap, which said DA NANG in gold letters, was old, dirty, and beat-up. All over Mac's clothes was the fine white powder of Sheetrock. His chest thumped when he spotted the manila folder from which Mac withdrew the deed to the farm. He handed the deed to Marcus.

"It's not going to do you much good. I pretty much destroyed the old homestead. You know, the one my mother's money paid for. I thought about burning it down to the ground, but I wanted you to have something to remember me by. You see, I know who my real father is. In return for money, you took me and my mother off grandfather Ashwood's hands. The Carlins had no money. Piss-poor, my father said. My real father, that is. You hated my mother and you hated me. Jesus, how we tried to please you. Then what do you do when you get caught with your pants down? I will never forget the awful look on her face when I told her I saw you with another woman. And, what do you do? You send *my* mother back to her home. And she went so you wouldn't take more of your hatred out on me. You bastard! And after all that, you had the gall, the fucking balls, to try and get me into the goddamn governorship so you could call the shots. You would have used Ashwood money to finance the campaign too. But even that wasn't enough for you. You also fucked my wife, you took advantage of her. Yeah, she told me all about it. Jenny is your daughter. How's that going to look, Judge, if it gets out? Alice says she has the guts to tell the truth, and you know what, Judge? I think she does. Alice has changed, in case you haven't noticed. Ah, you're thinking about Aunt Margaret." Mac clucked his tongue, shook his head. "Tonight you resign from the bench. You pension off Elias, and it damn well better be a handsome pension, as well as the other servants who've waited on you hand and foot all these years and were paid with Ashwood money. Don't even think about telling me you have money of your own. I know how much a Supreme Court justice earns, and it barely keeps you in Havana cigars, fine wine, and all those gourmet meals you're so fond of. If you don't do as I say," Mac said cheerfully, "I'll come back. I want to hear about your resignation on the eleven o'clock news."

Mac removed the cigarette from his mouth. He looked at it curiously before he dropped it on the fine, colorful Persian carpet, paid for with Ashwood money. He ground it to a pulp. He pushed his baseball cap farther back on his head. "In the South, Mr. Carlin, they have a saying. Every dog has his day. I just had mine. I can see myself out."

Outside the town house Mac did a tap dance before he settled himself in the car for the ride back to McLean.

Yody was in the kitchen cleaning the floor for the fifth time. When she saw Mac's headlights, she plugged in the percolator and ran to the living room to alert Alice, but the young woman was sound asleep on the sofa. On the cushion next to her was a box of photographs, along with several sports magazines.

"Something smells good in here," Mac said happily. "I just used up all my energy, so I now require something sinfully sweet. Whatcha got, Yody?"

"Double chocolate cake with double chocolate swirl ice cream with marshmallow and chocolate topping."

"Good. A double helping, but I'm going to take a shower first. Is Mrs. Carlin all right?"

"She's sleeping on the sofa. She's . . . very worried about you. A woman can tell these things. I allowed her to look at the box of pictures you keep on your desk. She seemed so . . . . lost. I saw her cry, Señor Mac." Yody's voice held something he'd never heard before. Was it possible she was censuring him? She smiled. He smiled.

"It's all right, Yody. Give me ten minutes, okay?" He was down in twelve, his cake and coffee on the end table next to his chair. The television was on, the voices muted. The *Monday Night Movie*, he thought—Ingrid Bergman and Humphrey Bogart in *Casablanca*. He knew Bogart would approve of his activities today.

Twenty minutes till the news. He lit a cigarette, wondering if Walter Cronkite would be solemn and bug-eyed when he announced Marcus Carlin's resignation. He was tingling with anticipation. The moment he saw the anchorman's face flash on the screen, he tapped Alice's rump. "Wake up, Alice. I think you might want to see this."

"Oh, Mac, I'm sorry, I didn't mean to fall asleep. What is it?" she asked sleepily.

"Watch," was all Mac said.

They watched.

"And this just in from the newsroom," Cronkite said in his best somber tone. He was slightly hunched over, almost as though he couldn't believe what he was about to say.

Alice gasped.

Mac laughed.

Cronkite droned on.

Alice clapped her hands in delight.

Mac beamed with pleasure. "I guess poor health is as good an excuse as any I can come up with. I wonder if the President will throw a fit? Not that I care, but usually he's the first to be notified."

"Are we both really free of him?" Alice asked in a disbelieving voice.

"Yes."

"I hope you don't mind that I was looking at these pictures. Yody said it was all right. I wasn't snooping, Mac. They were there on the table. They look . . . you look at them a lot, don't you?"

"Yes, I do. But that was another time, another place. I think I'm ready to put them away now."

"Tell me about these people, Mac," Alice said, picking up some of the photographs. "Which one is Lily?"

"This is Lily. Isn't she beautiful? That man standing next to her is the father of her child. His name is Eric Savorone and he's a doctor. This one is Sergeant Stevens. This is Freeze. This is Luke Farrell. It was the Fourth of July picnic. We took a picture of all the food. It went too. Thousands of guys showed up. We kind of put the war on hold that day. See this picture of Phil Pender and Rick? God, I'll never forget those guys. Someday I'll tell you about them, but not now."

"Who's this?" Alice said, holding up a picture of a girl in pink shorts and tee-shirt. "She's beautiful, whoever she is," Alice said sincerely. "Was she a WAC or a nurse?"

Mac looked at the picture of Casey Adams. He felt his throat constrict. He wondered if he was going to cry. He felt like it. "She's someone I used to know," he said around the lump in his throat.

Alice pretended not to see the torment in her husband's eyes. She gathered up the pictures and returned them to the box. She settled the lid around the four corners, making a production of it before setting it on the coffee table.

Alice looked at her watch. "Mac, it's three o'clock. I have to be at the foundation early. Jenny gets upset if she doesn't see me when she wakes up. Would you . . . Mac, would you just . . . hold me for a little while? I need someone right now. It's been a hell of a day."

"C'mere," Mac said, stretching out his arm. Alice wiggled closer and settled herself against him. "What do you call those things on your feet?" he asked curiously.

"Fuzzies." Alice giggled. "They make Jenny laugh. She has a pair too." Mac smiled. Alice burrowed deeper into the crook of his arm. She was asleep almost immediately.

It felt right.

Chapter 23

KNEE DEEP IN paperwork in her jungle-circus habitat, Casey picked up the phone before it had a chance to ring twice. As she brought the receiver to her ear she eyed Gertie, the green parrot. Gertie liked to peck at the phone, and sometimes Casey's ear.

"Luke! How good to hear your voice. Please tell me you aren't calling with bad news," Casey said anxiously.

"On the contrary. I'm calling to invite you to Squirrel Hill for Thanksgiving. Now that you drive, among other things, I thought you might be able to get a few days off. This long-distance romance is getting tiresome."

Casey laughed. "I have enormous phone bills. I'm scheduled to work on Thanksgiving. We're having a dinner catered here at the studio. I wish I could come," she said wistfully.

"I knew you were going to say that. Now you're going to make me spoil the surprise. I have a big gun to bring out, and when I spring it on you, I dare you to turn me down." Luke laughed. "I'm not complaining; hell, yes, I am complaining, but I haven't seen you since my visit to New York in May. It's all your fault too," Luke grumbled.

"Okay, okay, bring out your big gun."

"Singin and Maline are on their way as we speak. Mr. and Mrs. Singin Vinh. Is that good enough for you?" Luke laughed.

"Good enough! Good enough! I'll quit! I'll be there! I'll be there!"

"Atta girl! Will we make wild, glorious love or will we fight like cats and dogs? I need to know," Luke teased.

"We'll eat. Do they know about me . . . did you tell them?"

"No, they don't know. I don't think your Dr. Carpenter told them either. I planned to go the whole nine yards, you know, hide you in the closet and then spring you on them as we sit down to dinner. You know how childish I am. Do you think it will work?"

"Only if I fly there instead of drive. I've gotten five tickets over the past few months," Casey said proudly. "I paid them too."

"For speeding?" Luke asked incredulously.

"Of course not. For illegal parking. Once they towed my car, but Steve got it out for me. I'm back to taking buses. Oh, Luke, what if I can't get a flight!"

"Relax. Your ticket is being delivered to your office. I took the liberty of making a reservation when I heard from Singin."

"That's wonderful, Luke. I can't wait to see you. Is there anything I can bring?"

"Just your appetite and a lace nightie, one of those see-through affairs. I can pick up one if you don't have time to shop," Luke volunteered, laughter in his voice.

"Thanks, but I have one of my own. It's peach-colored." Casey laughed.

"I like black. I like black garter belts too."

"You're obscene." Casey giggled.

"Are you okay, Casey?"

"I'm fine. Overworked, but fine," Casey said. "Listen, this crazy parrot is getting ready to plunge at the phone so I have to hang up. I'll see you on Thanksgiving . . . and, Luke, thanks for inviting me. I'll look forward to seeing you." She hung up the phone just as Gertie lunged for it. "So there!" she said, brushing at the parrot.

Singin and Maline. It would be just like Luke to somehow get Alan to attend the dinner too. "I bet he's going to surprise me," she said under her breath. "Ohhh, I can't wait." Her mood darkened almost immediately when she envisioned the scene she would have to play out with Steve Harper.

Casey felt discomfited somehow. She played Luke's conversation back over in her mind. He'd been flip, cheerful, much the way he always was, but there was something in his voice, something she was having trouble identifying. Maybe it was because Luke was *too* flip, too cheerful. Too accommodating. He was sending a ticket for her. He would do that. If there was one thing Luke Farrell wasn't good at it, it was keeping a secret. If Singin and Maline were really coming, he would have hired a brass band or, at the very least, the Squirrel Hill High School band, and bragged about it. They talked every other day. He simply couldn't have kept this kind of secret. She was certain of it. Knowing Luke the way she did, he probably had another surprise of some kind for her. She sighed with happiness.

Unable to bear the suspense a moment longer, Casey left the room, careful to close the door behind her, to seek out Steve Harper. She found him in the employee kitchen, eating a can of cold Buitoni spaghetti. She went into her spiel immediately, ending with, "It's very important to me, Steve, and if you can't see your way clear to giving me the time off, then I'll have to resign."

"I don't see a problem with it, as long as you're still ahead on 'Show-and-Tell.' Listen, I have a list of possibles Morey Baker gave me yesterday. They're all serious contenders. I like the guy at the top of the list; he's making a real difference in the quality of life for children with Down's syndrome. I want to go with him as our lead the first of January. We can do a little promotion and get some mileage for the guy. December is a notoriously slow news month, so all in all, it's going to work out. The guy's a mover and a shaker, so you'll have to chase him around a bit. You do the background and Morey will put the lid on it. Then I want to schedule a second segment with the same guy for the end of January. He's setting up a foundation for Vietnam vets. Deal? How many days off do you want?"

"Deal. Just tomorrow and Thanksgiving. I'll be back Thursday evening and report to work Friday morning. I can't believe you ate that can of cold spaghetti," Casey muttered, shaking her head in disgust.

"I'll make up for it later. I guess I won't be talking to you again till after Friday, so have a nice Thanksgiving and enjoy your visit with your friends."

Casey thought he looked wistful. "I thought you were going

to ask me out on a date, or at the very least, take me to dinner," she blurted, and was instantly embarrassed.

"I was. I meant to. I even wanted to, but there's something in your eyes that I don't understand. I'm enough of an emotional cripple without . . . I don't mean to imply that you are . . . what I mean is, I don't think either one of us is ready for any kind of serious . . . you know," he said, shuffling his feet. "Besides, I'd rather have you for a friend. Hell, you know what I'm trying to say."

Casey did her best to smile. What was one more rejection? And he was probably right, she wasn't ready for anything other than work. That was why she'd held Luke at arm's length. She was still going to keep him at arm's length on her visit too. She was leaving the peach-colored nightie at home.

It was seven-thirty when Casey covered her typewriter and stacked her folders neatly in the wire basket Gertie loved to peck on. She ladled out water for both animals, sprinkled flaked shrimp on top of the water in the fish tank, and replaced the tube of Colgate toothpaste Izzy loved to decorate the bathroom with. She rinsed the coffeepot and carried the trash basket to the hallway. The only thing left to do was to take a quick peek at this marvelous "Show-and-Tell" subject who was at the top of Steve's list. She wondered how much chasing around she was going to have to do. She unfolded the sheaf of papers and put them in numerical order. As her eyes locked on the first line, she swayed dizzily. Senator Malcolm Carlin.

"I have to quit," she cried. "I can't do this!" Steve would want to know why. If she just up and quit, she wouldn't have to make an explanation. Two weeks' notice. He would want her to work on it until she left. No notice. She'd never get another job if she didn't give two weeks' notice. Oh God, she dithered, what am I going to do? "I can't do this," she wailed, sitting down next to the motorized car. "I just can't."

Izzy leaped through the banana trees, coming to sit next to her. With one hand he patted her shoulder, with the other he brushed her hair back from her forehead. He scampered away to return with a tissue. Then he was off again to return with a roll of Life Savers, which he laid at her feet. When she started to hiccup, he fetched his fat crayons and Maggie and Jiggs coloring book and laid them next to the Life Savers. She was still crying when the Colgate toothpaste was added to the pile of things. She stopped crying long enough to observe the chimp's offerings. She did her best to smile as she opened her arms.

The chimp laid his head on her breast, his arms wrapped around her neck. He was making mewling sounds and patting both of his hands against her back. She laughed then, to the chimp's delight. "Listen, fella, I'm taking you home with me tonight. Steve won't be back, and he'll never know. Get your jacket and forget the leash. You just hold my hand, okay? Dumb animals, my foot," she hissed to the fish tank as she closed the door behind her, leaving Gertie alone for the night.

THE MOMENT CASEY opened her front door, pandemonium broke loose. Sam and Gracie, catching the chimp's scent, started to howl and screech, scratching at her legs, their tails swishing furiously. Izzy, frightened out of his wits, secured a stranglehold on Casey's neck that was almost impossible to break. She could feel the furious beat of his little heart. Maybe this wasn't such a good idea after all, she thought.

Gracie hissed her disapproval the moment Casey lowered herself onto the sofa. Sam was alongside her immediately, yipping and sniffing at the same time. Gracie leaped to the back of the sofa, her paws snatching at the air, her back arching angrily. Izzy cowered against Casey. It occurred to Casey that Izzy wasn't safe. If she put the chimp up high, Gracie could get at him. If she put him down, both Sam and Gracie could attack him. Damn, this was one of her more stupid mistakes.

"All right, enough!" she shouted. "If you can't behave, you go in the bathroom. With the door closed!" Sam and Gracie looked at her. Izzy covered his eyes in fear. "Think about it!" Casey shouted again. "In case you forgot, I'm the one who buys the chicken and tuna." Her tone was only just short of brutal. Her roommates backed off. Gracie was back to normal. Sam was panting at her feet. Izzy hugged her tighter.

"It's okay, Izzy," Casey crooned. "I know exactly how you

feel. This is the outside world to you. I went through this once, but I had a nice man named Alan Carpenter to help me. You have me. It really is nice out here once you get past your fear. Friends . . . friends will make all the difference. I'm going to put you down now. Nothing is going to happen to you."

She reached for a section of the newspaper that she kept rolled into a tight cylinder. She used it when she wanted to be taken seriously. "Ladies, you will behave as such or you will feel this," she said, whacking the rolled paper on the edge of the coffee table.

Two sets of eyes watched as the intruder in their midst was set on the floor. Izzy hugged Casey's left leg. She pried him loose. Sam sniffed and yipped. Gracie pawed the air. Casey struggled to the kitchen with Izzy still attached to her leg.

It took an hour before Izzy was comfortable enough to let go of Casey's leg, and he only relinquished his hold when she set his dinner on the kitchen table. Her roommates stopped eating long enough to watch this strange phenomenon. Only Casey sat at the table. Only Casey used a spoon. Izzy ate his macaroni and cheese with gusto. The hot dog that was cut in pieces was his favorite. One hairy hand reached out to grab all the morsels. Instead of stuffing them in his mouth the way he usually did, he hopped off the chair. Casey watched as he sprinkled them in Sam and Gracie's dishes. She tried not to laugh. He was back on his chair a moment later banging his spoon for more macaroni and cheese.

"I guess the crisis is over," Casey muttered as she loaded the dishes in the dishwasher. When she turned it on and it gurgled to life, Izzy leaped from his chair to the top of the refrigerator. He screeched his disapproval at this strange sound. Casey turned it off. He leaped to the floor the moment the kitchen became silent.

The Yorkie advanced a step and then two until she was within easy reach of Izzy's long arms. She woofed softly once and then twice, her stubby tail wagging back and forth. Gracie slinked across the room on her belly until she was standing next to Sam. The three animals eyed each other. Izzy was perfectly still, his eyes going from the animals to Casey. She shrugged and waved her arms, palms up. "You're on your own." She laughed then.

How odd, Casey thought, that these three furry bodies could shake away her doom and gloom. How wonderful that they could bring a smile to her face. How amazing that by their presence alone she could feel whole and in control again. If she ever tried to explain the way she felt to anyone but Luke Farrell, they wouldn't understand. Luke would nod and say he knew it all along.

How much she shared with these animals: her hopes, her dreams, her agonies, her disappointments. She'd cried buckets while they snuggled next to her, comforting her, and she always emerged grateful and full of compassion. Everyone needed someone, whether it was human or animal. She felt blessed. Daily she told them how much they meant to her, how much she needed them, how glad she was that they welcomed her at the end of the day. It didn't matter that they could not understand. She understood.

Casey dropped to her knees for an hour of rollicking play, the way she did every evening when she came home. Even when she was exhausted she kept to the routine her animals expected. And when it was all over, each received a treat, a biscuit they carried to their beds and devoured. Izzy adapted easily, carrying his two Fig Newtons, to which he was addicted, to the chair in Casey's bedroom.

Casey changed her clothes, showered, and packed a small overnight bag while the animals dozed contentedly. The briefcase she'd tossed on the bed beckoned her. She started to tremble the moment she saw Mac's name. Crying had been a release back in the office, but she was past that now. Now she had to pull up her socks and act like the professional she was supposed to be. Mac would never recognize her. If Luke had walked right past her, so would Mac. She wanted to see him again. Needed to see him. The memory would have to last her a lifetime, unless she wanted to confess the truth. Part of her wanted to go to him, to slap his face, to tell him he'd lied to her and betrayed her. The other part of her wanted to melt in his arms, to tell him she'd never forgotten him, to tell him nothing mattered but the

two of them. But Mac had a family. She could never be a party
to breaking up a family.

Casey lit a cigarette and played variations of her fantasy
about their meeting. She lit a second cigarette and failed to
notice when her companions left the room. Memories were
wonderful sometimes, and sometimes they were terrible. She
was working on the terrible ones when the telephone at her
elbow rang. She listened to an airline representative tell her that
her flight to Pittsburgh was canceled. They had rescheduled her
for a special flight on Thanksgiving morning. Her return ticket,
they said, was unchanged. She would return Thanksgiving evening.

She dialed Luke's number. He picked it up on the third ring.
She could hear the delight in his voice, and found herself babbling about Izzy and her roommates. Luke laughed warmly.
Casey curled her legs underneath her and settled back for a
long, comforting talk. "What are you doing?"

"Reading a *JAMA* article on warts. It's amazing how we can
just shoot them off with a laser. If we had half this stuff in
Vietnam, we could have saved a lot more lives."

"I don't recall seeing too many wart problems," Casey said,
hoping to lightly ward off a long, lengthy discussion about the
time they'd spent in Asia. She needed to tell him about Mac and
the interview, but she didn't know how to bring up the subject.
Just blurt it out, she thought, get it out in the open and talk it
out with him. Luke could make sense out of anything.

She told him.

There was no gap in the conversation. Neither did his comment startle her or make her feel anything but glad that she had
brought it up. "Things like this are out of the realm of coinci-
dence. I think it's a good thing for you, Casey. You can't quit.
You started this phony identity thing and now you have to deal
with it.

"I had an answer to one of my letters concerning Lily today,"
Luke said, changing the subject. "Eric is in a French orphanage
in Saigon, just a stone's throw from where Lily's parents lived.
I got this from one of the economic-commercial officers at the
embassy. We've been corresponding for over a year now. Eric

was never taken to Thailand. I'm sorry to tell you this, but Lily's parents are dead. The story I got was they were on their way to the hospital and got caught in the cross-fire on the night it all happened, so Eric is truly an orphan. Jantzen also told me he's had other queries about Eric. He turned them over to a French nun in Saigon. Maybe Eric Savorone finally developed a conscience. Your letters I know about. You know, it makes me feel good that, in this world, three of us are trying to find Lily's son. I'm just as sure that any one of us would give that kid a wonderful home. I wonder if it will ever happen."

"If his real father is interested in him, then we don't stand a chance. The boy should be with his real father. God, I only wish Lily were here now."

"I've been thinking about going back," Luke said quietly. "I'm sick of warts and psoriasis. I made up my mind when I heard from Singin that I was going to talk to him. He did two years over there. That guy made a real difference. I think he wants to go back too. What about you, Casey? Ever think about it? I know you said you never wanted to see the inside of another hospital again, but don't you *think* about it?"

Something squeezed Casey's heart. "No," she said curtly, and a moment later, "once or twice," her voice soft, regretful.

"Okay, don't bend yourself into a pretzel. It was a question, that's all. How cold is it in New York?"

"Pretty cold. Fur coat weather. How is it in Pittsburgh?"

"We had snow flurries today. No accumulation though."

It was a strained conversation now, one neither one of them was comfortable with. It always ended this way, and then she cried when she hung up the phone. She wondered if Luke cried too. She was certain he did.

Chapter 24

TRAVELING TO SQUIRREL Hill to share Thanksgiving with Luke, Singin, and Maline was like a dream, Casey thought giddily. In her wildest fantasies she never thought this would happen. But in less than thirty minutes, according to the cab driver, she would be knocking on Luke's front door. Luke had offered to pick her up, but he said the turkey demanded his full attention, since he'd never cooked anything more than Spam and scrambled eggs. She thought about the Thanksgiving dinner Maline had prepared in her honor. She'd gone to so much trouble to make that day pleasant, to bring back memories for her. They were such wonderful friends, and she was so anxious to see them and for them to see her as she looked now. She'd never known why they hadn't come to the States for their wedding in the spring. Perhaps they'd gone to Spain to see Alan. Alan had never said, although she'd asked him repeatedly in her letters.

She thought about Alan then and wondered why she hadn't heard from him lately. She'd written three letters this month asking if it was all right to journey to Spain to spend Christmas with him the way they'd planned. She had to start thinking about a suitable Christmas present too. When was she going to shop? The studio was taking up all her free time. "Catalogues," she muttered. If she were lucky, she might be able to squeeze in a trip to Bloomingdale's. Steve had told her just yesterday that there would be no days off in December. She would be traveling to Washington, Virginia, and South Carolina. He'd also warned her that she would be spending nights at the studio preparing for the Mac Carlin interview. "I like this guy," Steve had said. "Consider it a mandate." She promised herself to do her best, whatever her best turned out to be. It was the real world now, with no place for memories, dreams, or would-haves, could-haves, or should-haves.

"Here we are, miss," the taxi driver said, pulling to the curb.

Casey paid him, adding a generous tip. When she stood on the sidewalk, she was aware for the first time that it was snowing lightly. Overhead the sky was gray and swollen. More snow. The path led to more of a patio than a front porch. Huge tubs of holly stood at each side of the door. She thought it a nice touch. She rang the bell, a huge brass lion's head whose nose was the button. She wondered where the door to Luke's office was, as he practiced out of his house. "To keep down overhead," he'd said back in Vietnam.

"Don't just stand there," Luke barked. "Come in, come in. My God, it's snowing!" He hugged her, and craned his head to see down the street. "It's sticking too. I bet you're going to be snowed in." He leered down at the little bag she was carrying.

"Not on your life." Casey laughed. "If I'm not in the studio tomorrow morning, I won't have a job. I'll walk back if I have to. Oooh, what's that delicious smell?"

"A culinary, gastronomical delight known as turkey with stuffing. I personally like the stuffing better than the turkey, as long as you slop giblet gravy all over it. I made extra," he said happily.

"I thought you couldn't cook," Casey said, taking off her coat.

"Hell, I thought so too. I'm following a recipe in a book. To the letter. No improvisations the way my mother does. She goes by the pinch-dab method. I prefer half a spoon, an eighth of a spoon, whatever. How about you?"

Casey laughed. "I'm no good in the kitchen, Luke, so don't expect any help from me."

"I wouldn't think of it," Luke said, his face a mix of horror and frustration. "I *am* a little worried about the gravy, though. I hate lumps. My mother always has lumps in her gravy. In her mashed potatoes too. My sister's is worse." He was fretting and shuffling his feet. "My pie-crust shell came away from the sides of the pan and it's cracked on the bottom."

"I wouldn't worry about it." Casey laughed. "A word of advice, Luke. Never confess your misdeeds in the kitchen and no one will notice."

"Advice noted. Okay. Get settled. How about a glass of wine? Listen, would you mind getting it yourself? It's right over there under the bar. Set out the glasses. Singin and Maline will be here pretty soon. I have to cut the vegetables for the salad. No, no, I don't want your help," he muttered.

"That's good, Luke, because I wasn't going to offer any. I'll just look around. Are your parents and sister coming for dinner?"

"God, no! My parents go to Florida for the winter every first of November, and my sister is skiing in Colorado. Look around. If you don't like the way I keep house, keep it to yourself, okay?"

"Sure. I never criticize. I like your apron." Casey giggled.

"Smartass," Luke mumbled as the door to the kitchen closed behind him.

It was a small, comfortable house. A bachelor's house done in muted earth tones. The chairs were low, deep, and comfortable. Ottomans added extra sitting space. The sofa, which she estimated to be a good seven feet long, was the color of fresh-cooked chocolate pudding before the top glazed over. Each table held a book, a newspaper, and cigarettes. Obviously, Luke read constantly. The den was small, with a free-standing, black-as-coal fireplace. A fire burned slowly. One entire wall was filled with bookshelves. Medical magazines and books were crammed into each shelf. They all looked worn and well-read. His desk was a nightmare, with papers everywhere. A morris chair in deep burgundy filled a corner. Next to it stood a square table with a lamp and a pile of medical books. Only one chair. That must have meant that this was Luke's room and not to be shared. She felt like an intruder. She backed up a step and turned around. If she'd continued to back out of the room, she would have missed *the wall*. The entire wall, from floor to ceiling, was filled with framed snapshots of Vietnam and the Fourth of July picnic. She felt a lump form in her throat. It must have taken Luke months to find all these frames. She started at the top. Tears formed in her eyes when she spotted the flowers she'd planted alongside the mean-looking huts everyone had lived in. The tears spilled down her cheeks at the sight of so many of Lily's namesake flowers in each row. She was tracing Mac's likeness with her index finger when she felt Luke's presence.

"I guess you can call this the Luke Farrell Memorial to Vietnam," he said quietly. "I chose this wall deliberately so I can see it when I sit at my desk. As much as I want to forget Vietnam, that's how much I don't want to forget it. We made a difference, Casey. All of us." His voice was so tortured, Casey felt her tears start anew.

"Now look what you've done. My makeup is smeared. Oh, Luke, you should go back. You'll never be happy unless you do."

"I know. I'm leaving January third. I have to spend Christmas with my family in Florida. I need to refer my patients to other doctors. Close up my house, take care of a few things, do some Christmas shopping, watch Guy Lombardo on New Year's Eve. You know, all that stuff you don't get to do while you're over there."

"I'll miss you."

"Yeah, well . . . Listen, you'd better go fix your face," Luke said quietly. "Our Asian guests will be here in a few minutes."

"You're a good person, Luke. They don't come any better than you." Casey reached up to kiss Luke on the cheek.

"I love you, Casey," Luke said. Even though his voice was light, almost teasing, Casey thought she'd never seen such misery in a person's eyes.

"Don't love me, Luke, please don't," she cried, and ran from the room. She was by the front door, grappling with her overnight bag, when the doorbell rang.

"Go, go," Luke urged. He waited until she was out of sight, taking her bag with her, before he opened the door to admit Singin and Maline Vinh.

"I wish we were here for other reasons," Singin said wearily after their initial greetings. "We planned this trip for so long,

looked forward to it. We had such wonderful plans, and now
. . . there is a cloud over our happiness."

"Where is she?" Maline asked anxiously.

Luke shrugged. "Doing whatever you women do in a bathroom, curling her eyelashes, combing her hair. Tell me, have
you seen any—"

"Not one. I think Alan wanted to surprise us. I didn't know
about his surgery until August. He did send one letter to me before he entered the hospital, saying he had to renege on his offer
to hold our wedding here in the spring. We thought at the time
he was on another urgent case. When his letter arrived from
Spain, I called him. He knew he was on borrowed time, even
then. I didn't expect . . . what I mean is I wasn't prepared . . ."
Singin's eyes fell on his bulky attaché case. "I said I would take
care of things. There's a will, and Alan said his last wishes are
chronicled. The service is Friday morning in New York, after
which we're flying out to California and then Seattle."

It was all said so breathlessly that Luke felt dizzy. Poor
Casey.

"You do think Lily will be able to handle it, don't you?"
Maline asked quietly.

Lily. They were still thinking of Casey as Lily. He felt even
dizzier, his hand reaching out to the closest table for support.
Obviously, Alan hadn't seen fit to confide in either Singin or
Maline when he cut Casey loose.

"Lily who?" Casey asked brightly, entering the room.

"Lily you, that's who. It sounds like a song, doesn't it?"
Maline said, stretching out her arms to embrace Casey, her face
wreathed in a smile. A moment later she stood back. "Let us
look at you. Oh, Singin, look, she's beautiful."

Singin stepped closer, elbowing his wife gently out of the
way. He too embraced and kissed Casey. "Very beautiful," he
murmured, studying her face critically. "I couldn't have done it
any better." He beamed. "You are happy, yes?"

"Very happy. It's like a miracle," Casey said.

"Come, sit here by me so we can talk," Maline said. "Better
yet, let us go for a walk in this beautiful snow while these men
prepare *our* dinner. Oh, so much room." Maline sighed. "Re-

member my tiny apartment? Singin and I *both* live in it now. If he leaves his toothbrush on the sink, the bathroom is cluttered. Hurry, hurry, I wish to make a snowball."

Luke and Singin watched from the window, huge smiles on their faces.

"Is that love I see shining in your eyes, old friend?" Singin prodded.

"You don't know *everything*, Singin," Luke bristled.

"Of course I do. We Thais are extraordinarily intuitive. So, it is love. Remarkable. I approve," he said, reaching for a celery stick filled with pimiento cheese. "Very good. I approve of this also. Tell me more. Tell me how best to break the news to Lily."

Damn, there was that Lily business again. "You just tell her, but not till after dinner."

Seeing the troubled look on Luke's face, Singin changed the subject. "Your apron is very amusing. I myself would never wear one. What does that mean, the saying on your apron?" Singin smirked.

"It means, in Yiddish, 'I know how to cook.' I picked it up at a garage sale. Well, actually my mother picked it up."

"Is she in love with you?"

"I'm sorry to say she isn't. She likes me a lot, but love, no. I think her heart belongs to someone else. We don't talk about it. Oh, hell, I do, but she doesn't respond. I mean she doesn't say she loves me back, that kind of thing. Anyway, I'm going back to Vietnam in January. I need to go."

"Yes, I myself feel the same way. Your medical people treated me wonderfully while I was there. They wanted me to stay. I too would go back, but Maline wishes to have a baby, and she can't do that alone. Perhaps you and Lily could put in a good word for me," he said slyly, his eyes on the filled celery sticks, wondering if he dared snatch another and ruin Luke's arrangement of vegetables.

"You know, Sing, I don't think I ever really thanked you for ... you know, giving up your practice and going to Vietnam to help out. There were days when the rest of us didn't know how to handle it. I mean the deformities. I get pissed to the teeth when I see all these demonstrations going on. One of these days

I'm going to blow up. I'm on the edge and I know it, that's why I have to go back. I want to be there, trying to make it a little better for our guys. We'd make a hell of a team, Sing."

"Yes, we would, old friend. But what about Lily?"

"Ah, yes, Lily," he said bitterly. "Did you ever see a dermatologist cry?"

"You're a surgeon. Dermatology is your elective," Singin sputtered.

"You're right. If I see another case of acne, I'm going to puke. You wanna hear something about my early days in surgical practice? As a favor to a colleague, I took over his practice for a week so he could take his first vacation in three years. His wife had threatened to divorce him if he didn't take the time off. I didn't want that on my conscience, so I said I would fill in for him. He said no problems, none of his patients needed anything but a little hand holding, that kind of thing. Hrumph," Luke snorted. "The first day, a forty-four-year-old man came to see me. He couldn't get out of the car. I had to examine him in the front seat. I called an ambulance and operated on him within an hour. He had a ruptured appendix. Three hours later he fucking died on me. Whatcha think of that? Here I am in this modern facility with every medical drug known to man, a sterile operating room, my expertise, and he fucking dies. I couldn't handle it. I came home here and fell apart."

Singin wrapped his arms around Luke. "It happens to all of us at one time or another. You aren't God and you can't save the world," he said quietly.

"The ones I lost *over there*, I lost because there was no way in hell anyone else could have saved them either. But a ruptured appendix! Well, at least I got it out of my system."

"I'm glad," Singin said.

"Now, Doctor," Luke said, "you set the table and I'll put a rush on the bird. Dinner is in ten minutes."

Two hours later Luke pushed his chair away from the table. "I cooked. I do not clean up. Singin and I are going to walk off this wonderful repast. When we get back, we expect coffee and liqueurs in the living room." He snapped his fingers twice to make his point. Casey threw a dish towel at him and Maline gave him the finger. Casey burst out laughing. Singin was so startled at his wife's behavior, he wagged a finger in her direction to indicate she should be ashamed. Her middle finger went up again. Luke guffawed as he pushed his friend through the door.

"This is the good old U.S. of A., Sing. Maline is a modern Thai so it stands to reason she will be a modern . . . whatever, while she's here. She did it in fun so don't get bent out of shape. You're among friends."

"Too damn modern," Singin sputtered.

"Forget it. Come on, let's check out the hill behind the church to see if there's enough snow to sled. There's an old Flexible Flyer in the attic. Jeez, I wonder if the runners are rusty."

"Candle wax will solve your problem," Singin said happily as he trotted along behind Luke. "It must have been wonderful growing up here," he said wistfully.

"It was. But that was then and this is now. I don't belong here anymore. I don't know how or why that happened." Luke turned to his friend. "I'm glad you could make it today, Sing, for whatever reason. I appreciate your listening."

"When it's my turn to unload, I hope you're as generous as I am." Singin grinned. "Look, Luke, there are children on the hill." He rushed ahead.

They were both huffing and puffing when they reached the top of the hill. "This is good, real good," Luke said happily. "See, there's just enough snow covering the grass. Hey, kid," he called to a six-year-old boy, "I'll give each one of you five bucks if you let us have a turn on your inner tube."

"Let's see the money, mister," a boy of ten or so said. Luke peeled off two five-dollar bills. "My treat," he said expansively. "Now, Sing, what you do is sit your ass in the tire and let it drag on the ground. This is going to be like greased lightning. If you see a tree coming up, roll out. You got all that?" Luke demanded as he took possession of a fat rubber inner tube.

Singin ticked off the points on his finger. "I have it down pat," he said solemnly.

"Hey, mister, you have to bring the tubes back up," the kid called, pocketing the money Luke gave him.

Luke peeled off two more fives and handed them over. "We're old men, kid, we could never make this hill again. We'll leave them at the bottom of the hill. Is it a deal?"

"Yeah, okay. Guess you are pretty old." The boy grinned.

"IT WAS THE most hair-raising, exhilarating, awesome, horrendous thing that ever happened to me!" Singin said to his wife. "And I made it to the bottom without having to roll out. Luke didn't make it to the bottom, but it only cost us ten dollars each. Luke paid. I loved it."

Maline smiled indulgently.

Casey poured coffee, Maline filled the brandy snifters. Casey thought it a perfect ending to a wonderful day. She held her brandy aloft. "To good friends," she said, clinking her glass against Luke's. "It was a wonderful dinner, Luke, more wonderful because you prepared it for us. Friends sharing this day is . . . I don't know . . . I think we're all blessed. I want to thank all of you for sharing this day with me."

"It was my pleasure," Luke said gruffly. Singin and Maline echoed his sentiments.

"I hate to say this, but if you want to make your flight, I think we're going to have to leave for the airport. The snow is coming down pretty heavily," Luke said fretfully. "Another hour and we might get held up on the highway."

"We can't miss our flight," Singin said, gulping at his coffee.

It was as though Luke's words were an instant command. Casey carried the cups and saucers to the kitchen.

"When are you going to tell her?" Luke hissed.

"I was just getting ready when you made your announcement," Singin said tightly. "I'll tell her in the car."

THE MEMORIAL SERVICE at St. John the Divine was filled almost to capacity by all those wishing to pay their final respects to Alan Carpenter. Casey sat dry-eyed. How, she wondered, had all these people found out about Alan's death? She must remember to ask Singin. She wanted to shed tears for Alan but her eyes remained dry. Singin was unashamedly wiping at his, as were many others. She turned then and saw Marcus Carlin. Their eyes met. She was the first to look away. She didn't see any tears glistening in his eyes. Of course he would be here, he and Alan were friends. What was he doing now that he retired? She wondered if he would speak to her, not that she cared one way or the other. Perhaps she should walk up to him when the service was over, before she caught a cab to take her to the studio.

To her left was Steve Harper. She watched as his shoulders slumped. He blew his nose, stuffing his handkerchief into his coat pocket. His shoulders remained slumped.

She, however, stood straight and tall the moment she realized Alan hadn't rejected her after all. Yesterday and all night she'd been too consumed with grief to think about anything but the fact that she would never see Alan again. She wished the minister would say something truly meaningful so she could draw strength from it in the days to come, but then how could he? He didn't know Alan. Alan had never come to this church. The urge to run to the front of the church and kick the minister was so strong, she found herself gripping the edge of her seat with both hands so that she wouldn't jump up.

"Thank you all for coming," the minister said.

Outside in the cold air, Casey turned up her coat collar. To her boss she said, "Don't wait for me. I'll catch a cab. I want to say good-bye to my friends."

Harper nodded and lumbered off. Maybe he would fire her now that Alan was dead. She realized she didn't care. She wished she didn't have to go into the studio at all, because today was the day she had to call Mac Carlin's office to set up an appointment for his interview.

Maline was crushing her, kissing both her cheeks and whimpering. "I'm so happy for you that things turned out so well. We will always be friends. I know it here," she said, tapping her chest. "I truly believe you were the reason Singin and I finally got together. It is nothing I can explain in words. Do you understand?"

"Of course. But it would have happened anyway, Maline.

How can I ever thank you for what you did for me? All those hours, all the time you sat with me . . . how do I . . ."

"I was trained to do whatever I did for you. It was my job. You now have a small piece of my heart. Singin's too. All we want for you is what you should want for yourself—happiness. Luke Farrell loves you very much. But if you do not love him in the same way, then you must look elsewhere for your happiness." She winked roguishly.

"So you really are a matchmaker." Casey smiled tearfully.

"It is my turn, Maline. This one, she is so selfish since she has come here," Singin said playfully. "We will meet again. Write to us, please, and let us know what you are doing and where you are. We must never lose touch. We must be friends all our lives. Maline and I will name our first child, if it is a girl, after you. A boy will be called Alan Luke Vinh."

"Oh, Singin," Casey cried tearfully as she hugged him tightly. "Yes, for all our lives we'll be friends. I wouldn't have it any other way. Have a safe trip and enjoy Disneyland."

"Good-bye, my friend," Singin said, kissing her one last time. Maline stepped in and squeezed her tight. "Promise," she whispered, "that we will always be friends."

"I promise."

Casey watched until the cab they climbed into was out of sight. She continued to wave, tears streaking down her cheeks. She brushed at them with her gloved hands.

When Casey turned away, her intention was to walk to the studio so she could clear her head. She wanted to think, and it was a way of postponing the inevitable call to Mac's office.

"Miss Ashley."

"Yes?" she said, turning around to meet Marcus Carlin's gaze.

"I need to talk to you about Alan. Would you care to have some breakfast with me, or perhaps a cup of coffee? It's rather important," he said when it looked as if she were going to refuse.

What was another hour out of her life? At least it would postpone the call. For sure Steve would fire her, though once again she realized she simply didn't care.

Sitting across from Marcus Carlin in a cracked leather booth in a coffee shop that smelled of old grease and cigarette smoke, Casey was stunned at the way he had aged since she'd seen him almost a year ago. She couldn't help but wonder if his resignation had anything to do with the bitter look in his eyes. He'd given the excuse for his retirement as poor health, but he didn't look sickly, just older.

Casey stared down at the cup of coffee in front of her, wondering if it was safe to drink. Marcus Carlin was staring at his cup too, probably wondering the same thing. He reached out and pushed his cup to the side. She noticed the fine white monogram on his cuff. She hadn't liked the man when Mac spoke of him so bitterly. She didn't like him at all when she'd met him last Christmas at Alan's house. Now, she liked him less and wasn't sure why.

The judge cleared his throat. "As you know, I'm Alan's lawyer. I drew up his will, and now I need to go over a few things with you."

"Why, Mr. Carlin? I have nothing to do with Alan's estate. And if it's your intention to ask me questions about Alan, I won't answer them. I really don't have much time, I have to return to the office," Casey said, preparing to get up. "It was nice seeing you again, and I'm sorry it was under these sad circumstances."

"Did you know about Alan's open heart surgery?"

"No, Mr. Carlin, I didn't. He told me he was going to retire to Spain to write his memoirs. Yesterday was the first I heard about it."

She had her coat on, her scarf tied around her neck. She was pulling on her gloves when the judge said, "You're Alan Carpenter's sole beneficiary. Aside from a few bequests to his domestic help and two fully paid medical scholarships, you will inherit his entire estate. It's quite sizable, even after inheritance tax. Around three million or so."

Casey's jaw dropped. "There must be some mistake," she said carefully. The judge watched as she pulled on her other glove. She licked at her dry lips. It appeared to the judge that she wanted to say something else but couldn't find the right words.

"It's no mistake. When I met you last Christmas, Alan and I and his lawyer finalized the will right there in his study. His cook and housekeeper witnessed his signature. You are a very wealthy woman, Miss Ashley."

"No," Casey said vehemently. "No. I don't want Alan's money. I could never take his money. He should never have done this," she added desperately. "I'm sorry, Mr. Carlin, but I have to get to the studio. Give it back, do whatever you have to do. I don't want it."

"It doesn't work that way, Miss Ashley. If you don't want it, you can do with it whatever you like *after* you take possession of it. I can't go back on . . . it isn't done," he said coldly. "I suggest you think about this and what it means to you. I'll call you in a day or so. In the meantime, I will call Richards, his lawyer, and get things under way."

Casey stared after the judge in stupefied amazement when he rose from the booth and marched out of the diner without paying the check. She laid two one-dollar bills on the table and left the diner. Her thoughts were in a turmoil.

When she paid the taxi driver and entered the studios of Tri State News, the only thing truly clear in her mind was that Alan hadn't rejected her. He'd been ill, certain he wouldn't live long, and therefore wouldn't tie her to him. The legacy was to make up for his lie. There was no way she was going to keep Alan's money.

"Glad to see you finally made it, *Miss Ashley*," Steve Harper snapped.

"Do you have a problem, Steve?" Casey snapped in return. "Why don't you just fire me? Look, I'm sorry about taking the time off, and I'm sorry about this morning. But if you hadn't given me the time off, I would have quit. That's how important all of this was to me. Now, shall we start over and say good morning like the civilized people we are, or should I turn around and walk out of here? I can stay late, as late as you need me to make up the time. I can be here by six tomorrow morning. It's your call," Casey said coldly.

"I'm sorry too," Steve muttered. "I want this thing locked up with the senator. I sent him a personal letter several weeks ago, and he hasn't responded. When was the last time you went through the mail?"

"Steve, I don't have time for the mail. You said Donna was doing the mail. Oh, I see. She's been out sick, and no one went through it. All right, I'll do the mail. Tell me this, do you want the mail done first or do you want me to call the senator and firm it all up?"

"Use your best judgment. I'm sorry about Alan, Mary. I hate funerals and memorial services. They remind me of my own mortality. Let's have lunch after the newscast."

"Okay," Casey muttered.

Izzy was perched on the edge of her desk. "He said I should make my own decision," she said to the chimp. "So, I'm going with the mail first."

There was no such thing as a mail tray at Tri State News. Mail was unceremoniously dumped into a cardboard carton that said EGGS in big red letters on the side. It was full, Casey saw. "Shit!"

Most of the letters were to the news anchor, Matthew Cassidy, who couldn't be bothered answering them. The job was left to Casey and Donna, a girl who came in part-time. Casey liked reading Cassidy's mail. A lady named Ettie constantly wrote to tell him about his ties and suggested he wear red once in a while. She went on to say he looked like a somber Baptist minister. She saw it then, under Ettie's letter. It was a long white envelope that said U.S. Senate on the upper left-hand corner.

Casey slit it with the letter opener. She didn't want to destroy the envelope. She was back in Vietnam reading a letter from Mac. Her eyes filled when she read the short note, which ended with, "Call my office to set up an appointment that will be mutually convenient." It was signed Senator Malcolm Carlin. She recognized his handwriting. She looked at the telephone number and instantly memorized it. She scanned the list of the various prestigious committees he sat on. "Well done, Mac," she whispered.

Her hand was on the phone a second later. You'll get his secretary or an aide. Senators never answer their own phones, she told herself over and over as she waited for the ringing phone to be picked up. A man answered, identified himself as Phil Benedict. Mac had called him Benny. "Senator Carlin, please. This is Mary Ashley from Tri State News in New York."

"Yes, Miss Ashley, we've been expecting your call. The senator isn't available right now. They're taking a vote on the Senate floor. I can have him return your call later."

"No, no, that isn't necessary. My time is free for the month of December, so if he can fit us in, we can work around his schedule. Do you handle his appointments, Mr. Benedict?"

"As a matter of fact I do. The senator and I were discussing this yesterday morning. Sunday is good for the senator. Monday too, but if, as your letter stated, you would like Mrs. Carlin and Jenny in the footage, it will have to be Sunday. They leave for South Carolina on Monday. The senator is booked up for the rest of the week. He only has a few hours the following week on Wednesday, and then he leaves for South Carolina too, to spend the holidays with his family. You said you require footage there. So, let's see, we can give you half a day on December twenty-first. You might like that. The plantation will be decorated for Christmas, and I understand there is to be a huge party for the children. Is any of this agreeable with you?"

Casey scribbled furiously. "Sunday is fine. Monday is fine too, but we need shots of Mr. Carlin with his family in the Senate building. Is it possible to do that first thing Monday morning? You said Mrs. Carlin is leaving on Monday."

"She's leaving mid-afternoon. The senator set aside time to take her to the airport. First thing Monday morning will be fine."

"Which half of the day on the twenty-first, on the plantation?" Casey asked briskly.

"The afternoon. The party starts at four. The senator is playing Santa." He laughed. Casey didn't.

"What time on Sunday?" Casey asked.

"I think you can pretty much pick the time. The senator

wants the interview done at the guest cottage. The main house is being closed up, even as we speak. Give me your phone number, and if there's any change, I'll call you immediately. Your home phone number will be helpful too. We tend to work late around here, and we just might need to call you late at night."

Casey gave him her phone number. "Let's say ten o'clock Sunday morning. I'll be down with the camera crew tomorrow evening."

"I guess that settles it then. It was nice speaking with you, Miss Ashley. You're certain you don't want the senator to call you back?"

"Yes, I'm certain," Casey said sharply.

"Good-bye, Miss Ashley," Benedict said coolly.

"Good-bye, Mr. Benedict," Casey said stiffly.

Casey looked at the scribbled notes and then at her watch. It was eleven-thirty.

In less than forty-eight hours she was going to see Mac Carlin.

She started to tremble.

Chapter 25

So THIS WAS where Mac lived. Casey looked around at the grounds, trying to imagine him romping about as a child. He hadn't liked it here. That much she did remember. She wondered why he was moving, and if he was trying to run from his past the way she was.

"Do you suppose they know the door is hanging by one hinge up there at the big house?" one of the cameramen said, jerking his hand in the direction of the stately looking mansion, as they stood in the doorway to the house where they were to meet the Senator and his wife and child. "That's not going to look good if you want a front shot of the house."

Casey adjusted the scarf around her neck with trembling hands which she immediately jammed into her bright red cashmere coat. She'd worked on her makeup for almost an hour this morning, trying to make it perfect. She'd brushed her hair for another hour before she swept it back with tortoiseshell combs. The crew had teased her unmercifully when she entered the hotel dining room to meet them for breakfast. To a man, the six-member crew joked that she was trying to impress the senator. They were dressed in jeans and heavy flannel shirts. *They* didn't have to impress anyone, they said. She'd bristled, but calmed down as soon as she had her first cup of coffee. She couldn't afford to act nervous or they'd never let her alone.

Thirty more seconds and she would see Mac. And his wife. The woman he lied about and their daughter. The woman he preferred to her. Anger rose in her then, hot and scorching.

She could hear his voice. The anger disappeared as suddenly as it arrived and left her feeling vulnerable. Introductions were being made. She was next. She fixed a smile on her face as she extended her hand in greeting. Her heart pounded in her chest. Dear God, he looked the same, exactly the way she remembered him. Their eyes met and she saw no recognition. For one brief moment she felt only relief and sadness, then the anger returned. She jerked her hand away and stuffed it into her pocket. "Senator," she said coldly—so coldly that the crew looked at her in shock and disbelief.

Mac backed up a step, his eyes on the young woman in the red coat. "This is my wife, Alice. And this is Jenny."

Casey smiled at the child before nodding curtly to her parents. She turned her back to follow the camera crew into the house. She could feel Mac's eyes on her back. She wanted to cry, to demand to know why she wasn't living here in this house with the two dogs bearing down on her instead of Alice. She reached down to scratch behind their silky ears. "And I'll just bet your names aren't Fred and Gus either," she said in a choked whisper. She whirled around and demanded of Alice, in the same cold, hostile tone she'd used before, "What are their names?"

"Why . . . the dogs you mean?" Alice said. "Fred and Gus. Is it important?"

"People like to see pets. Pets reflect stability. But we won't use the dogs."

"Why is that, Miss Ashley?" Mac asked curiously.

They were within a foot of one another, their eyes locked. *Liar. It was all a lie. You betrayed me. Liar. It wasn't a dream, it was a nightmare. Liar.* "Because I said so," Casey said. He senses something, Casey thought wildly. She could feel it.

Mac bristled then. He caught sight of the expression on his wife's face. God alone knew what Alice was thinking. "I don't have to do this show. Courtesy goes a long way, Miss Ashley."

This wasn't going the way she had planned at all. Everyone was uptight. Alice Carlin looked as if she were going to take a fit any second. The child was starting to get restless. Mac was angry. The crew didn't know what to do—finish laying the cable or stop until this, whatever it was, was over.

"I think you should decide now, *Senator*, before the crew

goes any further," Casey said bitingly. Once again their eyes locked. "I didn't ask for this job, it was foisted on me." She made the title "Senator" sound obscene.

"Then don't take it out on me," Mac snapped. What in the name of God was wrong with him? In his life he'd never spoken to a woman like this. Not even Alice, in their worst moments. Their eyes locked again. Something strange stirred in him. She was scratching the dogs' ears again. *They* liked her. Dogs were shrewd judges of character. It was *him*. He was bringing out the worst in her, and he didn't know why.

"Who should I take it out on?" Casey retaliated. *You lied to me, you bastard. You said we would get married and live happily ever after.* For sure she was going to get fired, she thought. No, she wasn't. She was going to quit. In about five minutes.

"I'm going to take Jenny outdoors until you all . . . decide what it is you're going to do," Alice said in a jittery voice. Mac nodded, his eyes never leaving Casey's tight, angry face.

When the door closed behind Alice and Jenny, Mac said, "Obviously something is going on here I don't understand. You didn't want this job, but you're here. Don't you like my politics? Is that it?"

"Actually, Senator, I don't like *you*," Casey said tightly.

"Why?" This was so stupid, Mac thought. Why am I putting up with this? It was obvious the crew was wondering the same thing.

Casey smiled. "You're a liar, and I despise liars. I put liars right up there with used car salesmen, Senator." There was such venom in her voice, Mac was speechless. The crew started to repack their gear.

"I do not lie, Miss Ashley. As a matter of fact I go out of my way so I *don't* have to tell a lie. I have never told a lie to my constituents."

"Did I say anything about your constituents, Senator? Perhaps you should search your conscience." Her voice was mocking now. Mac didn't know which was worse—her anger or this jaded mocking sound he was hearing. He felt like a fool. The crew thought him one too, he could see it in their faces. They might not approve of Mary Ashley's attitude, but their money was on their colleague. "You're a *politician*," Casey said, and that summed it all up in her eyes. Mac's too.

Casey turned to the crew. "I'm going back. I'll call the office and have them send someone else down here who is more compatible with the senator. She turned to Mac. "I like your dogs. I *really* like them. Good-bye, Senator."

"Wait," Mac said, desperate to know what was going on, certain he'd missed something important.

"For what?"

"Well, I . . ."

"Yes?" Their eyes locked. Casey smiled and did her best to fight back the tears pricking her eyelids.

"Do we . . . know each other? Did we meet somewhere, and was I rude to you? You . . ." He shrugged helplessly.

"You're not someone I want to know, Senator." Her eyes were full now and would spill over momentarily. One of the dogs whined softly. She turned and left the house, blinded with her tears, running headlong into Alice and Jenny. She muttered an apology as she ran to her car. Alice stared after her until the car was out of sight, her face furrowed in thought.

She was about to climb the steps to the porch when the crew emerged. She listened to the apologies and heard the words "stress" and "overload" mentioned several times.

Mac was standing in the middle of the room, a totally hopeless look on his face. "I don't know what happened, Alice. We called off the shoot by mutual agreement. There didn't seem much point in going through with it. She despises me. I saw it in her face, and I don't know why. I hate it when I don't understand something."

"Mac, did you put that box of pictures away yet?" Alice asked.

"They're on the desk. Why?"

She was back a moment later. Why was she doing this? Why was she helping her husband find a woman who would end her marriage and leave Jenny without a father? Because she cared about him and wanted his happiness, she realized. She had Jenny. Mac deserved to be happy, she told herself before she turned on the hallway light.

"Take a good look at this picture, Mac. This was the woman you knew in Vietnam. She's very pretty," she said with a catch in her voice. "Now watch this." She used Jenny's colored pencils. He watched with interest as Alice started to draw a bright red coat around the figure. With a yellow pencil she rearranged Casey's hair. With a fine-point pen she redefined Casey's new face the way she remembered it. "Voilà!" she said softly. "It was the tears in her eyes that convinced me. Eyes never lie, Mac. You can change the color, but you can't change emotion."

"Oh, God. She must have gone through unbearable hell. They said she was dead. I promised . . . so many things. The only one—" he said, his voice cracking. "The only one I kept was the dogs. I would have gone through with the divorce, Alice. You need to know that. I did love her, and I wanted to marry her. I lied to her. I didn't tell her about you, and I couldn't tell her about Jenny. She didn't have a happy childhood. Her parents left her in an orphanage. She never forgave them. We all betrayed her: her mother, her father, me, and God knows who else."

"Go after her or you'll lose her again. It's all right, Mac. Go after her," Alice urged.

He tried.

He thought his heart was going to beat right out of his chest. Of course it was Casey. The conversation now made sense. He drove like a maniac, certain he wasn't going to find her.

He was on the highway, passing the television van at ninety miles an hour.

Findherfindherfindherfindher.

Mac careened into the motel parking lot. Thank God he'd remembered Benny telling him where the crew was staying. There were no cars with out-of-state license plates in the lot. Should he wait? Was she driving a rental car or her own car? Did she stop here? Would she stop here? She'd only had a fifteen-minute head start on him. The way he'd been driving, he should have passed her along the way. If she was in the same emotional state he was in, she was probably halfway to New York by now. Jesus Christ, what should he do now? *I can't lose her again.* "I like your dogs," she'd said. He should have picked up on the whole thing the minute she'd asked for their names. *Carlin, you are the stupidest man who ever walked this earth.*

Mac was still sitting in the car when the van pulled alongside. He rolled down the window. "She isn't here. I don't have time to explain. Where would she go? You saw what happened back there. Would she drive back to New York or will she wait for you guys?"

"I don't know, Senator. She looked pretty pissed to me. I don't know what got into her. Mary's a hell of a nice person, and she's going to lose her job over this. Harper was real keen on getting you on film."

"Look, do . . . Mary a favor and blame it all on me. Say I couldn't get it all together and had second thoughts. Hell, I don't care what you tell him, just don't blame . . . Mary. Will you do that?"

"Why not?" they said in unison. "She rented a car after flying down here. We met up with her. It was a Ford Thunderbird. Maybe she decided to drive all the way back. Try I-95. She's not a fast driver. You can probably catch up to her."

"Thanks," Mac said, peeling out of the parking lot.

He didn't catch up to her. Or she hadn't been on the highway at all, but had gone to an airport or the Amtrack station and taken a plane or train back to New York.

He arrived in downtown Manhattan at five o'clock. There was so little traffic, he felt as if he had the city to himself. He even managed to find a parking space a block from Tri State News.

If he wasn't in such a flap, he would have laughed at the look of sheer terror on Steve Harper's face. "There's been a mix-up. I need to locate Miss Ashley right away. I need her home address."

"Senator, I can't give that to you. It's against policy."

"She won't mind. Trust me. I'll make sure she calls you, providing she's at home."

"I thought she was with you in Virginia. Where's the crew?"

"She was. They're on their way back. I just drove faster. Okay, thanks," Mac said, pocketing the address.

He knew he was too late even before the doorman told him

Miss Ashley came in and went out carrying two animal kennels.

"Two?" Mac asked, swaying dizzily.

"Yes, sir, two."

"Son of a bitch! Did she have a suitcase?"

"She went back for that. She put the kennels in her car and went back for her suitcase. She double-parked. I watched the car for her. Is something wrong?"

"Did she say where she was going?"

"No. She said good-bye and slipped me twenty bucks. Real nice lady."

You're a liar, she said. *I don't like you. You're a liar.*

Where would she go? She could be someplace as simple as around the corner and be lost to him forever. It was worth a try. Casey was the one thrown clear when the firebomb hit the jeep she was riding in. Who the hell was buried in France? Jesus, he'd wanted to believe, even tried to believe, but his faith wasn't strong enough. Lily must be the one in the grave. The thought didn't make him feel any better. Where would Casey go? Maybe Steve Harper would know.

"Christ, you missed her by ten minutes," Harper said. "She barreled in here and handed me the two kennels and told me to take care of her pets. She said they loved Izzy and Izzy needed company. I said okay because Izzy is lonely. She quit. What'd you do to her, Senator? I know something went on down there, and here you show up demanding her address and ten minutes later she blows in here, gives me her dog and cat, and then quits. You know what, Senator? I don't want you on my show. She was crying. Now, I'm busy, so if you don't mind. . . ."

"Yeah, I mind. Where would she go? Listen, this is very personal and very, very private. Please."

"I don't know. She just said she was going away. She said she was going to do what she was trained to do, not babysit some damn chimpanzee. That's all she said. I'm real disappointed in you, Senator," Harper blustered.

"I'm disappointed in me too, Mr. Harper," Mac said sadly.

With a knot in his throat, a pain in his chest, and tears streaming down his cheeks, Mac left.

* * *

IN HIS LIFE, Mac thought, he'd never been this tired, this weary, this heartsick. Not even back on the trail after a firefight or going three straight days with no sleep. All he wanted to do was sleep, to forget about this day and his part in it. His watch said it was three in the morning. "Of what century?" Mac groaned as he struggled from the car.

Yody's trailer was dark. He wondered if she won the Sunday-evening round-robin. He turned when he felt the cold air stir about him. Both dogs were on him in an instant, pawing and licking at him. He scratched their ears the way Casey had. "She was right here. I shook her hand, and I didn't know. I should have known," he said bitterly. "Which says diddly for me, guys. Come along, it's time for bed," he said wearily.

A night-light burned dimly in the kitchen, another lit the den and living room, and still another the hallway. He'd seen lights upstairs. Alice must be waiting for him. Damn, he didn't want to think about Alice, but he knew he had to. Would he have gone after Casey if Alice hadn't urged him to? Only after it was too late, he decided honestly.

He'd lost her again. God, what must she be thinking, what must she have gone through? All of this, he thought, looking around, must have been like a slap in the face to her. The dogs . . . Jesus. His head dropped to his hands. His shoulders shook as he tried to come to terms with his grief all over again. He needed the welcome release of tears. "I should have known," he said aloud. "Goddamnit, I should have known," he whispered to the dogs. "You liked her, I could tell. Where is she, where did she go?"

Alice Carlin backed away from the kitchen doorway. Her eyes were misty as she stared at her husband. She hadn't expected him to return so quickly. He must not have found her. She felt glad and sad at the same time. She wanted to go to her husband, to put her arms around him, to tell him it, whatever it turned out to be, would be all right. She knew though that Mac would never forgive her for intruding on his grief, the kind of grief he couldn't share with his wife. A wife in name only. Minutes later she was back in the room she shared with Jenny, who was running a high fever. She sat down on the chair, her eyes on her daughter. She picked up the Chatty Cathy doll that was Jenny's favorite. She stroked the matted hair, tears sliding down her cheeks.

Alice sensed his presence and turned. Her eyes questioned him as she placed a finger to her lips. In her fuzzy robe and fuzzy slippers she joined her husband at the top of the stairs. They sat down, like an old married couple, and shared the bottle of Coca-Cola Mac had taken from the refrigerator.

"Jenny's sick. She started to run a high fever around four o'clock. It happens fairly often. She gets ear infections and sore throats. I wasn't waiting up for you," she said defensively.

"You never told me Jenny gets sick a lot," Mac said.

"You weren't exactly interested for a long time. As you pointed out, she is my daughter, not yours. The doctor came out and gave her a shot. Children like Jenny are prone to . . . you know, they have problems." There was such sadness in Alice's voice, Mac drew her to him to comfort her.

"You're a good mother, Alice. I never thought . . . I don't know how you do it. You gave up everything I thought was important to you."

Alice grinned crookedly. "Maybe you have to go through childbirth to know what I feel as a mother. She was so defenseless. She had only me. My own parents weren't any more understanding than Marcus. We can talk about all of this now, Mac, if you want, but I don't think it's the right time. You're hurting badly. Why don't we talk about that? Maybe you'll feel better. I'm trying to help, Mac, I'm not . . . it's not that I want to know the sordid details so I can throw them back at you later on. Please believe me."

He told her the truth, leaving nothing out. "I felt something, but I didn't . . . it's done," he said sadly in a choked voice.

"There must be a way to find her, to set matters straight. You have to do it, Mac. How can you go on with your life with this hanging over your head?" Alice asked quietly.

"She doesn't need to hear me say any words. She saw everything she needed to see with her eyes. You were here with Jenny. She saw a family, she saw the dogs. She saw this guest cottage, the same kind of house we both said we wanted. She thinks it's our dream, yours and mine. Never hers. If there's one thing I know, it's that Casey Adams would never in any way do anything to break up this family. Never."

"Does that mean you aren't going to . . . do something?"

"Something? In a million years I'll never be able to find her. She doesn't want to be found. Why else is she calling herself Mary Ashley?"

"Maybe she'll go back to France. You could start there."

"You should go to bed, Alice. You have a busy day tomorrow."

"I can't sleep when Jenny is sick. If she isn't better tomorrow, I'll have to postpone our trip. A few days won't make much difference. I'm looking forward to the move. Jenny is very excited, but she's sad about leaving her new friends at the foundation. She adjusts well, so I'm not worried. I am worried about you, though. Is there anything I can do, Mac?"

The compassion in his wife's eyes under the bright hallway lighting stunned him. It was hard to believe this gentle-eyed woman in the fuzzy robe was the same woman he'd left behind when he went to Vietnam. He patted her hand comfortingly. "I'll deal with it, Alice. Off the top of my head I'd say we're a couple of misfits."

Alice smiled. "Are you just finding that out?"

"Pretty much so. I'm kind of slow in matters like this."

Alice handed the picture she was holding back to Mac. "Will you still be coming to South Carolina? If you don't, I'll understand. Try and get some sleep," she said in the same motherly tone she used with Jenny. "Daylight, for some reason, always makes things a little better."

"Maybe we'll be a family someday," Alice murmured to Jenny's Chatty Cathy doll. "Maybe."

Downstairs, Mac poured himself a drink, gulped it, and poured another and another and another until he passed out. It was the only thing he could think of to make his pain go away. He stayed drunk for three days.

* * *

"LET HIM ALONE, Benny," Alice said when he drove her to the airport. "Be there for him. The damn Senate can wait. Don't pressure him."

"Okay, Alice, but I thought he was moving to that apartment house in Arlington. Do you think I should move him or wait?"

"I'd mention it if the situation presents itself. Mac has to come up for air at some point. He'll realize alcohol isn't his answer. Mac is no fool, we both know that. Good-bye, Benny, thanks for the ride. You'll see that Yody gets on the plane at the end of the week, right?"

"Count on it. Good luck, Alice."

Alice debated a second before she leaned over and kissed Benny lightly on the cheek. "That's for being such a good friend to Mac. Visit sometime, okay?"

"You bet," Benny said, tweaking Jenny under the chin.

WHEN MAC SURFACED from his three-day alcoholic stupor, he moved to the apartment in Arlington with Benny's help. He didn't look back. He had a desk full of work and a letter to write. From there he would take it one day at a time. His little family would see him over the rough spots. Alice and Jenny were waiting for him. As long as he could see their beacon of light, he was going to be okay. He didn't know if he'd be willing to bet the rent on it though.

"Be happy, Casey, wherever you are. I'm going to try. If I don't succeed, I'll try harder," Mac murmured.

"Did you say something, Senator?" an aide to Senator Proxmire asked.

Startled, Mac looked around. "It wasn't important," Mac said evenly. "Thinking out loud, I guess. Sometimes it helps."

Proxmire's aide walked alongside Mac. "They say Tip O'-Neill does it all the time. So does my boss, but don't tell anyone." The aide grinned.

"My lips are sealed." Mac smiled. "When something is over, it's over." *It really is over for me. I'm alive and well. I'll survive.*

Chapter 26

HEAVY, SLASHING RAIN pelted the San Francisco Bay area. Casey hardly noticed. She only had eyes for her new passport. The picture was hers. The name on the passport said she was Casey Adams. All thanks to a young attorney named Oliver Preston, a Vietnam veteran. "No mean feat," he said when he handed it to her. "I feel like I personally dealt Goliath a mortal blow, and in a manner of speaking, that's exactly what I did to the U.S. Army. You're your own person now. You still retain dual citizenship. I respected your wishes in that matter and left the paperwork up to them. On the matter of your life insurance, well, the army is prepared to take the loss. Here in my hand are checks for all your medical bills, the ones paid by Dr. Carpenter. When I relieve you of my fee, you'll still have a tidy little nest egg. I think your Dr. Carpenter would understand."

"Marcus Carlin and Alan's lawyer in New York?"

"I'll handle everything. You signed your power of attorney, so there will be no problem. I'll carry out your wishes. Again, I think your Dr. Carpenter would be very proud to know you're donating all of your inheritance to Senator Carlin's foundation for Down's syndrome children in the name of Mary Ashley. I'll get on that right after . . . day after tomorrow really."

"I don't know how to thank you for all your help. I just walked in here out of the rain and fog, and there you were. I was one step away from jumping off the Bay Bridge a month ago."

"And now?" Preston asked curiously.

"Now I'm going to the bank and deposit these checks, and then I'm going to celebrate."

"Alone?"

"In a manner of speaking. I'll share it with my memories one last time. And then I'll start over tomorrow. Do you have a family, Oliver? I never asked."

"Yes. Great little wife, and a boy and a girl. They're my life."

"That's the way it should be. Don't ever let anyone break it up," Casey said softly. "Good-bye, Oliver, and thanks for everything."

"Listen," Oliver said, getting up from his desk. "What if I need to get in touch with you? Where will you be? What are you going to do?"

"What I do best. Right now, though, I'm going to try and catch some of your famous San Francisco fog." She laughed. Oliver thought the sound of her laughter was the saddest thing he'd ever heard.

"Good Luck, Casey."

"Thanks, Oliver."

THE AWFUL IN-COUNTRY smell was just as she remembered it. The heat and humidity just as paralyzing. Casey smiled. She was a veteran, she could handle it. Her bag full of cotton underwear, talcum, a fancy blue dress, and little else was at her feet. She could see the Twelfth Evac Hospital sign and underneath the letters CU CHI.

She heard the sound of choppers. "Incoming wounded," she said to the three young nurses at her side.

"Where?" the girls chorused in unison.

Casey pointed to the west.

"I can't see anything," one of the nurses said. "I don't hear anything either. How do you know that?" she asked suspiciously.

"I've been here before." Casey laughed. "Better get moving."

"We just got here. We're tired," they whined together.

"Tough. You're here to do a job, and you're going to do it. Get a move on. In case no one told you, I'm your superior. I'm tough, but I'm fair. Move your asses, girls. Those guys aren't going to wait to die till you get ready. In there and scrub up! Five minutes!"

"Jesus Christ, where did she come from?" one of the nurses demanded.

"Another planet," the second nurse said.

"She looks like a real bitch!" the third one said.

"Nah, she's a real pussycat. I'm the dragon. Move!" Luke Farrell roared.

"Hello, Luke," Casey said shyly.

"What name you going by these days?" Luke drawled.

"The same one I was born with, subject to change, of course," Casey drawled back.

"Can we talk about this later? The name change, I mean. This is a bad one. I don't want any of those kids dying on my table. How'd you find me? Triage!" he bellowed at the top of his lungs as the first chopper set down.

"I made a deal with the army. I said I'd come over here if they assigned me to your hospital. They said okay. Is that good enough for you?"

"Yeah. Easy, kid, hang on, we're gonna fix you right up," Luke said to a young kid with blond whiskers on a litter.

"You have the best doctor in the world, young man. You do what he says and hang on. I'll see you in a minute. Hang on now," Casey said.

"Yes, ma'am, I'll hang on."

"That's it, son," Luke said, running alongside Casey. "We got work to do, Adams."

"Yes, sir, that's why I'm here."

"The only reason?"

"Heck, no. I missed your homely face."

Their eyes met briefly.

"We're a good team. Farrell and Adams. Sounds like a dance team."

"How about Farrell and Farrell?" Casey laughed.

"Sounds even better," Luke said, taking his position behind the operating table.

"Next!"

Epilogue

Washington, D.C.

November 1984

CHILLING BLACKNESS.

Casey's hands flew to her mouth to stifle a cry of pain. Luke froze in his tracks, his back and shoulders stiffening.

"I thought . . . I expected . . . a statue . . . something . . . something white . . . something that would please the eye. This . . . this . . ."

"Is somber and reflective," Luke murmured. He was referring to the Vietnam Memorial with its manicured ramparts, two angled walls which sloped down into the ground from a height of ten feet at their junction. The carved names of the dead began and ended at the apex and were arranged in the order of their deaths from the years 1959 through 1975. "And contemplative. I can see it, now that I've gotten over the shock. Casey, look at it closely. Look at it with your mind, not your heart," Luke ordered.

"I am, Luke. It's ugly. It's cold, it's black. It's ambivalent, like this country's attitude toward the war." A sob caught in her throat. She leaned against her husband, her face full of despair.

"Like it or not," a vet said standing next to her, "it exposes the denial in this country's reaction to the war. I see . . ." the vet continued, "dignity, simplicity, elegance, something the war wasn't. I want to believe this is the beginning of our healing process."

Luke and Casey watched him walk away, muttering the same phrases over and over to anyone who would stop and listen.

"He's probably right," Luke said quietly.

"So many names. My God, so many names," Casey said softly, her hand outstretched to touch the names carved in the black granite. "I can see the reflection of myself, the trees, the people, the birds, the sky, the *other monuments, the world*." Her index finger traced the name Willard D. Craig and then the name Merle I. Cripe. Tears rolled down her cheeks. "It's not enough!" she cried.

"No, it isn't," Luke said, "but it's all we have for now. The more you look at this, the more you see reflected, the more I think this is . . . about as close to perfect as you can get. It's going to take a lot of getting used to, but someday this wall is . . . I don't know what it's going to be, but it's going to go down in history."

"What about that ragtag parade down Constitution Avenue?" Casey choked out the words, her fingers still tracing names of the fallen.

"It's a start, Casey. That's how we have to look at it. You're absolutely right, it's not enough, but it's all we have," Luke said, putting his arm around his wife.

"We have to find Rick's name. I'm not leaving here till we find it. Sue's name too. Are women's names on here? I want to see Mary Klinker's name and . . . and, the other one, oh Luke, I can't remember her name. . . ."

"We'll find them, Casey. We promised each other we wouldn't do this, and here we are doing exactly what we said we wouldn't do. Walk around with the children, and I'll find the names. Go on, Casey, the kids are getting restless."

"You're right. I'm sorry, honey," Casey said, stretching up on her toes to kiss her husband on the cheek. "We'll be back in ten minutes."

Luke squeezed his eyes shut. When he opened them he felt warm sunshine on his head. He looked around, disoriented for a moment, confused at what he was feeling and seeing reflected in the blackness in front of him. Casey was right, he could see the world, sparrows in flight, trees, monuments, sky, parents, brothers, sisters, the veterans strolling the Mall. He raised his eyes upward to feel the sun on his face. We're all being blessed, he thought.

The moment Luke found the name he was searching for, he pressed his finger so hard against the black marble that his nail cracked. It would have taken a derrick to dislodge him. When his wife returned, he guided her hand to the carved name: Richard Sanducci. He did cry then.

"Did you know that guy?" a voice behind them asked shakily.

Casey turned. "We all knew him. I was a nurse in Vietnam, my husband was a doctor. Were you there?"

"Yeah. Yeah, I was there. I knew Rick. Had a beer with him once. Saw him at that picnic in Da Nang. I was there when he was . . . when he . . . bought it. No one knew what to do. I mean that guy was like God, he wasn't supposed to die." The vet was shaking now, trembling, his eyes wild and frightened. He bent over clutching his stomach and then dropped to his knees, shaking worse. From out of nowhere a circle of bearded, fatigued veterans closed in.

Casey shot a look at her husband before she dropped to her knees. "It's okay," she said soothingly, "you're among friends." She pulled him close, stroking his hair, his back, his arms. "I went through this, so did my husband, and all these guys standing here. Is your family here?" she crooned. "Can we fetch someone?"

"What family?" the soldier said bitterly. "My wife couldn't handle it, so she took my kid and split. She got married again and won't even let me see my son. Said I was a bad influence with my nightmares, screaming fits, and . . . oh shit, she said it all. I lost every job I got. For the past year I've just been bumming."

"There are places you can go for help," Luke said softly. The circle of vets hooted sarcastically.

"There are places and then there are places. Here," he said, whipping a notebook and pen from inside his jacket. "This is a toll free number for you to call. If you can't make it there on your own, someone will come for you. This is a place where you'll get *real* help and be able to get your life back together. Before you know it, you'll have your son back. Trust me," Luke said seriously. When the ex-soldier still looked doubtful,

Luke said, "Remember that guy who threw the picnic in Da Nang? He heads up this foundation, oversees it. Won't cost you a cent. All you have to do is call."

"You shitting him, Doc?" one of the vets said coldly.

"No!" Casey said. "He's telling you the truth. You can all go if you need help. A support group isn't enough. There are people there, trained people who understand and know what you're going through. Why don't you give it a try? What do you have to lose?"

The soldier was on his feet, wiping his sweaty hands on his raggedy jeans. He nodded miserably. The paper Luke handed him was safe in his pocket.

"Thanks. I'll give it a try. Is this your son, Doc?"

"Yes."

"A man shouldn't lose his son. It's not right, it's not fair."

"No it isn't. Listen, I wrote my address on that paper. Let us know how you're doing, okay?"

"Yeah, yeah," the soldier called over his shoulder as he moved off with the small group of men clustered around him protectively.

"My hero," Casey said shakily. "He'll go, won't he, Luke?" She wiped at the tears rolling down her cheeks.

"I think so," Luke said.

"Don't cry, Mommy," seven-year-old Luke said.

"It's okay, honey, this is a good cry. Remember I told you sometimes people cry because they're happy? I'm crying because your daddy just did a kind, wonderful thing."

Luke Junior, a miniature replica of his father, stared up at his father adoringly.

"Mommy, can we get some ice cream now?" four-year-old Lily asked, tugging on her mother's skirt.

Casey didn't respond. Her eyes were on a small party approaching the wall from the left. A gaggle of reporters trailed behind, asking for an interview. She heard him say in a voice she remembered, "This is a private moment for me, gentlemen, please respect my wishes." She almost fainted, and probably would have but for Luke's tight grip on her arm.

He saw her then, his step faltering.

Luke released his grip on his wife's arm so he could heft Lily to his shoulders. "We knew this would happen someday. Can you handle it?"

Casey looked at her little family. Of course she could. She smiled and said, "Senator Carlin, how nice to see you again. You know Luke, and this is Luke Junior, and this little minx is . . . is named Lily." My God, her voice sounded normal. How, she wondered, was that possible? He looked just the way she remembered, a little older, a little grayer around the temples, but then so was she. She smiled again.

God in heaven, Mac thought. She was even more beautiful than he remembered. Her hand was outstretched, he had to take it in his own. He thought he could hear his heart beating inside his chest. "Casey, it's good to see you again." He had to look away. He couldn't bear to see the pain in her eyes. "Lily, you said." He wondered if anyone picked up on the catch in his voice. "Luke." Mac thrust out his hand. "I've been meaning to write you, to give you an update on all those guys you sent us. God, I can't tell you how satisfying, how rewarding it is to work with these vets. Thanks doesn't seem sufficient."

"It'll do," Luke said quietly.

"Where are my manners? This is Alice, my wife. Jenny, and this guy . . . this guy is Eric, Lily's son," Mac said proudly.

Casey's arms went out to the boy. He looked just like Lily. She kissed him and hugged him. "Oh, let me look at you. However did you find him, Mac? We tried and tried. You must be sixteen, all grown up." The urge to throw her arms around Mac was so strong she clutched at the boy instead. "Luke, look," she babbled, "it really is Lily's son. I named my daughter after your mother," she said to the startled boy.

Casey really looked at the boy then, all the memories rushing back to her. He was tall, with hazel eyes and light brown hair, probably inherited from Eric Savorone. At first glance he looked very American, with his sneakers, jeans, and sport coat. At second glance she could see his Eastern heritage in the shape of his eyes.

"Do you know my *real* father, Mrs. Farrell?" the boy asked

anxiously. Casey's eyes didn't waver in the uncomfortable silence that followed the boy's question.

"No, Eric, I don't. I know one thing, though. If your mother could have chosen a father for you, she would have chosen the one you have." The gratitude in Mac's eyes made her head spin.

Casey smiled, her eyes on Alice Carlin and her children. Her smile said, You have nothing to fear from me. Alice, her arms around both her children, smiled gently in return. Her smile said, I understand.

"Mac, it was good to see you again." She moved closer to kiss him lightly on the cheek. The faint scent of his after-shave tickled her nostrils. For one incredible moment she wanted to grab him and run as fast as she could. The moment passed. She stepped back to link her arm with her husband's.

"Keep in touch," Luke said gruffly.

"You too," Mac said just as gruffly.

The Farrells moved away.

"How was it?" Luke asked carefully, fearful of his wife's reply.

"It was fine, Luke. It's over." It was the first outright lie she'd ever told her husband. She buried it deep in her heart.

"PIZZA FOR EVERYONE," Alice said cheerfully.

"Go ahead, I'll get the car and catch up to you," Mac said.

Mac moved slowly until he was standing by the middle of the memorial. The crowds were gone now except for a few stragglers. He was alone, his reflection silhouetted in the blackness. Not quite alone, he thought. He could see the backs of Casey's little family walking away. An alien hand squeezed his heart. He fought with himself not to run after them, to grab her, to say the hell with everything and run off. Then the monument reflected only his solitary figure. Mac wiped his eyes.

Then dry-eyed, he walked the length of the memorial, muttering as he went along. "We won't let them forget. We did our best, Luke, Casey, Rick, me, all those guys. And *we'll* never forget."

Never.

About the Author

FERN MICHAELS is the New York Times best-selling author of the sizzling quartet of contemporary novels *Texas Rich, Texas Heat, Texas Fury,* and *Texas Sunrise,* as well as the steamy books in the Captive series: *Captive Passions, Captive Embraces, Captive Splendors, Captive Secrets,* and *Captive Innocence.* She is also the author of *Serendipity, Seasons of Her Life, To Have and to Hold,* the Kentucky trilogy, and the Sisterhood series.

www.fernmichaels.com